D0966249

TALES
OF
MYSTERY

TALES
OF
MYSTERY

Edited by BILL PRONZINI

BONANZA BOOKS
New York

Originally published, in a slightly different form, as *The Arbor House Treasury of Detective & Mystery Stories from the Great Pulps.*

Printed and Bound in the United States of America

Library of Congress Cataloging-in-Publication Data

Arbor House treasury of detective and mystery stories
  from the great pulps.
  Tales of mystery.

  Reprint. Originally published: Arbor House treasury of detective and mystery stories from the great pulps. New York : Arbor House, c1983.
  1. Detective and mystery stories, American. 2. American fiction—20th century. I. Pronzini, Bill. II. Title.
PS648.D4A68 1986   813'.0872'08   86-9750
ISBN 0-517-61819-2

h g f e d c b a

CONTENTS

ACKNOWLEDGMENTS

"Arson Plus," by Dashiell Hammett. Copyright © 1923 by Popular Publications, Inc.; © renewed 1950 by the Estate of Dashiell Hammett. First published in *Black Mask*. Reprinted by permission of the Harold Matson Co., Inc.

"The Mopper-Up," by Horace McCoy. Copyright © 1931 by Pro-Distributors Publishing Company, Inc. First published in *Black Mask*. Reprinted by permission of the Harold Matson Co., Inc.

"Red Pavement," by Frederick Nebel. Copyright © 1931 by Pro-Distributors Publishing Company, Inc. First published in *Black Mask*. Reprinted by permission of Mrs. Dorothy B. Nebel.

"The Living Lie Down with the Dead," by Cornell Woolrich. Copyright © 1936 by Popular Publications, Inc.; © renewed 1964 by Cornell Woolrich. First published in *Dime Detective*. Reprinted by permission of the Scott Meredith Literary Agency, Inc., 845 Third Avenue, New York, N.Y. 10022.

"Blue Murder," by Fredric Brown. Copyright © 1943 by Street & Smith Publications, Inc. First published in *The Shadow Magazine*. Reprinted by permission of the Scott Meredith Literary Agency, Inc., 845 Third Avenue, New York, N.Y. 10022.

"Hear that Mournful Sound," by Dane Gregory. Copyright © 1942 by Popular Publications, Inc. First published in *Detective Tales* as "Lynchville Had a Barber." Reprinted by permission of the author.

"Fatal Accident," by John D. MacDonald. Copyright © 1948 by Street & Smith Publications, Inc.; © renewed 1975 by John D. MacDonald Publishing, Inc. First published in *The Shadow Mystery Magazine*. Reprinted by permission of the author.

"See No Evil," by William Campbell Gault. Copyright © 1950 by Popular Publications, Inc. First published in *New Detective* as "See No Murder." Reprinted by permission of the author.

"Crime of Omission," by John D. MacDonald. Copyright © 1951 by Popular Publications, Inc.; © renewed 1978 by John D. MacDonald Publishing, Inc. First published in *Detective Tales*. Reprinted by permission of the author.

TALES
OF
MYSTERY

INTRODUCTION

They were seven by ten inches in size, printed on untrimmed woodpulp paper, with vividly colored enameled covers that, for the most part, depicted scenes of high melodrama. They contained stories just as vividly colored and melodramatic as their artwork, stories of mystery, detection, adventure, war on land and sea and in the air, life in the Old West, modern-day romance, science fiction, fantasy, and sometimes sadistic horror. They were the successors to the dime novels and story weeklies of the nineteenth century, mass-produced to provide cheap reading thrills for imaginative young adults and the so-called "common man," selling for a nickel or a dime in their early years and a quarter in their final ones. They flourished from the 1920s through the 1940s, and at the height of their popularity, in the mid-thirties, there were more than 200 different titles on the newsstands—titles such as *Black Mask, Dime Detective, Weird Tales, Thrilling Mystery, Big Chief Western, Crime Busters, Ace G-Man, The Whisperer, Captain Satan, G-8 and his Battle Aces, Pirate Stories, Gangland Stories, Zeppelin Stories*.

They were the pulps.

Their "father," the man who invented them, was cold, calculating, and avaricious Frank A. Munsey. (Munsey was widely disliked, especially by those who knew him well. One of the latter group wrote on the occasion of his death in 1925, "Frank Munsey contributed to the journalism of his day the talent of a meat packer, the morals of a money changer and the manner of an undertaker.") Munsey began his publishing empire inauspiciously enough in 1882, while still under thirty, with an eight-page fiction weekly of stories for children called *Golden Argosy*. It was not a success, and by 1889 he was in a severe financial bind. In an effort to get out of it, he shortened the title of his magazine to *Argosy* and began filling it with adventure stories for young adults. The revamped publication did well enough to allow him to start another magazine in 1891, this one named after himself. *Munsey's*, which was an inexpensive, illustrated, general periodical, was a success—so much so that Munsey again revamped *Argosy* to emulate his namesake in style and content.

It was in the mid-1890s that Munsey had his greatest inspiration: He restructured *Argosy* for the third time, turning it into an all-fiction magazine, and began publishing it on rough woodpulp paper. His ostensible reason for this move was that he felt any given piece of fiction was more important than what it was printed on, but in reality his reason was that pulp paper was much cheaper. By the turn of the century, *Argosy's* circulation topped 80,000 copies per month, and a few years later it soared to 250,000 copies. Munsey's profit from the early success of *Argosy* and *Munsey's* was estimated at nine million dollars, and he soon upped that figure substantially by introducing *The All-Story* (later *All-Story Weekly*) and *The Cavalier*—capital gains sufficient to warm the icy heart of any skinflint.

Munsey's prosperity did not go unobserved by other enterprising publishers, of course. Street & Smith, the dime-novel kings, brought out *Popular Magazine* in 1904 and followed it with *The Railroad Man's Magazine, People's Magazine, Top-Notch,* and such eventually long-lived titles as *Detective Story, Western Story,* and *Love Story.* Doubleday published *Short Stories;* the Butterick Company had *Adventure,* edited by Arthur Sullivant Hoffman (and, in an associate capacity, Sinclair Lewis); H. L. Mencken and George Jean Nathan founded a pair of spicy story books, *Parisienne* and *Saucy Stories*; William Clayton started his string of magazines with *Ace-High, The Danger Trail,* and *Ranch Romances.* More and more titles were introduced in the post-war years, forcing the dime novels and weeklies, which had hung on in diminishing numbers and with declining popularity, into extinction. By the early twenties, pulp magazines ruled the cheap-fiction roost.

The first detective story pulp appeared in 1915, when Street & Smith decided to convert their nickel thriller, *Nick Carter,* into a pulp that featured the adventures of Carter but also offered crime stories by other writers. They called their new magazine *Detective*

Story, published it semi-monthly, and charged a newsstand price of ten cents. Its circulation mounted slowly but steadily, and then burgeoned in the twenties when Street & Smith made it into a weekly. Its life span was longer than that of any other crime pulp: thirty-four years.

A curiosity, *Mystery Magazine* (thirty-two pages, eight by eleven inches in size, cheaply produced and poorly written) surfaced in 1919, but did not last long. The Mencken-Nathan duo launched *Black Mask* in 1920. The Munsey Company made its move into the field in 1924 with *Flynn's* (later *Flynn's Weekly Detective Fiction, Flynn's Detective Fiction Weekly,* and ultimately *Detection Fiction Weekly*). Edwin Baird founded *Detective Tales* in 1923 (not the same *Detective Tales,* it should be noted, that Rogers Terrill would later make into an important title for Popular Publications). William Clayton's *Clues: A Magazine of Detective Stories*—a more or less successful attempt to rival *Detective Story*—appeared in 1926. Another title designed along similar lines was Harold Hersey's *Dragnet Magazine* (1928), which was later sold to A. A. Wyn and retitled *Ten Detective Aces.*

It was in the thirties that the detective and mystery pulps proliferated and reached their largest audience. (Western magazines such as *Western Story, West,* and *Wild West Weekly* perennially led all pulps in total sales, but the crime weeklies, semi-monthlies, and monthlies ranked in aggregate as a close second.) Harry Steeger's Popular Publications, eventually the largest and most prominent of the pulp chain publishers, started *Dime Detective* in 1931 and followed it with *Detective Tales, New Detective, Strange Detective Mysteries,* and such sex-and-sadism or "weird menace" titles as *Dime Mystery, Horror Stories,* and *Terror Tales.* The Thrilling Group, founded by Ned Pines and editorially directed by Leo Margulies, which developed into a major rival of Popular and Street & Smith, launched *Thrilling Detective, Thrilling Mystery,* and *Popular Detective.* And a host of smaller publishers jumped on the pulp bandwagon with, among many other titles, *Private Detective Stories, Spicy Detective, Double Detective,* and *Star Detective.*

A number of "hero pulps," featuring crime fighters of extraordinary powers and/or physical capabilities, also commenced publication: *The Shadow, Doc Savage, Secret Agent X, The Phantom Detective, Operator #5, The Ghost,* and *The Masked Detective.* Master criminals of the megalomaniacal Fu Manchu sort also had their own magazines for a time, though the likes of *Doctor Death* (the first criminal lead character, established by Dell Publications in 1935), *Wu Fang,* *Dr. Yen Sin,* and *The Octopus* had short-lived careers.

The paper shortage of World War II killed off a large number of titles, including *Clues* and *Double Detective.* Others—notably, *Black Mask* and *Detective Fiction Weekly*—were purchased by chain outfits such as Popular Publications and thus underwent changes in editorial policy. A few new titles were introduced during and after the war, among them *Mammoth Detective, Mammoth Mystery, Hollywood Detective, Shock,* and *FBI Detective,* but the handwriting was already on the wall: the pulps were doomed. The advent of war may have ended the Depression in this country, but it also broke the back of the pulp giant; and in the war's aftermath, things began to change rapidly and radically everywhere. The publishing industry was especially vulnerable. Television and paperback books were the coming forms of cheap entertainment for the masses; there was little room for the pulps in the new and changing society.

Most titles were extinct by 1950. A few hardy ones—*Detective Tales, Dime Detective, Thrilling Detective, Popular Detective, Famous Detective, Crack Detective*—hung on a few years longer, but they could not compete with digest-sized mystery monthlies like *Manhunt,* which published better stories by better writers. When the last detective pulp died in 1957, hardly anyone noticed. And fewer still mourned the end of a great era.

But interest in that era, and in the pulps themselves, began to pick up again among collectors and students of popular culture—slowly at first, then with increasing fervor. In the seventies, some of the rarer pulps—*The Octopus, Wu Fang, Dr. Yen Sin,* early issues of *Weird Tales, The Shadow, Doc Savage,* and *Black Mask*—commanded high prices from dealers. (Prices have dropped somewhat in recent years, but desirable titles still fetch princely sums.) Histories and reminiscences of the pulps and the pulp years began to appear, among them Ron Goulart's informal history, *Cheap Thrills,* Frank Gruber's *The Pulp Jungle,* and Robert Jones's *The Shudder Pulps.* A number of paperback reprints of hero-pulp novels chronicling the adventures of Doc Savage, The Shadow, G-8 and his Battle Aces, The Phantom Detective, and others have also appeared; and small specialty publishers continue to do modestly well with books of pulp stories, mainly single-author collections and various works of horror, fantasy, and science fiction.

But few anthologies and collections of pulp crime fiction have been published, except for books by major figures (Dashiell Hammett, Raymond Chandler, Cornell Woolrich) and an occasional volume such as Ron Goulart's *The Hardboiled Dicks* (1965) or Herbert Ruhm's *The Hard-Boiled Detective: Stories from Black Mask Magazine* (1977). This dearth of anthologies is regrettable. To be sure, most pulp fiction was of poor quality; the stories were hastily written—many by hacks and many more by amateurs in order to satisfy the annual demand for millions upon millions of words during the boom years—and the bulk of them should be allowed to lie undisturbed in their mouldering pulp graves. There is, however, a substantial body of pulp work that *is* good, that *is* worth resurrecting: work by talented writers, many of whom went on to achieve success and acclaim as novelists after their training years in the pulp mill—Hammett, Chandler, Woolrich, Erle Stanley Gardner, Frederick Nebel, Horace McCoy, Frank Gruber, Robert Bloch, William E. Barrett, Fredric Brown, John D. MacDonald, William Campbell Gault and John Jakes, to name just a few.

This anthology is the first to offer a wide cross-section of pulp detective and mystery fiction from a variety of magazines, by some of the writers listed above and by others of unique ability who are generally unknown today: Norbert Davis, Dane Gregory, D. L. Champion. And it is only a small sampling of the material that deserves to be reprinted for the entertainment of modern readers.

I hope you enjoy the stories in these pages as much as I do. And I hope, too, that when you've finished the last of them, you'll join the growing number of aficionados whose fascination with that grand era leads us to champion the best it had to offer.

The pulps are dead; long live the pulps!

San Francisco, California   Bill Pronzini

DASHIELL HAMMETT

Arson Plus

THE MOST IMPORTANT of all the detective pulp magazines, in terms of quality—for part of its thirty-year life, anyway—and the development of the American school of realistic crime fiction, was Black Mask. And Black Mask's most important writer, of course, was Dashiell Hammett.

The magazine was founded in 1920 by, of all people, literateurs H. L. Mencken and George Jean Nathan—primarily because they were co-owners and co-editors of The Smart Set, a glossy jazz-age "magazine of cleverness" that was in constant financial straits. Mencken thought that by establishing "a new cheap magazine," he and Nathan could bail themselves out of debt. As it turned out, he was right. The first issue was dated April 1920 and was met with immediate favor by readers. As Mencken wrote to a friend a short while later, "Our new louse, the Black Mask, seems to be a success. The thing has burdened both Nathan and me with disagreeable work." Still later he stated that Black Mask was "a lousy magazine—all detective stories. I hear Woodrow [Wilson] reads it."

Mencken and Nathan sold Black Mask after six months, for a handsome profit. Phil Cody, Harry North, and George W. Sutton assumed command, and slowly the magazine began to undergo a transformation. The early issues were full of more or less genteel crime tales of the British drawing-room ilk, interspersed with standard adventure, Western, and "novelty" stories. But in 1923, as pulp biographer Ron Goulart puts it in Cheap Thrills: An Informal History of the Pulp Magazines (1972), "the real world began to invade Black Mask." It did so in the person of two young writers. Carroll John Daly was one; Hammett was the other.

Arson Plus

Hammett's first published story, "The Road Home," appeared in the December 1922 issue of Black Mask, *under his pseudonym Peter Collinson. The first "Continental Op" story was "Arson Plus," also as by Collinson, in the October 1, 1923 issue; the October 15 number contained "Crooked Souls," another Op novelette and Hammett's first appearance in the magazine under his own name. Two dozen Op stories (and the serialized versions of* The Dain Curse *and* Red Harvest) *followed, as did Sam Spade and the marvelous Maltese falcon and Ned Beaumont and* The Glass Key. *All in all, Hammett wrote thirty-one stories and four novels for* Black Mask *from 1922 to 1930, and in doing so altered forever the face of modern crime fiction.*

The Continental Op, fat, tough, and fortyish, was based on a man named James Wright, Assistant Superintendent of the Pinkerton Detective Agency in Baltimore, for whom Hammett had worked. And his methods, if not his cases, are based on real private-investigative procedures of the period. It was in these Op stories that Hammett honed his realistic style and plotting techniques, both of which would reach their zenith in The Maltese Falcon *(1929), unquestionably the finest "hardboiled" detective novel ever written.*

Even though it is his first recorded case, the Op is at his sharp-witted best in "Arson Plus"—probably the least known of the Op stories. (It was not included in either of the two "authorized" Continental Op collections, and has not appeared anywhere, at least to this editor's knowledge, since Ellery Queen reprinted it in one of his series of Hammett collections, Woman in the Dark, *in 1951.) It has been too long out of print.*

Before he began writing, Samuel Dashiell Hammett (1894–1961) worked as a clerk, stevedore, advertising manager, and served a fourteen-year stint, from 1908 to 1922, as an operative of the Pinkerton Agency. As prolific as he was in the twenties, he published just one novel after his Black Mask *years ended in 1930 (*The Thin Man, *1934, the weakest of his books) and no fiction at all during his last twenty-seven years of life. A variety of reasons has been put forth for this terminal dry spell: writer's block, a lack of new ideas, his steady consumption of alcohol, his close association with playwright Lillian Hellman. But whatever the true reason, it was known only to Hammett himself—and properly so. The stories and novels he did write are all that should matter to us.*

JIM TARR PICKED up the cigar I rolled across his desk, looked at the band, bit off an end, and reached for a match.

"Three for a buck," he said. "You must want me to break a *couple* of laws for you this time."

I had been doing business with this fat sheriff of Sacramento County for four or five years—ever since I came to the Continental Detective Agency's San Francisco office—and I had never known him to miss an opening for a sour crack; but it didn't mean anything.

"Wrong both times," I told him. "I get them for two bits each, and I'm here to do you a favor instead of asking for one. The company that insured Thornburgh's house thinks somebody touched it off."

"That's right enough, according to the fire department. They tell me the lower part of the house was soaked with gasoline, but the Lord knows how they could tell—there wasn't a stick left standing. I've got McClump working on it, but he hasn't found anything to get excited about yet."

"What's the layout? All I know is that there was a fire."

Tarr leaned back in his chair and bellowed:

"Hey, Mac!"

The pearl push buttons on his desk are ornaments so far as he is concerned. Deputy sheriffs McHale, McClump, and Macklin came to the door together—MacNab apparently wasn't within hearing.

"What's the idea?" the sheriff demanded of McClump. "Are you carrying a bodyguard around with you?"

The two other deputies, thus informed as to whom "Mac" referred this time, went back to their cribbage game.

"We got a city slicker here to catch our firebug for us," Tarr told his deputy. "But we got to tell him what it's all about first."

McClump and I had worked together on an express robbery several months before. He's a rangy, towheaded youngster of twenty-five or six, with all the nerve in the world—and most of the laziness.

"Ain't the Lord good to us?"

He had himself draped across a chair by now—always his first objective when he comes into a room.

"Well, here's how she stands: This fellow Thornburgh's house was a couple miles out of town, on the old county road—an old

8

frame house. About midnight, night before last, Jeff Pringle—the nearest neighbor, a half-mile or so to the east—saw a glare in the sky from over that way, and phoned in the alarm; but by the time the fire wagons got there, there wasn't enough of the house left to bother about. Pringle was the first of the neighbors to get to the house, and the roof had already fallen in then.

"Nobody saw anything suspicious—no strangers hanging around or nothing. Thornburgh's help just managed to save themselves, and that was all. They don't know much about what happened—too scared, I reckon. But they did see Thornburgh at his window just before the fire got him. A fellow here in town—name of Henderson—saw that part of it too. He was driving home from Wayton, and got to the house just before the roof caved in.

"The fire department people say they found signs of gasoline. The Coonses, Thornburgh's help, say they didn't have no gas on the place. So there you are."

"Thornburgh have any relatives?"

"Yeah. A niece in San Francisco—a Mrs. Evelyn Trowbridge. She was up yesterday, but there wasn't nothing she could do, and she couldn't tell us nothing much, so she went back home."

"Where are the servants now?"

"Here in town. Staying at a hotel on I Street. I told 'em to stick around for a few days."

"Thornburgh own the house?"

"Uh-huh. Bought it from Newning & Weed a couple months ago."

"You got anything to do this morning?"

"Nothing but this."

"Good. Let's get out and dig around."

We found the Coonses in their room at the hotel on I Street. Mr. Coons was a small-boned, plump man with the smooth, meaningless face and the suavity of the typical male house-servant.

His wife was a tall, stringy woman, perhaps five years older than her husband—say, forty—with a mouth and chin that seemed shaped for gossiping. But he did all the talking, while she nodded her agreement to every second or third word.

"We went to work for Mr. Thornburgh on the fifteenth of June I think," he said, in reply to my first question. "We came to Sacra

9

mento, around the first of the month, and put in applications at the Allis Employment Bureau. A couple of weeks later they sent us out to see Mr. Thornburgh, and he took us on."

"Where were you before you came here?"

"In Seattle, sir, with a Mrs. Comerford; but the climate there didn't agree with my wife—she has bronchial trouble—so we decided to come to California. We most likely would have stayed in Seattle, though, if Mrs. Comerford hadn't given up her house."

"What do you know about Thornburgh?"

"Very little, sir. He wasn't a talkative gentleman. He hadn't any business that I know of. I think he was a retired seafaring man. He never said he was, but he had that manner and look. He never went out or had anybody in to see him, except his niece once, and he didn't write or get any mail. He had a room next to his bedroom fixed up as a sort of workshop. He spent most of his time in there. I always thought he was working on some kind of invention, but he kept the door locked, and wouldn't let us go near it."

"Haven't you any idea at all what it was?"

"No, sir. We never heard any hammering or noises from it, and never smelled anything either. And none of his clothes were ever the least bit soiled, even when they were ready to go out to the laundry. They would have been if he had been working on anything like machinery."

"Was he an old man?"

"He couldn't have been over fifty, sir. He was very erect, and his hair and beard were thick, with no gray hairs."

"Ever have any trouble with him?"

"Oh, no, sir! He was, if I may say it, a very peculiar gentleman in a way; and he didn't care about anything except having his meals fixed right, having his clothes taken care of—he was very particular about them—and not being disturbed. Except early in the morning and at night, we'd hardly see him all day."

"Now about the fire. Tell us everything you remember."

"Well, sir, my wife and I had gone to bed about ten o'clock, our regular time, and had gone to sleep. Our room was on the second floor, in the rear. Some time later—I never did exactly know what time it was—I woke up, coughing. The room was all full of smoke, and my wife was sort of strangling. I jumped up, and dragged her down the back stairs and out the back door.

"When I had her safe in the yard, I thought of Mr. Thornburgh, and tried to get back in the house; but the whole first floor was just flames. I ran around front then, to see if he had got out, but didn't see anything of him. The whole yard was as light as day by then. Then I heard him scream—a horrible scream, sir—I can hear it yet! And I looked up at his window—that was the front second-story room—and saw him there, trying to get out the window! But all the woodwork was burning, and he screamed again and fell back, and right after that the roof over his room fell in.

"There wasn't a ladder or anything that I could have put up to the window—there wasn't anything I could have done.

"In the meantime, a gentleman had left his automobile in the road, and come up to where I was standing; but there wasn't anything we could do—the house was burning everywhere and falling in here and there. So we went back to where I had left my wife, and carried her farther away from the fire, and brought her to—she had fainted. And that's all I know about it, sir."

"Hear any noises earlier that night? Or see anybody hanging around?"

"No, sir."

"Have any gasoline around the place?"

"No, sir. Mr. Thornburgh didn't have a car."

"No gasoline for cleaning?"

"No, sir, none at all, unless Mr. Thornburgh had it in his workshop. When his clothes needed cleaning, I took them to town, and all his laundry was taken by the grocer's man, when he brought our provisions."

"Don't know anything that might have some bearing on the fire?"

"No, sir. I was surprised when I heard that somebody had set the house afire. I could hardly believe it. I don't know why anybody should want to do that. . . ."

"What do you think of them?" I asked McClump, as we left the hotel.

"They might pad the bills, or even go South with some of the silver, but they don't figure as killers in my mind."

That was my opinion, too; but they were the only persons known to have been there when the fire started except the man who had died. We went around to the Allis Employment Bureau and talked to the manager.

He told us that the Coonses had come into his office on June second, looking for work; and had given Mrs. Edward Comerford, 45 Woodmansee Terrace, Seattle, Washington, as reference. In reply to a letter—he always checked up the references of servants—Mrs. Comerford had written that the Coonses had been in her employ for a number of years, and had been "extremely satisfactory in every respect." On June thirteenth, Thornburgh had telephoned the bureau, asking that a man and his wife be sent out to keep house for him, and Allis sent out two couples he had listed. Neither couple had been employed by Thornburgh, though Allis considered them more desirable than the Coonses, who were finally hired by Thornburgh.

All that would certainly seem to indicate that the Coonses hadn't deliberately maneuvered themselves into the place, unless they were the luckiest people in the world—and a detective can't afford to believe in luck or coincidence, unless he has unquestionable proof of it.

At the office of the real-estate agents, through whom Thornburgh had bought the house—Newning & Weed—we were told that Thornburgh had come in on the eleventh of June, and had said that he had been told that the house was for sale, had looked it over, and wanted to know the price. The deal had been closed the next morning, and he had paid for the house with a check for $14,500 on the Seamen's Bank of San Francisco. The house was already furnished.

After luncheon, McClump and I called on Howard Henderson—the man who had seen the fire while driving home from Wayton. He had an office in the Empire Building, with his name and the title *Northern California Agent for Krispy Korn Krumbs* on the door. He was a big, careless-looking man of forty-five or so, with the professionally jovial smile that belongs to the traveling salesman.

He had been in Wayton on business the day of the fire, he said, and had stayed there until rather late, going to dinner and afterward playing pool with a grocer named Hammersmith—one of his customers. He had left Wayton in his machine, at about ten thirty, and set out for Sacramento. At Tavender he had stopped at the garage for oil and gas, and to have one of his tires blown up.

Just as he was about to leave the garage, the garage man had called his attention to a red glare in the sky, and had told him that it was probably from a fire somewhere along the old county road that paralleled the state road into Sacramento; so Henderson had taken the county road, and had arrived at the burning house just in time to see Thornburgh try to fight his way through the flames that enveloped him.

It was too late to make any attempt to put out the fire, and the man upstairs was beyond saving by then—undoubtedly dead even before the roof collapsed; so Henderson had helped Coons revive his wife, and stayed there watching the fire until it had burned itself out. He had seen no one on that county road while driving to the fire. . . .

"What do you know about Henderson?" I asked McClump, when we were on the street.

"Came here, from somewhere in the East, I think, early in the summer to open that breakfast-cereal agency. Lives at the Garden Hotel. Where do we go next?"

"We get a car, and take a look at what's left of the Thornburgh house."

An enterprising incendiary couldn't have found a lovelier spot in which to turn himself loose, if he looked the whole county over. Tree-topped hills hid it from the rest of the world, on three sides; while away from the fourth, an uninhabited plain rolled down to the river. The county road that passed the front gate was shunned by automobiles, so McClump said, in favor of the state highway to the north.

Where the house had been was now a mound of blackened ruins. We poked around in the ashes for a few minutes—not that we expected to find anything, but because it's the nature of man to poke around in ruins.

A garage in the rear, whose interior gave no evidence of recent occupation, had a badly scorched roof and front, but was otherwise undamaged. A shed behind it, sheltering an ax, a shovel, and various odds and ends of gardening tools, had escaped the fire altogether. The lawn in front of the house, and the garden behind the shed—about an acre in all—had been pretty thoroughly cut and trampled by wagon wheels, and the feet of the firemen and the spectators.

Having ruined our shoeshines, McClump and I got back in our car and swung off in a circle around the place, calling at all the houses within a mile radius, and getting little besides jolts for our trouble.

The nearest house was that of Pringle, the man who had turned in the alarm; but he not only knew nothing about the dead man, he said he had never even seen him. In fact, only one of the neighbors had ever seen him: a Mrs. Jabine, who lived about a mile to the south.

She had taken care of the key to the house while it was vacant; and a day or two before he bought it, Thornburgh had come to her house, inquiring about the vacant one. She had gone over there with him and showed him through it, and he had told her that he intended buying it, if the price wasn't too high.

He had been alone, except for the chauffeur of the hired car in which he had come from Sacramento, and, save that he had no family, he had told her nothing about himself.

Hearing that he had moved in, she went over to call on him several days later—"just a neighborly visit"—but had been told by Mrs. Coons that he was not at home. Most of the neighbors had talked to the Coonses, and had got the impression that Thornburgh did not care for visitors, so they had let him alone. The Coonses were described as "pleasant enough to talk to when you meet them," but reflecting their employer's desire not to make friends.

McClump summarized what the afternoon had taught us as we pointed our car toward Tavender: "Any of these folks could have touched off the place, but we got nothing to show that any of 'em even knew Thornburgh, let alone had a bone to pick with him."

Tavender turned out to be a crossroads settlement of a general store and post office, a garage, a church, and six dwellings, about two miles from Thornburgh's place. McClump knew the store-keeper and postmaster, a scrawny little man named Philo, who stuttered moistly.

"I n-n-never s-saw Th-thornburgh," he said, "and I n-n-never had any m-mail for him. C-coons"—it sounded like one of these things butterflies come out of—"used to c-come in once a week to-to order groceries—they d-didn't have a phone. He used to walk in, and I'd s-send the stuff over in my c-c-car. Th-then I'd s-see him once in a while, waiting f-for the stage to S-s-sacramento."

"Who drove the stuff out to Thornburgh's?"

"M-m-my b-boy. Want to t-talk to him?"

The boy was a juvenile edition of the old man, but without the stutter. He had never seen Thornburgh on any of his visits, but his business had taken him only as far as the kitchen. He hadn't noticed anything peculiar about the place.

"Who's the night man at the garage?" I asked him.

"Billy Luce. I think you can catch him there now. I saw him go in a few minutes ago."

We crossed the road and found Luce.

"Night before last—the night of the fire down the road—was there a man here talking to you when you first saw it?"

He turned his eyes upward in that vacant stare which people use to aid their memory.

"Yes, I remember now! He was going to town, and I told him that if he took the county road instead of the state road he'd see the fire on his way in."

"What kind of looking man was he?"

"Middle-aged—a big man, but sort of slouchy. I think he had on a brown suit, baggy and wrinkled."

"Medium complexion?"

"Yes."

"Smile when he talked?"

"Yes, a pleasant sort of fellow."

"Brown hair?"

"Yeah, but have a heart!" Luce laughed. "I didn't put him under a magnifying glass."

From Tavender we drove over to Wayton. Luce's description had fit Henderson all right, but while we were at it, we thought we might as well check up to make sure that he had been coming from Wayton.

We spent exactly twenty-five minutes in Wayton; ten of them finding Hammersmith, the grocer with whom Henderson had said he dined and played pool; five minutes finding the proprietor of the pool room; and ten verifying Henderson's story. . . .

"What do you think of it now, Mac?" I asked, as we rolled back toward Sacramento.

Mac's too lazy to express an opinion, or even form one, unless he's driven to it; but that doesn't mean they aren't worth listening to, if you can get them.

"There ain't a hell of a lot to think," he said cheerfully. "Henderson is out of it, if he ever was in it. There's nothing to show that anybody but the Coonses and Thornburgh were there when the fire started—but there may have been a regiment there. Them Coonses ain't too honest-looking, maybe, but they ain't killers, or I miss my guess. But the fact remains that they're the only bet we got so far. Maybe we ought to try to get a line on them."

"All right," I agreed. "Soon as we get back to town, I'll get a wire off to our Seattle office asking them to interview Mrs. Comerford, and see what she can tell about them. Then I'm going to catch a train for San Francisco and see Thornburgh's niece in the morning."

Next morning, at the address McClump had given me—a rather elaborate apartment building on California Street—I had to wait three-quarters of an hour for Mrs. Evelyn Trowbridge to dress. If I had been younger, or a social caller, I suppose I'd have felt amply rewarded when she finally came in—a tall, slender woman of less than thirty; in some sort of clinging black affair; with a lot of black hair over a very white face, strikingly set off by a small red mouth and big hazel eyes.

But I was a busy, middle-aged detective, who was fuming over having his time wasted; and I was a lot more interested in finding the bird who struck the match than I was in feminine beauty. However, I smothered my grouch, apologized for disturbing her at such an early hour, and got down to business.

"I want you to tell me all you know about your uncle—his family, friends, enemies, business connections—everything."

I had scribbled on the back of the card I had sent into her what my business was.

"He hadn't any family," she said; "unless I might be it. He was my mother's brother, and I am the only one of that family now living."

"Where was he born?"

"Here in San Francisco. I don't know the date, but he was about fifty years old, I think—three years older than my mother."

"What was his business?"

"He went to sea when he was a boy, and, so far as I know, always followed it until a few months ago."

"Captain?"

"I don't know. Sometimes I wouldn't see or hear from him for several years, and he never talked about what he was doing; though he would mention some of the places he had visited—Rio de Janeiro, Madagascar, Tobago, Christiania. Then, about three months ago—some time in May—he came here and told me that he was through with wandering; that he was going to take a house in some quiet place where he could work undisturbed on an invention in which he was interested.

"He lived at the Francisco Hotel while he was in San Francisco. After a couple of weeks he suddenly disappeared. And then, about a month ago, I received a telegram from him, asking me to come to see him at his house near Sacramento. I went up the very next day, and I thought that he was acting queerly—he seemed very excited over something. He gave me a will that he had just drawn up and some life-insurance policies in which I was beneficiary.

"Immediately after that he insisted that I return home, and hinted rather plainly that he did not wish me to either visit him again or write until I heard from him. I thought all that rather peculiar, as he had always seemed fond of me. I never saw him again."

"What was this invention he was working on?"

"I really don't know. I asked him once, but he became so excited—even suspicious—that I changed the subject, and never mentioned it again."

"Are you sure that he really did follow the sea all those years?"

"No, I am not. I just took it for granted; but he may have been doing something altogether different."

"Was he ever married?"

"Not that I know of."

"Know any of his friends or enemies?"

"No, none."

"Remember anybody's name that he ever mentioned?"

"No."

"I don't want you to think this next question insulting, though I admit it is. Where were you the night of the fire?"

"At home; I had some friends here to dinner, and they stayed until about midnight. Mr. and Mrs. Walker Kellogg, Mrs. John Dupree, and a Mr. Killmer, who is a lawyer. I can give you their addresses, if you want to question them."

From Mrs. Trowbridge's apartment I went to the Francisco Hotel. Thornburgh had been registered there from May tenth to June thirteenth, and hadn't attracted much attention. He had been a tall, broad-shouldered, erect man of about fifty, with rather long brown hair brushed straight back; a short, pointed brown beard, and a healthy, ruddy complexion—grave, quiet, punctilious in dress and manner; his hours had been regular and he had had no visitors that any of the hotel employees remembered.

At the Seamen's Bank—upon which Thornburgh's check, in payment of the house, had been drawn—I was told that he had opened an account there on May fifteenth, having been introduced by W. W. Jeffers & Sons, local stockbrokers. A balance of a little more than four hundred dollars remained to his credit. The cancelled checks on hand were all to the order of various life-insurance companies; and for amounts that, if they represented premiums, testified to rather large policies. I jotted down the names of the life-insurance companies, and then went to the offices of W. W. Jeffers & Sons.

Thornburgh had come in, I was told, on the tenth of May with $15,000 worth of bonds that he had wanted sold. During one of his conversations with Jeffers he had asked the broker to recommend a bank, and Jeffers had given him a letter of introduction to the Seamen's Bank.

That was all Jeffers knew about him. He gave me the numbers of the bonds, but tracing bonds isn't always the easiest thing in the world.

The reply to my Seattle telegram was waiting for me at the Continental Detective Agency when I arrived.

MRS. EDWARD COMERFORD RENTED APARTMENT AT ADDRESS YOU GIVE ON MAY TWENTY-FIVE. GAVE IT UP JUNE SIX. TRUNKS TO SAN

FRANCISCO SAME DAY CHECK NUMBERS ON FOUR FIVE TWO FIVE
EIGHT SEVEN AND EIGHT AND NINE.

Tracing baggage is no trick at all, if you have the dates and check numbers to start with—as many a bird who is wearing somewhat similar numbers on his chest and back, because he overlooked that detail when making his getaway, can tell you—and twenty-five minutes in a baggage-room at the Ferry and half an hour in the office of a transfer company gave me my answer.

The trunks had been delivered to Mrs. Evelyn Trowbridge's apartment!

I got Jim Tarr on the phone and told him about it.

"Good shooting!" he said, forgetting for once to indulge his wit. "We'll grab the Coonses here and Mrs. Trowbridge there, and that's the end of another mystery."

"Wait a minute!" I cautioned him. "It's not all straightened out yet—there're still a few kinks in the plot."

"It's straight enough for me. I'm satisfied."

"You're the boss, but I think you're being a little hasty. I'm going up and talk with the niece again. Give me a little time before you phone the police here to make the pinch. I'll hold her until they get there."

Evelyn Trowbridge let me in this time, instead of the maid who had opened the door for me in the morning, and she led me to the same room in which we had had our first talk. I let her pick out a seat, and then I selected one that was closer to either door than hers was.

On the way up I had planned a lot of innocent-sounding questions that would get her all snarled up; but after taking a good look at this woman sitting in front of me, leaning comfortably back in her chair, coolly waiting for me to speak my piece, I discarded the trick stuff and came out cold-turkey.

"Ever use the name Mrs. Edward Comerford?"

"Oh, yes." As casual as a nod on the street.

"When?"

"Often. You see, I happen to have been married not so long ago to Mr. Edward Comerford. So it's not really strange that I should have used the name."

19

"Use it in Seattle recently?"

"I would suggest," she said sweetly, "that if you are leading up to the references I gave Coons and his wife, you might save time by coming right to it."

"That's fair enough," I said. "Let's do that."

There wasn't a tone or shading, in voice, manner, or expression, to indicate that she was talking about anything half so serious or important to her as a possibility of being charged with murder. She might have been talking about the weather.

"During the time that Mr. Comerford and I were married, we lived in Seattle, where he still lives. After the divorce, I left Seattle and resumed my maiden name. And the Coonses *were* in our employ, as you might learn if you care to look it up. You'll find my husband—or former husband—at the Chelsea Apartments, I think.

"Last summer, or late spring, I decided to return to Seattle. The truth of it is—I suppose all my personal affairs will be aired anyhow—that I thought perhaps Edward and I might patch up our differences; so I went back and took an apartment on Wood-mansee Terrace. As I was known in Seattle as Mrs. Edward Comerford, and as I thought my using his name might influence him a little, I used it while I was there.

"Also I telephoned the Coonses to make tentative arrangements in case Edward and I should open our house again; but Coons told me that they were going to California, and so I gladly gave them an excellent recommendation when, some days later, I received a letter of inquiry from an employment bureau in Sacramento. After I had been in Seattle for about two weeks, I changed my mind about the reconciliation—Edward's interest, I learned, was all centered elsewhere; so I returned to San Francisco—"

"Very nice! But—"

"If you will permit me to finish," she interrupted. "When I went to see my uncle in response to his telegram, I was surprised to find the Coonses in his house. Knowing my uncle's peculiarities, and finding them now increased, and remembering his extreme secretiveness about his mysterious invention, I cautioned the Coonses not to tell him that they had been in my employ.

"He certainly would have discharged them, and just as certainly would have quarreled with me—he would have thought that I was having him spied on. Then, when Coons telephoned me after the fire, I knew that to admit that the Coonses had been formerly in my employ, would, in view of the fact that I was my uncle's only heir, cast suspicion on all three of us. So we foolishly agreed to say nothing and carry on the deception."

That didn't sound all wrong—but it didn't sound all right. I wished Tarr had taken it easier and let us get a better line on these people, before having them thrown in the coop.

"The coincidence of the Coonses stumbling into my uncle's house is, I fancy, too much for your detecting instincts," she went on. "Am I to consider myself under arrest?"

I'm beginning to like this girl; she's a nice, cool piece of work.

"Not yet," I told her. "But I'm afraid it's going to happen pretty soon."

She smiled a little mocking smile at that, and another when the doorbell rang.

It was O'Hara from police headquarters. We turned the apartment upside down and inside out, but didn't find anything of importance except the will she had told me about, dated July eighth, and her uncle's life-insurance policies. They were all dated between May fifteenth and June tenth, and added up to a little more than $200,000.

I spent an hour grilling the maid after O'Hara had taken Evelyn Trowbridge away, but she didn't know any more than I did. However, between her, the janitor, the manager of the apartments, and the names Mrs. Trowbridge had given me, I learned that she had really been entertaining friends on the night of the fire—until after eleven o'clock, anyway—and that was late enough.

Half an hour later I was riding the Short Line back to Sacramento. I was getting to be one of the line's best customers, and my anatomy was on bouncing terms with every bump in the road.

Between bumps I tried to fit the pieces of this Thornburgh puzzle together. The niece and the Coonses fit in somewhere, but not just where we had them. We had been working on the job sort of lopsided, but it was the best we could do with it. In the beginning we had turned to the Coonses and Evelyn Trowbridge because there was no other direction to go; and now we had something on them—but a good lawyer could make hash out of it.

The Coonses were in the county jail when I got to Sacramento. After some questioning they had admitted their connection with the niece, and had come through with stories that matched hers.

Tarr, McClump and I sat around the sheriff's desk and argued.

"Those yarns are pipe dreams," the sheriff said. "We got all three of 'em cold, and they're as good as convicted."

McClump grinned derisively at his superior, and then turned to me.

"Go on, you tell him about the holes in his little case. He ain't your boss, and can't take it out on you later for being smarter than he is!"

Tarr glared from one of us to the other.

"Spill it, you wise guys!" he ordered.

"Our dope is," I told him, figuring that McClump's view of it was the same as mine, "that there's nothing to show that even Thornburgh knew he was going to buy that house before the tenth of June, and that the Coonses were in town looking for work on the second. And besides, it was only by luck that they got the jobs. The employment office sent two couples out there ahead of them."

"We'll take a chance on letting the jury figure that out."

"Yes? You'll also take a chance on them figuring out that Thornburgh, who seems to have been a nut, might have touched off the place himself! We've got something on these people, Jim, but not enough to go into court with them. How are you going to prove that when the Coonses were planted in Thornburgh's house—if you can even prove that they were planted—they and the Trowbridge woman knew he was going to load up with insurance policies?"

The sheriff spat disgustedly.

"You guys are the limit! You run around in circles, digging up the dope on these people until you get enough to hang 'em, and then you run around hunting for outs! What's the matter with you now?"

I answered him from halfway to the door—the pieces were beginning to fit together under my skull.

"Going to run some more circles—come on, Mac!"

McClump and I held a conference on the fly, and then I got a car from the nearest garage and headed for Tavender. We made time going out, and got there before the general store had closed for the night. The stuttering Philo separated himself from the two men with whom he had been talking, and followed me to the rear of the store.

"Do you keep an itemized list of the laundry you handle?"

"N-n-no; just the amounts."

"Let's look at Thornburgh's."

He produced a begrimed and rumpled account book, and we picked out the weekly items I wanted: $2.60, $3.10, $2.25, and so on.

"Got the last batch of laundry here?"

"Y-yes," he said. "It j-just c-c-came out from the city t-today."

I tore open the bundle—some sheets, pillowcases, tablecloths, towels, napkins; some feminine clothing; some shirts, collars, underwear, and socks that were unmistakably Coons's. I thanked Philo while running back to the car.

Back in Sacramento again, McClump was waiting for me at the garage where I had hired the car.

"Registered at the hotel on June fifteenth; rented the office on the sixteenth. I think he's in the hotel now," he greeted me.

We hurried around the block to the Garden Hotel.

"Mr. Henderson went out a minute or two ago," the night clerk told us. "He seemed to be in a hurry."

"Know where he keeps his car?"

"In the hotel garage around the corner."

We were within ten feet of the garage, when Henderson's automobile shot out and turned up the street.

"Oh, Mr. Henderson!" I cried, trying to keep my voice level.

He stepped on the gas and streaked away from us.

"Want him?" McClump asked; and at my nod he stopped a passing roadster by the simple expedient of stepping in front of it.

We climbed in, McClump flashed his star at the bewildered driver, and pointed out Henderson's dwindling tail-light. After he had persuaded himself that he wasn't being boarded by a couple of bandits, the commandeered driver did his best, and we picked up Henderson's tail-light after two or three turnings, and closed in on him—though his car was going at a good clip.

By the time we reached the outskirts of the city, we had crawled up to within safe shooting distance, and I sent a bullet over the fleeing man's head. Thus encouraged, he managed to get a little more speed out of his car; but we were overhauling him now.

Just at the wrong minute Henderson decided to look over his shoulder at us—an unevenness in the road twisted his wheels—his machine swayed—skidded—went over on its side. Almost immediately, from the heart of the tangle, came a flash and a bullet moaned past my ear. Another. And then, while I was still hunting for something to shoot at in the pile of junk we were drawing down upon, McClump's ancient and battered revolver roared in my other ear.

Henderson was dead when we got to him—McClump's bullet had taken him over one eye.

McClump spoke to me over the body.

"I ain't an inquisitive sort of fellow, but I hope you don't mind telling me why I shot this lad."

"Because he was—*Thornburgh*."

He didn't say anything for about five minutes. Then: "I reckon that's right. How'd you know it?"

We were sitting beside the wreckage now, waiting for the police that we had sent our commandeered chauffeur to phone for.

"He had to be," I said, "when you think it all over. Funny we didn't hit on it before! All that stuff we were told about Thornburgh had a fishy sound. Whiskers and an unknown profession, immaculate and working on a mysterious invention, very secretive and born in San Francisco—where the fire wiped out all the old records—just the sort of fake that could be cooked up easily.

"Now, consider Henderson. You had told me he came to Sacramento sometime early this summer—and the dates you got tonight show that he didn't come until *after* Thornburgh had bought his house. All right! Now compare Henderson with the descriptions we got of Thornburgh.

"Both are about the same size and age, and with the same color hair. The differences are all things that can be manufactured—clothes, a little sunburn, and a month's growth of beard, along with a little acting, would do the trick. Tonight I went out to Tavender and took a look at the last batch of laundry—and there wasn't any that didn't fit the Coonses! And none of the bills all the way back were large enough for Thornburgh to have been as careful about his clothes as we were told he was."

"It must be great to be a detective!" McClump grinned as the police ambulance came up and began disgorging policemen. "I reckon somebody must have tipped Henderson off that I was asking about him this evening." And then, regretfully: "So we ain't going to hang them folks for murder after all."

"No, but we oughtn't have any trouble convicting them of arson plus conspiracy to defraud, and anything else that the Prosecuting Attorney can think up."

CARROLL JOHN DALY

Knights of the Open Palm

THE JUNE 1, 1923 issue of Black Mask is probably the most remarkable single issue of any pulp magazine. Its cover depicts a robed and hooded figure carrying a burning black cross, and bears the words "Ku Klux Klan Number"; nearly 100 of its 128 pages are devoted to stories, articles, and comments about the KKK—at least half of which are unabashedly pro-Klan.

The "Ku Klux Klan Number" was the brainchild of then-editor George W. Sutton, who wrote in an editorial that "the attempt to revive the old Ku Klux Klan—with new ideas and new purposes—was the most picturesque element that has appeared in American life since the war, regardless of whether we condemn its aims—whatever they may be—or not." He went on to explain that he had asked some of his best and most popular writers to "turn their muses loose on the Klan idea. We did not ask them to find out any more about the Klan than newspaper headlines would tell them. We wanted their stories to reflect only their reactions on the same Klan knowledge possessed by our readers" (emphasis Sutton's). And he concluded that the result was "an interesting collection of stories, including two novelettes—adventure, romance, humor, mystery, detective problems— with a sprinkling of vigorous articles for variety. We hope you'll enjoy this literary side-journey into the Invisible Empire."

The less said about most of this "literary side-journey," the better. But *there is one story in the issue that is worth attention—Carroll John Daly's "Knights of the Open Palm." It is an anti-Klan story, to be sure; even more important, from the historical point of view, it is the first fully realized hard-boiled private eye story, starring Race Williams and predating the "Arson Plus" debut of the Continental Op by four months. (An embryonic private eye, Terry Mack, also created by Daly, appeared two weeks earlier, in the May 15, 1923 issue of* Black Mask, *in a story called "Three Gun Terry.")*

Race Williams is a violent, crude, somewhat sadistic loner—a man of action, with no compunctions and no real vulnerabilities. In "Knights of the Open Palm," he says about himself, "I'm what you might call a middleman—just a halfway house between the dicks and the crooks. Oh, there ain't no doubt that both the cops and the crooks take me for a gun, but I ain't—not rightly speaking. I do a little honest shooting once in a while—just in the way of business. But my conscience is clear; I never bumped off a guy what didn't need it."

Daly wrote a total of fifty-three Race Williams stories for Black Mask *(and seventy-one stories for it altogether). They were enormously popular in the twenties and early thirties. In a poll conducted by editor Joseph T. Shaw in 1930, Daly was judged* Black Mask's *favorite writer; Erle Stanley Gardner finished second, with Hammett a somewhat distant third in the voting. (Many years later, Mickey Spillane would tell the world that Daly was one of his favorite writers, too, and sing the praises of Race Williams. Any similarity between the methods of Williams and those of Mike Hammer is purely intentional.)*

Born in Yonkers, New York in 1889, Daly was thirty-three years old when he created Race Williams. Before that he had studied law and stenography, worked as an assistant manager in a motion picture house, and finally owned and operated the first film theater on the boardwalk in Atlantic City. After his early successes in Black Mask, *he turned to full-time writing, of stories for the pulps and of such novels as* The Snarl of the Beast *(1927),* The Hidden Hand *(1928),* The Tag Murders *(1930), and* Murder from the East *(1935).*

He was a one-dimensional and melodramatic writer, however, and his popularity began to wane in the thirties as newer, better, and more sophisticated writers emerged in the pulps and in the book market. Although he continued to contribute to the pulps until their demise in the mid-fifties, his last novel published in the U.S. was in 1936; and his final four books appeared only in England and Canada. He died in 1958, a forgotten man who had been unable to transcend the hack level of pulp writing.

Still, some of Daly's early work for Black Mask *and other magazines has a good deal of energy and raw power. "Knights of the Open Palm" is not only a first but one of his (and Race Williams's) best stories.*

RACE WILLIAMS, PRIVATE Investigator, that's what the gilt letters spell across the door of my office. It don't mean nothing, but the police have been looking me over so much lately that I really need a place to receive them. You see I don't want them coming to my home; not that I'm over particular, but a fellow must draw the line somewheres.

As for my business; I'm what you might call the middleman—just a halfway house between the dicks and the crooks. Oh, there ain't no doubt that both the cops and the crooks take me for a gun, but I ain't—not rightly speaking. I do a little honest shooting once in a while—just in the way of business. But my conscience is clear; I never bumped off a guy what didn't need it. And I can put it over the crooks every time—why, I know more about crooks than what they know about themselves. Yep, Race Williams, Private Investigator, that's me.

Most of my business I hunt up and the office ain't much good except as an air of respectability. But sometimes I get a call, one client speaking to another about me. And that's the lay of it this time.

I was in my office straightening out the mail, and enjoying some of the threatening letters what the boys who lack a sense of humor had sent me, when this Earnest Thompson blows in. And "blows" ain't no fancy way of putting it neither; this guy actually blows and it's near five minutes before he quits blowing and opens up.

"Are you afraid of the Ku Klux Klan?"

That's his first crack out of the box.

"I ain't afraid of nothing."

I tell him the truth and then, wanting to be absolutely on the level, I ask:

"Providing there's enough jack in it."

He trots out a sigh like my words had lifted a weight from his chest.

"You don't happen to belong to that—that order?"

I think he was going to call it something else—but from the twitching of his mouth I get the idea that he went in some fear of that same order.

"No," I says. "I don't belong to any order."

Of course I'm like all Americans—a born joiner. It just comes to us like children playing; we want to be in on everything that's secret and full of fancy names and trick grips. But it wouldn't work with me; it would be mighty bad in my line. I'd have to take an oath never to harm a brother—not that I wouldn't keep my oath, but think of the catch in it. I might just be drawing a bead on a lad when I'd spot his button; then I'd have to drop my gun. Of course that ain't so bad, but that same lad mightn't be wise that I was one of the crowd and—blooey—he'd blow my roof off. No, I like to play the game alone. And that's why I ain't never fallen for the lure of being a joiner.

Well, this lad must of had the idea that half the country belonged to the Ku Klux and that the other half went about in fear of them, for when he finds out that I don't belong he beams all over and pump-handles me a couple of hundred times. Then he comes out with the glad tidings that a gent I helped out of trouble had told him about me; with that he opens up with the bad news. His son had been took by the Ku Klux.

His boy, Willie Thompson, who is only seventeen, goes hunting around in the woods a bit outside of the town they live in. Clinton is the name of the burg and it's in the West, which is all I'm at liberty to tell about it except that it's a county seat. Well, Willie stumbles across a bunch of the Klan and sees them tar and feather a woman—and what's more, he recognizes some of the Klan—this boy having an eye for big feet and an ear for low voices.

It appears that this woman had sold liquor to a member of the Klan who told her his poor old father was dying—you see, her husband ran a drugstore. Now wasn't that just too sweet of the boys? Of course they checked up a lot of other things against her, too, and give her warning to leave town in twenty-four hours. Yep, they give her all those little courtesies what a lady should expect. But the real secret of the story goes that one of the lads of the Night Shirt Brigade was in love with the woman and wanted to get hunk because she couldn't see him a mile.

Now, that's Earnest Thompson's side of the story and not mine, but at all events the town of Clinton was pretty well stirred up and some of the Klan were actually in jail for as much as ten minutes. But when the trial came off this Willie Thompson had been kidnapped. The father worried, of course, but he thought the boy would be back when the trial was over. That was two weeks ago; the trial had blown up and the boy never heard from again.

Why the whole thing seemed unbelievable. Think of it; here was this man with a good suspicion if not an actual knowledge of who had his son and he trots all the way to the city for me. Imagine if it had a been my boy—blooey—I'd a bumped that gang off one, two, three right down the line. But this lad was scared stiff; if he made a break to the authorities he got a threatening letter and—well, here he was.

But he made his offer a very alluring one: A good fat check, for this Thompson was a wealthy farmer. So I took the case and you should a seen his face light up.

"I didn't think that I could get anyone to defy the Klan," he takes me by the hand again. "I hope that you—that you won't give up when you find what you are up against."

Now that almost made me laugh.

"Don't you worry about me," I says. "And don't you worry about the boy. If he's alive and the Klan have him—why—I'll get him back to you in jig time; and no mistake about that."

Was I blowing a bit? Oh, I don't know. I'd said the same thing before and—well—I made good.

So the curtain goes up; he was to go back to Clinton that night and I was to follow in a day or two.

That night I trot down the avenue looking for some dope on this same Ku Klux Klan. I'd read a lot about it in the papers, but I didn't take much stock in it—mostly newspaper talk, it struck me.

It was in Mike Clancy's gin mill that I decided to get my information, for Mike belonged to every order under the sun.

But Mike shook his head:

"So you've fell for the lure, too?" he says sadly. "All the boys are crossing the river or going South to join the Klan—there's money in it and no mistake."

"Are you a member?" I ask him again.

"Not me," he shakes his head. "When it first hit the city I spoke to Sergeant Kelly about it. B-r-r-r-r-r! It ain't no order for an Irishman. Sure, it's the A.P.A. and worse. But if you must know about it why ask Dumb Rogers over there."

And he jerked his thumb toward a little dip what was sitting alone at a table in the corner.

And this same Rogers sure did give me an earful; that's how he got his name Dumb—he talked so much.

"The Klan?" he starts in. "I should say I did know about it. The boys is leaving the avenue by the carloads. You see they go South or West and join the Klan; then when there is a raid on and some lad is to be beat up, why the boys clean up a bit on the side. Suppose a jeweler is to leave town and don't and the Klan get after him—see the game—a ring or two is nothing to grab. And he dassen't say nothing—you write him a threatening letter or telephone him is better."

He paused a moment and looked at me.

"Don't tell me about the Klan—I know—I was a member and I was well on the road to making my fortune when they got on to me. They expelled me; threw me out like I wasn't no gentleman—that's what they done. And for why—just for going through a guy. Now, what do you think of that?" he demanded indignantly.

"That's tough, Rogers—tell me—how do you join?"

"Well, you got'a be white and an American and a Protestant—and you got'a have ten dollars—though if you've got the ten the rest of it can be straightened out. Yes, they got my ten, and what's more they got six-fifty for the old white robe—sixteen-fifty all together and they chucked me out—not so much as—"

But I interrupted him. I was after the passwords of the Klan and their greetings.

After a few more drinks he sure did open up; what with The

Exalted Cyclops, Klaliff, Klokard, Kludd, Kligrapp, Klabee, Kladd, Klexter, Klolkann, Kloran and a host of others I didn't know where I stood and had to call a halt. But I got the grip out of him, which was a shake with the left hand. Then he give me the salute which I take careful note of. It was copped from the Confederate Army and is made by placing the right hand over the right eye and then turning the hand so that the palm is in front.

"But remember the one important thing," Dumb Rogers points a boney finger at me. "When you meet another Klansman you always say, 'AYAK,' meaning, 'Are you a Klansman?' If you ever hear a lad pull that on you—you answer, 'AKIA'—'A Klansman I am.' The rest of it is a lot of junk and most of the boys can't remember it—but them's the two principal things."

Then he showed me a cheap little celluloid button which he wore wrong end out in the lapel of his coat. When he turned it about I seen the letters KOTOP which he explained meant, "Knights of the Open Palm."

Do you get it—why it looked like they were stealing the waiter's stuff. That order certainly must have been started by a dish carrier. But I took a good look at the back of that button—you couldn't tell nothing from it, but I sure would keep my eyes open when I seen a lad sporting a decoration that way.

Three days later finds me in Clinton, a little burg of three or four thousand and the county seat. But don't get the idea that it was a one-horse town; even the farmers went about in flivvers and some of the people went about in real sporty cars. You'd never take it for a town that was in the grip of some half-baked organization.

The hotel, though, was the regular thing; I guess it had stood the same way for twenty-five years; it was called the Clinton House, which don't show much originality.

And with all my plans for my work being secret I wasn't there above half an hour when Earnest Thompson blows in. He was all excited; the Klan had come out in the paper that they had nothing to do with the disappearance of Willie Thompson and those who thought different had better hold their tongues. He showed me the clipping and sure enough it was a direct threat at the whole town.

But that wasn't why he come. Since seeing me he had received an anonymous letter hinting that his son knew something about a suspected Klan murder over at a town twenty miles away.

"I think he did, too," Thompson said. "I think that he kept it from me, but was going to give the information out at the trial. He didn't tell me all he knew because he feared for my safety."

Of course that was news, but it wasn't good policy for him to drop right in on me. Why, if the Klan had half an eye out they'd know what was in the wind and results proved that they did.

That very night Old Thompson was visited in his home by a number of white-robed figures and—well—we'll put it down to the fear that something might happen to his boy—but anyway he out with the whole story of how he had hired me to come down. He may have had some excuse; his nerves may have been shot to pieces, but this same Thompson sure lacked guts.

And the next day he lights out of town and calls me up. He tells me what happened and how he was forced to tell and then up and begs me to stay on the case. And what's more, he promises to double the check. What do you think? I stayed on of course. I felt like bawling him out, but I didn't. The whole world might know why I was there and perhaps it wouldn't do this gang no harm to learn the sort of a man they had to deal with.

And that night the Klan honored me with a visit. Three of them there were and they must have put on their get-up in the hall. Yep, all dolled up like the heavy chorus in a burlesque show they walked in on me.

Two of them stood one on either side of the door, rubbing their knees together, acting like they was a couple of business men what didn't like playing the fool. But the third lad was different—he was the real thing and no fake about him. He was big and powerful as he swung across the floor and faced me. He stood so for a moment, glaring down at me through the slits in his white hood.

I just sat there in the chair looking him over and smoking; then I grinned. I couldn't help it. I could see the deadly threat coming.

"You are not a member of the Klan—The Great Invisible Empire?"

And he out with the last three words like he was announcing the batteries for the day's game at the Polo Grounds.

"No, I ain't," I tell him, pretending to wipe away a tear, "I wanted to join, but—well, you see I catch cold so easy. I got to stick to the pajamas."

But he never made a break, so I see I was wasting my time kidding that bird. So I made things easy for him.

"Don't try to figure it out," I says. "Come spill the sad news. Surely this ain't no pleasure call; out with the dirt!"

I don't know if he got it all or not, but he come out flat-footed and didn't make no more bones about it. And I'm giving him credit for a lad that talked like he meant business.

"You have caused the displeasure of the Klan; we want no hired gunmen in Clinton," he said. "You have twenty-four hours to leave town—twenty-four."

"You couldn't make that twenty-five," I chirp. "You see, I want to attend your next meeting and sort of bust things up."

Oh, I just wanted to get him mad.

And it worked!

"You have heard me." I can almost see him glare through the slits. "And be careful of that tongue of yours, for I have a gun—a gun that I draw and shoot in one second."

And then he finished things up with a string of oaths that, if not original, were at least well chosen.

But he was speaking my language now—this gun business—and I just stood up and faced him.

"Listen, Dough-head." And I wasn't talking for pleasure now. "So you have a gun that shoots in one second, eh? Well, let me give you some advice. If that's the best you can do you had better keep that gun parked. I'm telling you flat that you'd be exactly one-half a second too late."

His hand half lowered to his side.

"If you don't believe me try it," I encouraged. "Your two friends there can carry you out."

Was I bluffing? Say, I was talking gospel, and he knew it.

Then, when he didn't try nothing, I whipped out my gun and covered the three of them. And with that I make a grab and pull off the big lad's hood. I just wanted to get one look at his map and one look was enough—you could a picked him in a straw hat at Coney Island. He had a chin like one of the Smith Brothers or both of them—all whiskers and all hair and eyebrows.

"Listen, Feather-Face." I pound his ribs gentle like with the automatic. "You ain't dealing with no women nor a half-grown boy nor a distracted father now. You'll give me twenty-four hours, will you? Well, I'll give you twenty-four seconds to get out. And the next time you come around here I'll take that night-shirt off you and shove it down your throat—whiskers and all."

I was mad now and meant it. This white-hooded frightener of women and children couldn't come none of that high-falutin game on me, and what's more I didn't like the names he had called me.

"You've had one look at my gun," I told them as they sneaked out. "The next time you have cause to see it you'll see it smoking; now—beat it!"

Which they done. Say, them boys had never had such a shock in their lives. I just sat down on the bed and roared.

The next morning I find a little slip under my door; it's from the hotel manager and it asks me to leave. So the Klan had opened up. Of course I wasn't ready to go and I knew that they couldn't drive me out. You see, the town was about half and half; the authorities didn't side with the Klan nor they didn't come out against it; everybody was just sitting tight to see which way things was going to break. But if I was going to do a little gunning I'd need my night's sleep and if this manager was against me it would keep me pretty well on the jump. But I just shrug my shoulders and beat it downstairs, thinking things over.

I nod good morning to Jimmy O'Brien, the clerk. He's a real friendly lad and his handle tells me that he ain't no Klansman. There was no one else in the lobby, so I just wander to the doors and look out. And through them doors I catch a slant which is sure surprising even way off in that little Western town. Three men are coming down the street—single file—and there's about twenty-five feet between; right down the center of the main street they walk. Each has a gun swinging from his shoulder, but it don't hang over his back; it's swinging loose and mighty handy under the armpit—just a movement and it's ready to shoot.

The leader is a man which I place at over sixty; he's small but stocky—the other two must be in the thirties, big strapping giants of men.

I half turn as a figure comes to my side; it's Jimmy O'Brien. Of course I know that he's heard about my visitors last night. He was in the lobby when they beat it out.

"Who's the three desperadoes that take the middle of the road—more of the Klan?" I ask the clerk.

"No," says Jimmy. "That's Buck Jabine and his two sons. They are the only ones in town that openly defy the Klan. This Buck Jabine killed three men back in the old days—no, they ain't a family to fool with."

I could see that as they tramped up the street; they look business, all three of them.

"You see," Jimmy explained, "Buck talked against the Klan and then he began to get threatening letters. But he didn't leave town. He opened up with a warning that anyone found on his property after dark would be shot. This Buck shoots straight and quick—since that warning he ain't had no trouble—only letters. But they are coming here."

He breaks off suddenly.

The next minute they come in the door—one, two, three.

The old man takes one look around and then comes straight up to me.

"Stranger," he says, "I take it that you're Race Williams. Last night's doings got about a bit—shake—my name is Buck Jabine."

With that he sticks out his fin and the two sons do the same, though there ain't a yip out of them.

"I hear you ain't none too friendly with the boys, neither," I try to make things pleasant.

But he don't smile; he just looks at me. He's a chap what takes things seriously.

"Well," Buck just stroked his chin, "I just wanted to shake hands with you and tell you that I have a place out in the country—about two mile. Any time you want a place to sleep peaceful walk out—the house will be open to you day and night. I don't take no sides, mind you. Buck Jabine is only interested in his own family—he don't stand for no interference—but my house is open to you, wide open."

I thank him and then tell him about the manager's little note—just in the way of light conversation, you know. I've made up my mind to stick at the hotel.

36

"When they put me out of a bum joint like this, they'll put me out in a cloud of smoke," I tell Buck.

"Hump!"

He strokes his chin again; then turns sudden and struts straight into the manager's office.

I try to get sociable with the sons, but don't make a go of it. I'm looking for dope on the Klan, but there is nothing doing. Oh, they're friendly enough, but don't go in for conversation. They don't even open up with a grin when I make wise cracks about night shirts and pajamas. They just stare at me. I could see that I'd have a right down sociable time over at their place.

"Yes" and "No" and a few "I don't reckons" is the best I gather, though once one of them opens up enough to ask me the time. So I guess the old man does the talking for the family; all together, it looks like a closed corporation.

And then Buck trots out of the office and the manager is right on his heels. My, but that manager is all smiles and tells me how it was all a mistake and begs me to stay on. And he means it, too, for behind that smile he looks real worried. Of course I ain't so stupid but that I know that this Buck Jabine has something to say about it and I sort of pity the manager. He's between Buck and the Klan and he ain't got much choice. Still, I think he was doing the right thing. He couldn't tell if the Klan would get him or not, but Buck— well, one look at Buck was enough; him and that family of his was all business.

"Ain't you worried about something happening to your house while you're away?" I ask Buck when he's leaving.

He just gives me the up and down for a minute and then he draws back his upper lip; I think it was meant for a smile, but I ain't sure. Then he chirps:

"There ain't no danger; Sarah's home and the boys' women. No, there ain't no danger."

With that they all file out and tramp down the center of the street—the same single file. So I see that this is sure one nice little family.

Now, this Klan ain't as secret as what I had thought. After Buck leaves, Jimmy, the clerk, up and gives me quite an earful. Sometimes them birds have even paraded right down Main Street and more than once they have taken out some citizen and tarred and feathered him. Then they'd bring the victim back and dump him out of a car right in the center of the Square by the fountain. See'n' they'd forget to put his clothes on again would seem like they lacked modesty.

When there were any deaths about the State due to the Klan's midnight playfulness, why the Klan would come out in the paper denying it and announcing that they would expel any member who had a hand in it. Which is real generous of them, you'll admit; open-handed and fair-minded, to be sure. And then Jimmy outs with some real news: there's a Klan meeting that night. It's an open secret that they're taking in new members. So I see it ain't a falling organization but a growing one and I'd better work fast.

All day long that hotel is watched—there ain't no doubt about it. Three lads in the front and one out in the back. People what drop in dodge me like they would the plague and the general feeling is that I'm a marked man. Well, they may get me; the thing's possible; but if they do, the local undertaker is going to have more business than he's had in years.

Jimmy's a good scout and when he goes off duty about noontime he sneaks up and has a chat with me. So I take him into my confidence to a certain extent, and I believe if he didn't have a wife and kid he'd a been with me forty ways from the ace.

But he tells me where the Klan meeting place is and how people don't dare go near it. Then he tells me that he has a bicycle and after I bit I get his promise to hide it in a barn down the street behind the hotel; the fellow what owns the barn goes by the label of Dugan—enough said!

I watch out pretty carefully all evening and I don't see more than one chap watching the back of that house—so at nine o'clock I'm ready to pull off my little trick; I'm bent on joining in the festivities of the Klan.

There's a little partition off the back of the hotel and I get Jimmy to slip me in there unnoticed. Out in the dark of the tiny rear window I can see the solitary figure about ten yards away; it's a lonely little alley and no one else passes by. So I spring my game. I take my pillowcase, which I've made to look like a Klan hood, and, slipping it over my head, I light a candle and stand there in the open window; after a bit I give the Klan Salute—then I beckon the distant figure to me.

As I say, the whole Klan is a child's game, and that duck comes to me on the run; he most likely thinks that things are arranged for tar and feathering me. As for me, well—I just club my gun and bat him over the head and he falls pretty—right in a nice dark spot.

Five minutes I wait and then, when there's nothing doing I step out the window and beat it down the alley. A few minutes later I'm on the bike, speeding out toward the open country and in the direction which Jimmy give me where lays what is known as the Klavern or meeting place.

All I need now is the regulation night shirt and I've laid plans to get that. Jimmy has seen the gang going to the meetings and knows the place that they stop their cars and put on the regalia. And what's more, he'd told me about a lad whose business kept him late in town. It was this cluck that traveled alone in a Ford that I was looking for.

I guess I got to that spot a bit ahead of time. It was just around a bend in the road and very lonely. There was a nice place well back in the bushes where I parked my bike and waited. The night was dark, but I could see fairly well and in the course of twenty minutes about three cars pulled up and the occupants got all rigged out in their ghostly costumes. They'd just slip on the white robe and then crown themselves with the hood. If one party was decorating themselves there the next party would stop farther down the road.

After that I waited near an hour and then my man comes; all alone in a Ford he is and in some hurry. He don't even get out of the flivver, but tries to do the lightning change right in the car.

Say! I caught him with one arm in and one arm out of the shirt. Surprised! Why, he opened and closed his mouth just like a fish and a pretty far gone fish, too.

"None of your lip," I tell him when he started to spout about the terrible things that would happen to me. "You know me, kid."

I tickled his chin with my gat.

"I handled three of your breed last night. Come! jump out of that night shirt or they'll bury you in it."

No laughter in my voice then—when I'm gunning I'm a bad man—none worse!

Enough! He showed good sense and handed over the whole

outfit. It didn't take me more than a couple of minutes to bind him with the rope I had brought; then I tied him to a tree out of view of the road and, jumping into his car, I drove away.

A few hundred yards or more down the road I see the turn I'm looking for and a short drive down a rough lane and things are starting. A white-robed figure holds up his hand and stops me; of course in my robe he takes me for one of the clucks. I spot this lad for the Klexter, the outer guard.

"White and Supremacy," I say like a regular.

After that it's gravy; I go through my stuff which I got from Dumb Rogers. After a Salute he passes me and I turn into a field where there is near fifty cars parked.

Here I have to go through the speeches again with the Klarogo, the inner guard. But everything is rosy and pretty soon I pass down a narrow glade and into the Klavern itself. It was a fairly large open space surrounded by the thick woods—a good place to scatter if the cops come, I guess. There were near a hundred gathered about and when I slip in the show is already on.

"Imperial One, the men who seek admission to our legions stand prepared," a voice suddenly booms out, and with that all the robed figures gather about in a circle.

Then a lad with a cross all lit up breezes in and behind him march about eight lads—the candidates—looking for their ten dollars' worth. And they got it; in wind at least. I never heard so much talking in my life.

The Head Goblin, a bird fixed up in white and scarlet, lets off steam about sending everybody to hell while the Klan took care of law and order. It was bum stuff, most of it, and if I'd 'a been one of the candidates I'd 'a hollered for my money back.

The members is not called brothers or anything like that; they are called citizens and the initiation is called being naturalized, and they take an oath which would knock you cock-eyed for length, bad English and rotten principles. And then the new citizens swear never to tell anything nor give any evidence against a Klansman unless he's committed rape, willful murder or treason. Hot dog! Burglars, counterfeiters, and check-raisers welcome—also arson might be appreciated—I don't know. But I sure do see why Dumb Rogers was sore and why all the crooks are joining.

Then the little buttons are given out with no extra charge but lots more wind; those buttons must have been worth all of ten for a cent—when I was a kid we use to pick better in a nickel's worth of popcorn.

But I don't get no real dope; not a mention of the boy nor a mention of me, which sure hurts my pride. Then I get the how of their puffing off the real dirt without being openly to blame. Committees is appointed, but they don't say what for. See the lay of it? If you have an enemy—why get on a committee—it's hot stuff!

The real fellows who just enter the Klan because they are born joiners don't know half the time why they are beating up some helpless old man or weak woman. They just do it. Why—God alone knows. They forget their manhood and listen to all the wind about cleaning up the world and making it safe for the white race. And all for ten bucks. Oh, I'm a pretty tough egg—none tougher, I guess, but I felt as white as my robe in comparison with most of that gang.

And just when I'm wondering what good this whole show is going to do me, outside of improving my morals, I get a real shock. There's a commotion outside the circle and the outer guard rushes in and following him is—is my victim of the Ford.

Some excitement then and I can see my finish unless I duck and—and I ducked. In the excitement it was easy to slip back through the circle of white figures and into the thick foliage. I lay low there, where I can see what's going on. I'm not leaving yet— no—not me! I still got unfinished business. There sure will be a few dead Kleagles, to say nothing of a couple of Klodards and one thing and another, if this bunch get mussy with me.

You see, I suspect they'll unmask, looking for me, but no such thing. After they quiet down a bit the lad what thinks I wronged him starts around the circle, examining all the uniforms. He must have spilt soup or something on his, else how could he tell it? But he has no luck and after a little more talk they just bust up the meeting and beat it. The fear of Race Williams has been placed in their hearts. So I lay there a while, cussing my hard luck.

I'm wondering if they'll search the woods, but they don't. However, I shake my night-shirt so as to be free and easy for gun-play; but these boys are not bent on committing suicide. About ten minutes pass and the chug of the motors has died away and I'm just about thinking of going back to town, when two white-robed figures suddenly enter the deserted glen. But they don't look around none, just lay off a bit. Then one of them, wanting a smoke, pulls off his hood and—and it's Feather-Face. Now, I got this bird sized up. Where he is, there is trouble.

Backing slowly out of the woods, I decided to sneak around and see if I can hear what they're saying. The moon is fairly bright, so I got to be mighty careful. And then, as I turn and go slowly through the trees, I hear the chug-chug of a motor. I peer through the trees and there by the roadside is a car—none of your flivvers this time, but a big touring car. The motor stops and a lad gets out and passes through the wood within ten feet of me. He ain't got no hood nor robe on, but I can't get a slant at his map.

I turn and follow him and as I reach the end of the clearing I hear him say to the others:

"Ed'll be here in ten minutes and then—"

"Sh!" cautions another voice.

But I don't wait to hear no more. I got ten minutes and I'm flying down the road to the place I left my bike. I ain't got time to duck in and out among the trees, but I don't meet no one, which ain't so much my luck as his.

And the bike's there and in less than ten minutes I'm about twenty feet behind that car, hidden in the bushes, ready to do a six-day race.

Five minutes later we all breeze off together—the four of them in the car and me following on the bike—none of us showing lights.

Now, the first part of that ride is not so bad, for they ain't bent on speed and the road is fairly level—but the moon goes behind a cloud and I got to hang close. On top of that we come to an upgrade and things are not so good. Then they turn up a steep and winding road and the bike ain't no good any more—at least it's no good to me.

It looks like I'm stumped as I stand there panting and listening to the throb of the distant motor—and then the throb stops sudden—not just dies away. I look up the side of that hill and suddenly I see a light—it just flashes for a moment and is gone. Enough—I park the bike in the woods and start in to hoof it.

Twenty minutes later I'm at the top of a steep hill—on the other side of me is a cliff and below a roaring mountain stream. I can hear the water dashing by far below. And then out comes the moon and about fifty feet away I see a log cabin almost on the very edge of the steep cliff. A little ways from it I see the big car.

There ain't no one in sight and I just duck around that cabin, trying to look in; but there's nothing doing. Oh, I can catch the flicker of light from between some of the cracks in the logs, but can't see in. There is only one window and that is boarded up. I try the door softly, but it's locked tight; then I go round back with half an idea of climbing to the roof in the hope of finding a crack big enough to peer through.

And then when I get around the side I hear the door open—it creaks mighty loud. Only a second and footsteps are coming around to the back. Both guns ready, I back to cover behind the opposite corner of the cabin and wait. The moon is fine and I see two men plainly as they approach the edge of the cliff, forcing a lithe figure of a boy between them. His arms are bound, but his legs ain't, and he's pleading with them in a low voice.

"I won't never tell about the murder—I won't never say a word about who done it."

His feet are giving from under him and they help him along.

"You're right—you won't never tell."

One of the men give a gruff laugh.

"Here, you, Ed, give him the knife and get the job done," he says to his companion.

"Oh, push him over," Ed answers, and I seen his stomach ain't strong for such work, for his voice breaks a bit.

"Here—give me the knife."

The other has a sneer in his tones. The next instant I see a flash of steel in the air above the boy.

Crack!

Yep, it's my gun what speaks and that lad goes out like a light. The other lad draws a gun and looks around him bewildered. But he don't see nothing; leastwise in this world he don't. I get him right through the head—there ain't no mistake where I land in that distance. He drops the wrong way—staggers a bit and I hear his body crashing down the cliff, tearing loose the rough stones as it goes.

Oh, I ain't a killer, but remember, there were four of them, that left two more to be accounted for yet; it wouldn't do to wound a lad and then have him pop up again when you least wanted to see him.

The boy just stands there—swinging back and forth on his weak legs—and I'm afraid he'll go over too.

"Lay down, you fool!" I says, and he drops like a log and lays still.

Then I wait. I know those gentlemen in the cabin must have heard the shots and be coming. Like a movie picture villain, a figure looms up from the side of the cabin; sneaking slowly along, the flash of nickel plainly visible in his hand. And like a movie villain he fades out of the picture. I got him.

"Number three," I says and wait; the party ain't over yet.

And then there's a step behind me; like a foot upon dried twigs.

Like a shot I turn and in the rays of the moon spot the evil, sneering map of Feather-Face. His gun spoke ahead of mine—I knew that from the red-hot burn that shot along my temple—just above the ear it seemed to hurt most.

Of course I fired—emptied both guns, I guess. But I didn't see nothing when I shot—there were dancing, blazing lights before my eyes and then darkness—a deadly black darkness followed by a sinking feeling. It had stuck on my feet while I shot, but now I knew I was slipping; every minute I expected to hear the gun bark—but didn't.

Then there was the chug-chug of a motor—the grinding of hurriedly shifting gears; my firing had scared Feather-Face off. With that thought I sagged to the ground—everything went black.

When I come-to again I was in the cabin and several men were leaning over me. One of them was in uniform and I recognized him for the Chief of Police of Clinton.

I hear them talking a minute; how they had come across Willie Thompson staggering down the road and how they had come out to the cabin; and I gathered that Feather-Face had beat it—then curtains again.

I was all right—that is, to a certain extent—when I come-to

again. But I was in the coop, which was not so good. Yep, I opened my eyes in the jail at Clinton and a doctor was bending over me.

He had a real friendly face and his talk was good.

"You sure did for that gang," he said. "I hope you come out of it all right. Oh, not your head—it must be as hard as rock—you're all right there. I mean this little killing. You have a good lawyer—none better—and the judge has no use for the Klan. Thompson has told him his story—and it's not a pretty one. Man, I tell you you have a first-class lawyer. I hear that it's fixed up to release you on bail—on a writ of habeas corpus, they call it."

"Then I'll get out all right," I said, relieved, for I had the idea that the Klan ran the town.

"Oh, the judge is with you, but the Klan—you see, there is a threat about town—death to the party that goes on your bail—and the trouble is that the people fear the Klan. They have a habit of making good on these little threats. Why, no one can visit you—the Klan's orders again—of course they wouldn't forbid you medical attention."

"Then no one will have the nerve to go my bail?"

I sure was some surprised.

"That remains to be seen." He shook his head, but there didn't seem to be much hope in his voice.

But he didn't tell me then that there also was a threat to storm the jail and there was much talk about asking for the State troops to be sent over.

And that's that. I didn't get much time to think; my mouthpiece sure did work fast, for by that afternoon I was hustled out of the jail by the Chief of Police and three or four other highly nervous gentlemen and rushed into court.

Some court; just one long, low-ceilinged room with great big windows on either side of it. It was warm and the windows were open and the bright sun shone in. But the faces about me—there was nothing bright and comforting about them; hostile, hard faces they were and a murmur, a threatening murmur of disapproval, ran through the room as I was led before the judge's bench. The Judge was hard too, but his face was honest and almost defiant as he looked over the crowded courtroom.

My lawyer was there and talking, but I didn't get much of what he said, but I guess the Judge was hurrying things along; the people looked like they might act up bad any minute. The District Attorney was objecting to everything—I wasn't surprised—I'd heard that he was mighty close in with the Klan.

Then the Judge came out flat-footed and named the bail—not a large sum, neither; and he hammered on the bench as a low rumble of protest went up from the packed courtroom.

Then my lawyer says, slow and calm:

"Your honor, I have the bondsman here."

My, you could hear a pin drop when he said that, and half the court stood up and looked around where the lawyer had pointed toward the door at the rear.

There comes a sudden rattling of windows from both sides; I look first at one of the big windows and then the other. There, on the two opposite window sills, had appeared the huge, stalwart frames of the Jabine boys. Motionless as statues they stood with their rifles swung loose beneath their armpits.

"Buck Jabine!"

I hear the hoarse whisper go up from ten voices at once. And I look toward the back door of the courtroom.

Right through the swinging doors had come Buck Jabine, his head erect, his eyes looking neither to left nor right. Straight between that path of gaping, angry faces, he made his way until he reached the bench. Not a hand was raised to stop him—not a mouth voiced even anger. You see, everyone there knew Buck Jabine and the boys. Two minutes later and everything was Jake.

So it was that I left the courthouse a free man and joined the procession of the Jabines. I was third in that single-file line as we made our way up the Main Street and out into the open country toward the Jabine farm. Not a word did we speak—just hoofed it along. I wondered then if I made as forbidding an appearance as the family.

Thompson and his son were at the Jabine house and such a welcome you never did see. And the Jabines took it all without a smile—they were all business and no mistake.

Of course I got the low down on the whole affair from the Thompsons. Willie Thompson had made some discoveries about the murder at the town twenty miles away—it was Feather-Face and his three friends what had pulled it off in the name of the Klan. There was robbery behind it and Willie had come across that little cabin in the hills and seen them splitting some of the swag. Enough! They nailed him and was just waiting for things to blow over a bit before they bumped him off and let his body float away below the cliff.

After that things happened in town. The real story came out and I was never even brought before the Grand Jury. It appears that even with the truth most of the Grand Jury wanted to hold me at first—you see, they were thick with the Klan. Then things started.

Ten members of the Klan who were on the Grand Jury up and resigned from the Klan; they come out flat and told the Judge how they felt and how they had joined the organization just like they would have joined any other fraternal organization. The end of it was that the Judge discharged me without my ever showing up in court.

You see, it was better for me not to be seen about too much. The Klan was slipping and members were leaving it every day; and what's more, an Anti-Klan organization was forming, though Buck Jabine would have nothing to do with either one of them. Altogether things were bad in Clinton; both factions went around armed and defiant. The Klan had sure lost its grip.

But of Feather-Face nothing was heard; both sides sought him now equally bent on vengeance. I could see that Feather-Face's position was not an enviable one—still, he kept clear of Clinton.

"There weren't no harm in the old order," Jabine opened up to me one evening. "My father was in the Klan back in the Sixties. But this modern Ku Klux Klan was a money-making graft bent on raising religious and racial hatred. Of course half the crime laid to their doors wasn't true, but it gave others the opportunity to masquerade under their name. You can't defy law and order and the rights of your fellow-man without the criminal element sneaking in. Robbery, murder, private vengeance—that's all what could come of it. And it took you—you, a stranger, to show it all up in its proper light."

And from then until the day I left that was all Buck Jabine had to say on the subject.

The night that the Thompsons, father and son, came to the house in their little car to drive me to the station, Buck said:

"I have arranged for the train to stop at Haddon Junction, five miles down. You see," he turned to Old Thompson, "the folks of Clinton were planning to give Race Williams, here, a little send-off and it won't do. The Klan spirit is dead. Why bring it up again? There are enough left to make trouble if any popular demonstration is shown. The Klan is slipping—slipping fast and I say let it slip."

Well, I was agreeable, though I think Willie Thompson—who had become somewhat of a hero about town—was disappointed and felt badly about it. But the cash transaction was all that interested me. I had mailed the check which Thompson had given me along to my New York bank and—well—I didn't have no doubts on it—but I'd be glad to get home and do a little drawing on it.

So I shook hands with Buck and got a few grunts out of the Jabine boys. Then I said good-bye to the ladies—I didn't mention the ladies before, but it will be enough to say that they were sure some Amazons and would make a good showing in a free-for-all. And—well—I was off. Old Thompson and me in the front seat and Willie Thompson in the rear. It sure felt good to be on the go again with my twin gats parked nicely about me.

At nine-thirty he was only about a quarter of a mile from the station and ten minutes to catch the train, when we have trouble. Blooey! Both the rear tires go like a couple of cannon; so sudden did it come that I had half drawn my gun.

Then I watched the two of them stall around a minute. I could see the one light of the little station shining in the distance, so I decided to hoof it. These lads treated an automobile like a steam-roller—only one spare tire and an inner tube on hand. They'd be a half-hour at least; what with scratching their heads and pulling up their pants.

I wouldn't listen to their protests about waiting over another night and I wouldn't let one of them come along to the station with me; they weren't fit to be separated—too slow-thinking birds they were. No, sir, I was booked for the city and going through.

So I swung out my suitcase and after a couple of handshakes started down the road. I hoofed it fast, but I got a-thinking while I walked; got a-thinking as I looked down and kicked some mighty dirty-looking pieces of glass and half a broken bottle from the road.

I could hear the train coming along and see her headlight flashing down the tracks as I reached the station. Now, there was no station master at this Haddon Junction and only one light on the north side of the station—the side the train was approaching from. So, bag in hand, I started to pass under that light and out onto the platform—then I stopped dead—that broken bottle had suddenly loomed up before me as big as life. I just ducked back and made my way cautiously around the other side of the station. Not really suspicious, you understand—only careful. And that's the secret of why I hope to die in bed.

Bang! Like that! I duck into a chap who is coming slowly from around the south end of the station. We hit with a crash and both step back a pace; he out on the platform toward the tracks.

Was he quick? Well, he never had no chance. Mind you, he had his gun in his hand, but he never used it. Just as clean as a whistle I had pulled and shot him straight between his bloodshot eyes. The train roared into the station as he fell and in the light of the headlight as it flashed by I got a look at his face. Oh, I knew it before, even in the dull light of the moon. Yep, you hit it—it was Feather-Face. You recollect I once told him that he'd be half a second too late.

And then the brakeman swung out on the step; I climbed aboard; he swung his lantern and we were off.

"Thought I heard a shot," the brakeman said as he climbed up the steps behind me, where I struggled with the door.

You see, I couldn't tell what he had seen and I wanted to hear if he had any comments to make. I had half an idea that I had already done enough shooting to please the people of Clinton.

"Yep."

I turn and look the man over as the train gains headway.

"Yep, a dog snapped at me—a dirty dog—I killed him—with this."

With that I shoved my gun out under his chin sudden as I watched to see how he took it.

"Thought I saw a figure—a human figure."

He lays down his lantern and stretches his hand up toward the emergency strap.

Then in the dim light from his lantern I catch the glimpse of a tiny button beneath his coat—yep, his lapel is half twisted around and I take a chance that the letters on that button are KOTOP.

Looking him straight in the eyes, I suddenly raise my right hand and place it over my right eye, palm in—then I reverse the hand, giving him the Klan salute.

His hand lingers for a moment on the bell, but I see that his fingers loosen their grip.

"Ayak," he says.

"Åkia," I answer.

His hand drops from the bell and without another word he turns and enters the forward car. I stand so a moment; then with a grin I slip into the rear car. After all that is said against the Klan, I sure got to admit that there are times when it serves its purpose.

HORACE
McCOY

The Mopper-Up

TWO EVENTS MADE Black Mask *the great, pioneering magazine it was in the detective field. One was the decision of Dashiell Hammett to submit the bulk of his early work for publication in its pages; the other was the hiring, in 1926, of Joseph T. "Cap" Shaw as its new editor.*

Shaw, a former Army captain in World War I, had never read or even heard of Black Mask *when he accepted new publisher Ray Holland's offer to take editorial control. He did not care for what he found; it seemed to him the magazine had no direction—except, that was, for the stories written by Hammett. Immediately, taking Hammett as his model, he began not only to reshape the magazine but to establish a whole new style of detective writing: what later became known as the "Black Mask school." In his introduction to* The Hard-Boiled Omnibus, *his 1946 anthology of what he felt were the best stories he purchased during his ten years at the magazine's helm, Shaw described this new style as "hard, brittle ... a full employment of the function of dialogue, and authenticity in characterization and action. To this may be added a very fast tempo, attained in part by typical economy of expression."*

He went on to say that the writers he developed—Raymond Chandler, Frederick Nebel, Raoul Whitfield, George Harmon Coxe, Paul Cain, and Norbert Davis, among others—"observed the cardinal principle in creating the illusion of reality; they did not make their characters act and talk tough; they allowed them to. They gave the stories over to their characters, and kept themselves off the stage, as every writer of fiction should. They did not themselves state that a situation was dangerous or exciting; they did not describe their characters as dead-shots, or infallible men. They permitted the actors in the story to demonstrate all that to the extent of their particular and human capabilities. As a consequence, they wrote convincingly."

Shaw was constantly on the lookout for writers who could follow these principles, who could join Hammett as regulars in the Black Mask *schoolroom, and among the first he encouraged was a young Texan named Horace McCoy. (Shaw stated in 1932 that McCoy was one of the writers "who helped establish the* Black Mask *standard.") He published McCoy's first story, "The Devil Man," in the December 1927 issue, and bought sixteen more over the next seven years, most of which feature flyer Jerry Frost and the fictional branch of the Texas Air Border Patrol known as "Hell's Stepsons." The Frost stories are generally good, but none quite matches McCoy's only novelette about Texas Ranger Tom Bender, "The Mopper-Up."*

Bender is one of the toughest characters ever to appear in the pages of Black Mask; *for sheer recklessness, few pulp detectives can match him. Yet "The Mopper-Up" is more than just a rough-and-tumble action yarn. It also contains elements of the symbolism and understated characterization that was to mark much of McCoy's later work, and lyrical passages of a type that Shaw considered "almost too fine writing." All in all, it exemplifies McCoy's creative imagination, which later gave us that American classic about marathon dance contests,* They Shoot Horses, Don't They? *(1935).*

Born in 1897, Horace McCoy worked as a newspaperman in Dallas in the 1920s and also earned a national reputation as a little-theater actor. In 1931, he moved to Hollywood in an effort to break into motion pictures as both an actor and a writer; he succeeded in the latter goal only after the publication of They Shoot Horses, Don't They?, *but then went on to attain a successful position as a screenwriter that lasted for twenty years. He published a number of other novels, including* No Pockets in a Shroud *(1937),* Kiss Tomorrow Goodbye *(1948), and* Scalpel *(1952), none of which had the same literary quality or the same impact of his first. He died in Los Angeles in 1955.*

The Mopper-Up

ON THROUGH THE dusk and into the night they worked. Their clothes were splattered with grease and their ears and lips were purple, for winter was on and the weather was two above. The bluest norther of the year had been brewed in a devil's cauldron in the Rockies and it boiled out and came rolling down through Raton Pass to roar across the flats of the Panhandle and lash and sting and freeze.

The crew of *Excelsior No. 1* was gaunt and tired and half-frozen, for they worked in a field that was squarely in front of the great slot through which the northers slid, but they cursed loud and kept on.

"Let's go with the bit, you ——— ! The land's crazy with oil!"

Black gold down below.

A sixth of ninety days' production split eleven ways for the crew.

The rainbow's end for a roughneck who's slaved his life away.

Parties and liquor and sweet times for a hairy-handed tool dresser.

A warm apartment and a soft bed for a rig-man who's used to cots.

"Keep that steam up, you ——— ! The land's crazy with oil!"

Nobody believed in them because the livestock was freezing to death and a man had to hump himself to keep alive.

But the geologist told the chief operator it was a cinch and the chief operator believed him. He told the crew there was a lake of oil under there a mile wide, a mile deep and five miles long and that it was on a perfect anticline and would flow for years with never a chance for anybody to suck it out from under them.

He was a plunger and he had faith and he pleaded and threatened and cursed and kept his crew working through the coldest winter the plains country had known in twenty years. Night and day they tugged and heaved under gasoline flares in a mighty race with time for it was the discovery well that got the cream of production.

They spudded her in on a Monday night and by Wednesday they were down three hundred and fifty feet. Thursday they set in three hundred and fifty feet of eighteen-inch casing and cemented it with a hundred and fifty sacks of Trinity Portland. Friday they hooked up the storage tanks and by Saturday the cement was hard enough to drill through.

The wind swirled about their legs and ate through their cotton gloves and flurries of snow flecked their faces but they didn't mind because they were getting close to home.

The following Monday they made their water shut-off three feet below the last water and got ready to blow. At noon the chief yelled: "Swab 'er!" and they let the swab go down to two thousand feet. It came out with a rush. Everybody yelled. A hell of a kick under there. The tank man moved over to the big valve in the well-head and they sent the swab down again.

It wrenched free of the tubing, rode high-wide-and-handsome in the rigging and a deluge erupted from the hole.

The deluge was black and soft as velvet and blew over the top of the derrick.

They shouted and pounded one another in the back. The tank man forgot about the valve and jumped out and did a war dance crying over and over again: "Hot damn! Hot damn." He was thinking about his wife and three kids in Abilene who were up against it hard but stringing along on his gamble. A roughneck had to run over to the valve to close it. The deluge was trapped in twin flow pipes and gushed into the storage tanks with a soft squishy sound that was sweet music to their ears.

Excelsior No. 1 was running five thousand barrels a day.

The news was out at twilight and by dawn the march towards Rondora had started. It hadn't been in the papers yet but there are old-timers who can smell an oil strike five hundred miles off; and in their wake traveled the others: operators, scouts, vaga-bonds, thieves and women. The country was locked in by winter and everybody knew the going would be hard but there was gold at the end of the road, so they came on.

The ground spawned rigs . . . and in a little while the town was hemmed in by a palisade of hundred-feet derricks.

Spring.

Geese were going north and the aspen were budding into leaf. The creeks were running high in their banks from the melting snow, red squirrels chattered and blue jays screamed in strident notes. Light breezes came down from Raton Pass to whisper a magic message and the country popped alive. Jack-rabbits sat up lazily, their long ears flopping; the flowers went red and yellow and green; the grass grew tall and the cattle went out to graze. The mesquite and the chaparral stirred themselves and the blue came back to the sage.

Up and down the land had gone the fame of Rondora. Millions were there. All a man had to do was to take a hammer and chisel and bring in a gusher. They came from everywhere for the weather was warm and they could travel light. They settled like locusts and attracted no attention because everybody was thinking of something else . . . and it wasn't long before the grifters and gangsters and gamblers were running things.

II

W H E N T O M B E N D E R hopped a train north he was wearing a white hat that had silk lining as red as the *alegria* stain that saves your face from the sun.

It was big and hadn't been broken in yet and felt like a house sitting on top of his head. He hated to break in a new hat but his old one wasn't fit to wear to a town like Austin after he got through with those vaqueros. One of them had pushed a .44 bullet through the crown and Tom Bender knew it was only by the grace of God it wasn't his skull.

They were as slick a gang of greasers as a man ever clapped an eye on and they fought like wildcats but he brought four of them in alive. They had been running wet hosses, stampeding them off a hacienda in Nuevo Leon and then cutting out a few to swim across the river and sell to shady dealers in Texas. The whole country knew about it and everybody told Tom Bender they were *maldito Indios* and that if he went after them he was in for a lot of trouble.

He trapped them on the mud flats south of Rinera where the river cuts through wide cottonwood bottoms and called on them to surrender. They wanted to fight, so he accommodated them, killing one and plugging another before the others stuck their hands in the air and quit. It was a hell of a battle and there was no reason for it because he already had his orders to come to Austin.

After he put them in jail he caught a train for the capital. He didn't know why the Adjutant-General had called him and he didn't care because summer was just around the bend in the south and the Rio Grande country in the summertime was hot and cruel. The air was like the devil's own breath and the ground got hard and a man's feet stayed blistered all the time. Any kind of a job anywhere else was a picnic and Tom Bender liked picnics.

He was the issue of a frontier ancestry that had driven the Indians west of the Pecos to clear settlements for log cabins, a civilization of contrasts: hard, kind and tragic. The measure of an aristocrat was the nerve he had and the speed with which he could bark an Injun in his tracks and pitch a buffalo on his head with one ball.

Tom Bender's people were aristocrats and when they died that was all the heritage they left him.

That was enough.

When he hit Austin his body throbbed happily and he had a song in his heart for it was a passionate attraction he felt for the city. He swung along the street with the gait of a man to whom the feel of a pavement is a strange and mysterious thing, and everybody's eye was on him. They could tell by the walk of him that he was a fighting man and they knew by the brown of his face that he was from the south. Women looked at him but he paid no attention because he didn't know women could talk with their eyes. . . .

He went straight to the capitol and entered a dim, musty office in the east wing. Doubled up in a swivel-chair behind a massive desk was the Adjutant-General, lean and limber, and smoking a cigar. He said: "Hello, Tom," in a preoccupied tone but didn't get up or offer to shake hands.

There was a bluish haze hanging from the low ceiling, the office reeked with the smell of cigars and Tom Bender knew that when the smoke hung thick like this the Adjutant-General was getting ready to crawl somebody's frame. The thing to do was to let him alone and say nothing.

Bender sat down inelegantly in a Jacobean chair and waited. After a while he lighted a cigarette and as he began to puff the Adjutant-General said he had a trip for him and it was too bad he couldn't give it to somebody he didn't like. Bender asked him how was that and the Adjutant-General said it just looked like a hell of a way to reward him for getting those vaqueros.

Tom Bender laughed and said that was all right, the look on the Rinera sheriff's face was enough.

Then the Adjutant-General got up and stood by the desk. He looked down at the brim of Tom Bender's new white hat and said he was glad of that because he had a lulu now and he didn't mean maybe. Hell was popping over at Rondora. The old settlers had got enough of gangsters and gamblers and were about to take things into their own hands. The Adjutant-General said it was vigilante stuff.

Tom Bender nodded and declared that was the way with them ———— boom towns. They were so busy trying to get rich that the riff-raff had the place by the tail before they knew it.

"That's it exactly," the Adjutant-General said. "Last week a couple of bums put on a shooting match on the main stem and accidentally killed a twelve-year-old girl. Neither one of them was hit but a bullet ricocheted and got the daugher of Jeff Peebles. He couldn't get any satisfaction from the sheriff so he's got the whole town steamed up. It's a tough place."

Tom Bender looked up, bared his teeth wisely and said they were all tough but that some were tougher.

"Then Rondora's tougher," the Adjutant-General said. "I want you to get over there and head off trouble. There may be some even after you get there."

Tom Bender looked up, bared his teeth a little and said: "Yeah—there may be at that."

He was a good officer and scared of nothing but when he got in a tight corner he unlimbered his guns and started blasting.

The Adjutant-General glared down and snapped: "And, by ———! I don't want you to make a shooting gallery out of that town, either!"

Tom Bender grinned and spread his hands placatingly.

"All right," he said; "—no shooting gallery."

It was easy to agree to anything when a man's insides felt as if they had soaked up a lot of sunshine and he knew he had a day or two to play before he went back to work.

The Adjutant-General wrinkled his brow studiously and said: "I think maybe I better get Klepper down from Fort Worth to help you."

"Naw," said Bender, shaking his head; "you leave Klep be. I'll take a crack at it by myself. If I need help I'll holler."

"Well—" said the Adjutant-General, "all right. But I want results. I want the place mopped up."

"I'll mop 'er up," Bender said. "I'll get right over there tomorrow."

"No, you won't," his superior said quickly. "You have lunch with me and I'll put you on the train. There's a 1:15 train out for Amarillo that makes connections. I'll take you myself—I want to know you're on it."

Every time Tom Bender was turned loose in Austin he hit the high spots. He didn't get in often but when he did he took all they had and yelled for more.

"Don't rush me," he said, grinning. "I just got here. I know a lot of people here. I got to say hello to my friends."

The Adjutant-General frowned through a geyser of smoke.

"Tom," he said slowly, "you're a hell of a good man but the next time you get tight and wake up in Oklahoma City I'm going to kick you off the staff if I get impeached for it."

Bender grinned boyishly and slanted his head with his left eye closed from the thin finger of smoke that pried at it.

"Naw," he said disdainfully; "I ain't gonna get tight. I just wanna look around. I'll catch that train for sure."

"All right—but if you don't it'll be just too bad. I'm telling you, Rondora's hot. They're ready to start stringing 'em up to telephone poles."

"That'd be swell," Bender said; "yes, sir—that'd be swell."

The Adjutant-General meditated a moment and then gave up trying to be serious.

"Hell," he said, and sat down.

III

TOM BENDER UNLOADED at Rondora the next night an hour after sunset when the drilling rigs were ablaze with lights. The rigs were thrown around the town in an uneven circle, a glow

58

about the floor of each derrick, a lone light gleaming up near the
double board, another ninety feet in the air to light the top of the
stands and another above that on a gin pole which shone dully
down on the crown blocks.

It was an unearthly spectacle and looking at it Tom Bender
could believe those who said there was no arrangement of lights
that could look like this. His nostrils were filled with the cloying
smell of a breeze that has blown over hundreds of pools of oil and
his ears vibrated to a slow boom that was like the ringing of a great
bell from far off. Somewhere out there they were running surface
casing in the holes and beating it with sledges.

He was unconscious of the people around him until he heard a
voice say: "Taxi to the hotel," and felt somebody tug at his glad-
stone. He released it and followed a man across the gravel to a
flivver that was parked in front of the station. The man hoisted
the bag up and slammed it down hard in the space between the
hood and the fender and then started back to the train from which
people were still emerging.

The way he handled the bag got Tom Bender's dander up because
it was a present from the Adjutant-General and he was as careful
of it as he was of his watch. He yelled: "Hey!" and the driver
stopped. Bender strode over with blood in his eyes and asked him
where he was going. The driver replied shortly that he was going
to get some more passengers and walked away muttering to himself.

"Hey!" Bender yelled again. When he faced him this time the
yellow glare of the station lamps revealed deep lines in his face.
Tom Bender was spoiling for a good ruction and he didn't care
where it started. "How long you gonna be?" he challenged.

"Aw, I dunno," the driver responded lazily. "You in a hurry?"

"You're ——— right I'm in a hurry!" Bender snapped. The
driver wasn't very big and Bender knew if he slammed him one
he'd probably break him in two.

The driver's fingers were spread and working and his face was
alight with belligerency but he knew this was too much man for
him to take on single-handed. In a minute his fingers grew still,
he relaxed a little and tried to take it good-naturedly.

"In that case," he said; "I guess we better be rolling."

"Yeah," said Bender, still a little sore; "in that case we better be
rolling."

They rolled.

Rondora was booming. It was a settlement of drab one- and two-story buildings squatting upon the prairie with only a railroad to keep it alive. It was the sort of town that can be found nowhere but on the west Texas flats, and had the hand of fortune stayed itself Rondora probably would have gone on for generations on end creating not even a flicker of interest from the world outside. People were born, lived and died in the same house—that sort of town. Quick riches had increased the tempo of life and geared it too high for old-time fashions. She was an old chassis with a new and powerful motor and anybody who stopped to think would have known she couldn't stand a pace like this without bursting somewhere.

The single important street teemed with people. Automobiles were parked nose-first at the curbing and crowds were gathered on the corners and in the drug stores. Some of them were in the habiliments of the field and some of them were in plain trousers and shirt sleeves but all of them had money in their pockets and were looking for things to buy. From somewhere came the noisy discord of an electric piano. Conversation was loud, laughter was boisterous and women drove slowly up and down the street in closed cars, sitting alone in the shadows, and stealing surreptitious come-hither looks at the men on the sidewalks.

Bender grinned and remarked that Rondora was sure a hot burg. The driver laughed pleasantly and agreed but added it sure as hell was gonna cool off now.

"I know you," he said with a touch of pride. "You're Cap'n Tom Bender."

Bender admitted it, looked at the driver and said he didn't remember him.

"Nope," the driver explained; "but I was up to Denton seven or eight years ago when Willie Braun barricaded himself in that house and dared the cops to come and get him."

It was a six-hour gun battle with a train robber and Bender said he remembered it all right.

"I was standing pretty close when Braun shot your legs out from under you," the driver went on. "You laid flat on your belly in the street and blew his head off."

The Mopper-Up

Tom Bender didn't have to be reminded of that. He grunted and said nothing but the driver looked at him enviously and under the look Bender expanded and forgot all about the unpleasantness of a few minutes before. The driver asked him if he were in town on business and Bender said he had come up from the Rio Grande just to spend a vacation. He could tell from the way the driver laughed that he didn't believe it.

Bender asked him if he knew where Jeff Peebles lived and the driver said he did. He asked if Bender wanted to go out there.

"Later," he said. "I got plenty of time. Take me to the hotel first."

Up towards the end of the street they stopped before the hotel and a Negro bell-boy dashed out and got the bag. Bender told the driver to wait and went inside. The lobby was narrow and small but it was filled. All the seats were taken and there were women sitting around with diamonds on their fingers as big as dimes. Rondora had about ten times more people than it could care for.

Bender signed the register at the desk and the clerk explained that the hotel was pretty crowded and asked him if he was particular about a room. Bender said he wasn't just so it had a bed and a tub and the clerk handed a key to the Negro and said: "505."

On the way to 505 the bell-boy tried to get solicitous and confided that if the big gentleman wanted anything to pass the time or get anything to drink all he had to do was call number Four. He held up his badge to show the number but Bender flipped back his own coat lapel and said: "I like mine best because it's gold."

When the Negro saw the little star in the circle his eye popped and he shut up.

The room was plain and severe but it had a bed and a tub so Bender didn't complain. A guy got shoved in a lot of funny places when he was a Ranger, and anyway he consoled himself with the thought that he wouldn't be here long. He didn't like Rondora and when he didn't like a town he got right to work.

He washed his face, combed his hair, stuck a Police Positive .38 in his shoulder-holster, a blue-barreled .45 automatic in his hip pocket holster and came downstairs. The driver asked him if he was ready to go to Jeff Peebles and Bender said yes.

The driver turned off to the east and after a few blocks the town petered out and ran off into the sage. There were scores of rigs nearby and the din was terrific. Tall, gaunt skeletons they were and up close they looked like bad dreams. The smell of crude oil was strong and occasionally some roughneck sang out in profane music.

Jeff Peebles lived in a plain cottage and Bender had to cross a footbridge to reach the gate. He went up and knocked at the front door.

It was partly opened by an angular woman. Her face was sharp and she wore a plain print cotton dress, her hair was pulled tightly down about her ears and parted in the middle. In the light of the lamp in the front room Bender could see it was heavily streaked with gray and that her face was wan and lifeless. Jeff Peebles' millions had come too late.

She stared out apprehensively, as if she were half-afraid and Bender said:

"I'm looking for Mr. Peebles."

She shook her head slowly and replied: "He ain't here."

"Well," Bender asked; "where could I find him?"

She shook her head again.

"He ain't here," she repeated in that flat tone that was instantly monotonous.

"Yessum, I know he ain't here. But where is he?"

She looked at him with wide, sharp eyes and she started to shake her head when Bender said, "I'm Captain Bender of the Rangers. It's pretty important."

The woman now evidenced a slight animation. She stepped back and opened the door a little, saying: "Come in, Captain Bender. Come in."

"No'm," he said; "I just wanna locate Mr. Peebles."

"He's off to a meeting," she said, her voice sounding as if it were struggling from great depths to reach the surface. "You can wait here if you want to or you can go down to the Odd Fellows' Hall. That's where the meeting is. The Odd Fellows' Hall."

"Thanks," he replied. "I'll run on down there."

"That's all right, Captain," she said. "You come back any time you want to."

"Thanks," Bender said. He went out the gate, latched it and

62

recrossed the narrow footbridge to the car. He said to the driver: "Drop me at the Odd Fellows' Hall."

Going back he asked the driver if he knew anything about the shooting of Jeff Peebles' daughter. The driver said he didn't know any more than anybody else. They killed the girl all right and the sheriff arrested two guys named Botchey Miller and Pack Patton but they were released on bail or something right away.

Bender asked him where it happened.

The driver replied that the girl was killed down the street from the hotel in front of the *Happy Hour Club*.

"What kind of a dump is that?" Bender asked.

"Well," the driver explained; "it's supposed to be a pool-hall but they run it wide open. You can find any kind of a game and get any kind of a drink. I mean, strangers and everybody can."

"Who runs it?"

"Botchey Miller," the driver said. "Patton runs the *Fishtail Club* out on the Amarillo road."

"Roadhouses too?" said Bender.

"Sure. Botchey's got one out beyond Jeff Peebles' place about two miles."

Bender nodded and said, "I gather from that the boys don't like each other—Miller and Patton."

"I'll say they don't," the driver said. "Didn't they try to kill each other?"

Bender laughed and told him that wasn't always a fair test. He explained that gun-fighting was like boxing or golf or anything else; after it was finished it was all over and there was no use having hard feelings.

"Well, Botchey and Pack don't figure that way," the driver said. "They're at each other's throats and everybody knows it."

He turned a corner and stopped the flivver before a notion store. He said the Odd Fellows' Hall was upstairs.

"Okey," Bender said, getting out. "How much I owe you?"

"Just a buck," the driver said and Bender gave him a dollar bill and said: "Come back to the hotel at ten o'clock. I'll be wanting to ride some more then."

The driver said he would, and Bender turned around to look for the steps that led to the Odd Fellows' Hall.

IV

THE STAIRS WERE long and wide and went straight up with no landing to break the climb. In the hall above a globe shed a pale and insufficient glow. Bender saw a chink of light shining through a crack in one of the doors and he went over. He could hear the hum of conversation inside and he listened for a moment but couldn't make out what they were saying so he knocked on the door.

A man in shirt sleeves and with a light beard opened it, holding one hand on the knob and bracing the other against the wall suspiciously. He gruffly asked Bender what he wanted.

He said he wanted to see Jeff Peebles.

"He ain't here," came the answer. The man tried to shut the door but Bender jammed his foot at the bottom of it and told him to wait a minute. He pushed inside with little effort.

The man surveyed him with ill grace and said in a sharp tone: "You're liable to get throwed out on your ear, guy."

Tom Bender grinned and complacently remarked that he'd been thrown out on his ear before. He told the man to go get Peebles. The man told him to go to hell and looked around as if he needed help.

The room was deep and cavernous and there were a dozen or more men inside, all of them looking in the direction of the door. Two of them stepped off a small rostrum at the end of the hall and walked down the aisle between the chairs, their feet clumping loudly on the board floor.

One was willowy and cadaverous and wore a cheap suit with yellow square-toed shoes. The other was younger but both were agitated. As they came up Bender asked which was Jeff Peebles and the cadaverous man said he was. Before Bender had a chance to say anything else he told him to state his business and make it snappy.

The hall bristled with defiance and the attitudes of the men indicated they were in no mood for horseplay, so much as he disliked to Bender flipped back his coat lapel and flashed his badge.

"I'll make it plenty snappy," he told them straight from the shoulder. "I'm Tom Bender. Peebles, come outside. I wanna talk to you."

Peebles recognized the authority but he shook his head grimly and declared whatever had to be said could be said right there.

The other men arose and sauntered down. Bender saw trouble coming and his mood was truculent.

"Okey," he said. "I'm here to take charge."

The men exchanged glances, amused, and Peebles said sarcastically:

"Well, you're just outta luck. We've decided to handle this ourselves."

"Let's talk about it," Bender suggested but Peebles shook his head, pressed his thin lips together and said talk wouldn't do any good because everything was settled.

A few of the men chorused: "Yeah," and a deep bass voice from behind said: "You're damned right."

Tom Bender knew what his chances were without any long thinking. There was a great strength latent in the group but all of them were sensible and might yet be reasoned with. But if they got out carrying the torch there would be hundreds of irresponsible men to fall in and care not where the flame touched.

"Bender," Peebles said; "my girl was killed. The men who killed her were arrested but it didn't take. Now we're gonna have justice."

Tom Bender worked back against the door and said: "You can't get justice with a mob—that's no good. I'm down here to take charge and I will but I got to have a chance. Leave me be and I'll mop up this burg so ———— clean you can eat your dinner off the sidewalks."

Nobody paid much attention to what he said because they all felt like fighting. Old Jeff Peebles shook his head and looked at Bender through narrow-slitted eyes, the puzzled look of a man who faces a strange thing he knows he must deal with.

In a low voice he said: "Get away from that door, Bender—we're going out!"

Behind him there was a milling of feet. Somebody cried: "Here we go!" and another voice shouted: "We'll show these bootleggers something!"

Tom Bender was pressed flat against the door working his elbows to clear his coat from in front so he could get to his guns unimpeded and saying in a tense voice:

"There ain't gonna be no mob stuff—I'm telling you that! I

know the girl got killed . . . and that the town's filled with bootleggers and gamblers . . . but I'm gonna handle it my own way and
you might as well get that straight!"

The men surged and carried Peebles a step forward. He turned
and spread his thin arms saying ". . . Wait," and faced Bender
again. The big Ranger had his feet planted wide, there was a heavy
scowl on his face and his hands were on his hips. A little excited,
Peebles shrilled: "Get outta the way!"

Bender didn't budge. He felt immensely relieved that he had
got set for action without touching off an explosion and he knew
he had the upper hand now. He told Peebles to cool off in a tone
that was almost banter.

"All right," the old man rasped; "I'm gonna count three and if
you don't move we'll move you. . . . One. . . . Two. . . ."

Jeff Peebles took a step forward and a blue-black .45 automatic
came into the Ranger's hand. He pointed it at Peebles' belly and
said:

"Okey—but I'll plug the first guy that gets in close!"

Old Jeff Peebles' eyes went shut in high, impotent rage, the
muscles in his face and neck twitched violently and for a moment
Bender thought he was coming on anyway. He said: "By —— !"
through his clenched teeth and fell back a step.

There were loud mutterings from the others but none of them
wanted any of him. He had a gat in his hand, guts in his belly and
the tradition of the Texas Rangers behind him. That was what
held them off though Bender was not conscious of it—that tradition.

He was only conscious that his friend was the blue-black automatic around whose broad butt his long fingers were wrapped and
that it felt nice and warm and comfortable in his hand. He waved
the barrel in a semi-circle and told them to back up and sit down.
They backed up but they didn't sit down because they were waiting
on old Jeff Peebles to take the lead. Old Jeff was holding his ground
and looking as if he would like to paw up the floor. Bender knew
as long as he was up anything might happen.

"That goes for you too, Peebles," he said. "Back up and sit down."

Jeff Peebles glared at him in silent ferocity trying to decide
whether he would lose caste by retreating. Bender knew what was
going on in the back of the old man's mind but he didn't say

anything because he didn't give a damn. . . . Finally Peebles grunted and went over to a chair. Bender put his gun away and followed him and they sat down side by side at the same time like a pair of robots. The men all breathed easier because they would rather have a Ranger with them than against them.

He sat among them, strength of their strength, and with the authority to act. He could have given them commands and they would have been obeyed with no questions asked but he gave no commands. He looked at old Jeff Peebles and asked him what he wanted done.

The quiet request made it difficult for old Jeff and in that moment Bender's triumph was complete. Old Jeff cleared his throat, embarrassed, and said vaguely: "Well . . . I dunno, Cap'n. Things are pretty bad."

Bender said they were and that he was ready for suggestions. After a little while old Jeff said maybe it would be better if the Cap'n used his own judgment and then he looked at the other men for approval.

It was noisy and emphatic.

They all came downstairs feeling that the problem was solved and they tried to get in close to Bender to shake his hand. He laughed and told them gruffly to get the hell on home and leave him be.

V

RANGER TOM BENDER cruised through the open double doors of Botchey Miller's *Happy Hour Club*.

It was a long, wide room with a partition separating half of it. The front half contained pool tables and domino tables and both were well patronized. Voices came above the click of the balls and the slap of the dominoes on the wood.

Tom Bender went through the portières into the rear half.

Here were dice tables, a chuck-a-luck game, a keno game and a stud poker game going full blast. Dealers were at each game, wearing green eye shades and small black sateen aprons and a number of hard-looking workmen were waiting their chances to play.

Bender sauntered over to one of the dice tables and watched a boisterous roughneck who smelled of cheap perfume throw a double ace for ten dollars, a double six for twenty dollars and then get six for a forty-dollar point. He lunged all around it but no six, and eventually tossed a four-tray for craps. The roughneck rubbed his hands, backed out and said nothing, and the space was quickly filled by another eager gambler.

A waiter passed by with a tray filled with drinks and Bender stopped him and asked where Botchey was. The waiter said he was in the back and Bender asked him where the back was. The waiter pointed to a door and went on.

Bender went to the door and opened it without knocking.

It was a little office lighted by a single light that was suspended from the rafter on a single cord and the glow was deflected down by a shade to cut through the smoky atmosphere in a lurid shaft. Three men were inside. Two of them were sitting at a table looking at magazines and the third was leaning back in a chair with his feet propped up against an opened drawer.

He was forty, sallow and hook-nosed. He wore a soft hat, no coat, his sleeves were rolled up and his collar was open.

None of them got up as Bender entered. They stirred and the man at the desk said: "All right?"

Bender stopped beside the table and said he was looking for Botchey Miller. The man at the desk stood up and walked over slowly saying: "I'm him, brother."

Bender nodded and said: "I'm Tom Bender, Captain, Texas Rangers."

Botchey Miller's face took on a puzzled look and the two men at the table closed their magazines and looked around.

Miller said: "Ranger, hunh? Well, what's it all about?"

"Nothing much," Bender drawled; "only you're out of a job. This joint is closing."

Miller's lips worked in and out like a fish breathing and Bender took a step closer to the table where the two men were sitting. One of them was dark and wore a blue suit and a small black bow tie. He was scowling and biting his lower lip. The other man was younger and had a pleasant face. Bender asked him what his name was and he said Eddie Price.

Bender asked the dark man the same question but he leered and tried to get hardboiled.

"Ah, hell, tough guy," he said. "What's coming off here?"

"I asked you a question," Bender said evenly.

The man guffawed and looked at Botchey. "Say, Botchey," he called, "these Rangers are sure big tough babies, ain't they?" Miller laughed because he didn't know what else to do.

Bender flattened a great hand against the dark man's mouth and nearly slapped him out of the chair. He scrambled up, his eyes blazing, and made a move to his hip pocket. Bender laid his .38 Police Positive across his hip and the yellow light glinted along the barrel.

"What's your name?" he repeated.

Unintelligible growls came from the man's throat and words finally took form. "Wright,——you!" he cried. "You got a nerve—"

"Yeah," Bender said. He looked at Miller, who was standing stiff and straight as a tent pole. "All right, Miller, clean the house out. You're closing tight as a drum."

Botchey Miller was boiling inside and his eyes were swimming in anger, but he managed to say: "Aw, hell . . . I got to have a chance. Let's talk this over."

Bender shook his head and kept his .38 across his hip. Wright and Price were a little way in front of him and both of them were itching to go after their guns, but they were afraid to.

"Talkin's out," Bender snapped. "You're closing right now. Are you gonna do this or am I?"

"Well," Miller sneered, "since you're so —— tough suppose you do it."

"Okey. Your roadhouse is closing, too. I'm going out there later and if it's open I'll roll you guys good."

He turned around and walked out.

Outside Tom Bender stopped in the middle of the floor and raised his voice.

"Everybody listen," he said. In a minute or two there was quiet and they all were looking at him. "Cash in your chips and get out quietly. This joint is closing for good. There ain't no argument . . . cash in and beat it."

Tall, square-built, his eyes unwavering, he stood there loosely and looked out at them . . . and they began to do his bidding. There were mutterings and an undercurrent of antipathy, but he conveyed to them a quiet force and although he hadn't told them who he was everybody sensed that he was a Ranger. They began to shuffle . . . and in a little while the room was devoid of customers. A few of the dealers and two or three waiters stood around. The rear door opened and Botchey Miller ambled out, smiling sourly.

"Miller," Bender said, "keep this place shut down. Tomorrow I'm gonna start a bonfire with your furniture."

Botchey Miller said between his teeth: "You'll never get away with this—you'll never get away with it."

Tom Bender grinned and told him he'd been getting away with it for fifteen years.

"You close that roadhouse tonight or I'll fix it for you," he said.

"Aw, lissen—" Miller said, "you—"

"You heard me. You guys catch a rabbit."

He walked out.

The taxi driver kept his appointment and at ten o'clock straight up he parked his flivver in front of the hotel and started inside. At precisely the same moment the Negro bell-boy came through the lobby paging Mr. Bender. The driver spotted him and came over, but Bender told him to wait a moment and answered the page. The bell-boy took him over to the desk and said that gentleman there was waiting for him.

He was bulky, a little fat and wore a greenish suit and a wide black hat with the brim curled in cowboy style. He introduced himself as Jim Lovell, the chief of police, and asked if they couldn't go where they could talk.

Bender asked him what was the matter with right here and the chief said he'd rather not.

"All right, then," said Bender; "we'll go to my room."

They went upstairs and Jim Lovell sat down and made himself comfortable and asked him bluntly if he didn't know he was violating all ethics by not reporting to the chief of police.

Just as bluntly Bender told him he wasn't a damn bit interested in ethics.

"I know," Lovell said, "but just the same I'm the chief here even if you are a Ranger. I might be able to help you."

"I don't need any help," Bender said. "A job like this is a cinch for me."

"Cinch huh?" Lovell drawled, lifting his eyes.

"Yeah—a cinch."

Lovell laughed a little and said there ought to be some way out that wasn't so violent. He was acquainted with Botchey Miller and after all Botchey wasn't such a bad egg. He didn't see any use in getting hard without some reason and he thought Botchey ought to have a couple of days to get his business straight.

Bender began to get sore and he told Lovell it didn't make a —
—— what he thought, that he was running the show.

Lovell's face turned red as a beet and he declared loudly that he had some rights in the matter and that if Bender didn't hold off a while and co-operate with him he'd wire the Adjutant-General and raise some hell.

That sounded like a funny story to Tom Bender and he laughed and told him to go right ahead and wire. He had his orders and he wasn't afraid of any wire.

"Look here," he said, "these guys have been splitting wide open for months. Did you know that not three hours ago old Jeff Peebles had a mob together to clean the place up?" Jim Lovell winced a little and Bender went on: "Now, there ain't gonna be no more foolishness. They're shutting down pronto."

Lovell nodded and said all right, his only reason for saying anything was to try to head off a war. Bender asked him what he meant.

"Well," he said, "you know you can't lock everything tight without something happening. As long as you got an oil field you're gonna have bootlegging and gambling . . ."

"Yeah, I know. There'll be hip-pocket bootlegging and a man'd be a damn' fool to think he could stop that. There'll be dice shooting and poker games, too . . . but that'll be when the boys get together. I ain't trying to stop that. It's these organized gangs I'm after."

"Well," Lovell said, "I've warned you. Now there's just one more thing: you want me to help you or not?"

"Thanks," Bender said dryly. "I'll handle it. I wanna know all my trouble's in front."

Lovell jumped up, his cheeks scarlet and asked him what the hell he meant by a crack like that. Bender told him it meant any —————— thing he wanted it to mean.

His enmity was brutal and open and Lovell choked with rage. For a minute it seemed that the old over-ripe hatred between police chiefs and Rangers would come to a head. Lovell was excited but Bender was impassive and relaxed because he knew the Rondora chief wouldn't start anything. To have done that would have been mutely to testify to something Bender already suspected—that he was on Botchey Miller's payroll.

Lovell finally decided there wasn't anything he wanted to do about it. He said, compressed: "All right . . . all right . . ." and walked out, slamming the door.

For a moment Bender stood there looking at the door, the inside of him rising and falling slowly like an infallible barometer that recorded trouble close at hand. With a lurch the inside of him settled and he felt heavy . . . and in the next moment energy flowed into him as if he had drained it from the floor.

He rushed to the door, flung it open and went downstairs. The driver was waiting.

"Let's go!" he said.

Three miles out on the Amarillo road stood a two-storied, high-gabled house alone in the open country. Once upon a time it had been a pretentious dwelling but now it made no pretense. It was a mile beyond the frontier of the drilling rig lights.

This was Pack Patton's notorious dive—the *Fishtail Club* and it was lighted from top to bottom, making no effort to hide the secret of what went on inside. It was pretty generally known that in the basement was a big still and that upstairs were rooms and gambling apparatus.

Bender went up the wide front stairs two at a time but at the front door he was met by three men who had their hats off. One of them, heavy-set and with thick jowls, intercepted him as he started inside and told him he'd have to show his card. The other two men crowded around him close.

Bender said he didn't have a card and asked him who the hell he was. The man replied that his name was Patton.

"You're just the guy I'm looking for," Bender retorted. "I see you was expecting me."

Patton leered and said he always made it a rule to meet distin-guished guests. He said he was sorry but the club was closed.

"You're ———— right it's closed," Bender said. "It's closed for good. I wanna go in and look around."

"Sorry," Patton said; "you can't go in."

Bender nodded.

"Yeah," he said; "I'm going in."

He started in and somebody grabbed his arm. Bender whirled around, reaching for his .38 with right hand and swinging out with his left. It struck something hard and they closed in on him and tried to throw something over his head.

He gave up trying to get the .38 and lashed out hard, struck one of them and heard him grunt. He fell back, still swinging and something hit him a powerful lick behind the head and he thought it was going to snap off. A white explosion ascended in front of him and he staggered. As he did he came out with his .45 from his hip pocket and shook his head desperately to clear the mists and locate one of his assailants. In a moment he saw a form before him and he leveled the .45 and squeezed the trigger.

The narrow alcove lighted in a great red glare, a man swore loudly, doubled up and pitched on to the floor. A moment later Bender saw a form running up the steps and was about to shoot when he recognized the driver of the taxi. He wanted to shout a warning but before he could the driver had swung a heavy tire tool against one of the men's heads and knocked him back against the wall. He followed it up swinging and grunting, the man trying to get his gun out and the driver banging away with the tire tool.

Tom Bender looked at the third man who stood before him and looked down the muzzle of his gun. It was Patton, his face contorted in the pale light.

"Get your hands up," Bender rasped.

Patton swore and raised them and Bender reached out and searched him carefully. He took a nickel-plated pistol out of his coat pocket. The door surged with people from the inside who had been attracted by the shot and Bender yelled:

"Get the hell back in there!"

The men in the lobby groaned and the taxi driver came over beside Bender and said: "Where do we go from here?"

"Keep these guys right here," Bender said, passing over Patton's gun. "I'm going inside."

He pushed his way in. There were perhaps a dozen persons within the dance space, some of them women. Everybody was excited and several already had made their exits through the rear.

"Everybody beat it!" Bender said. "The joint is pinched!"

"By ——— !" somebody yelled. "There's a coupla guys out there dying! Why don't you call the ambulance?"

Bender looked coldly in the direction of the voice. "You call it," he said. "I'm busy."

He walked across the dance-floor to the steps leading upstairs. This was his element and his powerful figure dominated the foreground. He went up the steps and in the corridor he reached for his gun and walked on. He opened a door and stepped inside a brilliantly lighted room that was equipped with a dozen tables and gambling devices.

There were five employees inside, regarding him calmly. They seemed not in the least disturbed.

"All right, boys," Bender said; "this is the finish. Get out."

One of them asked if this was a pinch. Bender told him it wasn't if he got the lead out and beat it. Three of them marched out without a word, but the other two changed their eyeshades for hats and told Bender so long.

Bender followed them out, went down the hall and looked inside three other rooms. They were all dark, but from the light outside he could see they were comfortably furnished and all the beds wore silk spreads.

When he came back downstairs the lower floor was emptied. Employees had deserted Patton in his hour of need and he stood alone and captured by a taxi driver.

Bender went in the kitchen. The Negro chef was hurriedly putting on his pants and when he saw the Ranger he began to jabber and protest his innocence.

"Never mind," Bender said. "You go on home and don't take any more jobs like this. How do I get downstairs?"

The Negro pointed to a door in the wall beside a big gas stove

74

and Bender went over and opened it. A flight of narrow steps was revealed. Gun in hand, Bender rolled down them. The cellar smelled strongly of raw mash and before him he saw two great copper stills. The lights were on but nobody was there.

"Hey!" he yelled.

He came back upstairs. The Negro was on his way out.

"Anybody down there?" he asked.

"Naw, sir," the Negro said. "They come up a while ago and went outside."

"Sure?"

"Yes, sir, I'm sure."

"Okey. Beat it."

The Negro went out and left him alone in the kitchen. Bender looked around. In the corner was a basin of waste paper and trash. Bender grinned and went over and stood beside it. He put his gun in his pocket and lighted a cigarette.

He flipped the match in the trash box and came back to the lobby.

The taxi driver, charged with a sudden responsibility, was proving himself trustworthy. He had Pack Patton covered but there were a lot of people on the ground at the foot of the steps looking on with great curiosity. The man Bender had shot was stretched out on the floor on his face and there was another man slumped in the corner with blood pouring from his head.

"Get downstairs," Bender told Patton. He said to the taxi driver: "Take him to the car and if he tries any monkey business let him have it."

"Sure," the driver said.

"———— !" Patton swore and then erupted a stream of obscenity.

Bender stooped down and picked up the dead man. He worked him over his shoulder, followed Patton and the driver to the car. He flopped the dead man in the back.

Bender went back to get the other man. The driver had beaten him into unconsciousness and Bender couldn't tell how badly he was hurt. As he came back to the car the people surged around him and headlights flooded the road as all the traffic stopped. There were shouts and murmurs and the discord of excitement.

Bender paid no attention. He put the other man in the back and told Patton to get in front. Patton swore again and crawled in. The driver put the gun in his pocket and got under the wheel.

"Just what the hell is this raid?" Patton gritted.

"Nothing," Bender said. "You tried to get funny—that's all. Now you're going to jail."

He got in the back and spread the men out so he could sit down.

On his right side was a dead man, on his left an unconscious man and both heads were down with their chins on their chests.

Patton swore again and said: "You killed a man, you big—" and Bender reached around with his hand and slapped him on the side of the head."

"Pipe down," he said; "or I'm liable to bump you."

The driver grinned and cut on the switch. "He's piped," he said.

"What'd you hit that guy with?" Bender asked.

"A spring leaf," the driver said. "I was mad and I guess I hit him too hard."

"Yeah," Bender said dryly. "I guess I owe you a dinner for that. Let's be rolling."

The crowd gathered around the car. One man came in close, stuck his head under the top, saw the men in the back seat and said:

"Well, I'll be—! Looks like a cyclone hit 'em."

"You said it, brother," the driver clipped over his shoulder.

The car jerked away down the road, rolled a few hundred feet and pulled into a dirt road. The driver reversed it, turned around and started back.

A puff of smoke vomited from the *Fishtail Club* and a roll of flame pushed out and licked its way upward.

"———— !" Patton cried. "The place is one fire! The place is on fire!"

Bender looked out and nodded.

"Yeah," he said; "the cook must of left in a hurry."

Patton kept raving like a mad man and would have jumped out of the car but he knew that would be exactly what Tom Bender wanted for the big Ranger was waiting for a chance to mow him down.

When he returned to the hotel forty-five minutes later the main street was nearly deserted. The great wide glow that had spread over the heavens had attracted everybody and the fire had become the chief interest.

Bender went to sleep with his automatic under his pillow.

But his sleep was fuddled and semiconsciously he knew why. He had gone to bed wound up and taut and that was bad business. It had happened before and he had had bad dreams but even while he was having the dreams he was conscious of the reason. He always told himself the next time he got in a fight he would sit around and cool off before he went to bed but always in the morning he had forgotten.

Only half asleep, he heard noises. Somebody was raising the windows.

He lay still and prized his eyelids up a little and saw two shadowy forms coming through from the fire-escape. In a moment they were still and he lay there, hardly breathing, until the white beam of a flashlight struck him in the face.

He had the impulse to jump up and cover them but he had sense enough to fight that back because he knew they were waiting for him and ready and he wasn't.

They slowly walked over and he could tell from the way they held the light that they were nervous too.

They came close by the bed and he could hear them breathing. They were snorting like horses after a run and making enough racket to wake the dead. Whoever it was certainly was overanxious. When the light went out this time Bender opened his right eye and saw a man above him big as all outdoors and got a gleam of something steely in his hand.

The man was fixing to knife him.

Like a flash he slid out of bed backwards, pulling his automatic out from under the pillow with him and when his foot struck the floor he knew this was no time to play around.

He flicked his gun down and squeezed the trigger a couple of times and in the light of the explosion he saw an agonized face and imagined he could hear the bullets thud home with a soft plunk like he had shot a piece of liver.

He dropped down quickly to use the bed as a barricade but before he could hide himself or fire at the second man there was

77

another crack, sharper and more staccato than his, and a finger of flame reached out and went through his right arm and he knew he was shot.

He fell to the floor and tried to push his gun over to his left hand but his right hand wouldn't respond. He had a frantic moment and his arm was numb and dead and somehow he got the crazy idea that he had been sleeping on it and that it was asleep. Then he knew that couldn't be . . . so he reached over with his left hand and got the automatic and stuck his hand up to rub out the other assailant.

The assailant could see better than he could and he fired again over the bed, the bullet singing by Tom Bender's head and biting off a lot of plaster behind him.

Bender turned the nose of his automatic down and got the bead and then *crack—crack* came from the window sill. The man across the bed spun around like a toy top and fell with a loud noise and somebody jumped down off the sill and ran into the room.

Bender crawled up saying: "Who is it? Who is it?"

"Cap'n? Cap'n?" the man said.

Bender switched on the light on the table by the bed and there stood the taxi driver, gun in hand, his cap on side-wise and excitement in his eyes.

"For ———— sake!" Bender rasped. "Where the hell did you come from?"

"I saw 'em, I saw 'em," he said. "I knew they were up to something so I followed 'em up the fire-escape. When Botchey shot at you I located him and gave him the works."

Bender swore and grinned.

"By ———— !" he said in a nasty bass, "you're the ———— guardian angel I ever had."

The taxi driver came over and said: "Look—you're shot!"

Blood was pouring down Bender's forearm and the upper part of his pajama sleeves was stained crimson.

"Yeah," he said. "Call a doctor or something for these guys."

The taxi driver went to the telephone and Bender went around the bed.

Botchey Miller on his side on the floor, a hole in his temple and one in his neck, but he was still breathing. Bender had to pull the

other man off the bed to identify him, and he slid to the floor in a
heap.

It was Jim Lovell, the chief of police. His right hand relaxed and
stretched out and came close to a six-inch stiletto that lay gleaming
on the floor. Lovell was hit once below the right eye and the bullet
had ranged upward and come out at the back of his head.

Bender pitched his gun on the bed and sat down and looked at
the men. Then he picked up the stiletto and held it up. The taxi
driver came over and Bender said: "They was fixing to park that
in my back."

The taxi driver nodded. Bender squinted his eyes and stared at
him. He wrapped his left fingers around his right arm just below
the shoulder and squeezed hard to try to stop some of the pain.

"Say," he said; "what the hell is your name?"

"Rusty Minton," the driver said. "Why?"

Bender winced as a surge of pain rolled down his arm.

"Nothing," he said; "only I thought it was about time you and I
got acquainted."

VI

T H E N O O N W H I S T L E S blew and Rondora paused for
lunch but the Grand Jury did not adjourn because they were looking at records and listening to a Ranger captain tell them plain
facts about organized crime and boom towns.

Tom Bender sat there in a long room of dim coolness, his right
arm bandaged from shoulder to elbow where a .38 bullet had
plowed through a muscle, and explained how the keys he had
found in Botchey Miller's pocket fit a safety deposit vault that had
contained the records now before them.

Those records made the Grand Jury gasp. They revealed how
Lovell, the former chief of police, who now lay in the morgue, had
been taking money from Miller and also how lesser officials were
involved. Bender told them he had looked for these lesser officials
but couldn't find them and it was his guess they had blown for
good. . . .

The Grand Jury indicted Pack Patton and no-billed Tom Bender and Rusty Minton, a taxi-driver. It adopted a vote of thanks for the latter pair and everybody shook hands and dispersed.

They asked Bender to remain over so they could throw a banquet or something but Bender told them he was still sleepy and that now that everything was quiet he thought he'd run over to Amarillo and hit the hay.

They thought he was too modest and said so but Bender laughed and told them so long.

He went back to the hotel and asked the clerk to get him transportation for Amarillo on the one o'clock bus. At five minutes to one he came downstairs and scores of persons crowded around the pointed him out and said flattering things. Bender got hot under the collar and quietly told a couple of them to get the hell away from there.

It seemed that the bus would never come. He felt that his hands and feet were unaccountably large and that in a minute or two . . . and then the big gray bus poked its ugly nose around the corner and drove up.

The crowd moved and from its midst came the taxi driver. His face was flushed, his eyes were wide but his attitude was one of mingled happiness and confusion.

"Say, Cap'n," he babbled; "guess what—the mayor's just appointed me chief of police!"

"That so?" Bender asked. "Well," he went on seriously; "you been a machine-gun sergeant in France and you got guts. Just keep these crooks in line and stay honest. Don't shoot until you have to, but when you do, try to hit something." He grinned. "That way, you may get to be mayor."

Rusty Minton gulped.

"I can handle it all right," he said, "but the mayor comes to me out of a clear sky. I didn't ask for this job."

"Well, you want it or not?"

"Sure—I'm tickled to death. But how'd he come to me?"

Bender's eyes twinkled.

"Search me," he said.

"All aboard," shouted the driver.

"So, long," Bender said.

Rusty Minton's mouth popped open as the truth broke over him like a rainbow. He would have gone after the bus but it was out of sight.

"Ugh!" he said to himself. "Wottaguy!"

FREDERICK
NEBEL

Red Pavement

DURING CAP SHAW'S ten-year editorial reign, a good many private eyes battled their way through the pages of Black Mask *in pursuit of truth, justice, and the American Way—Daly's Race Williams, Hammett's Continental Op, Chandler's Carmady, Raoul Whitfield's Ben Jardinn, Roger Torrey's McCarthy, Norbert Davis's Ben Shaley, and Dwight V. Babcock's Maguire, to name the most prominent. But with the clear exceptions of the Continental Op and Carmady, none of these dicks was in the same league with Frederick Nebel's slightly jaded, slightly shady "Tough Dick" Donahue.*

Donahue made his debut in the November 1930 issue, in a story called "Rough Justice," and appeared in fourteen more cases until his "retirement" in 1935. He was not the most active of Nebel's pulp detective characters—the team of police captain Steve MacBride and news hound Kennedy appears in thirty-seven Black Mask *stories, and another private eye, Cardigan, is featured in forty-three novelettes published in* Dime Detective—*but he is certainly the toughest. A former New York City cop who was fired for raiding the wrong gambling joint, Donahue works for the Inter-State Detective Agency and is not above using illegal methods to achieve his goals. "I've been up against crooks, guns, and I've double-crossed them to get what I wanted," he says in one story. "That's what my game is. It's not a polite business of question-and-answer bunk. You work against crooks and you've got to beat them at their own game."*

Toughness is only one of the elements that make the Donahue stories memorable. They are also vivid portraits of the New York underworld at the end of Prohibition. And they are rich in the street slang of the period, as well as spiced with an underplayed sense of gallows humor.

Six of the Donahue stories comprise Nebel's only collection, Six Deadly Dames, *first published by Avon books in 1950 and reprinted by Gregg Press in 1980 as part of their series of mystery fiction revivals. "Red Pavement" is not included in that book. It is, in fact, reprinted here for the first time anywhere since its original publication in the December 1932 issue of* Black Mask.

Louis Frederick Nebel (1903–1966) began selling regularly to the pulps when he was in his teens, using his own name and such pseudonyms as Eric Lewis and Grimes Hill. Instead of attending college, he worked in the Canadian North Woods and on a tramp steamer in the Caribbean, and traveled extensively in Europe, where he met his wife Dorothy in 1928. In the early thirties, Nebel wrote his only three novels, Sleepers East *(which was filmed three times, once as* Sleepers West*),* But Not the End, *and* Fifty Roads to Town. *But he was a short story writer at heart, and because at this time he also began making sales to such slick magazines as* Collier's, American, *and* Liberty, *he abandoned novels and, in 1937, the pulps as well. He was a successful slick writer for more than twenty years, with only a few of his stories for these magazines having criminous themes. Ironically, however, his final few stories marked a belated return to the mystery field: they were published in such genre periodicals as* Ellery Queen's Mystery Magazine *in the late fifties and early sixties.*

DONAHUE HAD STOPPED in the dark, windy street to cup his hands over a match. He heard the door bang, and looking up from the match's glow, he saw the drunk reel towards him across the sidewalk. He stepped aside, still maneuvering his hands in the wind to get a light, and had the flame leaning steadily towards his cigarette when he heard the grunt and the sound of the man piling headfirst into the gutter, near a fire-hydrant.

The door opened again. Tossing the match away, Donahue saw a head thrust out, the shadow of a face beneath a fedora; then the head withdrew and the door banged shut. He stood for half a moment quite complacently enjoying the first drags of smoke and watching the drunk's awkward efforts. The wind came from the west, up West Tenth Street and smack against his back, flapping the long skirt of his belted camel's hair and humming past his rigid Homburg.

"Here," he said, at length.

He swung to the curb, grabbed a wandering arm and hauled the man to his feet. He grinned good-humoredly.

"Steady, brother. Another dive like that and—Stead-y!"

" 'S all right—'s all right, brother. Must have been somethin' I ate. 'S trouble with restaurants these days: you can't depend on nothin' any more."

"Come on; I'll steer you to a subway."

The man grunted. "Idea." He reeled around and poked Donahue's arm. "An' not only restaurants, brother." His lower lip pouted; he teetered back on his heels. " 'S damn' shame, 's what!"

"Come on; snap out of it."

"Sure. Where was we goin'?"

"Subway. I'll pilot you to Sheridan Square."

"Swell idea. Le's go. . . . You goin' uptown, too?"

"Yeah."

They went along the dark street, past the pale glow of a speakeasy areaway; went on—the man bouncing along on his heels like a marionette and Donahue keeping a firm grip on his arm. He was no great bundle to handle; short, bony-faced, with a gray, hard pallor. New clothes, cheap but substantial. And he was very drunk. The whites of his eyes rolled into view frequently. They reached West Fourth Street and the drunk stopped resolutely.

"T' hell with subway. Le's get taxi. *Taxi!*" he yelled.

Brakes squealed and a cab stopped on the opposite side of the street. Donahue hadn't bargained for this, but traffic was flowing past and he did not care to see the drunk run down. He steered him through the traffic and put him into the cab.

"Where d' you want to go, friend?"

"Hell. You're comin' uptown, ain't you? Come on!"

Donahue shrugged and climbed in and the man said: "Penn Station, Jymes."

The cab started off and the drunk leaned against Donahue's

shoulder. "Gonna meet her, brother. Gonna make her my wife. Penn Station, train at 9:02. She come a long ways. To meet me." He poked himself, hiccoughed. "Be my wife."

He swung away, heaved over on one side and dragged awkwardly at a hip pocket. He drew out a small wallet and a big .38 revolver. His lip drooped and he said:

"Here, hold this rod a minute, brother."

Donahue took it, hefted it; guns were in his trade and he liked the feel of this one.

The drunk had taken a small snapshot from his wallet. "Her picture, mister." He looked, oddly enough, like a yokel just then.

Donahue glanced sketchily at it, then said, hefting the gun: "You want to look out for this rod. What the hell are you packing a cannon like this around for?"

"Ah," the drunk said, and winked with tremendous spirit. He closed his hand over his gun and thrust it into his overcoat pocket. His teeth bared in a drunken grimace and he stared grimly before him. "I gotta pack it," he said.

Donahue was good-humored, twisting a smile off his lips. "I know, but look at it this way: here you show me, a perfect stranger, a rod the State of New York says you're not allowed to pack. Of course, personally I don't care who packs a rod, but if I'd turned out now to be a city cop instead of a private dick—well, where'd you be?"

"Uh," said the drunk. "Yeah, I get you. I gotta be careful. I gotta—" He stopped short, fell against Donahue, gripped his arm. "You—you're a private detective?"

"Yeah."

"Good! Listen, brother—now listen." He tugged at his wallet, counted out some bills. "Here. Here's a hundred bucks. Listen, now. I gotta meet this gal. But I'm drunk, see? I'm stewed. Some swell lousy pals o' mine got me stewed. Tell you what. You meet my gal, tell her I been detained on business. You take her to a hotel—make it the *Grandi*, and she gets a room there. Me, I'll get me a Turkish bath, get straightened out. Hey, wait now! How the hell do I know you're a private dick?"

Donahue chuckled, showed him plenty of identification. He was frank. "This is easy money," he said.

"A hundred bucks. Count 'em. I—jeeze—I got to get straightened out. You see, I just come back from South America—struck it rich—and these fine, nice, lousy pals o' mine . . ."

Grinning, Donahue pocketed the hundred dollars. "Now wait, brother. You'd better lend me that picture of the girl. Tell me her name. Also, I'll have to have your own name."

"Sure! Sure I'll"—he sought his wallet again—"lend you the picture. Name's Laura and she's—"

Donahue had his little book out. "And your name."

He turned, by instinct more than anything else, and saw the long black shape of the touring car draw up and crowd in close. But he hadn't time to get a word out of his mouth. He hadn't time to snap his hand to his gun.

A gun crashed four times.

Donahue flung back against the side of the cab, ducking. The driver ducked and slewed in his seat and the cab careened, brakes screamed, but at the same time there was a tremendous bounce as the wheels went over the curb. The right front mudguard crashed against a building wall. The car recoiled and glass shattered.

Donahue was pitched forward out of the seat. He struck the glass partition between tonneau and driver's seat and collapsed on the floor, facing backwards. The drunk piled down on top of him violently and Donahue felt something warm and liquid slap his cheek. He straight-armed the drunk off, hauled himself up and dropped to the seat, hot and shaking all over. His client was gurgling on the floor, in the darkness there.

The driver was pressing his forehead down on the upper rim of the wheel. The man on the cab's floor was groaning and gurgling, and up and down the street autos, trucks, were stopping; the shots, the sound of the crashing taxi had frozen a few pedestrians into immobility and they remained thus.

"Brother . . ."

Donahue got a flashlight on and sprayed light down on the man's face. He shut the flash off immediately, grimacing.

"Brother . . ." The tone was curiously sober.

"That's all right—that's all right."

"Listen. Go meet her. It'll be tough, her comin' alone. Go meet her. Here . . . take this wallet. Key inside—for bag—"

Donahue snapped: "Cut out talking."

"Here, take it."

"Will you shut up!"

He felt a hand pawing at his own.

"Take it. You'll recognize her by the picture. There's some dough in it. Give it to her. Here. There's a baggage check in it. I got a bag at the station. Get it. Give it to her. Tell her to get out of town—go home again—I'm sorry—"

Donahue found himself taking the wallet, shoving it into his pocket.

And he heard the broken voice go on: "Don't tell—the—cops. It ain't her fault. She—don't—know—and—"

"For ——— sake, shut up!"

It was hard to listen to the gurgle of a dying man. There was no reason why he had to listen to it. The man was a stranger.

"Hey, there!"

That was a voice outside the cab,—loud and challenging.

Donahue pushed open the door and climbed out and a cop came up to him, stopped and eyed him with a hard stare.

"What the hell happened?"

Donahue's thoughts were on the sprint. In his pocket lay the hundred dollars representing his fee for promising to meet and conduct to the *Hotel Grandi* one named Laura something. He did not know the man's name—nor the girl's. He had a rather thorough opinion of a harness-bull's imagination. To tell this cop the truth as it had happened would, in the clear sound of words, seem fantastic. He would not expect the cop to believe him. Part of the truth might get by. The fact of the matter was he had seen an easy way to make a hundred dollars, had taken the case as a joke; and the joke had turned into tragedy.

"Take a look in the cab," he said.

The cop snapped on a flashlight and poked into the tonneau. Donahue watched him, his eyes narrowed.

"Hey!" the cop yelled; then he backed out, spun around. "That guy's dead."

Donahue said: "A curtained touring car yanked up alongside us and let go. The guy inside got it."

"Who's the stiff?"

"I'm damned if I know."

The cop towered with rage. "What the hell are you trying to hand me?"

"I picked him up in a gutter downtown. He was soused. Like a drunk, I couldn't get rid of him. So we took a cab."

The driver looked out, choked: "F-four shots!"

"You," the cop said to Donahue, "are lying!"

"So what should I do now? Break down?"

There was no turning back now. He had the man's wallet. To turn the wallet over now would be to put himself in a very serious jam.

The cop twirled his nightstick and laughed unpleasantly.

"Okey, guy, okey. Be wise, be wise. . . . Hello, Coake," he said to another cop who had come up on the run.

"Hello, Donlin. What the hell?"

"A stiff inside."

"Who's this?"

"A wise bimbo."

Donahue said: "You cops!" with hopeless irony, and chuckled.

A car drew up at the curb and a stoutish man alighted without haste and came across the sidewalk slapping gloves he held in one hand across the palm of the other.

"I heard shots."

"Yeah," Donlin said. "Pike what's inside."

The stoutish man looked into the cab, backed out and said: "Well, well," in a merry voice. "And who's—"

Donahue was leaning against the building wall, eyes cold but watchful.

The stoutish man said: "Well, well, Donny!"

Donahue's "Hello, Kelly," was not enthusiastic.

"He's a wise bimbo," Donlin growled.

Kelly McPard grinned broadly. "Hell, he's all right. Just has a habit of being Johnny-on-the-spot. So what happened, Donny?"

"Ask precious," Donahue said, indicating Donlin.

Donlin told him, and then said: "And this guy right away starts to act dumb."

McPard made a face, as though all this was unpleasant business. "Tsk! tsk! Well—well, suppose we get the Morgue bus. Did you frisk the stiff?"

"No," Donlin said.

"Better." He backed away from the cab, turned casually and looking up the street, said to Donahue: "What about it?"

"It's blind to me." Donahue shrugged. "I told the cop everything I know."

Kelly McPard kept looking up the street and said thoughtfully: "Ye-es, I suppose so. . . . Well?" This was directed at Donlin, who had come out of the cab.

"Only this." Donlin held the .38 auto in his hand.

"Full?"

"Yup."

McPard sighed and said to Donahue: "Mind running over the station house?"

"I gave the cop all the dope. I was headed uptown. You know where I live."

McPard shrugged. "Okey."

"What!" yelped Donlin. "You gonna let this ape—"

"Ah," drawled McPard, "he's all right. We don't need him." There was curious laughter back of his voice, a wily dip to his head. "Run along, Donny. I wouldn't think of pestering you." And there was still that curious sense of laughter.

Donahue walked away.

2

HE HAD DECIDED a dozen times in the space of as many minutes to turn the wallet over to McPard. And in the end he hadn't. He was Irish, and that may have accounted in some measure for the sentimental streak beneath the tough hide. That—or the fact that he and Kelly had a habit of playing hide and seek with each other. Within limits he trusted McPard. Kelly was square. But he had long wanted something on Donahue, and this would have been too good a chance.

It was two minutes to nine when he heaved out of a taxi at Penn Station. He slapped swing doors open, went down into the main rotunda. The only 9:02 train would arrive downstairs. He went down and saw a man in a cap marking on a blackboard that the

9:02 was expected to arrive at 9:15. He worried a cigarette between his lips and cast a quick glance over the waiting people. The small wallet felt hot and oily in his palm; he kept that hand religiously in his overcoat pocket. Shop windows were bright and cheerful in this subterranean cavern, but the air was always stuffy, second-hand, winter or summer. He prowled around, looking. He pushed into a soda counter, entered a telephone booth, took out the wallet. It contained two hundred and twenty dollars. There was the girl's picture. She looked young, brown-haired, nice. On the back was inscribed: "Love to Charlie from Laura." The snap wasn't very old. And there was a baggage check. He replaced the articles in the wallet, the wallet in his pocket.

"Tough," he said, thinking of the picture.

He went out and looked at the blackboard again. His watch checked with the electric one above: 9:12. Then the man with the cap was megaphoning: "Blah . . . from . . . blah . . . Columbus . . . Wheeling . . . blah . . . was due at 9:02 . . . blah . . . Track . . . blah!"

People got up and moved down the corridor. Donahue tailed along, looking around. His eye lit on a small young man leaning against a stone pillar. There was a sensation of something clicking as the little man's eyes met his own. Then they dropped, a foot ground out a cigarette and the little man sauntered off, whistling. Donahue tried to catch sight of him a moment later, but was unable.

People were coming up the stairway from the train level below. Donahue watched and saw her but did not immediately go to her. She was very small, with a startled, pretty face. A porter was beside her, holding a bag and asking something. She kept shrugging and peering eagerly at the faces. It was minutes before the crowd went away, and then she stood there alone with the porter drooping beside her. Donahue cast another look around, then went over to her.

"Laura?"

There was a frightened smile. "Yes!"

"He couldn't meet you. He sent me. . . . I'll take that, porter." He took the bag and gave the porter a quarter. "This way, Laura—"

"But—"

He was pointing: "We have to go to the checkroom first." He flung a look over either shoulder.

"How is Charlie? Why couldn't he come?"

"Yes," he said, making believe he misunderstood. "The checkroom's upstairs. Have a nice trip?"

"Oh, long. Lonesome."

"There it is over there."

He gave the check to the man at the counter and received a small yellow handbag that looked new. Gripping it in his left hand, the girl's suitcase in his right, he started off.

"Come on. We'll get a taxi."

They got one in the tunnel and rode out into Seventh Avenue. Donahue had given the address of his apartment-hotel. He was glad the girl didn't talk. She sat quietly in a corner. He sat in the other, his arms folded and his face in a hard, brown study. Presently the cab stopped and the hotel doorman let them out. Donahue lugged the bags and they went up to his apartment. He could tell by the way she looked when they entered his rooms that she expected to see Charlie there. She turned on him as he was closing the door.

She said, weakly: "Something—something's—"

"Ssh!" He skated the bags into one corner and scaled his hat on to a divan. He went on into the bathroom, looked at himself in the mirror and thought: "Of all the saps, Donahue, you're the berries—with all the trimmings." He turned, strode out of the bathroom with his coat's long skirt slapping his calves. He walked straight to the center of the room and stood there grinding the heels of his hands slowly together and regarding the girl with a glazed introspective look.

There was a little cry—"Oh!" And small white fingers suddenly against cheeks from which the color was ebbing.

He took a step and laid a big hand on either of her small rounded shoulders. "He's dead, Laura." That was the easiest way—right out with it. He felt the rounded shoulders twitch and he saw her looking up at him with a peculiarly abstracted expression. Then she stepped back and began walking up and down the room, swiftly, quietly, with her eyes fixed on the carpet. Suddenly she dived on to the divan and lay there—still, motionless, without a move, without a quiver.

He grabbed the back of a chair and dragged it across the carpet, planked it down in front of the divan. He sat down and scrutinized the palms of his hands, turning them this way and that.

He said, as if talking aloud to himself: "He asked me to meet you. That bag there: he asked me to give it to you. He said you should go home again. He said he was sorry he couldn't meet you. He gave me some money to give to you—to get back on, I guess."

She broke into sobbing and he got up and entered the bathroom and washed his hands. The running water dimmed the sound of her sobbing. He washed his hands over and over again, throwing secret glances at his image in the mirror. After a while he turned to the room and saw her sitting up. Her hat was askew, her face smeared with tears. She sniffled, stared straight ahead of her with blank, wet eyes.

"Where can I see his body?"

"I wouldn't," he said.

"I want to."

"You can't."

She looked up at him. "Why?"·

"It was his dying wish that you shouldn't."

Her tone was dull: "How did it happen?"

"He was shot. I guess it was an accident." He tossed the wallet to the divan. "His money's in that and the key to his bag. I'll get you a room in the hotel. I brought you to this apartment because I thought it'd be easier."

"Who—who are you?"

"My name's Donahue. I'm a private detective."

"You knew Charlie well?"

"I never saw him before. I just saw him when he was dying."

"And—and you did this—for him—for me? You did this for strangers?"

He frowned and turned away. He was glad she didn't rave and carry on hysterically. She wasn't that kind. All her emotion remained inside, locked up, torturing her. You could see that much in the stunned white face, tell it by the dull, listless monotony of her words. Then she was feeling at her throat.

"Do you—you mind if I stay here till I can get a train?"

He shivered. He wanted to get her into another room, out of sight; he wanted to get her out of the city as soon as possible. He had done enough. He didn't want to have a strange girl on his hands.

She was saying: "I hate to ask it. I—I'm not that kind of a girl, you understand. But—but I'm afraid to stay alone. I'm just—afraid. Coming like this—from a small town—I've never been in a big city. And I'm afraid to be alone. I'm ashamed to ask you, but . . ." She moved her shoulders wearily and then covered her face with her hands.

"Okey," he said after a while. "Sure. Stay here. I never thought of that." He nodded. "Bedroom's in there."

He picked up her suitcase and Charlie's bag and carried them into the bedroom. He frowned and muttered to himself, but when he reappeared in the living room these manifestations of his ill-humor were absent. She was standing, a small, lone, pitiful spectacle.

"In there," he said.

She smiled wistfully. "You're so good, Mr. Donahue—so good." She dragged her feet past him and entered the bedroom, closing the door quietly.

He crammed a pipe and lit up, took to pacing with slow, long strides, his face wrapped in thought. A few moments later he heard a sharp outcry. His nape bristled, his eyes narrowed and he whipped to the connecting door, flung it open.

She was on her knees, shaking, her eyes wide. She looked up at him and grimaced and pointed downward. He crossed the room and looked down into Charlie's open bag.

It was crammed with money—hundreds, thousands of dollars.

3

THE CONNECTING DOOR was closed—locked. He had heard the girl turn the key quietly on the bedroom side. It amused him more than anything else. There was a single in-a-door bed in the living-room, if he wanted to use it later. But the divan would do. He was interested in neither, though, at the moment. Coming out of the little pantry that contained nothing more than an icebox and a sink, he tried the Scotch highball while heading for a mohair easy chair. Dropping into the chair, the dim glow of the floor lamp behind made his smooth black hair shine but kept his face mostly in shadow.

Fourteen thousand five hundred dollars. He looked at the connecting door: the money was behind that door. He drew on his pipe and heard, far away, the thresh of a southbound Elevated train.

Charlie Stromson was his name. It was like this: He'd known her in Revelation, Ohio, six or seven years ago. She was the cashier in the Center Square General Store. Charlie worked in the Sportsman's Exchange, the game and fish store; he was a wizard at repairing guns and fly rods and mounting fish or birds. Then he got it into his head that there was gold in South America. They became engaged, and he went off to find a fortune.

He wrote her three months later from New York, that he was leaving for South America to get their fortune. That was the last she heard of him for three years. Then there was a letter from Montevideo. He'd made his fortune and he named a date when she was to meet him in New York. She sent a letter care of the General Post Office, New York, saying she would meet him on the appointed date. She'd shown Donahue the letter post-marked at Montevideo. It told of hardships in the jungle, of privation, months and years away from any civilized town.

Donahue muttered: "Um," and took a long drink. The sound of a knock on the corridor door made him lower the glass slowly and stare. He had removed his shirt—his suspenders looped around his hips—and was in worn leather slippers. He got up, went to the secretary, put the drink down and picked up his gun. He crossed to the door.

"Who's there?"

"It's Kelly, Donny."

Donahue thrust his gun into his hip pocket. He threw a look at the closed bedroom door, then turned the key in the one before which he stood and opened it.

McPard looked neat in his blue overcoat and soft gray hat. His shoes shone. His cheeks were pinked up by the wind outside and his smile bloomed whimsically in his cherubic face. He wandered in, cast his smiling, twinkling eyes around the room. Donahue closed the door and stood for half a moment eying McPard's back.

"Park, Kelly. . . . Drink?"

"No, thanks." McPard sat down on a straight-backed chair, drew a white linen handkerchief from his pocket, unfolded it and blew his nose quietly. "That guy who was bumped off, Donny. . . ." He patted his nose gently, put away the handkerchief.

Donahue drew his eyes away from the bedroom door. "Yeah?" He walked across to the secretary and scooped up his drink and carried it on to the divan. "Yeah, Kelly?"

"Hell, now, Donny"—he made a palliating gesture with his hands—"why not give me the straight of it?"

"I did, Kelly."

"I know, I know. Straight as a crooked line. I don't say you had anything to do with his death, Donny; you know I wouldn't say a nasty thing like that."

"I know; you wouldn't like to hurt my feelings."

McPard grinned. "Exactly!" He leaned back, crossed his legs. "It didn't take us long to place him. I didn't expect much, but anyhow I wandered through Rogues' Gallery and—sure—there was his mug—there it was."

Donahue snapped a look at the bedroom door. "I don't believe it, Kelly."

"So his mug led to his record. He did a three-year stretch."

Donahue stood up, growled: "That's something you thought up!"

McPard chuckled absently. "Yeah, I thought you'd say that. But it's no go, Donny. I guess you weren't so hot as a bodyguard."

"Bodyguard?"

McPard stood up and regarded Donahue affectionately. "Come, now, Donny—don't try to kid me. I just want the truth. When did this mug hire you, where did he live, and who bumped him off— and where," he added, smiling whimsically, "was the dough bunked?"

"You know so much about this, Kelly: tell me."

"There was around twenty thousand involved. This mug blew into New York from the wide open spaces about three and a half years ago. He got tangled up in the wrong end of town. One night this egg and two pals walked into a gambling joint uptown and collected twenty thousand bucks in a handbag they swiped from the joint's office. In the mix-up one of the customers got shot and spent a month in the hospital. One of this egg's pals did the shooting. They scrammed out with the dough, this egg hauling the bag. Cops were bearing down. The two pals got big-hearted and told the egg to take the bag and beat it—they'd meet later.

"Well, he beat it. He waited in their hide-out for a week, but they didn't show up; they were waiting for the tail to cool and besides a couple of dicks were working that street and the pals were afraid. The egg finally leaves the hide-out. We pick him up two weeks later on a loitering charge, not knowing who he is—and then he's identified by the guy who was shot. But he won't squeal on his pals—no names, nothing. And he swears he doesn't know where the money is. He gets three years. He comes out six weeks ago and tonight he's bumped off. He was afraid of that, I guess, so he hired a private dick."

Donahue shot back: "The only reason a guy like that would hire a private dick would be so he wouldn't have to pack a rod himself. Well, this guy packed a rod. You saw it. And besides, since when have I been so hard up that I'd rent out to a heel?"

"You mightn't have known."

"I didn't know what he was. I picked him out of the gutter down near Sheridan Square. He was plastered. He couldn't stand up so I thought the best way to get rid of him would be to shove him in a subway train. Well, I walked him a couple of blocks and then he got the taxi idea. I didn't want to go with him, but you know how drunks are—and, anyhow, I was headed uptown and it meant a free ride. I never saw him before in my life. I didn't know his name."

McPard seemed politely bored. "Anyhow, Donny—anyhow, what I came here for in the first place was to tell you that Inspector Overhill wouldn't take my word for it that you were on the up and up. So you better put a shirt on."

"Listen, Kelly—"

McPard shrugged. "What's the use? Overhill wants to see you. I'll wait." He added: "Meantime, if I were you, kid, I'd think it over. This Charlie Stromson left some dough. Overhill's very eager about knowing where. Besides, when a guy hires another for a bodyguard he usually tells the bodyguard the names of the guys that are after him and what they look like."

Donahue swung around, glowering: "I told you—"

"That's right, that's right. You told me you weren't hired. Tsk, tsk! I keep forgetting." His eyes danced with a wily blue twinkle. "I'm waiting."

Donahue cursed him, put on a shirt and tie. His eyes darted to the bedroom door. No sound there. McPard had not even noticed the door.

"Okey," Donahue said, swinging the overcoat over his arm.

They went down in the elevator. Going across the lobby, McPard pulled out a packet of cigarettes, took one, said: "Have one, Donny?"

Donahue took one and McPard struck a match and they lit up from it. Outside, they climbed into a taxi. It turned left into a side-street, then down Park Avenue, which lower became Fourth.

Overhill, a blond man with big ears, a Roman nose and a wicked pair of eyes, said: "There you are, Donahue," and kicked shut a desk drawer upon which his foot had been propped. He scanned some sheets, leaned back and made a pyramid of his fingers.

"Well, Kelly, what's the dope?"

"Donny's in the dark."

Overhill planted his elbows on the desk. "You knew this man, Donahue. You were riding with him and the cock-and-bull story you handed Kelly doesn't go over—not at all. Now I'm not here to waste my time or patience on a private dick. I don't want a song and dance. I want to get the guys that killed him and I want to recover a certain amount of money. This Stromson cached about twenty thousand before he was imprisoned. He got it when he came out and these two heels went after him to get it. He hired you—"

Donahue broke in: "As for wasting time, Inspector, mine's as important to me as yours is to you. Kelly went over all that and I told him what I'm telling you: I never saw this guy before until I picked him out of the gutter tonight."

"You're lying, Donahue."

"Did you get me down here to pinch me?"

Overhill frowned. "Of course not. I got you down—"

"I know—to hand me a lot of crap. Well, keep it. Any time something happens within a hundred blocks of where I happen to be, you damned blockheads get me down here and put on an act. I'm getting fed up on it!" He glared. "And if I'm lying, you prove it. You go ahead and prove that I knew this bird, that I was acting as his bodyguard when he was bumped off. Prove it! And when you prove it, get out a warrant for my arrest or a subpoena as a material witness—"

"Here, here!" Overhill said. "Don't get all steamed up—"

"Oh, don't get all steamed up! Maybe I should take it as an honor!"

McPard shook his head. "Tsk, tsk! All over nothing. We're just your friends, Donny—"

"Oh, yeah!" Donahue said, nodding his head. "Yeah. Like"—he drew a forefinger across his throat—"this."

He pivoted and strode to the door.

"Hey," Overhill said, "where you going?"

But Donahue did not reply. The door banged after him.

Overhill shrugged. "No use, Kelly. We haven't anything on him. He knows it."

Kelly McPard smiled whimsically and rosebuds bloomed on his cherubic cheeks. "Some day, Ed . . . some day I'm going to make Donny say Uncle."

4

WHEN DONAHUE SAILED into his apartment the first thing he noticed was that the bedroom door was open. The next thing he noticed was that the bed had not been slept in.

The girl was not there.

Both bags were gone—the suitcase and Charlie's handbag.

His eyes brown and hard, he cruised around the apartment. There was no sign of a struggle. Nothing was overturned, no rugs had been scuffled. He stopped in the center of the living-room and his thoughts went round and round. She had listened, heard Kelly and himself talking. Afterwards she had slipped out. No note of thanks, no note of explanation.

The phone rang and he answered it. "No, don't send it up. I'll be right down."

The clerk at the desk was mysterious when Donahue confronted him downstairs. "A lady left this letter for you with instructions that I should give it to no one but you." He smiled. "She emphasized—'no one but Mr. Donahue.' "

"What time was that?"

"About forty minutes ago."

"Thanks, Herbert. You're a great guy."

He walked to a corner of the lounge and opened the letter beneath a shaded wall light. It read:

Dear Mr. Donahue:

I heard the conversation between you and that man. He was a detective, I guess. I am sorry. I wanted to open the door and tell him you were innocent but I was afraid. I am taking the bags to the Penn Station. I thought that I better get Charlie's bag out of your apartment in case some policemen came back. I will wait at the information booth in the station until midnight, in case you come back. Then you can come over and tell me what to do. If you don't come, I will check the bag and throw away the check. I don't want it. Then I will take the first train home I can get. The way you talked to that man, I know you would not want me to show up. But I am very grateful to you for everything.

Laura.

He crumpled the letter and stuffed it into his pocket. She had used her head, taking the bag out. But—he cursed—it would be like her to throw away the money! He stalked out of the hotel, hailed a taxi and climbed in. Ten minutes later he climbed out at Penn Station and made his way to the information booth. She was not there. He looked all around, ventured into the waiting-room, came back to the information booth. He sought out every nook in the station, re-covered the waiting-room and returning to the information booth stood with his hands in his pockets and regarded the floor darkly.

It began to occur to him that his position was not as secure as he had felt it to be when he walked out of Overhill's office. Certain people had seen him take the girl into the hotel earlier that evening. The clerk was a good fellow, but the cops could make him talk. If she turned up a corpse, they would be able to get a fair likeness of her for the tabs. Certain people in the hotel would recognize her . . .

He shook his head, made a sound in his throat and strode long-legged out of the station. He stood for a moment on the curb, the wind hooting and clapping about him. A cab drew up.

"Taxi?"

Donahue said: "Maybe that's a good idea." He climbed in and said: "Sheridan Square."

He leaned back, his hands way down in his pockets and his shoulders hunched. The more he thought of it, the less he liked it. He took the letter out of his pocket, tore it up into little bits and let them fly out the window. He did not go quite as far as Sheridan Square.

"Stop here," he said, and got out at Hudson Street and West Tenth.

He made his way slowly down West Tenth Street, bending his head into the wind that blew from the river. He was frank with himself. No mock heroics. The guy with the death gurgle in his throat asked you to do something, and like a sap you did it. The girl turned out to be a pop-eyed little thing from the sticks. You broke the news to her as gently as you could. You didn't have to be gentle about it, but you were, anyhow. Then you felt relieved: it was simple, and you'd put her on the train back, tomorrow, brush your hands together and—finish. Hell!—you would. The yellow handbag turns out to be a plant, the girl is more shocked than you are. You still are able to get over that. "Take this dough, little one, go home and bury it for another five years. Then use it." But then Kelly had to turn up. . . .

No. No mock heroics. Not tonight. Not now, especially. There was one thing essential, paramount, vital: this girl must not turn up a corpse. Not under any circumstances must the cops find her; not alive, if possible, certainly not dead. So Donahue was frank with himself. He was not being gallant—not now. He was intent on saving his skin, his license to operate, his sense of superiority born of his always having been on the right side of the fence when the cops got gay. When you got right down to it, the girl as a personality meant nothing to him; she was significant only for the fact that her death would bring the cops down on him. And, he reflected, a girl wandering around with almost fifteen thousand dollars was certainly a potential corpse.

He recognized the glow of the areaway speakeasy across the street. He moved on, and in a minute he saw the fire-hydrant. He continued to the end of the block, crossed to the southeast corner and came back up West Tenth on the south side of the street. By this time he had his gun in his overcoat pocket, his fingers gripping it loosely.

He remembered the door, not because it was unlike the other doorways in that block but because it lay diagonally across the sidewalk from the fire-hydrant. He remembered considering how neatly the drunk would have opened his head had he struck the hydrant.

Going up to the door, he put his left hand on the knob and turned it. The door gave but he did not immediately throw it open. He stood deliberating for half a minute. He threw a glance up and down the street. Then he opened the door swiftly the length of his arm, stepped in while his right hand came out with his gun; shifted deftly and quietly on his feet and in a second had the door shut behind him, without a sound.

For the space of a minute he did not move. He stood rock-still, his gun held level with the lapel of his coat pocket, his breath bated and his ears straining. The hall was black as pitch but there was, beyond in the darkness, an oblong of slightly lighter darkness that seemed familiarly like the night outside. He went towards it. The oblong was a door. The door was open. It led into a small yard. Standing not too close to the doorway, he could smell the damp earth. After a moment he slipped into the yard and hugged the outside wall.

It was a sort of hollow square. A high board fence separated it from the yard back of the house on the next street. The house he had entered had a wing extending on either side as far as the fence. These wings made the east and west side of the hollow square, the fence made the south, the part through which he had come made the north.

There was an outside wooden stairway up the front of the west wing, with a platform at the top, and a door. On this door was a spider-web of light, as if a green shade, cracked with age, had been drawn down over the glass panel. Otherwise there was no light, no sound of life or even hint of it, within the hollow square.

He crossed to the foot of the wooden stairway, looked on the building for a button. There was none. A railing went up the outside of the stairway, supported at intervals by a post. He started up, keeping close to the face of the house. He paused on the next to last step and listened. The night had an emptiness about it; street sounds, not nearby, had a bell-like clarity.

He took the last step rapidly, rapped soundly on the glass panel. His right hand shoved the gun back into his pocket and remained there. The door opened, a blowzy fat man in an undershirt stood there outlined against light made hazy by skeins of tobacco smoke. He was sleepy and halfway through a yawn, and Donahue shoved him backward, stepped in and said:

"Now sit tight, everybody."

It was a large room, dusty, smelling of liquor, tobacco, old perspiration. There was a round table in the center with a drop light, green-shaded, above it. Poker chips were on the table, stacks of silver and bills; and around the table three men in shirt sleeves. The skeins of tobacco smoke wound sluggishly around their heads. They did not move. The three of them leaned with their elbows on the table. One had a deck of cards, ready to deal. They had about them the beady-eyed immobility of rats at bay.

"Sit down, you," Donahue muttered.

The fat man pawed his way around to the fourth chair and sat down. His fat eyes popped and he wore an injured expression.

Donahue said in a dead-level voice: "I may be up the wrong alley. Who runs this scatter?"

The fat blowzy man looked very pained.

"You?" Donahue said.

"Well, that is, now—as you would say—if some boys want to play a little cards and drink a bit—" He stopped and sat back and looked injured again. "I don't see—that is, as I would say—"

"Hell," chopped off the man at his left. He had a face the color of cement and looked quite as hard. His pale hard eyes were steady on Donahue. The man next to him made whistling lips but no sound came forth. He wore a gray hat and an innocent, youthful expression. The man on his right had a bald head and a red neck.

This man fidgeted and then said: "You a dick?"

"Suppose I am?" Donahue said.

"Well, I'd say, then, we only spoke to the skipper last week and he said he'd lay off. He's gettin' his cut. He and Henry—"

"Of course," the fat man nodded. "Me and Bill there—" He looked around indignantly. "Me and Bill are okey with the skipper."

The man with the pale hard eyes growled: "This guy ain't no dick! Damn it, this guy ain't no dick!" He shoved back his chair.

"I wouldn't do that," Donahue said.

The man subsided, but his pale eyes glowered. The youthful man in the gray hat went on making whistling lips but still no sound was heard. He kept looking at the cards in his hands.

Donahue said: "It's about Charlie Stromson."

The man in the gray hat choked. This startled everybody at the table. The man broke into a violent fit of coughing and the pale-eyed man towered in his chair. The other sneezed, choked, and finally sat with his eyes running water.

Donahue said: "You get up, put your coat on."

The man rose, put his coat on and stood sniffling and wiping his eyes.

"Pull your hat down a little more."

The man did so.

"Okey," Donahue said. "Now sit down again and—and this goes for all of you—keep your hands on the table." His voice lowered, his eyes were fixed hard on the man in the gray hat. "When Stromson pitched out of the street door tonight, why did you open the door and then duck back?"

The man sneezed. "I didn't open no door."

The fat man and the bald man both looked very innocent and the pale-eyed man stared hard and bitterly at the man in the gray hat. He seemed about to explode, but didn't. Instead, he tore a card in two and slapped the pieces angrily down on the table.

Donahue was grim. "No song and dance. I'm in the right scatter and I'm going to get what I came after. I'm looking for the woman. I'm looking for fourteen thousand five hundred bucks. I'm looking for the guys that bumped off Charlie Stromson."

The pale-eyed man forgot himself. He jumped to his feet and

his chest swelled, his eyes got doubly large and hard and they had a white whiplash look in them.

"Who the hell bumped off Charlie Stromson?" he bellowed.

"Sit down, you."

The man sat down—but sitting, he towered, his jaw thrust out like a slab of cement.

The blowzy fat man insisted: "This man's a dick! I tell you he's a dick! Listen, now listen—" He stopped and threw a peevish look around the table. "May as well tell him. I'm going to tell him." He looked up at Donahue. "This Stromson was here. He got tight here. He was here, see, and about eight-thirty he goes. He goes out about eight-thirty. He gets halfway down the steps and falls. 'Louie' "—he nodded towards the man in the gray hat—"Louie goes out and sees. I guess he picks him up. Anyhow, in a few minutes Louie comes back. This is on the up and up. Louie comes back and says, 'Hell, Charlie's in bad shape.' I say, 'Well, Louie, maybe you and Beef ought to look after him.' And Louie says, 'I told Charlie. I said we ought to look after him, but he says he can take care of himself.' So we think, well, Charlie'll be all right and we sit down to play. That's God's honest."

Donahue said: "Why did Charlie come here?"

The fat man shut up like a clam. The pale-eyed man had undergone a considerable change of expression. He stared at the table with a bright, concentrated look. He was thinking—hard. He looked up suddenly to find Donahue eying him with keen scrutiny.

"You," Donahue said, "and this mug in the gray hat were the two pals that stuck up that gambling joint with Charlie. He bunked his dough before he went up to stir and you two smart sweethearts chiseled in when he came out."

The man in the gray hat choked on this and went into another fit of coughing.

"Will you stop that!" the pale-eyed man cried.

Donahue's voice picked up an edge, swiftly. "I'm not going to monkey around here. I'm no precinct dick. I'm just a sap that walked into a jam out of which I'm getting nothing but a headache and a swell chance of taking a rap for a stunt you eggs pulled off tonight. Well, I don't take raps. Where's the jane?"

The pale-eyed man leaned back. "Guy, we been here in this joint since eight o'clock. You ain't worryin' us. We didn't know this umpchay was bumped off till you told us." He grinned, seemed confident and suddenly sure of himself. "We're strictly kosher, and there's a phone over there if you want to call the cops. See if we care."

The fat man began fussing like an old woman: "Now, now, Beef, don't go makin' the gentleman mad. Of course, that is to say, well, I'm okey with the skipper and all that—but if I cause him any trouble, it'll mean a bigger cut. Me and Bill here"—he indicated the bald, red-necked man—"like to play square with everybody."

Louie, the man in the gray hat, moved nearer to the pale-eyed Beef, and the pair assumed an attitude of mixed hostility towards the operators of the joint. And Beef said:

"I don't care. This palooka ain't goin' to faze me none. I'm clean. You guys know me and Louie been in this dump since eight or before."

Donahue remained silent for a long moment. Then he shrugged, grinned and put his gun in his pocket. The fat man sighed and smacked his hands together.

"Now, now, sir, that is what I would call—well, so to speak, that is—"

Donahue was at the door. He said: "Fourteen thousand five hundred bucks are floating around somewhere." He was noisy going down the stairway. He did not go far. There were many nooks in the dark hollow square. He pressed back into shadows and waited.

5

TWENTY MINUTES ELAPSED. Then Beef and Louie appeared on the landing. Both wore hats and coats. The door closed behind them and their feet came down the stairway. They did not go towards the door leading to West Tenth. They went around the bottom of the stairway and passed through a hole in the board fence. Donahue went after them. In the street, they walked into a cigar store. Donahue went on, walking rapidly. At the corner he climbed into a cab and said:

"Just wait here a minute."

He watched through the rear window, and when he saw Beef and Louie come out of the cigar store accompanied by two others, he said:

"Drive around the corner and park."

In a minute the four men, walking briskly, crossed Hudson Street and got into a cab on the east side.

"When that Checker starts," Donahue told the driver, "swing around and tail it. Don't get too close—but don't lose it."

The tail led up the West Side, went across town at Fortieth as far as Madison, and then north. It made a right turn into the Fifties, swinging in with a few eastbound cars. The Checker stopped at the next block and Donahue, passing in his cab, saw the four men get out. He let his cab cross to the east side of Park, then got out, paid up, tipped generously and walked back to the west side of the avenue. The four men, he saw, had started walking west. They walked in pairs, Louie and Beef in front. A little farther on, they turned and climbed a brownstone stoop, opened a door and disappeared. Donahue waited a couple of minutes, then went up the steps, opened the door there and entered a high, narrow corridor.

There was the sound of a piano being played lazily. Muffled drone of voices. A girl reached for Donahue's hat and coat. He gave her a quarter but kept both. At the end of the corridor was a wooden door with a glass port high up. He went down and looked through the glass. There was a chummy bar inside, half a dozen men. Beef and Louie and the others were not present.

Donahue pushed open the door. There was a wide door at the right, a dim-lit room beyond. A man was drowsing over piano keys, playing lazy rhythm. A girl was leaning on the piano singing in a whisper.

Donahue said: "Rye high," to the bartender. Turning, he caught a glimpse of a small young man leaving the other end of the bar, heading for a curtained doorway at the rear. Donahue moved slowly, then a little faster as the curtains opened and closed. He pulled them aside. There was a small lighted sign halfway down the hallway: *Men's Room.*

Donahue took two long running steps. The small man turned around. Donahue had his gun out. He did not stop. With his left hand he grabbed the small man by the collar and hustled him into the men's room. The door swung shut.

"Quick, you!" Donahue clipped in a hoarse whisper.

"Look out now—"

"You're the nice-faced punk I saw at Penn Station tonight! Where is she?"

"I don't know what—"

There were voices coming down the hall. Donahue rushed the man into one of three closets. The cabinets had half-doors, with two feet of open space at the bottom. Inside, he snapped the catch and kept his gun jammed in the small man's back. Several men entered. He heard them talking, laughing. In a few minutes they went out.

"Now," Donahue said, "spill it!"

"You're hurting me!"

"Oh, am I? Listen, you! There's an open window leading to an alley. If you don't yap, I'll let you have a bellyful and take that window out. Quick, now!"

"Honest, I don't know anything."

Donahue took a big gun from the man's pocket. "You're just an angel, I suppose. You're going to be an angel for me, sweetheart. Where's the jane? By —————— where is she?"

He had the man by the throat now. He pressed hard, while his knee kept the man pinned to a sidewall of the cabinet. The man twisted and writhed, his tongue stuck out and his eyes bulged.

"Where is she?"

"Leggo—"

Donahue eased up. "Now."

"Upstairs."

"How'd she get here?"

"I—brought her."

"Who wanted her?"

The man shook his head and Donahue went to work on his throat again.

It came out—choked: "Hagin . . ."

"He upstairs?"

"Ugh—yeah."

Donahue said: "Okey, sweetheart. Now don't think you're going to waltz right after me and . . ."

He struck with the man's gun—on the head, a short, hard chopping blow. The man sank without a sound. Donahue pushed him against the back wall of the cabinet. He did not unlock the door. He got down on hands and knees and crawled out. Looking at the outside of the door, he saw that the indicator said: *Occupied.*

He put a gun in either pocket and left his hands on them. He went out into the corridor and began climbing the stairway. In the hallway above, he stood for a moment, then went to the rear and peered through a windowpane there. He unlocked and opened the window. There was a fire-escape outside, leading to a court below. He left the window open. The lazy sound of the piano seemed far away.

Moving up the hall, he listened at doors. At the third from the rear, on the left, he listened longest. Then he retraced his steps to the door nearest the rear window. He tried it. It was open and he entered a large bedroom. A small bed lamp glowed. The room was empty, and an open door gave into another room that was dark. He moved into it on soft rugs and saw a long, thin sliver of light where sliding doors had not quite closed. He returned to the bedroom, took stock of his bearings, then turned out the bed lamp. All was in darkness now. Looking through the open door, he could see the thin sliver of light. He moved towards it.

The slit was not large enough for him to see through. He counted four or five different voices. There was a heated argument, everyone was talking at once. He pried the doors apart, a bare half-inch, noiselessly. Now he saw Beef and Louie and the two men they had picked up downtown. The four were in a dangerous huddle around a blond burly man, at the far side of the room.

Donahue pulled out his guns. He worked the doors apart another inch. No one noticed him. Bit by bit he got them far enough apart to enter. He entered and stood quite silent. He saw the girl on a couch. She looked unconscious. Her hair was down and her clothes were twisted. He stood waiting, the guns in his hands, level with his hips.

It was the burly blond man who saw him first. The others stopped talking.

"Hold that pose, all of you," Donahue said.

"It's him!" muttered Beef.

Donahue said: "So you and Louie were just a couple of home-loving card players. Fighting over the split, huhn?"

The burly man began: "These mutts—"

"You're Hagin," Donahue said.

"I'm Hagin. These mutts walked in on me. Let me walk out of this huddle and it's worth a thousand bucks to you."

"Put the thousand on the table."

Hagin took out a wallet, emptied it. "I got only nine hundred here. I'll get the rest up. Now lend me one of those rods and I'll teach these grifters a lesson."

"You sit right down in that chair," Donahue said. "You other guys hold that pose."

Hagin dropped down into the chair, his eyes wide. "Why, you dirty—"

"Pipe down. There's a lot of dough flying loose around this burg tonight. Most of it I can't touch. So I'll touch what I can." He moved slowly to the table, caught up the sheaf of bills with the two end fingers of his left hand. "Somebody's got to pay my taxi fare. You, Hagin—you were the guy ran that joint Stromson and these two heels crashed that night. Right?"

"Right! And now these two bums tango in here with a couple of punks—"

"Pardon me. I want to get this straight. It figures, then, that the little punk downstairs was the guy you sent after Stromson. He got Stromson and then he went to Penn Station to head off the jane. You didn't know just where the dough was bunked. You figured the jane might know. I got to her ahead of the punk. The punk tailed us, camped on my doorstep. I went out. The jane went out later and he clamped on to her and brought her here. What I can't figure out is"—he looked at Beef—"where you guys horn in."

Beef growled: "Stromson took the rap for us and kept his trap shut. When he come out, we crowded him. He bunked the dough in the country before he went up. We knew he took the rap and he kept his jaw shut. We dickered and he offered us two grand apiece and that was okey by us. Then for some goofy reason he takes a boat to South America, soon as he's out of stir, and comes back on the same boat. We try to roll him for some dough by gettin' him into a card game. We get him drunk three nights runnin', but he won't play. And we don't know where he's bunked the dough.

"There was a little guy hangin' around Bill and Henry's for a

109

week. Bill says he's hidin' out. This little guy leaves about half an hour before Stromson does tonight. Stromson was bellyachin' about a jane he had to meet at Penn Station. When you bust in there tonight we know there's only one guy'd be after Stromson. Hagin. So up we come, after Stromson's dough. The little guy's Hagin's punk. We saw him downstairs but didn't let on. You drop them guns, fella, and you get a third of the dough. Hagin's got it."

"You're a damn' liar!" Hagin said. "I haven't got it."

Beef snarled: "You bum, you got it! When we crashed in here the jane was out cold!"

"If I got it," Hagin growled, "why the hell would the jane be out cold?"

She was lying now with her eyes open.

Donahue said to her: "Get up, put your hat and coat on and go out. Got the wallet?"

She shook her head.

Donahue said: "Hagin, give her the wallet."

"It's in the desk drawer," he said.

Donahue said: "Get it, Laura. See he hasn't taken anything out."

She got up and made her way to the desk, took out the wallet, examined it. "It's all here."

"Where're your bags?"

"I checked them at the station. I thought it would be best to check them. After I checked them a little man followed me to the information booth. Then he said he'd shoot me if I didn't go with him. He brought me here."

Hagin said: "I only tried to get the checks out of her."

"He's got them!" Beef snarled.

"No," the girl said, "I've got them." She turned down the left cuff of her coatsleeve. She said to Donahue: "I couldn't make up my mind whether to give them up or not."

Donahue said: "Which one is for the little bag?"

"This one," she said, holding up a cardboard square.

"Put it on the table. These rats would run you down for it, no matter where you went."

She sighed. "I guess you're right. I don't want it anyhow."

Hagin stared at it. Beef and the others stared at it—hungrily.

The girl had her hat on.

Donahue said to the men: "This hurts, but it's my only out." He motioned to the girl. "Come on. Go through those rooms and into the hall. There's a back window open. Go down the fire-escape, through the alley. Get a cab, get your suitcase, go to a hotel and leave on the first train you can get. I won't be seeing you again."

She came very close to him. "Thanks," she said. "Thanks for everything."

He waited fully two minutes, then began backing out. The men remained like images. They couldn't understand his letting almost fifteen thousand dollars slide by. He reached the next room, turned and sped swiftly to the bedroom. The hall was empty. He went out the window, down the fire-escape, through the alley. He breathed thankfully. The girl had gone.

He grabbed a taxi and rode to Penn Station. The driver passed a stop-light and was held up for five minutes by a long-winded cop. Presently he moved on. It was dark and deserted in front of the station. No trains were moving, and inside the station it was quite deserted also. He didn't see the girl. She would have been here already, he reasoned.

He saw four men heading for an exit. He started, then stopped. The four men walked swiftly in close formation and passed out through the doors. Donahue broke into a fast walk. He reached the doors and pushed one open when a vicious snarl of gunfire broke loose in the street. The mad sound of a sub-machine-gun was touched up with the bark of heavy pistols.

He saw four men lying on the sidewalk. A car roared on the get-away. One of the four figures moved and the gun in his hand blazed four times. The car turned suddenly, heeled over on its rubber, hurtled diagonally across the street with full power on. It struck a building and seemed to bounce back into the street. He couldn't tell definitely. Because the car exploded in a sheet of flame. The fourth man on the sidewalk was motionless again, on his back now, his arms outflung. It looked like Beef.

Donahue was on his way, blocks north, by the time police arrived, to find the pavement red.

Next day the papers had it. Hagin and the punk had shot it out with the other four, using a Thompson gun. But their get-away had been tragically incomplete. Six dead men in the street . . .

One of the papers got waggish. "Apparently," it said, "there was something sentimental about it. It would appear that the gun fight started over a suitcase containing a lot of woman's clothes, no piece of which bears any identification."

Donahue, reading it, said: "These women . . . these women!"

PAUL CAIN

Parlor Trick

WHO WAS THE hardest of the hard-boiled writers for Black Mask? Who wrote the sparest, starkest, toughest prose of them all?

The answer, without any doubt, is Paul Cain.

Cain's style, as pulp authority Ron Goulart wrote, at times "becomes as sparse and clipped as that of a McGuffey's Reader." In an afterword to a recent reprint edition of Cain's only novel, Fast One (1933), critic Irvin Faust says that Cain "hasn't the time or patience for excess baggage. He picks up his literary scalpel and scrapes away conjunctions as if they were bad merchandise . . . He digs into the page with a hard sentence: simple, declarative, exact."

"Parlor Trick" (July 1932), one of the few short-shorts to appear in Black Mask during Cap Shaw's editorship, was Cain's third published story. And, arguably, his best. In these few thousand words, there is more tension, menace, and raw realism than in most hard-boiled novels. It is a perfect portrait in microcosm of the way gangsters lived and loved and died in the last days of Prohibition. Given the same theme and plot elements, Hemingway could not have written it any better.

Not much in the way of specific information is known about the man who signed his fiction Paul Cain. His real name was Peter Ruric; he was a successful Hollywood screenwriter (The Night of January 16, Grand Central Murders, Mademoiselle Fifi); and he also wrote, of all things for the hardest of the hard-boiled writers, verbose and rather amusing articles on gourmet cooking. ("No one but a Spaniard can make a fried egg look so terrible and taste so good."—"Viva las Castañetas," Gourmet

113

Magazine, June 1951.) He published seventeen stories in Black Mask *in the early thirties, five of which were later bridged together to form* Fast One, *and one each in* Star Detective *and* Detective Fiction Weekly. *His only other book, a collection of seven* Black Mask *stories called* Seven Slayers, *was published in digest paperback form in 1946 and later reprinted by Avon Books in 1950. A blurb on the back cover of the original edition describes Cain/Ruric as "slender, blond, bearded, 30-odd years old," and goes on to say, "He spent the bulk of these years in South and North America, Africa, the Near East, Europe. He was, intermittently, a bosun's-mate, a Dada painter, a gambler and a 'no' man in Hollywood. He writes as he has lived—at high speed, and with violence."*

Yes, indeed.

I KNOCKED ON the door at the end of the hall. It was cold in the hall, almost dark. I knocked again, and Bella's voice said: "Come in," faintly; then she said: "Oh—it's locked." The key scratched in the lock and the door opened and I went into the room.

It was very hot in there. It was dark, with only a little light from a gas heater. There was a little more light that came through a short corridor from the kitchen, but it was pretty dark.

Bella closed the door and went over to the davenport and sat down. She was near the heater, and the yellow light flickered over the lower part of her face.

I took off my coat and put it on a chair. Bella kept scraping her teeth lightly over her lower lip. Her teeth were like a little animal's and she ran them over her soft lower lip rapidly, like an animal. The light from the heater was bright on the lower part of her face.

I went through the short corridor to the kitchen. The bathroom door was open; I glanced in as I passed and Gus Schaeffer turned his head and looked over his shoulder at me. He was standing at the basin with his back to the door and when he turned his head to look at me his face was awful. His skin was damp and gray and his eyes had something leaden and dying in them.

I said: "Hi, Gus," and went in to the kitchen.

There was a man sitting on one of the benches at one side of the narrow breakfast table. The table was set lengthwise into a niche, with a bench at each side, and the man on one of the benches was sitting with his back in the corner of the niche, his knees drawn up, his feet on the outside end of the bench. His head was back against the wall and his eyes and mouth were open. There was a thin knife-handle sticking out of one side of his throat.

Gus came out of the bathroom and stood behind me in the doorway.

There were several nearly empty glasses on the table. One had fallen to the floor, broken in to many glittering pieces.

I looked at the glass and I looked up at the man again. I think I said: "———" very softly.

"I did it. I did it and I didn't know it. I was blind . . . " Gus was clawing at my arm.

Bella came through the corridor and stood behind him. She looked very scared, very beautiful.

She said huskily: "Gus was terribly drunk. Frank said something out of turn and Gus picked up the knife and stuck it in to his neck. He choked—I guess—"

She looked at the dead man, and then her eyes turned up white in their sockets and she fainted.

Gus turned around and almost fell down trying to catch her. He said: "Oh, baby—baby!" He took her up in his arms and carried her back into the living room.

I followed him in and switched on the lights. He put Bella on the davenport. I watched him bend over her and flick ice water across her face with his fingers, from a pitcher; he rubbed her hands and wrists, and tried to force a little whiskey between her clenched pale lips. He kept saying: "Oh baby—baby," over and over. I sat down.

He sat on the edge of the davenport and looked at me while he rubbed and patted Bella's hands.

"You better telephone," he said. Then he looked at Bella a long time. "I did it—see—I did it; only I didn't know about it. I was cockeyed—"

I nodded. I said: "Sure, Gus," and I leaned forward and picked up the telephone.

Gus was looking at Bella's white beautiful face. He bobbed his head up and down mechanically.

I said: "What's the best play—self-defense?"

He turned suddenly. "I don't care—no play at all." He dropped her hand and stood up. "Only I did it myself. She didn't have anything to do with it. She was in here. . . . " He came towards me, shaking his finger at me, speaking very earnestly.

I said: "Maybe I can get Neilan. The longer we let it go, the worse it'll be."

I dialed a number.

Neilan was a short chubby man with a strangely long face, a high bony forehead. He and Frank had been partners in a string of distilleries for almost five years. He said: "When did *you* get here, Red?"

"Bella called me up and told me something had happened—I live around the corner."

I was sitting near the door that led in to the kitchen. Bella was sitting in the middle of the davenport, leaning forward with her elbows on her knees, staring vacantly into the brightness of the heater. Gus was sitting in a straight-backed chair in the middle of the room.

Neilan had been walking around looking at the pictures on the walls. He sat down straddling an arm of the davenport.

"So you were so drunk you don't remember?" Neilan was looking at Gus.

Gus nodded. Bella looked up at him for a moment and nodded a little and then looked back into the fire.

There was a light tap at the door and it opened and a big man came in quietly and closed the door behind him. He wore glasses and his soft black hat was tilted over the back of his head, I think his name was McNulty, or McNutt—something like that. He said: "Ed's downstairs with a couple of the boys."

"They can wait downstairs." Neilan turned his head a little and looked at Bella out of the corners of his eyes. "So Gus was so drunk he don't remember?"

Gus stood up. He said: "—— damn it! Pat—I was so drunk I

didn't know any better, but I wasn't so drunk I don't know it was me. Lay off Bella—she was in here. . . . "

"She didn't say so."

Bella said: "I was nearly asleep and I could hear Gus and Frank talking in the kitchen and then they didn't talk any more. After a while I got up and went out in the kitchen—Frank was like he is now, and Gus was out—with his head on the table."

Her chin was in her hands, and her head bobbed up and down when she talked. Gus was sitting down again, on the edge of the chair.

Neilan grinned at McNulty. He said: "What do you think, Mac?"

McNulty went over to Bella and reached down and put one big finger under her chin and jerked her head back.

"I think she's a liar," he said.

Gus stood up.

McNulty turned as if that had been what he wanted. He hit Gus very hard in the face, twice. Gus fell down and rolled over on his side. He pulled his knees up and moaned a little.

McNulty took off his coat and folded it carefully and put it on a chair. He went to Gus and kicked him hard in the chest and then kicked his head several times. Gus tried to protect himself with his arms. He didn't make any more noise but put his arms up and tried to protect himself. He tried to get up once and McNulty kicked him in the stomach and he fell down and lay quietly. In a little while, McNulty stopped kicking him and sat down. He was panting. He took off his hat and took a handkerchief out of his pocket and wiped his face.

I looked at Neilan. "I called you," I said, "because I thought you'd give Gus a break. . . . "

He said: "You ought to of called the police. They'd be after giving Gus a break, and your lady friend here"—he jerked his head at Bella—"with a length of hose."

Bella was leaning back on the davenport with her hands up to her face. She stared at Gus and tried to look at McNulty.

McNulty smiled, said: "Sure—why don't you call a cop? Frankie had everybody from the Chief down on his payroll—they'll have to go back to working for the city." He was out of breath, spoke unevenly.

Bella stood up and started to go towards the door, and Neilan stood up too, and put one hand over her mouth and one on her back. He held her like that for a minute and then he pushed her back down on the davenport.

McNulty got up then and stooped over and took hold of the back of Gus' shirt collar and pulled him up a little way.

McNulty said: "Come on, boy—we'll get some air."

Gus' shirt collar started to tear and McNulty cupped his other hand around the back of Gus' neck and jerked him up on his feet. Gus couldn't stand by himself; McNulty stood there holding him with his arm around his shoulders. Gus' face was in pretty bad shape.

McNulty said: "Come on, boy," again and started guiding Gus towards the door.

Neilan said: "Wait a minute, Mac."

McNulty turned and stared vacantly at Neilan for a minute and then pushed Gus down in a big chair. He sat down on the arm of the chair and took out his handkerchief and wiped Gus' face.

Neilan went out into the kitchen. He was out there two or three minutes without making any noise, then he snapped off the light and came back. He turned off the lights in the living room too, and it was dark except for the faint yellow light from the heater.

Neilan went back and sat down at the end of the davenport, out of the light. The light rippled over Bella's face, and after a while, when my eyes were used to the darkness, I could make out dark shapes where McNulty and Gus sat—and Neilan.

It was so dark and quiet except for the sharp sound of Gus' breathing. There wasn't anything to look at except Bella and she was leaning back with her eyes closed and her face very still.

It got on my nerves after several minutes and I said: "What's it all about, Pat?"

Neilan didn't answer, so I leaned forward in my chair, but I didn't get up. I sat there with all my muscles tight.

Then I heard something moving out in the kitchen. I don't know whether anybody else heard it, but I know there was sound out there like something moving across the floor.

I stood up and I couldn't speak. I didn't hear the sound again but I stood there without moving, and then Bella started talking. She talked in a conversational tone, with her head back, her eyes closed:

"Frank came here to see me. He's been coming to see me every night for four nights. He brought along a lot of lousy whiskey and got Gus drunk, and he got drunk too. He wouldn't give up."

She stopped talking a moment and the light beat up and down on her face. She was very beautiful then.

"He made a crack tonight while Gus was in the bathroom about telling Gus about Red and me. . . . "

She opened her eyes and looked towards me in the darkness a minute, and then closed her eyes and went on:

"I was scared. I called Red while they were raising hell in the kitchen and he came over and I let him in. We listened to them for a few minutes from in here in the dark, and then when Frank got to talking about what a great guy Red was, and started getting dirty about it, Red went in there very quickly and killed him. I guess Gus was too far gone to see it or know anything about it."

She stopped talking again and it was quiet.

"Then Red beat it and I stayed in here a while and then I went out like I told you and woke up Gus. He thought I did it, I guess. I called Red again. . . . "

Neilan got up and went over and switched on the lights.

McNulty got up too and stood there blinking, staring stupidly at Bella.

I went over and got my hat and coat and put them on. I stood looking at Bella for a while after I had put on my coat. She was still leaning back with her eyes closed. She was one of the most beautiful women I have ever seen.

Neilan opened the door and McNulty and I went out into the hall. It was very cold there after the intense heat of the room. Then Neilan closed the door and the three of us went downstairs.

There was a small touring car at the curb, with the side-curtains on. There were two men whom I had never seen before in the front seat, and another man on the sidewalk. The engine was running.

McNulty opened the door and got in the back seat, and then I got in, and then Neilan. There wasn't anything else to do. I sat between them, and Neilan said: "Let's go."

We went down the street slowly. The man who had been standing on the sidewalk didn't get into the car; he stood there looking after us. I turned around a little and looked at him through the rear window; as we turned the corner, he went on back up the street, the other way.

When we got out of town a ways we went faster. It was very cold.

I said: "Hurry up."

Neilan turned and grinned at me. I could see his face a little as we passed a street light. He said: "Hurry up—what?"

"Hurry up." The cold was beginning to get in to the pit of my stomach, and my legs. I wanted to be able to stand up. I wanted it standing up, if I could.

Neilan glanced out the rear window. He said: "I think our tail light's out."

The car slowed, stopped. We were pretty well out in the country by that time and the road was dark.

Neilan said: "See if we've got a tail light, Mac."

McNulty grunted and reached up and opened the door and heaved himself up into the door. He stooped and put one foot out on the runningboard, and then Neilan reached in front of me very quickly. There was a gun in his hand and he put it close to McNulty's back and shot him three times. The explosions were very close together. McNulty's knees crumpled up and he fell out of the car on his face.

The car started again and the man who sat next to the driver reached back and slammed the door shut hard.

Neilan cleared his throat. He said: "Frank's number has been up a long time. He's been tipping our big deliveries, South; we haven't got a truck through for two months."

I could feel the blood getting back into my arms and legs. I wasn't so cold and I could breathe without pain.

"McNulty was in it with him. McNulty was in the outfit downstate. We found out about that last night."

We rode on for a little while and nobody said anything.

"If the dame sticks to her beef," Neilan went on, "the scarcer you are, the better. If she doesn't, Gus'll stand it. You can't do yourself any good around here any more anyway."

Pretty soon we stopped at a little interurban station where I could get a car in to the city.

I had to wait a while. I sat in the station where it was warm, and thought about Bella. After a while the car came.

CORNELL
WOOLRICH

The Living Lie Down With the Dead

THROUGHOUT THE 1930S, Black Mask's *primary rival in the pulp detective field was* Dime Detective, *edited by Kenneth S. White of Popular Publications. When it was inaugurated in 1932,* Dime Detective *was advertised as a magazine of "mystery . . . thrills . . . terror" and published as many eerie, neo-gothic melodramas as it did stories of hard and brittle realism. But the success of Cap Shaw's magazine soon forced Popular to launch a new publication,* Dime Mystery, *for its terror stories so that White could concentrate on buying fiction for* Dime Detective *that was more in keeping with the* Black Mask *formula.*

Dime Detective *remained an imitator, however, even though White was a good editor and even after Shaw left* Black Mask *in 1936 as the end result of a dispute with his publishers. Ironically, White, who had been jealous of Shaw's success, became the editor of* Black Mask *himself when Popular Publications bought the title in 1940. Both magazines ended their days in the early fifties, rather ignominiously publishing, for the most part, second-rate pulp action stories under such titles as "Pardon My Poison Platters," "You're the Crime in My Coffin," and "Hollywood Knife Life."*

During the mid-thirties rivalry between the two magazines, White succeeded in luring some Black Mask *writers into his stable. Frederick Nebel created Cardigan, his "Cosmos Agency dick," for* Dime Detective, *and kept him active long after Nebel dropped out of* Black Mask. *Norbert Davis wrote for* Dime Detective; *so did Carroll John Daly, Erle Stanley Gardner, and George Harmon Coxe. White also encouraged a number of other pulpsters, including Frederick C. Davis, John Lawrence, T. T. Flynn, John K. Butler, and William E. Barrett (who later became the bestselling author of, among other novels,* Lilies of the Field).

White's most important "find" among the newer writers was Cornell Woolrich. He was not the purchaser of Woolrich's first pulp crime story— that honor went to the editor of Detective Fiction Weekly, *who bought and published "Death Sits in the Dentist's Chair" in his August 4, 1934 issue—but White did buy many of Woolrich's early stories. One of them, published in the April 1936* Dime Detective, *was "The Living Lie Down with the Dead," a story which ranks with the best of that early work and yet has never before been reprinted in its original form. (A heavily edited and less effective version appeared in* Ellery Queen's Mystery Magazine *in 1955, under another title.)*

Woolrich was evidently obsessed by the idea of being buried alive; that theme is the basis for this story and for another, "Graves for the Living," and to a lesser degree can be found in some of his other nightmarish works. "The Living Lie Down with the Dead" is a potent brew of steadily mounting suspense and horror, in which a pair of crooks devise and carry out what they consider to be a foolproof plan to steal a fortune in jewels from a sealed mausoleum. Ah, but the best laid plans of mice and ghouls . . .

Cornell George Hopley Woolrich (1903–1968) was a tragic figure who lived most of his life in New York City hotel rooms, both alone and with his domineering mother. He suffered a life-long sense of unfulfillment and doom, which perhaps explains his ability to vividly express palpable dread in his fiction; no writer past or present rivals him in the evocation of pure terror, as such novels as The Bride Wore Black *(1940),* Black Alibi *(1942), and* Phantom Lady *(1942, as by William Irish)—and such short stories as "Papa Benjamin," "The Screaming Laugh," and the one you are about to read—eloquently attest.*

Critic Francis M. Nevins, Jr., who has been responsible for the modern revival of much of Woolrich's work—Ballantine Books reissued ten of his best novels in 1982–1983, to considerable acclaim—calls Woolrich "the Poe of the twentieth century and the poet of its shadows." It is both an apt description and a proper one.

The Living Lie Down With the Dead

THE DEPRESSION HAD given Miss Alfreda Garrity a bad fright. The one of '93, not the last one. She saw banks blow up all around her, stocks hit the cellar, and it did something to her common-sense, finishing what a knock-out blow from love had begun ten years before; it made the round-topped, iron-hooped trunk lying in a corner of her hotel-room look good.

Her father, the late railroad president, Al Garrity, had left her well-provided-for for life, but when she got through, everything she owned was in that trunk there in the room with her—$90,000 in old-fashioned napkin-size currency. She had a new lock put on it, and a couple of new bolts on her room-door, which she hadn't been through since the night she was jilted, wedding-dress and all, five hundred and twenty weeks before. She'd taken a considerable beating, but no depression could get at her from now on, and that was that.

So far so good, but within a year or so a variation had entered her foolproof scheme of things. Some blood-curdling rumor of inflation may have drifted in to her from the world outside. There was a guy named Bryan doing a lot of talking about silver. Either that, or the banknotes, beginning to show the wear and tear of being taken out, pawed over and counted every night at bedtime, lacked attractiveness and durability for purposes of hoarding. After all, she lay awake worrying to herself, they were only pieces of printed paper. One day, therefore, she cranked up the handle on the wall-telephone ('96) and called one of the better-known jewelry firms down on Maiden Lane.

The manager himself showed up that afternoon, bringing sample-cases under the watchful eye of an armed guard. A $5,000 diamond brooch found its way into the trunk to glisten there unseen under all the dog-eared packets of crummy banknotes. Pretty soon they were just a thin layer solidly bedded on a sparkling rockpile. By 1906 she had to quit that—she'd run out of money and the rocks went to work for her. Their value doubled, tripled, quadrupled, as the price of diamonds skyrocketed. In that one respect, maybe she hadn't been so batty after all.

Meanwhile, she never stepped out of the room, and the only one she allowed in it was an old colored maid who brought her meals to her—and never dreamed what was in that mouldy old trunk in the corner. But all during the Twenties, sometimes at night an eery figure would glide silently about the room, flashing prismatic fire from head to foot, a ghost covered with diamonds. There wasn't space enough on the rustling white bridal-gown to put them all, so she'd spread the rest around her on the floor and walked barefooted on a twinkling carpet of pins, brooches, brace-lets, ring-settings, getting the feel of them. Sometimes tiny drops of red appeared on the sharp points of the faceted stones.

She knew her number was going to be up soon, and it got so she couldn't bear the thought of parting from them, leaving them behind. She called her lawyer in, the grandson of the man who had been her father's lawyer, and told him her wishes in the matter, made out her will. She was to be buried in the vault her father had built for himself fifty years before; she was to go into it in her bridal-dress, face veiled, and no one must look at her face once the embalmers were through with her. There must be a glass insert at the top of the coffin, and instead of being placed horizontally as in Christian burial, it was to be left standing upright like the Egyptians used to do. And all the diamonds in the trunk were to be sealed into the tomb with her, were to follow her into the next world; she wanted them left directly in front of the glass-slitted sarcophagus, where she could look at them through all eternity. She had no heirs, no relatives, nobody had a claim on them but herself, and she was taking them with her.

"I charge you," she wheezed hectically, "on your professional honor, to see that this is carried out according to my instructions!"

He had expected something dippy from her, but not quite as bad as all that. But he knew her well enough not to try to talk her out of it, she would only have appointed a different executor—and good-bye diamonds! So the will was drawn up, signed, and attested. He was the last one to see her alive. She must have known just when it was coming. The old colored crone couldn't get in the next morning, and when they broke down the door they found her stretched out in her old yellowed wedding-gown, orange-blos-som wreath, satin slippers, and all. This second bridegroom hadn't left her in the lurch like the first.

The news about the diamonds leaked out somehow, although it was the last thing the lawyer had wanted. The wedding-dress bier set-up was good copy and had attracted the reporters like flies to honey in the first place. Then some clerk in his law-office may have taken a peek while filing the will and let the cat out of the bag. The trunk had been taken from the room, secreted, and put under guard, but meanwhile the value of its contents had spurted to half a million, and the story got two columns in every evening paper that hit the stands. It was one of those naturals. Everybody in the city was talking about it that first night, to forget about it just as quickly the next day.

Unfortunately for the peace of Miss Garrity's soul, there were two who took a professional interest in the matter instead of just an esoteric one. Chick Thomas' eye lighted on it on his way to the back of the paper where the racing charts were. He stopped, read it through once, and looked thoughtful; then he read it a second time and did more thinking. When he'd given it a third once-over, you could tell by his face he had something. He folded the paper tubularly to the exclusion of everything else but this one item and called it to the attention of Angel Face Zabriskie by whacking it ecstatically across his nose. There was no offense in the blow, only triumph. "Get that," he said, sliding his mouth halfway toward his ear to pronounce the two words.

Angel Face read it and got it, just the way Chick wanted him to. They looked at each other. "How d'ya know it ain't just a lot of malarkey? Her mouth won't admit or deny it, it says here."

"Which proves they're going through with it," opined the cagey Chick. "He don't want it advertised, that's all. If they weren't gonna do it, he'd say either yes or no, one or the other. Don't you know mouths by now? Anytime one of 'em won't talk it means you've stolen a base on him."

Angel Face resumed cutting his corns with a razor-blade. "So they're turning over the ice to the worms. So what's the rush? Let her cool off a while first before we get busy on the spade-work—if that's what you got in mind."

Chick got wrathful. "No wonder I'm stuck here in a punk furnished-room, teaming up with you! You got about as much imagination as the seat of my pants! Don't you know a haul when you see one? 'What's the rush?' he mimicked nasally. "No rush at all! Wait a week, sure, why not? And then find out somebody else has beat us to it! D'ya think we're the only two guys reading this paper tonight? Don't you think there's plenty of others getting the same juice out of it we are? Five hundred grand ain't unloaded into a cemetery every day in the week, you know. If I'd listen to you we'd prob'ly have to get in line, wait our turn to get near it—"

Angel Face tossed aside the razor-blade, shook a sock out and began putting it on. "Well, what's the answer?" he asked not unreasonably. "Hold up the hearse on its way out there? How do we know it'll be in the hear—"

"Naw," snapped Chick, "it won't be in the hearse in the first place, and there'll prob'ly be enough armed guards around it to give an imitation of a shooting-gallery if we tried that; that mouth of hers is no fool. And point that kick of yours the other way, will ya, it's stuffy enough in here already!" Angel Face obligingly swiveled around the other way on his chair while he finished clothing his pedal extremity. "Naw, here's the idea," resumed Chick, "it come to me just like that while I was reading about it." He snapped his fingers to illustrate the suddenness of the inspiration. "To be johnny-on-the-spot and ring the bell ahead of all the other wise guys, one of us goes right into the burial-vault all dressed in wood instead of the stiff they think they're planting. That's one angle none of the others'll think of, I bet!"

Angel Face threw a nauseated look up at him from shoe-level. "Yeah? Well, as long as you thought of it, you're elected."

His roommate squinted at the ceiling in exasperation. "They ain't burying her in sod! Don't you know what a mausoleum is yet? They're like little stone or marble houses. I've seen some of 'em. They got more room inside than this two-by-four rat-hole we're in now. They're just gonna leave her standing up in there. Wait, I'll read it over to you—"

He swatted the paper across his thigh, traced a finger along the last few lines of print at the bottom. "The burial will take place at eleven o'clock tomorrow morning at the Cedars of Lebanon Cemetery. The services will be strictly private. To discourage curiosity-seekers, Mr. Staunton has arranged for a detail of police to bar outsiders from the grounds both before and during the ceremonies. Whether the fantastic provisions of the will are to be carried out in their entirety and a huge fortune in jewelry cached in the crypt, could not be learned. It is thought likely, however, that because of the obvious risks involved it will be allowed to remain in the vault only a short time, out of regard to the wishes of the deceased, and will then be removed to a safer place. Funeral arrangements completed at a late hour last night, it is learned on good authority, call for the use of a specially constructed coffin with a glass 'pane' at the top, designed and purchased several years ago by Miss Garrity herself and held in readiness, somewhat after the old Chinese custom. The body is to be left standing upright. Pending interment, the remains have been removed to the Hampton Funeral Parlors—"

Chick flicked his hand at the paper. "Which just about covers everything we needa know! What more d'ya want? Now d'ya understand why we gotta get right in with it from the beginning? Outside of a lotta other mugs trying to muscle in, it says right here that they're only liable to leave it there a little while before they take it away again, maybe the very next day after, for all we know. We only got one night we can be dead sure of. That's the night after the funeral, tomorrow night."

"Even so," argued Angel Face, "that still don't prove that two guys can't get at it just as quick from the outside as they can if one's outside and one's in."

"Where's yer brains? If we both stay outside we can't get to work until after dark when the cemetery closes, and even then there's a watchman to figure on. But if one guy's on the inside along with a nice little kit of files and chisels, he can get started the minute they close the works up on him, have the whole afternoon to get the ice out of the strongbox or trunk or whatever they put it in. Y'don't think they're gonna leave it lying around loose on the floor, do ya? Or maybe," he added witheringly, "you was counting on backing an express-van up to the place and moving it out trunk and all?" He spat disgustedly at an opening between two of the floor-boards.

"Well, if the shack is stone or marble like you said, how you gonna crack it?"

"It's got a door just like any other place, ain't it?" roared Chick. Then quickly dropping his voice again, "How d'ya get at any door, even a bronze one? Take an impression of the key that works it! If we can't do that, then maybe we can pick the lock or find some other way. Anyhow that part of it's the least; it's getting the ice all done up ready to move out in a hurry that counts. We gotta be all set to slip right out with it. We can't hang around half the night showing lights and bringing it out a piece at a time."

"Gee," admitted Angel Face, "the way you tell it, it don't sound so bad, like at first. I kept thinking about dirt being shoveled right on top of the coffin, and all like that. It ain't that I'm yellow or anything—"

"Naw," agreed his companion bitingly, "orange! Well we'll settle that part of it right-off before we do anything else, then we'll go up and look the place over, get a line on it." He produced a shining quarter, newly minted, from somewhere about his person. "I'll toss you for who goes in and who stays out. Heads it's you, tails it's me. How about it?"

Angel Face nodded glumly. The coin flashed up to within half a foot of the ceiling, spun down again. Chick cupped it neatly in his hollowed palm. He held his hand under the other's nose. Miss Liberty stared heartlessly up at them.

"O.K. Satisfied?" Chick dropped the coin back into a vest-pocket, not the trouser-pocket where he kept the rest of his small change. He'd had it for years; it had been given to him as a souvenir by a friend who had once been in the business, as an example of the curious accidents that beset even the best of counterfeiters at times. It had come from the die with a head stamped on each side of it.

Angel Face was a little white around the gills. "Aw, I can't go through with it, Chick, it's no use. It gives me the heebies even to think about getting in the box in her place."

"Take a litle whiff of C before you climb in, and it'll be over with before you know it. They don't even lie you down flat, they just stand you up, and you got glass to look through the whole time— it's no different from being in a telephone-booth." Then, still failing to note any signs of enthusiasm on the other's face, he kicked a chair violently out of the way, flung back his arm threateningly. "All right, blow, then! G'wan, ya yellowbelly, get outa here! I'll get me another shill! There's plenty of guys in this town would do more than that to get their mitts on a quarter of a grand worth of ice! All y'gotta do is stand still with a veil on your dome for half a day—and you're heeled for the rest of your life!"

Angel Face didn't take the departure which had been so pointedly indicated. Instead he took a deep abdominal breath. "All right, pipe down, d'ya want everyone in the house to hear ya?" he muttered reluctantly. "How we gonna get in the place to look it over, like you said?"

Chick was already down on his heels unbuckling a dog-eared valise. "I never believe in throwing away nothing. I used to have a fake press-card in here someplace. I never knew till now why I hung onto it. Now I know. That and a sawbuck oughta fix it for us to see this grave-bungalow. We're a couple reporters sent up to describe it for our paper ahead of time." He shuffled busily through a vast accumulation of pawn-tickets, dummy business cards, fake letters of introduction, forged traveler's checks, dirty French postcards, and other memorabilia of his salad days. Finally he drew something out. "Here it is. It got me on a boat once when the heat was on, and I ducked across the pond—"

"Can two of us get by on one?" Angel Face wanted to know, studying it.

"Naw, cut out a piece of cardboard the same size and scribble on it, stick it in your hatband. I'll just flash this one, the gateman up there prob'ly won't know the diff." He kicked the valise back under the bed. "Let's go. Stick a pencil behind your ear and scratch something on the back of an envelope every now and then—and keep your trap shut; I'll do the rest of it."

They went trooping down the rickety rooming-house stairs, two gentlemen bound on engrossing business. They checked on the Cedars of Lebanon Cemetery in a directory in a candy store on the corner, and Chick bought three or four bars of very inferior milk-chocolate done up in tinfoil, insisting that it be free of nuts, raisins, or any other filling. He stuck one piece in each of his four vest-pockets, which was as close to his body as he could get it.

"It'll melt and run on ya," warned Angel Face as they made their way to the subway.

"Whaddya suppose I'm doing it for?" gritted the master mind tersely. "Will ya shuddup or d'ya want me to hang one on your loud-talking puss!"

"Aw, don't get so tempermental," subsided Angel Face. Chick was always like this when they were on a job. But he was good just the same, had that little added touch of imagination which he himself lacked, he realized. That was why he teamed with him, even though he almost always was the fall-guy.

They rode a Bronx train to the end of the line, walked the rest of the distance on foot. Chick spoke once, out of the side of his face. "Not so fast, relax. These newspaper punks never hurry."

The cemetery was open. They slouched in, strolled up to the gatekeeper's lodge. Angel Face looked about him in surprise. He had expected rows of mouldering headstones, sunken graves, and cockeyed crosses. Instead it looked just like a big private estate. It was a class cemetery, no doubt about it. The most that could be seen from the perimeter was an occasional group of statuary, a tasteful pergola or two, screened by leaves and shrubbery. There were even rustic benches of hewn logs set here and there along the winding paths. It was just like a park, only cleaner. Tall cypress trees rustled in the wind. The set-up perked him up a lot. It wasn't such a bad place to spend a night—salary, $250,000. He let go a bar or two of *Casey Jones* and got a gouge in the ribs from Chick's elbow.

The gatekeeper came out to them and Chick turned on the old personality. "Afternoon, buddy. We been sent up here to get a story on this tomb the old crow with the di'monds is going into tomorrow. We been told not to come back without it, or we lose our jobs." He flashed the press-card, jerked his head at the one in Angel Face's hatband, put his own away again.

"What a way to earn a living," said the gatekeeper pessimistically. "Nearly as bad as my own. Help yourselves. You follow this main path all the way back, then turn off to your left. The Garrity mausoleum is about fifty yards beyond. You'll know it by the—"

Chick's paw dropped fraternally on the old codger's shoulder. "How about giving us a peek inside? Just so we can get a rough idea. You know yourself we haven't got a chance of getting near the place tomorrow. We don't want to take pitchers or anything, you can search us, we have no camera." Angel Face helpfully raised his arms to frisking position, dropped them again.

"I couldn't, gents, I couldn't. The gatekeeper stroked the silver stubble on his face. "It would cost me my job if the trustees ever got wind of it." He glanced down sideways at the ten-spot poking into his breast-pocket from Chick's dangling hand. "How's chances?" the latter slurred.

"About fifty-fifty." The old man grinned hesitantly. "Y'know these plots are private property. I ain't even supposed to butt into 'em myself—" But his eyes were greedily following the second sawbuck going in to join the first. Even Angel Face hadn't seen his partner take it out, he was that smooth.

"Who's gonna know the difference, it won't take a minute. We'll be out again before you know it." A third tenner was tapped down lightly on top of the other two.

The old man's eyes crinkled slyly. "I ain't supposed to leave my post here at the gate, not till we close up at six—" But he was already turning to go back into the lodge for something. Chick dropped one eyelid at Angel Face. The old man came out again with a hoop of thick ponderous keys slung over his arm. He looked around him craftily. "Come on before anyone sees us," he muttered.

They started down the main path one on each side of him; Chick took the side he was carrying the keys on. He took out a chocolate-bar, laid open the tinfoil, and took a very small nibble off one corner. Then he kept it flat up against his moist palm after that, holding it in place with his thumb.

"See that you get all this now," he ordered Angel Face across their guide's shoulders. "The Captain's putting himself out for us." Angel Face stripped the pencil from his ear, held the back of an envelope in readiness. "He takes the rough notes and I polish 'em up, work 'em into an article," explained Chick professionally.

"You young fellas must get good money," remarked the old man.

"Nothing to brag about. Of course, the office foots the bill for any extra expenses—like just now." Even an old lame-brain like this might figure thirty-dollars a pretty stiff tip coming from a leg-man.

"Oh, no wonder," crackled the old fellow shrewdly. "So that's it!"

Chick secretly got rid of the distasteful morsel of sweet stuff he'd been holding in his mouth, took out a second chocolate-bar and stripped it open, nipped it between his teeth. The gateman didn't notice that he now had two, one in each hand. He kept his palms inward and they didn't extend beyond his fingertips.

They turned off the main path without meeting anyone, followed a serpentine side-path up over a rise of ground, and just beyond came face-to-face with a compact granite structure, domed and about ten feet high. The path ended at its massive bronze door, flanked by two hefty stone urns and guarded by a reclining angel blowing a trumpet.

"Here she is," said the gatekeeper, and once again looked all around. So did Chick, but for a different reason. Not very far ahead he could make out the tall iron railing that bounded the cemetery; the Garrity mausoleum, therefore, was near its upper limits, on the side away from town. He peered beyond, searching hurriedly for an identifying landmark on the outside by which to locate it. It wasn't built up out there, just open country, but he could make out a gray thread of motor highway with a row of billboards facing his way. That was enough, it would have to do. He counted three of them, then a break, then three more.

He turned his attention quickly to the key the old man was fitting into the chunky door, lavishly molded into bas-reliefs of cherubs and what-not but grassgreen from long exposure to the elements. The old man was having a lot of trouble with it, but Chick didn't dare raise his eyes to watch what was going on, kept his head down. When it finally opened and the key dropped back to the ring again, his eye rode with it like something stuck to it, kept it separate from all the rest even after it was back in with them again, told it off from the end ones on each side of it. It was the fifth from one end of the bunch and seventh from the other, unless and until the old man inadvertently shifted the entire hoop around, of course—which would have been catastrophic but wasn't very likely. The hoop was nearly the size of a bicycle-wheel.

Chick tilted his head out behind the old man's back, caught Angle Face's eye and gave him the office. The gatekeeper was lugging the squealing, grinding door open with both arms, and the keys on the ring fluttered like ribbons with every move he made. Angel Face said, "Here, I'll help ya," as the door gave an unexpected lurch outward and he fell back against the gatekeeper. It was the old jostle-and-dip racket, which they'd had down to a science even before they were in long pants. Chick flipped that one certain key out from the rest with the point of his nail, deftly caught it on one bar of soggy chocolate, and ground the other one down on top of it. "Oops, sorry!" said Angel Face, and jerked the gateman forward again by one lapel, as if he'd been in danger of falling over, which he wasn't. Chick separated the two slabs, the released key fell back in line again, and by the time he had trailed into the dank place after the other two he had the tinfoil folded back in place again and his handkerchief wrapped around the two confectionery-bars to protect them from further softening through bodily warmth; they were in his breast-pocket, now, which was least liable to be affected.

The gatekeeper didn't linger long inside the place with them, but that wasn't necessary now any more. The floor of the vault was three feet below ground level, giving it a total height of about thirteen feet on the inside. Half a dozen steps led down from the doorway. The interior was in the shape of a cross, outlined by bastions of marble-faced granite that supported the dome. The head and one arm already contained coffins supported on trestles, Al Garrity and his wife respectively. Hers was evidently to go into the remaining arm. Macabre purple light filtered downward from a round tinted-glass opening in the exact center of the dome, so inaccessible from the floor that it might have been on some other planet. Even so, you could hardly see your hand in front of your face a short distance away from the open door. The place was icy cold and, once the door was closed, apparently air-tight. Chick wondered how long the supply of oxygen would last if anyone were shut up in there breathing it. Probably a week; certainly more than twenty-four hours. It was too leading a question to put the gate-keeper, especially in Angel Face's presence. He kept the thought to himself.

"You'd think," he heard the latter complain squeakily in the gloom, "they'd punch a winder or two in a place like this, let some light in."

"This one's about fifty years old," the old man explained. "Some of the newer ones they put up since has more light in 'em. There's one even has electric tapers at the head of the bier, going day and night, worked by battery."

"Ain't it unhealthy to leave the coffins above ground like this?" Chick asked.

"The bodies are preserved, embalmed in some way, I understand, before they're put in these kind of places. I s'pose if you was to open up one of these two they got here already you'd find 'em looking just like the day they got here. They don't change any, once there here."

A sound resembling *"Brrh!"* came from Angel Face's direction; he retreated toward the doorway rather more quickly than he'd come in. Chick took note of that fact, he could see that more build-up was going to be in order.

On the way out he sized up the thickness of the wall, where the entrance cut through it. A good solid two feet. And where the bastions encroached on the interior, God only knows! Pickaxes and even dynamite would have been out of the question. The only possible way was the one he'd decided on.

Angel Face was scribbling away industriously on the back of an envelope when he came out after him, but his face looked pretty strained. Chick pointed to the inner side of the bronze door, which faced outward while it stood ajar; the keyhole ran all the way through. He furtively spread two fingers, folded them again. A key for each, that meant. If it was intended for encouragement, it didn't seem to do much good, and Chick didn't care to risk asking the old man whether a key used from the inside would actually work or not. Who the hell had any business letting themselves out of a tomb? And apart from that, he had a hunch the answer would have been no anyway.

"Well," said the old man as he took leave of them at the door of his lodge, "I hope you two young fellas hev gotten what you came out here after."

Chick slung an arm about his shoulder and patted him reassuringly. "Sure did, old-timer, and much obliged to you. Well, be good."

"Hunh," the old reprobate snorted after them, "fat chance o' being anything but around these diggin's!"

They strolled aimlessly out the way they had come in, but with the ornamental stone and iron gateway once behind them Chick snapped into a sudden double-quick walk that rapidly took them out of sight. "C'mon, pick up your feet," he ordered, "before he feels for that pocket where he thinks he's got something!" He thrust the three tenners that he had temporarily loaned the old man back into his own trousers.

"Gee!" ejaculated Angel Face admiringly.

"He's too old to enjoy that much dough anyway," his partner told him.

It was dusk already when they came out of the subway. Chick, who was somewhat of a psychologist, wisely didn't give his companion time to argue about the undertaking from this point on. He could tell by the other's long face he was dying to back out, but he wouldn't give him the chance to get started. If he stayed with the idea long enough, he'd get used to it, caught up by the rush of their preparations.

"Got dough?" he demanded as they came out on the sidewalk.

"Yeah, but listen Chick—" quavered the other.

"Here, take this." Chick handed him two of the tens. "Go to a hardware store and get an awl and a screw-driver, good strong ones; better get each one separately in a different place."

"Wha—what's the idea?" Angel Face's teeth were clicking a little, although it was warm by the subway entrance.

"That's to let air in the coffin; shut up and let me do the talking. Then get a couple of those tin boxes that workmen carry their lunches in; get the biggest size they come in"—he saw another question trembling on his partner's lips, quickly forestalled it—"to lug the ice away in, what d'ya suppose! If two ain't enough, get three. Get 'm so one'll fit inside the other when I bring 'em out there tomorrow night. Now y' got that? See that y' stick with it. That's your part of the job. Mine'll be to take these candy-bars to a locksmith, have a pair of duplicate keys made, one for each of us—"

This, judging by the change that came over Angel Face's incorrectly named map, was the first good news he had heard since they had scanned the paper that morning.

"Oh, that's different," he sighed, "as long as I get one, too—"

"Sure, you can take it right in with you, hang it round your neck on a cord or something, just to set your mind at rest. That's what

I tried to tip you off back there just now, the keyhole goes all the way through. But don't try using it ahead of time and ditching me, or I'll make you wish you'd stayed in there—"

"So help me, Chick, you know me better than that! It's only in case something goes wrong, so I won't be left bottled up in there for the rest of me—"

"Y' got nothing to worry about," snarled Chick impatiently. "I'll contact Revolving Larry for you and getcha a few grains of C. By the time you're through dreamin' you're Emperor of Ethiopia you'll be on your way out with the sparklers."

Angel Face even seemed to have his doubts about this angle of it. "I dunno—I never been a user. What does that stuff do to ya?"

"It'll make you stay quiet in the box, that's all I'm interested in. Now g'wan and do what I told you, and wait for me back at the room. I'll meet you there by twelve at the latest. This corpse beauty-parlor she's at oughta be closed for the night by then. We got a jimmy home, haven't we?

He didn't wait to be told but left with a jaunty step, bustling. Angel Face moved off slowly, droopily, like someone on his way to the dentist or the line-up.

Chick knew just where to have the keys made. He'd had jobs done there plenty of times in the past. It was in the basement of a side-street tenement and the guy kept his mouth closed, never asked questions, no matter what kind of a crazy mold you brought him. Chick carefully peeled the tinfoil off the warped chocolate-bars.

"Big fellow, ain't it," said the locksmith, examining the impression. "How many you gonna need?"

"Two, but I want 'em made one at a time. Bring the mold out to me after you finish the first one, the second one's gotta be a little different. "He wasn't putting anyone in the way of walking off with half-a-million dollars' worth of jewels under his nose, maybe only an hour before he got there. To hand Angel Face a key that really worked was like pleading for a double-cross. He'd see that he got out all right, but not till he was there to let him out.

"Take about twenty minutes apiece," said the locksmith.

"I'll wait. Get going on 'em."

The locksmith came back with one completed key for inspection, and the two halves of the mold, which he had to glaze with some kind of wax. "Sure it works, now?" Chick scowled.

"It fits that, that's all I can tell you."

"All right, then here's what you do now." He scraped a nailful of chocolate off the underside of each bar, trowelled it microscopically into the impression, smoothed it over, obliterating one of the three teeth the key had originally possessed. "Make it that way this time." He tucked the first one away to guard against confusion.

The locksmith gave him the mold back when he'd finished the job; and Chick kneaded the paraffined chocolate into a ball, dropped it down the sewer. Angel Face's key had a piece of twine looped to it, all ready to hang around his neck. An amulet against the horrors, that was about all it was really good for. At that, probably even the real one wouldn't work from the inside, so the deception was just an added touch of precaution.

Chick knew just where to put his finger on the peddler known as Revolving Larry, a nickname stemming from his habit of pirouetting to look all around him before making a sale. Chick passed him on the beat where he usually hung out, gave him the office. They met around the corner in a telephone booth in a cigar store about five minutes later. "Does C give you a jerky or a dreamy kick?" Chick breathed through a slit in the glass.

"Depends on how strong the whiff is," muttered Larry, thumbing through a directory hanging on a hook.

"Gimme a couple grains the kind you sell the saps, all baking soda."

Larry did his dervish act, although there was no one in the place. "Lemme in a minute," he muttered. Chick changed places with him in the booth, and Larry bent his leg and did something to one of his heels, holding the receiver to his ear with one hand. He handed Chick a little folded paper packet through the crack in the door, and Chick shoved a couple of bills in to him behind his back, turning to face the front of the store. Then he walked out, ignoring the frantic pecks on the glass that followed him. "Wholesale price," he growled over his shoulder.

The Hampton Funeral Parlor was on Broadway, which gave him a pretty bad jolt at first until he happened to glance a second time at the classified listing in the directory he was consulting. There was a branch chapel on the east side; it was the nearer of the two to the hotel she'd lived in. He played a hunch; it must be that one. A conservative old crow like that wouldn't be prepared for burial in a district full of blazing automobile sales-rooms. Even the second one, when he went over to look at it, was bad enough. It was dolled up so that it almost looked like a grill or tap-room from the outside. It had a blue neon sign and colored mosaic windows and you expected to see a hat-check girl just inside the entrance. But after midnight it was probably dark and inconspicuous enough for a couple of gents to crack without bringing down the town on their heads. He managed to size up the lock on the door without exactly loitering in front of it. A glass-cutter was out; in the first place the door-pane was wire-meshed, and in the second place it had to be done without leaving any tell-tale signs, otherwise there might be an embarrassing investigation when they opened up in the morning. Embarrassing for Angel Face, anyway. A jimmy ought to do the trick in five minutes; that kind of place didn't usually go in for electric burglar-alarms.

When he went back to the room he found Angel Face pacing back and forth until the place rattled. At least he'd brought in the lunch-boxes, the awl, and the screw-driver. Chick examined them, got them ready to take out, looked over the jimmy and packed that too. Angel Face's frantic meandering kept up all around him. "Quit that!" he snapped. He opened a brown-paper bag crammed with sandwiches he'd brought in with him. "Here, wrap yourself around these—"

Angel Face took out a thick chunk of ham and rye, pulled at it with his teeth once or twice, gave up the attempt. "I ain't hungry, I can't seem to swaller," he moaned.

"You're gonna be hungry!" warned Chick mercilessly. "It's your last chance to eat until t'morra night about this time. Here's your key, hang it around your neck." He tossed over the dummy with the two teeth. "I got some C for you too, but you take that the last thing, before you step in."

When they let themselves out of the house at one A.M., Angel Face followed docilely enough. Chick had also done a little theatrical browbeating and brought up a lot of past jobs which Angel Face wouldn't have been keen to have advertised. It hadn't seemed to have occurred to him that neither would Chick, for that matter. He wasn't very quick on the uptake. Chick glanced at him as they came out the front door of the rooming-house, swept his hat off with a backhand gesture and let it roll over to the curb. "They don't plant 'em in snap-brim felts, especially old ladies—and I ain't wearing two back when I leave!" Angel Face gulped silently and cast longing eyes at his late pride and joy. "You can get yourself a gold derby by Wednesday, like trombones wear, if you feel like it."

They had walked briskly past the Hampton Chapel, now dark and deserted, as if they had no idea of stopping there at all, then abruptly halted a few yards up the side-street. "Stay here up against the wall, and keep back," breathed the nerveless Chick. "Two of us ganged up at the entrance'd make too much of an eyeful. I'll whistle when I'm set."

Chick's cautious whistle came awfully soon, far too quickly to suit him. He sort of tottered around to where the entrance was and dove into the velvety darkness. Chick carefully closed the door again so it wouldn't be noticeable from the outside. "It was a push-over," he whispered, "I coulda almost done it with a quill tooth-pick!" He went toward the back, sparingly flickering a small torch once or twice, then gave a larger dose to the room beyond. "No outside windows," he said. "We can use their own current. Turn it on and close the door."

Angel Face was moistening his lips and having trouble with his Adam's apple, staring glassy-eyed at the two shrouded coffins the place contained. Otherwise it wasn't so bad as it might have been. Black and purple drapes hung from the walls, and the floor and ceiling were antiseptically spotless. The embalmers, if they actually did their work here, had removed all traces of it. Of the two coffins, one was on a table up against the wall, the other on a draped bier out in the middle, each with an identifying card pinned to its pall.

"Here she is," said Chick, peering through the glass pane, "all ready for delivery." Angel Face looked over his shoulder, then jerked back as though he'd just had an electric shock. A muffled veiled face had met his own through the glass. He turned sort of blue.

Chick went over to the second one, against the wall, stripped it, and callously sounded it with his knuckles. "This one's got some-body in it too," he announced jubilantly.

He unburdened himself of his tools, went back to the first coffin, and started in on the screws that held the lid. He heaved it a little out of line so that it overlapped the bier. "Get down under it and get going on some air-holes with that awl. Not too big, now! They'll have to be on the bottom so they won't be noticeable."

"Right while—while she's in it?" croaked Angel Face, folding to his knees.

"Certainly—we don't wanna be here all night!"

They gouged and prodded for a while in silence. "You ain't told me yet," Angel Face whimpered presently, "once I'm in it, how do I get out again? Do I hafta wait for you to come in and unscrew me?"

"Certainly not, haven'tcha got any sense at all? You take this same screw-driver I'm using in with you, under your arm or some-where. Then you just bust the glass from the inside, stretch out your arms, and go to work all down the front of it yourself."

"I can't reach the bottom screws from where I'll be, how am I gonna bend—"

"Y'don't have to! Just get rid of the upper ones and then heave out, it'll split the rest of the way. I'm not gonna put them back all the way in."

He was still down underneath when he heard Chick put down the screw-driver and dislodge something. "There we are! Gimme a hand with this." He straightened up and looked.

A rather fragile doll-like figure lay revealed, decked in yellowed satin and swathed from head to foot in a long veil. They stood the lid up against the bier. "Get her out," ordered Chick, "while I get started on that second one over there." But Angel Face was more rigid than the form that lay on the satin coffin-lining, he couldn't lift a finger toward it.

"When the second coffin was unlidded, Chick came back and without a qualm picked up the mortal remains of Miss Alfreda Garrity with both arms. He carried her over to the second one, deposited her exactly on top of the rightful occupant, whipped off the veil, and then began to push and press downward like a ship-ping-clerk busily packing something in a crate. Angel Face was giving little moans like a man coming out of gas. "Don't look, if y'feel that way about it," his partner advised him briskly. "Get in there a while and try it out."

It took him ten minutes or so to screw the lid back on the one that now held the two of them, then he carefully dusted it with his handkerchief and came back. Angel Face had both legs in the coffin and was sitting up in it, hanging onto the sides with both hands, shivering but with his face glossy with sweat.

"Get all the way down—see if it fits!" Chick bore down on one of his shoulders and flattened him out remorselessly. "Swell!" was the verdict. "You won't be a bit cramped. All right, did you punch them air-holes all the way through the quilting? If you didn't you'll suffocate. Now we'll try it out with the lid and veil on. Keep your head down!'

He dragged the veil over from beside the other coffin, sloshed it across the wincing Angel Face's countenance, and then began to pack it in and straighten it out around him, like a dutiful father tucking his offspring into bed. Then he heaved the heavy lid up off the floor, slapped it across the coffin, and fitted it in place. He peered down through the glass pane, studying the mummified onion-head that showed below. He retreated and gauged the effect from a distance, came back again on the opposite side. Finally he dislodged the lid once more. Angel Face instantly sat up, veil and all, like a jack-in-the-box. He tossed the veil back and blew out his breath.

"D'ja have any trouble getting air?" Chick wanted to know anxiously.

"There coulda been more ventilation."

"All right, stay there, we'll let a few more in to be on the safe side. Rest your head again, the closer I can bring 'em to your muzzle the better." He went to work from below with the screwdriver.

Angel Face suddenly yelped "Ow!" and reared up again, rubbing his ear.

"Good!" said Chick. "Right next to your face. If I put any more in the bottom'd look like a Swiss cheese. All right, get out and stretch, it's your last chance. Here's your bang of C. Sniff it quick."

Angel Face took the small packet, gratefully scrambled over the side.

Chick was examining the glass insert in the lid. "It's kinda thick at that. I think you better take something in with you to make sure of smashing it. I lamped one of them patented fire-extinguishers outside, wait a minute—"

When he came back he had a small iron mallet with two or three links of filed-off chain dangling from it. "Just a tap from this'll do the trick for you. There's room enough to swing your arms if you bring 'em up close to you. One more thing and we're set: watch your breathing, see that it don't flutter the veil. I'm gonna bulge it loose around you, so it won't get in the way of your beak." He scrutinized the other shrewdly. "Gettin' your kicks yet?"

Angel Face was standing perfectly still with a foolish vacant look on his face. There hadn't been enough cocaine in the dose to affect anyone used to it, but he wasn't an addict. "No wonder they call 'em attics," he admitted blithely. "I'm way up over your head. Gee, everything looks pretty!"

"Sure," agreed Chick. "Lookit the pretty coffin. Wanna get in? Come on."

"Oke," said Angel Face submissively. He climbed back in of his own accord. "How do I steer it?" he wanted to know.

"Just by lying still and wishin' where y'wanna go," the treacherous Chick assured him. He tucked in the large screwdriver, point-downward, under one armpit, the iron mallet under the other, once more arranged the veil about his henchman's head and shoulders, this time leaving a large pocket through which he could draw breath without moving it. "I'm in Arabia," was the last thing the voluntary corpse mumbled. "Come over'n see me sometime."

"Don't forget to have the ice loose when I show," ordered Chick. "See ya t'morra night about this time." He put the lid back on, and ten minutes later it was screwed as firmly in place as though it had never been disturbed. One coffin was as silent as the other. He gathered up his remaining tools and turned to go, with a backward glance at the one bier in the center. He could hold out, sure he could hold out. The C would wear off long before the funeral in the morning, of course, but that was all to the good. In his own senses he'd be even surer not to give himself away.

Chick turned the lights out and silently eased out of the room. He locked the front door on the inside, so they wouldn't even know it had been tampered with, let himself out of one of the ornamental windows on the side-street, pulled it closed after him. They'd probably never even notice it had been left unlatched all night.

He was standing across the street next morning at half past ten when the funeral procession started out for the cemetery. So were a sprinkling of others, drawn by curiosity. The dumbells probably thought the jewels were going right with her in the coffin. Fat chance. He saw it brought out and loaded onto the hearse, the tasselled pall still covering it. So far so good, he congratulated himself; they hadn't tumbled to anything after opening the parlor for the day, not even the air-holes on the bottom, and the worst was over now. Forty minutes more, and even the worst boner Angel Face could pull wouldn't be able to hurt them. He could bust out and stretch to his heart's content.

Only one car followed the hearse, probably with her lawyer in it. Chick let the small procession get started, then flagged a taxi and followed. Even if outsiders hadn't been barred during the duration of the services, he couldn't have risked going in anyway, on account of the danger of running into that gatekeeper again, but it wouldn't do any harm to swipe a bird's-eye view. The hearse and the limousine tailing it made almost indecent time, considering what they were, but he didn't have any trouble keeping up with them. He got out across the way from the main entrance just as they were going through, and parked himself at a refreshment-stand directly opposite, over a short root-beer.

The gates were closed again the minute the cortege was inside, and the two guys loitering in front were easily identifiable as dicks. Chick saw them turn away several people who tried to get in. Then they came forward, the gates swung narrowly open again, and a small armored truck whizzed through without slowing down. There, Chick told himself, went Miss Garrity's diamonds. Smart guy, her lawyer; nobody could have tackled that truck on the *outside* without getting lead poisoning.

He hung around until the hearse, the limousine, and the truck had come out again, about twenty-five minutes later. They were all going much slower this time, and the gates stayed open behind them. It hadn't taken them long. You could tell the old doll had no relatives or family. The two dicks swung up onto the limousine running-boards and got in with the lawyer—and that was that. He and Angel Face had gotten away with it! Now there could no longer be any possible slip-up.

At midnight, with the big tin lunch-box that held two other ones under his arm, he bought more sandwiches. Not to feed the imprisoned Angel Face, but to spread out on top of the rocks when they were packed in the boxes, in case any nosey cops decided to take a gander.

It was a long ride to the end of the line, but he knew better than to take a taxi this time. The stem along the motor highway around and to the back of the Cedars of Lebanon, to where those bill-boards faced the mausoleum, was even longer, but he had all night. In about thirty minutes he caught up with them, three and then a blank space and then three more, lighted up by reflectors.

He turned off the road to his right and went straight forward, and in about ten minutes more the tall iron pike-fence of the cemetery blocked him. There wasn't a living soul for miles around; an occasional car sped by, way back there on the road. He pitched the telescoped lunch-boxes up over the fence, then he sprang for the lateral bar at the top of the railing, and chinned himself up and over. It wasn't hard. He dropped down soundlessly on the inside, picked up the lunch-boxes, and in another five minutes he was slipping the key into the bronze door.

You could tell how thick it was by how far the key went in. It went in until only the head showed, and the head was an awkward size—not quite big enough to slip his whole fist through and turn, and yet too big for just thumb and fingers to manage like an ordinary key. He caught it between the heels of his palms and tried grinding it around. It wouldn't budge. No wonder the gate-keeper had had a tough time of it yesterday afternoon! He gave it more pressure, digging in the side of his feet to brace him as he turned.

Had they changed the lock after the services? Had the choco-late-mold gotten just a little too soft and spread the impression? Maybe he should have brought a little oil with him. He was sweat-ing like a mule, half from the effort and half from fright. He gave a final strangling heave, and there was a shattering click—but it wasn't the door. He was holding the key-handle in his bruised paws, and the rest of it was jammed immovably in the lock, where it had broken off short.

No one had ever been cursed the way that locksmith was for bungling the job. He swore and he almost wept, and he clawed and dug at it, and he couldn't get it out—it was wedged tight in the lock, not a sixteenth of an inch protruded. Then he thought of the glass skylight, up on the exact center of that rounded inaccessible dome. He went stumbling off through the darkness.

It was nearly three when he was back again, with the length of rope coiled up around his middle under his coat. He unwound it, paid it out around him on the ground. There weren't any trees near enough, so he had to use that angel blowing a trumpet over the door. He put a slip-knot in the rope, hooked the angel easily enough, and got up there on the periphery of the dome. Then he brought the rope up after him. He got up on the dome by cat-walking around to the opposite side from the angel and then pulling himself up with the rope taut across the top. One big kick and a lot of little ones emptied the opening of the violet glass. The crash coming up from inside was muffled. It was pitch-black below. He dropped the rope down in, gave it a half-twist around his wrist, let himself in after and began to swing wildly around going down it.

Suddenly all tension was out of the rope and he was hurtling down, bringing it squirming loosely after him. He would have broken his back, but he hit a large wreath of flowers on top of a coffin. One of the trestles supporting it broke and it boomed to the floor. He and gardenias and leaves and ribbons and velvet pall all went sliding down it to the mosaic floor. An instant later the stone angel's head dropped like a bomb a foot away from his own. It was enough to have brained him if it had touched him.

He was scared sick, and aching all over. "Angel!" he rasped hoarsely, spitting out leaves and gardenia petals, "Angel! Are y'out? J'get hit?" No answer. He fumbled for his torch—thank God it worked!—and shot streaks of white light wildly around the place, creating ghastly shadows of his own making. Her mother's coffin was there in one wing and her father's in the other, like yesterday, and the rocks were there in an old trunk, with the lid left up. And this—this third coffin that he'd hit, that he was on now. Angel Face should have been out of it by now, long ago—but it was still sealed up! Had he croaked in it?

Bruised as he was he scrambled to his feet, widly swept aside the leaves and flowers and the velvet pall, flicked his beam up and down the bared casket. A scream choked off in his larynx—there was no glass insert, no air-holes. It was the other coffin, the one he'd put her in with the unknown!

What followed was a madhouse scene. He set the torch down at an angle, picked up the chipped angel's head, crashed it down on the lid again and again, until the wood shattered, splintered, and he could claw it off with his bare, bleeding hands. There beneath his eyes was the gaunt but rouged and placid face of Miss Alfreda Garrity, teeth showing in a faintly sardonic smile. She could afford to smile; she'd put one over on them, even in death—landed in her own tomb after all, through some ghastly blunder at the mortician's. Maybe he'd been the means of it himself: those two palls, each with a little card pinned to it. He must have transposed them in his hurry last night, and the box with the two in it weighed as much as the big one she'd ordered for herself. And they hadn't looked! Incredible as it sounded, they hadn't looked to make sure, had carried it out with the pall over it, and even here hadn't uncovered it, in a hurry to get rid of the old eccentric, forgetting to give her the eternal gander through the glass at her rocks that she'd wanted!

What difference did it make how it happened, or that it had never happened before and might never happen again after this— it had happened now! And he was in here, bottled up in his stooge's place, with a broken rope and nothing to cast it over, no way of getting back up again! Not even the mallet and screwdriver he'd provided the other guy with! The scream came then, without choking off short, and then another and another, until he was out of them and his raw vocal cords couldn't make any more sounds and daylight showed through the shattered skylight, so near and yet so out of reach. He began banging the angel's head against the bronze door, until it was just little pebbles and the muscles of his arms were useless.

It was afternoon when they cut through the door with blow-torches. Cops and dicks had never looked so good to him before in his life. He wanted twenty years in prison, anything, if only they'd take him out of here. He was, they told him, pretty likely to get what he wanted—with his past record. He was groveling on the floor, whimpering, half batty, picking up shiny pieces of jewelry and letting them dribble through his fingers again. They almost felt sorry for him themselves.

Her lawyer was there with them, too, breathing smoke and flame—maybe because some little scheme of his own had miscarried. "Outrageous! Sickening!" he stormed. "I knew something like this was bound to happen, with all that damnable publicity her will got—"

"Other coffin," the haggard Chick kept moaning, "other coffin." His voice came back when someone gave him a shot of whisky, rose to a screech. "The other coffin! My partner's in it! There's a living man in it, I tell you! They got them mixed. Phone that place! Stop them before they—"

One of the dicks raced off. They met him near the entrance, as they were leading Chick out. His face was a funny green color, and he could hardly talk either now. "They—they planted it at three o'clock yesterday afternoon, at Hillcrest Cemetery, out on Long Island—"

"In the ground?" someone asked in a sick voice.

"Six feet under."

"God in Heaven!" shuddered Staunton, the lawyer. "What abysmal fools these crooks are sometimes! All for a mess of paste. They might have known I wouldn't put the real ones in there, will or no will! They've been safely tucked away in a vault since the night she died." He broke off suddenly. "Hold that man up, I think he's going to collapse."

Holocaust House

PULP DETECTIVES CAME in all shapes and sizes, from all sorts of backgrounds, and had any number of skills, quirks, and physical deformities. Some were downright odd. William E. Barrett's Ken McNally, for instance, was a rich playboy who led a double life, sometimes operating a sleazy tattoo parlor under the name Needle Mike in order to gather information on criminal activities. Nat Perry, the creation of Edith and Ejler Jacobson, was a hemophiliac known as The Bleeder. Bruno Fischer's Calvin Kane had a deformed body and scuttled like a crab from corpse to corpse. Bill Long, one of Wyatt Blassingame's many series characters, was a circus performer who joined forces with a retinue of sideshow freaks to do battle with evildoers.

And then there were Doan and Carstairs.

Doan was short, looked fat but wasn't, and owned a smile as innocent as a baby's; he was a cheerful alcoholic who never suffered hangovers no matter how much he'd had to drink the night before; he appeared to be a nice, pleasant individual, and on rare occasions he was. Carstairs, on the other hand, was a dog. A real dog, that is, a massive fawn-colored Great Dane whom Doan won in a poker game. A creature of breeding and dignity, Carstairs hated Doan's bibulous life-style and considered him a low, uncouth person, not at all the sort he would have chosen for a master. Doan, a trained and case-hardened private eye, did most of the sleuthing. Carstairs usually went along for the ride, although he did help to save Doan's bacon on occasion.

The Doan and Carstairs series, authored by Norbert Davis, is a fine

*example of the wackier side of detective fiction—one of the few successful
blends of screwball humor and hard-boiled violence. "Holocaust House,"
which initially appeared as a two-part serial in* Argosy *in 1940, was the
first of only two Doan and Carstairs pulp novelettes; the other, "Cry
Murder!", was published in* Flynn's Detective Fiction *in 1944. But the
duo also stars in the three novels Davis published under his own name,*
The Mouse in the Mountain *(1943),* Sally's in the Alley *(1943), and*
Oh, Murderer Mine *(1946). (Davis's fourth novel,* Murder Picks the
Jury, *was a collaboration with W. T. Ballard that appeared in 1947 under
the joint pseudonym of Harrison Hunt; it was an expansion, evidently
written by Ballard alone, of Davis's nonseries novella "String Him Up!",
published in* Double Detective *in 1938.) Although Carstairs plays only
a small role in "Holocaust House," Doan is at his best in the wild and
woolly caper involving odd explosive devices, frozen corpses, wild dogs, a
snowbound house in the Rocky Mountains, and an assortment of the weird
and wonderful characters that regularly sprang from Davis's fertile
imagination.*

*Norbert Davis (1909–1949) was among the most talented of all the
writers who specialized in pulp fiction. He sold his first story, "Reform
Racket," to Cap Shaw and* Black Mask *in 1932, while studying law at
Stanford University, and followed it with hundreds more sold to a wide
range of mystery, detective, adventure, and Western publications. In addition to Doan and Carstairs, he created such series sleuths as Ben Shaley,
Doc Flame, Bail Bond Dodd, the Judge, Jim Daniels, and another brilliantly screwball private eye, Max Latin. A Western series character, the
enigmatic Major Cain, starred in several novelettes, one of which, "A
Gunsmoke Case for Major Cain," became the basis for a Wild Bill Elliot
movie called* Hands Across the Rockies *(1941). Davis abandoned the
pulps in 1943–1944, when he began to have success with humorous stories
for such magazines as* The Saturday Evening Post.

*His fiction was fast-paced, occasionally lyrical in a hard-edged way, and
often quite funny (particularly in the Doan and Carstairs and Max Latin
stories). His private life, however, was tragic. A string of marital failures,
the death of his agent, declining sales to the slick magazines, and other
personal pressures led him to take his own life by carbon monoxide poisoning in 1949.*

CHAPTER I
WHERE WAS I?

WHEN DOAN WOKE up he was lying flat on his back on top of a bed with his hat pulled down over his eyes. He lay quite still for some time, listening cautiously, and then he tipped the hat up and looked around. He found to his relief that he was in his own apartment and that it was his bed he was lying on.

He sat up. He was fully dressed except for the fact that he only wore one shoe. The other one was placed carefully and precisely in the center of his bureau top.

"It would seem," said Doan to himself, "that I was inebriated last evening when I came home."

He felt no ill effects at all. He never did. It was an amazing thing and contrary to the laws of science and nature, but he had never had a hangover in his life.

He was a short, round man with a round pinkly innocent face and impossibly bland blue eyes. He had corn-yellow hair and dimples in his cheeks. At first glance—and at the second and third for that matter—he looked like the epitome of all the suckers that had ever come down the pike. He looked so harmless it was pitiful. It wasn't until you considered him for some time that you began to see that there was something wrong with the picture. He looked just a little *too* innocent.

"Carstairs!" he called now. "Oh, Carstairs!"

Carstairs came in through the bedroom door and stared at him with a sort of wearily resigned disgust. Carstairs was a dog—a fawn-colored Great Dane as big as a yearling calf.

"Carstairs," said Doan. "I apologize for my regrettable condition last evening."

Carstairs' expression didn't change in the slightest. Carstairs was a champion, and he had a long and imposing list of very high-class ancestors. He was fond of Doan in a wellbred way, but he had never been able to reconcile himself to having such a low person for a master. Whenever they went out for a stroll together, Carstairs always walked either far behind or ahead, so no one would suspect his relationship with Doan.

He grunted now and turned and lumbered out of the bedroom

in silent dignity. His disapproval didn't bother Doan any. He was used to it. He got up off the bed and began to go through the pockets of his suit.

He found, as he knew he would, that he had no change at all and that his wallet was empty. He found also in his coat pocket one thing that he had never seen before to his knowledge. It was a metal case—about the length and width of a large cigarette case, but much thicker. It looked like a cigar case, but Doan didn't smoke. It was apparently made out of stainless steel.

Doan turned it over thoughtfully in his hands, squinting at it in puzzled wonder. He had no slightest idea where it could have come from. It had a little button catch at one side, and he put his thumb over that, meaning to open the case, but he didn't.

He stood there looking down at the case while a cold little chill traveled up his spine and raised pin-point prickles at the back of his neck. The metal case seemed to grow colder and heavier in his hand. It caught the light and reflected it in bright and dangerous glitters.

"Well," said Doan in a whisper.

Doan trusted his instinct just as thoroughly and completely as most people trust their eyesight. His instinct was telling him that the metal case was about the most deadly thing he had ever had in his hands.

He put the case carefully and gently down in the middle of his bed and stepped back to look at it again. It was more than instinct that was warning him now. It was jumbled, hazy memory somewhere. He *knew* the case was dangerous without knowing how he knew.

The telephone rang in the front room, and Doan went in to answer it. Carstairs was sitting in front of the outside door waiting patiently.

"In a minute," Doan told him, picking up the telephone. He got no chance to say anything more. As soon as he unhooked the receiver a voice started bellowing at him.

"Doan! Listen to me now, you drunken bum! Don't hang up until I get through talking, do you hear? This is J. S. Toggery, and in case you're too dizzy to remember, I'm your employer! Doan, you tramp! Are you listening to me?"

Doan instantly assumed a high, squeaky Oriental voice. "Mr.

Doan not here, please. Mr. Doan go far, far away—maybe Timbuktu, maybe Siam."

"Doan, you rat! I know it's you talking! You haven't got any servants! Now you listen to me! I've got to see you right away. *Doan!*"

"Mr. Doan not here," said Doan. "So sorry, please."

He hung up the receiver and put the telephone back on its stand. It began to ring again instantly, but he paid no further attention to it. Whistling cheerfully, he went back into the bedroom.

He washed up, found a clean shirt and another tie and put them on. The telephone kept on ringing with a sort of apoplectic indignation. Doan tried unsuccessfully to shake the wrinkles out of his coat, gave up and put it on the way it was. He rummaged around under the socks in the top drawer of his bureau until he located his .38 Police Positive revolver. He shoved it into his waistband and buttoned his coat and vest to hide it.

Going over to the bed, he picked up the metal case and put it gently in his coat pocket and then went into the front room again.

"Okay," he said to Carstairs. "I'm ready to go now."

It was a sodden, uncomfortable morning with the clouds massed in darkly somber and menacing rolls in a sky that was a threatening gray from horizon to horizon. The wind came in strong and steady, carrying the fresh tang of winter from the mountains to the west, where the snow caps were beginning to push inquiring white fingers down toward the valleys.

Doan stood on the wide steps of his apartment house breathing deeply, staring down the long sweep of the hill ahead of him. Carstairs rooted through the bushes at the side of the building.

A taxi made a sudden spot of color coming over the crest of the hill and skimming fleetly down the slope past Doan. He put his thumb and forefinger in his mouth and whistled. The taxi's brakes groaned, and then it made a half-circle in the middle of the block and came chugging laboriously back up toward him and stopped at the curb.

Doan grabbed Carstairs by his studded collar and hauled him out of the bushes.

"Hey!" the driver said, startled. "What's that?"

"A dog," said Doan.

"You ain't thinkin' of riding *that* in this cab, are you?"

"Certainly I am." Doan opened the rear door and shoved Carstairs expertly into the back compartment and climbed in after him. Carstairs sat down on the floor, and his pricked ears just brushed the cab's roof.

The driver turned around to stare with a sort of helpless indignation. "Now listen here. I ain't got no license to haul livestock through the streets. What you want is a freight car. Get that thing out of my cab."

"You do it," Doan advised.

Carstairs leered complacently at the driver, revealing glistening fangs about two inches long.

The driver shuddered. "All right. All right. I sure have plenty of luck—all bad. Where do you want to go?"

"Out to the end of Third Avenue."

The driver turned around again. "Listen, there ain't anything at the end of Third Avenue but three abandoned warehouses and a lot of gullies and weeds."

"Third Avenue," said Doan. "The very end."

CHAPTER II
EXPLODING CIGAR

THE THREE WAREHOUSES—like three blocked points of a triangle—looked as desolate as the buildings in a war-deserted city. They stared with blank, empty eyes that were broken windows out over the green, waist-high weeds that surrounded them. The city had been designed to grow in this direction, but it hadn't. It had withdrawn instead, leaving only these three battered and deserted reminders of things that might have been.

"Well," said the taxi driver, "are you satisfied now?"

Doan got out and slammed the door before Carstairs could follow him. "Just wait here," he instructed.

"Hey!" the driver said, alarmed. "You mean you're gonna leave this—this giraffe . . ."

"I'll only be gone a minute."

"Oh no, you don't! You come back and take this—"

Doan walked away. He went around in back of the nearest warehouse and slid down a steep gravel-scarred bank into a gully that snaked its way down toward the flat from the higher ground to the north. He followed along the bottom of the gully, around one sharply angling turn and then another.

The gully ended here in a deep gash against the side of a weed-matted hill. Doan stopped, looking around and listening. There was no one in sight, and he could hear nothing.

He cupped his hands over his mouth and shouted: "Hey! Hey! Is there anyone around here?"

His voice made a flat flutter of echoes, and there was no answer. After waiting a moment he nodded to himself in a satisfied way and took the metal case out of his pocket. Going to the very end of the gully, he placed the case carefully in the center of a deep gash.

Turning around then, he stepped off about fifty paces back down the gully. He drew the Police Positive from his waistband, cocked it and dropped down on one knee. He aimed carefully, using his left forearm for a rest.

The metal case made a bright, glistening spot over the sights, and Doan's forefinger took up the slack in the trigger carefully and expertly. The gun jumped a little against the palm of his hand, but he never heard the report.

It was lost completely in the round, hollow *whoom* of sound that seemed to travel like a solid ball down the gully and hit his eardrums with a ringing impact. Bits of dirt spattered around his feet, and where the case had been there was a deep round hole gouged in the hillside, with the earth showing yellow and raw around it.

"Well," said Doan. His voice sounded whispery thin in his own ears. He took out his handkerchief and dabbed at the perspiration that was coldly moist on his forehead. He still stared, fascinated, at the raw hole in the hillside where the case had rested.

After a moment he drew a deep, relieved breath. He put the Police Positive back in his waistband, turned around and walked back along the gully to the back of the warehouse. He climbed up the steep bank and plowed through the waist-high weeds to the street and the waiting taxi.

The driver stared with round, scared eyes. "Say, did—did you hear a—a noise a minute ago?"

"Noise?" said Doan, getting in the back of the cab and shoving Carstairs over to give himself room to sit down. "Noise? Oh, yes. A small one. It might have been an exploding cigar."

"Cigar," the driver echoed incredulously. "Cigar. Well, maybe *I'm* crazy. Where do you want to go now?"

"To a dining car on Turk Street called the *Glasgow Limited*. Know where it is?"

"I can find it," the driver said gloomily. "That'll be as far as you're ridin' with me, ain't it—I hope?"

The *Glasgow Limited* was battered and dilapidated, and it sagged forlornly in the middle. Even the tin stack-vent from its cooking range was tilted drunkenly forward. It was fitted in tightly slant-wise on the very corner of a lot, and as if to emphasize its down-at-the-heels appearance an enormous, shining office building towered austere and dignified beside it, putting the *Glasgow Limited* always in the shadow of its imposing presence.

The taxi stopped at the curb in front of it. This was the city's financial district, and on Sunday it was deserted. A lone street car, clanging its way emptily along looked like a visitor from some other age. The meter on the taxi showed a dollar and fifty cents, and Doan asked the driver:

"Can you trip that meter up to show two dollars?"

"No," said the driver. "You think the company's crazy?"

"You've got some change-over slips, haven't you?"

"Say!" said the driver indignantly. "Are you accusing me of gypping—"

"No," said Doan. "But you aren't going to get a tip, so you might as well pull it off a charge slip. Have you got one that shows two dollars?"

The driver scowled at him for a moment. He tripped the meter and pocketed the slip. Then he took a pad of the same kind of slips from his vest pocket and thumbed through them. He handed Doan one that showed a charge of a dollar and ninety cents.

"Now blow your horn," Doan instructed. "Lots of times."

The driver tooted his horn repeatedly. After he had done it

about ten times, the door of the *Glasgow Limited* opened and a man came out and glared at them.

"Come, come, MacTavish," said Doan. "Bail me out."

MacTavish came down the steps and across the sidewalk. He was a tall gaunt man with bony stooped shoulders. He was bald, and he had a long draggling red mustache and eyes that were a tired, blood-shot blue. He wore a white jacket that had sleeves too short for him and a stained white apron.

Doan handed him the meter charge slip. "There's my ransom, MacTavish. Pay the man and put it on my account."

MacTavish looked sourly at the slip. "I have no doubt that there's collusion and fraud hidden somewhere hereabouts. No doubt at all."

"Why, no," said Doan. "You can see the charge printed right on the slip. This driver is an honest and upright citizen, and he's been very considerate. I think you ought to give him a big tip."

"That I will not!" said MacTavish emphatically. "He'll get his fee and no more—not a penny!" He put a ragged dollar bill in the driver's hand and carefully counted out nine dimes on top of it. "There! And it's bare-faced robbery!"

He glared at the driver, but the driver looked blandly innocent. Doan got out and dragged Carstairs after him.

"And that ugly beastie!" said MacTavish. "I'll feed him no more, you hear? Account or no account, I'll not have him gobbling my good meat down his ugly gullet!"

Doan dragged Carstairs across the sidewalk and pushed him up the stairs and into the dining car. MacTavish came in after them, went behind the counter and slammed the flap down emphatically.

Doan sat down on a stool and said cheerfully: "Good morning, MacTavish, my friend. It's a fine bonny morning full of the smell of heather and mountain dew, isn't it? Fix up a pound of round for Carstairs, and be sure it's none of that watery gruel you feed your unsuspecting customers. Carstairs is particular, and he has a delicate stomach. I'll take ham and eggs and toast and coffee—a double order."

MacTavish leaned on the counter. "And what'll you pay for it with, may I ask?"

"Well, it's true that I find myself temporarily short on ready cash, but I have a fine Swiss watch—"

"No, you haven't," said MacTavish, "because I've got it in the cash register right now."

"Good," said Doan. "That watch is worth at least fifty—"

"You lie in your teeth," said MacTavish. "You paid five dollars for it in a pawn shop. I'll have no more to do with such a loafer and a no-good. I've no doubt that if you had your just deserts you'd be in prison this moment. I'll feed you this morning, but this is the last time. The very last time, you hear?"

"I'm desolated," said Doan. "Hurry up with the ham and eggs, will you, MacTavish? And don't forget Carstairs' ground round."

MacTavish went to the gas range, grumbling under his breath balefully, and meat made a pleasantly sizzling spatter. Carstairs put his head over the counter and drooled in eager anticipation.

"MacTavish," said Doan, raising his voice to speak over the sizzle of the meat, "am I correct in assuming I visited your establishment last night?"

"You are."

"Was I—ah—slightly intoxicated?"

"You were blind, stinking, pig-drunk."

"You have such a pleasant way of putting things," Doan observed. "I was alone, no doubt, bearing up bravely in solitary sadness?"

"You were not. You had one of your drunken, bawdy, criminal companions with you."

MacTavish set a platter of meat on the counter, and Doan put it on top of one of the stools so that Carstairs could get at it more handily. Carstairs gobbled politely, making little grunting sounds of appreciation.

Doan said casually: "This—ah—friend I had with me. Did you know him?"

"I never saw him before, and if my luck lasts I'll never see him again. I liked his looks even less than I do yours."

"You're in rare form this morning, MacTavish. Did you hear me mention my friend's name?"

"It was Smith," said MacTavish, coming up with a platter of ham and eggs and a cup of coffee.

"Smith," said Doan, chewing reflectively. "Well, it's a nice name. Don't happen to know where I picked him up, do you?"

"I know where you said you picked him up. You said he was a stray soul lost in the wilderness of this great metropolis and that you had rescued him. You said you'd found him in front of your apartment building wasting away in the last stages of starvation, so I knew you were blind drunk, because the man had a belly like a balloon."

"In front of my apartment," Doan repeated thoughtfully. "This is all news to me. Could you give me a short and colorful description of this gentleman by the name of Smith?"

"He was tall and pot-bellied, and he had black eyebrows that looked like caterpillars and a mustache the rats had been nesting in, and he wore dark glasses and kept his hat on and his overcoat collar turned up. I mind particularly the mustache, because you kept asking him if you could tweak it."

"Ah," said Doan quietly. He knew now where he had gotten the instinctive warning about the metal case. Drunk as Doan had been, he had retained enough powers of observation to realize that the mysterious Smith's mustache had been false—that the man was disguised.

Doan nodded to himself. That disposed of some of the mystery of the metal case, but there still remained the puzzle of Smith's identity and what his grudge against Doan was.

CHAPTER III
THE TEMPESTUOUS TOGGERY

AT THAT MOMENT the front door slammed violently open, and J. S. Toggery came in with his head down and his arms swinging belligerently. He was short and stocky and bandy-legged. He had an apoplectically red face and fiercely glistening false teeth.

"A fine thing," he said savagely. "A fine thing, I say! Doan, you bum! Where have you been for the last three days?"

Doan pushed his empty coffee cup toward MacTavish. "Another cup, my friend. I wish you'd tell the more ill-bred of your customers to keep their voices down. It disturbs my digestion. How are you, Mr. Toggery? I have a serious question to ask you."

"What?" Toggery asked suspiciously.

"Do you know a man whose name isn't Smith and who doesn't wear dark glasses and doesn't have black eyebrows or a black mustache or a pot-belly and who isn't a friend of mine?"

Toggery sat down weakly on one of the stools. "Doan, now be reasonable. Haven't you any regard for my health and well-being? Do you want to turn me into a nervous wreck? I have a very important job for you, and I've been hunting you high and low for three days, and when I find you I'm greeted with insolence, evasion and double-talk. Do you know how to ski?"

"Pardon me," said Doan. "I thought you asked me if I knew how to ski."

"I did. Can you use skis or snow-shoes or ice skates?"

"No," said Doan.

"Then you have a half-hour to learn. Here's your railroad ticket. Your train leaves from the Union Station at two-thirty. Get your heavy underwear and your woolen socks and be on it."

"Why?" Doan asked.

"Because I told you to, you fool!" Toggery roared. "And I'm the man who's crazy enough to be paying you a salary! Now, will you listen to me without interposing those crack-pot comments of yours?"

"I'll try," Doan promised.

Toggery drew a deep breath. "All right. A girl by the name of Shiela Alden is spending the first of the mountain winter season at a place in the Desolation Lake country. You're going up there to see that nothing happens to her for the next three or four weeks."

"Why?" Doan said.

"Because she hired the agency to do it! Or rather, the bank that is her guardian did. Now listen carefully. Shiela Alden's mother died when she was born. Her father died five years ago, and he left a trust fund for her that amounts to almost fifty million dollars. She turns twenty-one in two days, and she gets the whole works when she does.

"There's been a lot of comment in the papers about a young girl getting handed all that money, and she's gotten a lot of threats from crack-pots of all varieties. That Desolation Lake country is as deserted as a tomb this time of year. The season don't start up there for another month. The bank wants her to have some

protection until the publicity incident to her receiving that enormous amount of money dies down."

Doan nodded. "Fair enough. Where did her old man get all this
dough to leave her?"

"He invented things."

"What kind of things?"

"Powder and explosives."

"Oh," said Doan, thinking of the deep yellow gouge the metal
case had left in the hillside. "What kind of explosives?"

"All kinds. He specialized in the highly concentrated variety like
they use in hand grenades and bombs. That's why the trust he left
increased so rapidly. It's all in munitions stock of one kind and
another."

"*Ummm,*" said Doan. "Did you tell anyone you were planning on
sending me up to look after her?"

"Of course. Everybody I could find who would listen to me.
Have you forgotten that I've been looking high and low for you
for three days, you numb-wit?"

"I see," said Doan vaguely. "What's the girl doing up there in
the mountains?"

"She's a shy kid, and she's been bedeviled persistently by cranks
and fortune hunters and every other kind of chiseler." J. S. Toggery
sighed and looked dreamily sentimental. "It's a shame when you
think of it. That poor lonely kid—she hasn't a relative in the world—
all alone up there in that damned barren mountain country. Hurt
and bewildered because of the unthinking attitude of the public.
No one to love her and protect her and sympathize with her. If I
weren't so busy I'd go up there with you. She needs someone
older—some steadying influence."

"And fifty million dollars ain't hay," said Doan.

J. S. Toggery nodded, still dreamy. "No, and if I could just get
hold of—" He snapped out of it. "Damn you, Doan, must you
reduce every higher human emotion to a basis of crass
commercialism?"

"Yes, as long as I work for you."

"Huh! Well, anyway she's hiding up there to get away from it all.
Her companion-secretary is with her. They're staying at a lodge
her old man owned. Brill, the attorney who handles the income

from the trust, is staying with them until you get there. There's a caretaker at the lodge too."

"I see," said Doan, nodding. "It sounds interesting. It's too bad I can't go."

Toggery said numbly: "Too bad you . . . What! *What!* Are you crazy? Why can't you go?"

Doan pointed to the floor. "Carstairs. He disapproves of mountains."

Toggery choked. "You mean that damned dog—"

Doan snapped his fingers. "I've got it. I'll leave him in your care."

"That splay-footed monstrosity! I—I'll—"

Doan reached down and tapped Carstairs on the top of his head. "Carstairs, my friend. Pay attention. You are going to visit Mr. Toggery for a few days. Treat him with consideration because he means well."

Carstairs blinked balefully at Toggery, and Toggery shivered.

"And now," said Doan cheerfully. "The money."

"Money!" Toggery shouted. "What did you do with the hundred I advanced you on your next month's salary?"

"I don't remember exactly, but another hundred will do nicely."

Toggery moaned. He counted out bills on the counter with trembling hands. Doan wadded them up and thrust them carelessly into his coat pocket.

"Aren't you forgetting something, Mr. Doan?" MacTavish asked.

"Oh, yes," said Doan. "Toggery, pay MacTavish what I owe him on account. Cheerio, all. Goodbye, Carstairs. I'll give you a ring soon." He went out the door whistling.

Toggery collapsed limply against the counter, shaking his head. "I think I'm going mad now," he said. "My brain is simmering like a teakettle."

"He gets me that way too," said MacTavish. "Why do you put up with him?"

"Hah!" said Toggery. "Listen! If he wasn't the best—the very best—private detective west of the Mississippi, and if this branch of the agency didn't depend entirely on him for its good record, I would personally murder him!"

"I doubt if you could," said MacTavish.

"I know it," Toggery admitted glumly. "He could take on you and me together with Carstairs thrown in and massacre all three of us without mussing his hair. He's the most dangerous little devil I've ever seen, and he's all the worse because of that half-witted manner of his. You never suspect what he's up to until it's too late."

CHAPTER IV
WELCOME TO DESOLATION

DOAN ROLLED HIS head back and forth on the hard plush cushion, opened his eyes and blinked politely. "You were saying something?"

The conductor's face was red with exertion. "Yes, I was sayin' something! I been sayin' something for the last ten minutes steady! I thought you was in a trance! This here is where you get off!"

Doan yawned and straightened up. He had a crick in his neck, and he winced, poking his finger at the spot.

The roadbed was rough here, and the old-fashioned tubular brass lamps that hung from the arched car top jittered in short nervous arcs. The *whaff-whaff-whaff* of the engine exhaust sounded laboriously from ahead. The car was thick and murky with the smell of cinders. Aside from the conductor, Doan was the only occupant.

Doan asked: "Do you stop while I get off, or am I supposed to hop off like a hobo?"

"We'll stop," said the condutor.

He might have been in telepathic communication with the engineer, because that's just what they did right then. The engine brakes screeched, and the car hopped up against the bumpers and dropped back again with a breath-taking jar, groaning in every joint.

"Is he mad at somebody?" Doan asked, referring to the engineer.

"Listen, you," said the conductor indignantly. "This here grade is so steep that a fly couldn't walk up it without his feet were dipped in molasses first."

Doan took a look at the empty seats. "You didn't make this trip especially on my account, did you?"

"No!" The conductor was even more indignant at the injustice of it. "We got to run a train from Palos Junction through here and back every twenty-four hours in the off season to keep our franchise. Otherwise you'd have walked up. Come on! We ain't got all night to sit around here."

Doan hauled his grip from the rack, pausing to peer out the steamed window. "Is it still raining?"

The conductor snorted. "Raining! It's rainin' down on the coast maybe, but not here. You're eight thousand feet up in the Rocky Mountains, son, and it's snowin' like somebody dumped it out of a chute."

Doan was no outdoorsman, and he hadn't taken what J. S. Toggery had said about skis and snow-shoes at all seriously.

"Snowing?" he said incredulously. "Why, it's still summer!"

"Not up here," said the conductor. "She'll make three feet on the level, and it's driftin'. Get goin'."

Still incredulous, Doan hauled his bag down the aisle and through the end door of the car. This was the last car, the only passenger coach, and when he stepped out on the darkness of the platform the snow and the wind slapped across his face like a giant icy hand. Doan sputtered indignantly and went staggering off balance down the iron steps and plumped into powdery wet coldness that congealed above the level of his thighs.

The engine whistle gave a triumphant, echoing scream.

The conductor was a dim, huddled form with one gaunt arm stretched out like a semaphore. His voice drifted thinly with the wind.

"That way! Through snow-sheds . . . along spur . . ."

The engine screamed again, impatiently, and bucked the train ahead.

Doan had dropped his bag, and he scrambled around in the snow trying to find it. "Wait! Wait! I've changed my mind."

The red and green lights on the back of the car blinked mockingly at him, and the conductor's howl came blurred and faint through the white swirling darkness.

"Station . . . quarter-mile . . . snow-sheds . . ."

The engine wailed like a banshee, and the snow and the darkness swallowed the sound of it up in one gulp.

"Well, hell," said Doan.

He spat snow out of his mouth and wiped the cold wetness of it off his face. He located his bag and hauled it out into the middle of the tracks. He had a topcoat strapped on the side of the grip, and he unfastened it now and struggled into it. He was thinking darkly bitter thoughts about J. S. Toggery.

With the collar pulled up tight around his throat and his hat pulled down as far it would go over his ears, he stood huddled in the middle of the tracks and looked slowly and unbelievingly around him. He had a range of vision of about ten feet in any given direction; beyond that there was nothing but snow and blackness. There was no sign of any other human, and, aside from the railroad tracks, no sign that there ever had been one here.

"Hey!" Doan shouted.

His voice traveled away and came back after a while in a low, thoughtful echo.

"This is very nice, Doan," said Doan. "You're a detective. Make a brilliant deduction."

He couldn't think of an appropriate one, so he shrugged his shoulders casually, picked up his bag and started walking along the track in the direction the conductor had pointed. The wind slapped and tugged at him angrily, hauling him first one way and then the other, and the frozen gravel of the roadbed ground under his shoes.

He kept his head down and continued walking until he tripped over a switch rail. He looked up and stared into what seemed to be the mouth of an immense square cave. He headed for it, kicking through the drifts in front, and then suddenly he was inside and out of the reach of the wind and the persistent, swirling snow.

It began to make sense now. This high square cave was a wooden snow-shed built to keep the drifts off the spur track on which he was standing. If the rest of the conductor's shouted information could be relied on, the station was a quarter mile further along the spur track.

Doan nodded once to himself, satisfied, took a new grip on the handles of his bag and started trudging along the track. It had been dark outside, but the darkness inside the shed was black swimming ink with no slightest glimmer to relieve it. It was a darkness that enclosed Doan like an envelope and seemed to travel along ahead of him, piling up thicker and thicker with each step he took.

He lost his sense of direction, tripped over the rails and banged against the side of the shed, starting up echoes that clattered deafeningly.

Swearing to himself in a whisper, Doan put his bag down on the ground and fumbled around in his pockets until he found a match. He snapped it alight on his thumbnail and held it up in front of him, cupping his hands protectively around the wavering yellow of the flame.

There was a man standing not a yard away from him—standing stiff and rigid against the rough boards of the shed wall, one arm out-thrust awkwardly as though he were mutely offering to shake hands. His eyes reflected the match flame glassily.

"Uh!" said Doan, startled.

The man didn't say anything, didn't move. He was a short, thick man, and his face looked roughened and bluish in the dim light.

"Well . . . hello," Doan said uncertainly. He felt a queer chill horror.

The man stayed there, unmoving, his right hand outthrust. Very slowly Doan reached out and touched the hand. It was ice-cold, and the fingers were as rigid as steel hooks.

Doan went backward one stumbling step and then another while the shadows jiggled weirdly around him. Then the match burned his fingers and he dropped it, and the darkness slapped down like a giant soft hand. It was then that he heard a noise behind him—a stealthy skitter in the gravel, faint through the swish of the snow against the shed walls.

Doan turned his head a little at a time until he could see over his shoulder. He stood there rigid while the darkness seemed to pulsate with the beat of his heart.

There were eyes watching him. Luminous and yellow and close to the ground, slanted obliquely at their corners. There were three pairs of them.

Doan stood there until the breath ached in his throat. The paired eyes didn't move. Doan exhaled very slowly and softly. He slid his hand inside the bulk of his topcoat, under his suit coat, and closed his fingers on the butt of the Police Positive.

Just as slowly he drew the revolver from under his coat. The hammer made a small cold click. Doan fired straight up in the air.

The report raised a deafening thunder of echoes. The eyes blinked and were gone, and a voice bellowed hollowly at Doan out of the blackness:

"Don't you shoot them dogs! Damn you, don't you shoot them dogs!"

The voice came from somewhere in back of where the yellow eyes had been. Doan dropped on one knee, leveling the revolver in that direction.

"Show a light," he ordered. "Right now."

Light splayed out from an electric lantern and revealed long legs in baggy blue denim pants and high snow-smeared boots with bulging rawhide laces. The yellow eyes were back of the legs, just out of the throw of light from the latern, staring in savage watchfulness.

"Higher," said Doan. "Higher with the lantern."

The light went up by jerks like a sticky curtain on a stage, showing in turn a clumsy-looking sheepskin coat, a red hatchet-like face with fiercely glaring eyes, and a stained duck-hunter's cap with the ear flaps pulled down. The man stood as tall and stiff as some weird statue with his shadow stretched jagged and menacing beside him.

"I'm the station master. This here's company property. What you doin' on it?"

"Trying to get off it," said Doan.

"Where'd you come from?"

"The train, stupid. You think I'm a parachute trooper?"

"Oh," said the tall man. "Oh. Was you a passenger?"

"Well, certainly."

"Oh. I thought you were a bum or something. Nobody ever comes up here this time of year."

"I'll remember that. Come closer with the light. Keep the dogs back."

The tall man came slowly closer. Doan saw now that he had only one arm—the left—the one that was holding the lantern. His right sleeve was empty.

"Who's our friend here?" Doan asked, indicating the stiff frozen figure against the wall.

The tall man said casually: "Him? Oh, that's Boley, the regular station master. I'm his relief."

"He looks a little on the dead side to me."

The tall man had a lean gash of a mouth, and the thin lips moved now to show jagged yellow teeth. "Dead as a smoked herring."

"What happened to him?"

"Got drunk and lay out in the snow all night and froze stiff as a board."

"Planning on just leaving him here permanently?"

"I can't move him alone, mister." The tall man indicated his empty right sleeve with a jerk of his head. "I told 'em to stop and pick him up tonight, but they musta forgot to do it. I'll call 'em again. It ain't gonna hurt him to stay here. He won't spoil in this weather."

"That's a comforting thought."

"Dead ones don't hurt nobody, mister. I've piled 'em on trench parapets and shot over 'em. They're as good as sandbags for stoppin' bullets."

"That's a nice thought too. Where's this station you're master of?"

"Right ahead a piece."

"Start heading for it. Keep the dogs away. I don't like the way they look at me."

The light lowered. The tall man sidled past Doan, and his thin legs moved shadowy and stick-like in the lantern gleam, going away.

Doan followed cautiously, carrying the grip in one hand and the cocked revolver in the other. He looked back every third step, but the yellow eyes were gone now.

The shed ended abruptly, and the station was around the curve from it, a yellow box-like structure squashed in against the bare rock of the canyon face with light coming very dimly through small, snow-smeared windows.

The tall man opened the door, and Doan followed him into a small square room lighted with one unshaded bulb hanging behind the shining grillwork of the oval ticket window. Yellow varnished benches ran along two walls, and a stove gleamed dully red in the corner between them.

Doan kicked the door shut behind him and dropped his grip on the floor. He still held his revolver casually in his right hand.

"What's your name?" he asked.

"Jannen," said the tall man. He had taken off his duck-hunter's cap. He was bald, and his head was long and queerly narrow. He stood still, watching Doan, his eyes gleaming with slyly malevolent humor. "You come up here for somethin' special? There ain't no place to stay. There's a couple of hotels down-canyon, but they ain't open except for the snow sports."

Doan jerked his head to indicate the storm outside. "Isn't that snow?"

"This here is just an early storm. It'll melt off mostly on the flats. In the winter season she gets eight-ten feet deep here on the level, and they bring excursion trains up—sometimes four-five hundred people to once—and park 'em on the sidings over weekends."

There was a whine and then a scratching sound on the door behind Doan.

The tall man jerked his head. "Can I let my dogs inside, mister?"

Doan moved over and sat down on the bench. "Go ahead."

Jannen opened the door, and three shadowy gray forms slunk through it. They were enormous beasts, thick-furred, with blunt wedge-shaped heads. They circled the room and sat down in a silent motionless row against the far wall, watching Doan unblinkingly with eyes that were like yellow, cruel jewels.

"Nice friendly pets," Doan observed.

"Them's sled dogs, mister."

"What dogs?" Doan asked.

"Sled dogs—huskies. See, sometimes them tourists that come up here, they get tired of skiin' and snow-shoein' and then I pick me up a little side money haulin' 'em around on a dog sled with the dogs. Lot of 'em ain't never rid behind dogs before, and they get a big kick out of it. Them are good dogs, mister."

"You can have them. Do you know where the Alden lodge is from here?"

Jannen's lips moved back from the jagged teeth. "You a friend of that girl's?" His voice was low and tight.

"Not yet. Are you?"

Jannen's eyes were gleaming, reddish slits. "Oh, yeah. Oh, sure I am. I got a good reason to be." With his left hand he reached over and tapped his empty right sleeve. "That's a present from her old man."

Doan was watching him speculatively. "So? How did it happen?"

"Grenade. I was fightin' over in China. It blew up in my hand. Tore my arm off. Old man Alden's factory sold the Chinks that grenade. It had a defective fuse."

"That's not the girl's fault."

Jannen's lips curled. "Oh, sure not. Nobody's fault. An accident. Didn't amount to nothin'—just a man's right arm tore off, that's all. Just made me a cripple and stuck me up in this hell-hole at this lousy job. Yeah. I love that Alden girl. Every time I hear that name I laugh fit to bust with joy."

His voice cracked, and his face twisted into a fiendish grimace. The dogs stirred against the wall uneasily, and one of them whimpered a little.

"Yeah," Jannen said hoarsely. "Sure. I like her. Her old man skimped on that grenade job, and skimped on it so he could leave that girl another million. You'd like her too, mister, if an Alden grenade blew your right arm off, wouldn't you? You'd like her every time you fumbled around one-handed like a crippled bug, wouldn't you?

"You'd like her every time the pain started to bite in that arm stump so you couldn't sleep at night, wouldn't you? You'd feel real kind toward her while you was sleepin' in flop houses and she was spendin' the blood money her old man left her, wouldn't you, mister?"

The man was not sane. He stood there swaying, and then he laughed a little in a choking rasp that shook his thin body.

"You want me to show you the way to the lodge? Sure, mister. Glad to. Glad to do a favor for an Alden any old time."

Doan stood up. "Let's start," he said soberly.

CHAPTER V
MISS MILLION-BUCKS

DOAN SMELLED THE smoke first, coming thin and pungent down-wind, and then Jannen stopped short in front of him and said:

"There it is."

The wind whipped the snow away for a second, and Doan saw the house at the mouth of a ravine that widened out into a flat below them. The walls were black against the white drifts, and the windows stared with dull yellow eyes.

"Thanks," said Doan. "I can make it from here. If I could offer some slight compensation for your time and trouble . . ."

Jannen was hunched up against the wind like some gaunt beast of prey, staring down at the house, wrapped up in darkly bitter thoughts of his own. His voice came thickly.

"I don't want none of your money."

"So long," said Doan.

"Eh?" said Jannen, looking around.

Doan pointed back the way they had come. "Goodbye, now."

Jannen turned clumsily. "Oh, I'm goin'. But I ain't forgettin' nothin', mister." His mittened left hand touched his empty right sleeve. "Nothin' at all. You tell her that for me."

"I'll try to remember," said Doan.

He stood with his head tilted against the wind, watching Jannen until he disappeared back along the trail, his three huskies slinking along like stunted shadows at his heels. Then he shrugged uneasily and went down the steep slant of the ridge to the flat below. The wind had blown the snow clear of the ground in places, and he followed the faint marks of a path across the stretch of frozen rocky ground.

Close to it, the house looked larger—dark and ugly with the smoke from the chimney drifting in a jaunty plume across the white-plastered roof. The path ended at a small half-enclosed porch, and Doan climbed the log steps up to it and banged hard with his fist against the heavy door.

He waited, shivering. The cold had gotten through his light

clothes. His feet tingled numbly, and the skin on his face felt drawn and stiff.

The door swung open, and a man stared out at him unbelievingly. "What—who're you? Where'd you come from?"

"Doan—Severn Agency."

"The detective! But man alive! Come in, come in!"

Doan stepped into a narrow shadowed hall, and the warmth swept over him like a soft grateful wave.

"Good Lord!" said the other man. "I didn't expect you'd come tonight—in this storm!"

"That's Severn service," Doan told him. "When duty calls, we answer. And besides, I'm overdrawn on my salary."

"But you're not dressed for—Why, you must be frozen stiff!"

He was a tall man, very thin, with a sharp dramatically haggard face. His hair was jet-black with a peculiarly distinctive swathe of pure white running back slantwise from his high forehead. He talked in nervous spurts, and he had a way of making quick little half-gestures that had no meaning, as though he were impatiently jittery.

"A trifle rigid in spots," Doan admitted. "Have you got some concentrated heat around the premises?"

"Yes! Yes, surely! Come in here! My name is Brill, by the way. I'm in charge of Miss Alden's account with the National Trust. Taking care of the legal end. But of course you know all about that. In here."

It was a long living room with a high ceiling that matched the peak of the roof. At the far end there was an immense natural stone fireplace with the flame hooking eager little blue fingers around the log that almost filled it.

"But you should have telephoned from the station," Brill was saying. "No need to come out tonight in this."

"Have you a telephone here?" Doan asked.

"Certainly, certainly. Telephone, electricity, central heating, all that. . . . Miss Alden, this is Mr. Doan, the detective from the Severn Agency. You know, I told you—"

"Yes, of course," said Shiela Alden. She was sitting on the long, low divan in front of the fire. She was a small, thin girl with prim features, and she looked disapprovingly at Doan and then down at the snow he had tracked across the floor. She had lusterless stringly brown hair and teeth that protruded a little bit, and she wore thick horn-rimmed glasses.

"Hello," said Doan. He didn't think he was going to like her very well.

"This seems all very melodramatic and very unnecessary," said Shiela Alden. "A detective to guard me! It's so absurd."

"Now, not at all, not at all," said Brill in a harassed tone. "It's the thing to do—the only thing. I'm responsible, you know. The National people hold me directly responsible for your well-being. We must take every reasonable precaution. We really must. I'm doing the best I know how."

"I know," said Shiela Alden, faintly contemptuous. "Pull up that chair, Mr. Doan, and get close to the fire. By the way, this is Mr. Crowley."

"Hello, there," said Crowley cheerfully. "You're hardly dressed for the weather, old chap. If you plan to stay around here I'll have to lend you some of my togs."

"Mr. Crowley," said Brill, "has a place over at the other side of Flint Flat."

"A little hide-out, you know," said Crowley. "Just a little shack where a man can hole in and soak up some solitude now and then."

He had a very British-British accent and a hairline black mustache and a smile full of white teeth. He was every bit as handsome as those incredible young men who are always driving the latest sport motor cars in magazine advertisements. He knew it. He had brown eyes with a personality twinkle in them and wavy black hair and an expensive tan.

"Mr. Crowley," said Brill, "got lost in the storm this afternoon and just happened—just happened to stumble in here this afternoon."

"Right-o," said Crowley. "Lucky for me, eh?"

"Very," said Brill sourly.

Crowley was sitting on the divan beside Shiela Alden, and he turned around and gave her the full benefit of his smile. "Yes, indeed! My lucky day!"

Shiela Alden simpered. There was no other word for it. She wiggled on the cushions and poked at her stringy hair and blinked shyly at Crowley through the thick glasses.

"You must stay the night here, Mr. Crowley."

"Must he?" Brill inquired, still more sourly.

Shiela Alden looked up, instantly antagonistic. "Of course! He can't possibly get home tonight, and we have plenty of room, and I've invited him!"

"A little blow like this," said Crowley. "Nothing. Nothing at all. You should see it scream up in the Himalayas. That's something!" He leaned closer to Shiela. "But of course there's no chance to stumble on to such delightful company when you're in the Himalayas, is there? I'll be delighted to stay overnight, Miss Alden, if it won't inconvenience you too much. It's so kind of you to ask me."

"Not at all," said Shiela Alden.

Doan was standing in front of the fire with his arms out-spread, gradually thawing out, and now someone tugged uncertainly at his sleeve.

"You're—the detective?"

Doan turned to look at another girl. She was small too, smaller even than Shiela Alden, and she had a soft round face and full lips that pouted a little. She had blond hair, and her eyes were very wide and very blue and they didn't quite focus.

"This is Miss Alden's secretary," Brill said stiffly. "Miss Joan Greg."

"You're cute," Joan Greg said, swaying just slightly. "You're a cute little detective."

"Cute as a bug's ear," Doan agreed.

"Joan!" Shiela Alden said sharply. "Please behave yourself!"

Joan Greg turned slowly, still keeping her hold on Doan's arm. "Talking—to me?"

"You're drunk!" Shiela Alden said.

Joan Greg made the words carefully with her soft lips. "Shall I tell you just what you are—you and that thing sitting beside you?"

The tension in the room was like a wire stretched to a breaking point, with them all standing and staring at Joan incredulously. She was swaying, and her lips were twisting to form new words, while her eyes stared at Shiela Alden with glassy, unblinking hate.

"I'll—kill—her," said Joan Greg distinctly.

CHAPTER VI
DANGEROUS LADY

"MISS GREG!" BRILL gasped, horrified. But he did not make a move. He just stood, gaping.

"Wait until I get warm first, will you?" Doan asked casually.

Joan Greg forgot all about Shiela Alden for the moment. She swayed against Doan and said: "You're just the cutest little fella I've ever seen. Lemme help you out of your coat."

Brill stepped forward. "I'll do—"

"No! No! Lemme!"

Fumblingly, she helped Doan take off his topcoat and staggered back several steps holding it in front of her.

"Gonna—hang it up. Gonna hang the nice cute little detective's coat up for him."

She went at a diagonal across the room, missed the door by ten feet, carefully walked backward until she got a new line on it, and made it through. They could hear her in the hall, stumbling a little.

"I could use some of that," Doan said.

Brill stared at him. "Eh?"

Doan made a motion as though he were lifting a glass.

"Oh!" Brill said. "A drink! Yes, yes. Of course. Kokomo! Kokomo!"

A swinging door squeaked, and light showed through the archway opposite the entrance to the hall. Feet scraped lumberingly on the floor, and a man came in through the archway and said in a surly voice:

"Well, what?"

He had shoulders as wide as a door and long thick arms that were corded with muscle. He was wearing a white apron over blue denim trousers and a checked shirt, and he had a tall chef's hat perched jauntily over the bulging shapeless lump that had once been his left ear. He carried a toothpick in one corner of his pulpy lips, and his eyes were dully expressionless under thick, scarred eyebrows.

"Ah, yes," Brill said nervously. "Bring the whisky, Kokomo, and—and a siphon of soda."

"You want ice?"

"I've had mine tonight already," Doan said.

"No," Brill said. "No ice."

Kokomo lumbered back through the archway and appeared immediately again carrying a decanter and a siphon on a tray with a stacked pile of glasses.

Brill took the tray. "Mr. Doan, this is Kokomo—the cook and .caretaker. This is the detective, Kokomo."

"This little squirt?" said Kokomo. "A detective? Hah!"

Brill said: "Kokomo! That's all!"

"Hah!" said Kokomo, staring down at Doan. He moved his big shoulders in a casual shrug and padded back through the archway. The swinging door squeaked shut behind him.

"Really, Mr. Brill," Shiela Alden said severely. "It seems to me that I have grounds for complaint about your choice of employees."

Brill threw his hands wide helplessly. "Miss Alden, I've told you again and again that our Mr. Dibben had been handling all your affairs and that he was injured when an auto ran over him and that his duties were suddenly delegated to me without the slightest warning and that he hadn't made any note of the fact that you intended to come up here.

"When you called me I had to find a man at once who would act as caretaker and cook and open this place up for you. This man Kokomo had excellent references—a great deal of experience—all that. You must admit, Miss Alden, that in spite of his uncouth appearance, he is a very good cook, and it's very difficult to get servants to come clear up here . . ."

Shiela Alden wasn't through. "And I don't think much of your choice of a secretary, either."

Brill lifted his hands. "Miss Greg had the very finest references. There was nothing in them whatsoever that indicated she was—ah—inclined to drink too much."

"Lonely country," Crowley said. "Brings it on. Seen it happen to a lot of chaps in Upper Burma. Probably be all right as soon as she gets back to civilization, eh? By the way, Mr. Doan, how on earth did you find this place? I mean, I got jolly well lost myself, and I can't see how a stranger could find his way here."

Doan had filled a glass half with whisky and half with soda and was sipping at it appreciatively. "The station master brought me around—not because he wanted to. He seemed a bit sour on the Alden name."

"And that's another thing!" Brill said worriedly. "The man's a crank—dangerous. He shouldn't be allowed at large. He holds some insane grudge against Miss Alden, and he might—might . . . I mean, I'm responsible. I tried to talk to him, but all he did was threaten me. And those damned dogs. Mr. Doan, you had better investigate him thoroughly."

"Oh, sure," said Doan.

Brill ran thin nervous fingers through his hair, mussing up the blazed streak of white that centered it. "I don't like you coming up here in this wilderness, Miss Alden. It's a great responsibility to put on my shoulders." He fumbled in his coat pocket and brought out a shiny metal case.

Doan stiffened, his glass half-raised to his lips. "What's that you've got there?"

"This?" said Brill. "A cigar case."

The case was an exact duplicate of the one Doan had found in his pocket—his deadly present from the mysterious Mr. Smith.

Brill snapped the catch with his thumb, and the case opened on his palm, revealing the six cigars fitted into it snugly.

Doan released his breath in a long sigh. "Where," he said, clearing his throat. "Where did you get it?"

Brill was admiring the case. "Nice, isn't it? Just the right size. Eh? Oh, it was a present from a client."

"What was his name?"

"Smith," said Brill. "As a matter of fact, that's a strange thing. We have several clients whose name is Smith, and I don't know which one of them gave me this. Whoever it was just left it on my secretary's desk with a little note saying in appreciation of services rendered and all that and signed, *Smith*."

"What was in it?" Doan asked.

Brill looked surprise. "Why, cigars."

"Did you smoke them?"

"Well, no. You see, I smoke a specially mild brand on account of my throat. I gave the ones in the case to the janitor, poor chap."

"Poor chap?" Doan repeated.

"Yes. He was killed that very night. He had a shack on the outskirts of the city, and he was running a still of some sort there—at least that's what the police think—and the thing blew up and blasted him to bits. Terrific explosion."

"Oh," said Doan. He watched thoughtfully while Brill selected a cigar and put the case back in his coat pocket.

"Well," said Brill, making an effort to be more sociable. "Let's think of something pleasant . . ." His voice trailed off into a startled gulp.

Joan Greg had come quietly in from the hall. She was holding Doan's revolver carefully in her right hand. She was walking straighter now, and she came directly across the floor to the front of the divan. She stopped there and pointed the revolver at Shiela Alden.

"Here!" Crowley shouted in alarm.

Doan flipped the contents of his glass into Joan Greg's face. Her head jerked back when the stinging liquid hit her. She took one uncertain step backward, and then Doan vaulted over the couch and expertly kicked her feet from under her.

She fell on her back, coming down so hard that her blond head bounced forward loosely with the impact. Doan stepped on her right wrist and twisted the revolver from her lax fingers.

Joan Greg turned over on her stomach and hid her face in her arms. She began to cry in racked, gasping sobs. The others stared at her, and at Doan with a sort of frozen, dazed horror.

"More fun," said Doan, slipping the revolver into his waistband. "Does she do things like this very often?"

"Gah!" Brill gasped. "She—she would have . . . Why—why, she's crazy! Crazy drunk! Where—where'd she get that gun?"

"It was in my topcoat pocket," Doan said. "Careless of me, but I didn't think there were any homicidal maniacs wandering around the house."

Shiela Alden's face was paper white. "Get her out of here! She's fired! Take her away!"

"Yes, yes," said Brill. "At once. Terrible. Terrible thing, really. And I'll be blamed—"

"Take her away!" Shield Alden screamed at him.

Doan leaned over and picked Joan Greg up. She had stopped

crying and she was utterly relaxed. Her arms flopped laxly. Her eyes were closed, and the tears had made wet jagged streaks down her soft cheeks.

"She's passed out, I think," Doan said. "I'll take her up and lock her in her bedroom."

"Yes, yes," Brill said. "Only thing. This way."

Crowley was bending anxiously over Shiela Alden. "Now, now. It's all over. Gives a person a nasty feeling, I know. Saw a chap run amok in Malay once. Ghastly thing. But you're a brave girl. Just a little sip of this."

Brill led the way across the living room and down the hall to a steep stairway with a rustic natural-wood railing. Brill went on up it and stopped at the first door in the upper hallway. He was still shaky, and he edged away from the limp form of Joan Greg as a man would avoid contact with something poisonous.

"Here," he said, pushing the door open and reaching around to snap on the light. "This—this is awful. Miss Alden is sure to complain to the office. What do you suppose ailed her?"

Doan put Joan Greg down on the narrow bed under the windows. The room was stiflingly hot. He looked at the windows and then down at Joan Greg's flushed face and decided against opening one. While he was looking down at her, she opened her eyes and stared up at him. All the life had drained out of her round face and left it empty and bitter and disillusioned.

"What's the trouble?" Doan asked. "Want to tell me about it?"

She turned her head slowly away from him and closed her eyes again. Doan waited a moment and then said:

"Better get undressed and into bed and sleep it off."

He turned off the light and went out of the room, transferring the key from the inside of the lock to the outside and turning it carefully. He tried the door to make sure and then put the key in his pocket.

Brill was wringing his hands in a distracted way. "I—I can hardly bear to face Miss Alden. She will blame me. *Everybody* blames me! I didn't want this responsibility. . . . I've got to go down and out-wait that scoundrel Crowley."

"Why?" Doan asked.

Brill came closer. "He's a fortune hunter! He didn't get lost today! He came over here on purpose because he's heard that Miss

Alden was here! She's an impressionable girl, and I can't let him stay alone with her down there. The office would hold me accountable if he—if she . . ."

"I get it," Doan said.

"I don't know what to do," said Brill. "I mean, I know Miss Alden will be sure to resent—But I can't let him—"

"That's your problem," said Doan. "But I'm not supposed to protect her from people who want to make love to her—only the ones that don't. So I'm not out-waiting our friend Cowley. I'm tired. Which is my bedroom?"

"Right there. You'll leave your door open, Mr. Doan, in case—in case . . ."

"In case," Doan agreed. "Just whistle, and I'll pop up like any jack-in-the box."

"I'm so worried," said Brill. "But I must go down and see that the scoundrel doesn't . . ."

He went trotting down the steep stairs. Doan went along the hall back to the bedroom Brill had indicated. It was small and as neatly arranged as a model room in a display window, furnished with imitation rustic bed, chairs and bureau.

It, too, was stiflingly hot. Doan spotted the radiator bulking in the corner. He went over and touched it experimentally and jerked his fingers away with a whispered curse. It was so hot the water in it was burbling. Doan looked for the valve to turn it off, but there was none.

He stood looking at the radiator for some time, frowning in a puzzled way. There was something wrong about the whole setup at the lodge. It was like a picture slightly out of focus, and yet he couldn't put his finger on any one thing that was wrong. It bothered Doan, and he didn't like to be bothered. But it was still there. An air of intangible menace.

He discovered now that he had left his grip downstairs. He didn't feel like going and getting it at the moment. He wanted to think about the people in the house, and he had always been able to think better lying down. He shrugged and headed for the bed. Fully dressed, he lay down on top of it and went to sleep.

CHAPTER VII
NICE NIGHT FOR MURDER

WHEN DOAN AWOKE, he awoke all at once. He was instantly alert, but he didn't make any other motion than opening his eyes. The heat in the bedroom was like a thick oppressive blanket—fantastic and unreal against the shuffling whine of the storm outside.

Doan stayed still and wondered what had awakened him. His bedroom door was still open, and there was a dim light in the hall. A timber creaked eerily somewhere in the house. The seconds ticked off slowly and leadenly, and then a shadow moved and made a rounded silhouette in the hall in front of the bedroom door.

Doan moved his hand and closed his fingers on the slick coolness of his revolver. The shadow thickened, swaying a little, and then Joan Greg came into sight. She was moving along the hall with mincing, elaborately cautious steps. She had evidently taken Doan's advice about going to bed. She was dressed in a green silk nightgown that contrasted with her blond hair. She stopped opposite Doan's doorway and looked that way.

Her soft lips were open, twisted awry, and there was a dribble of saliva on her chin. Her eyes were widened in mesmerized horror. She was holding a short broad-bladed hunting knife in her right hand.

"That's fine," said Doan quietly. "Just stand right where you are."

The knife made a ringing thud falling on the floor. Joan Greg drew a long shuddering breath that pulled the thin green silk taut across her breasts. The cords in her soft throat stood out rigidly.

Then she crumpled like a puppet that has been dropped. She was an awkwardly twisted heap of green silk and white flesh, with the gold of her hair glinting metallically in the light.

Doan swung cat-like off the bed and reached the doorway in two long steps. He didn't look down at Joan Greg, but both ways along the hall. One of the doors on the opposite side moved just a trifle.

"Come out of there," said Doan. "Quick!"

The door opened in hesitant jerks, and Crowley peered out at him. He was wearing nothing but a pair of blue shorts, and his wedge-shaped torso was oily with perspiration. His face was a queer yellowish green under its tan.

"So beastly hot. Couldn't get the windows open. I thought—I heard—"

"Come here."

Crowley moistened his lips with a nervous flick of his tongue. He came forward one step at a time. "What—what's the matter with her?"

"Stand right there and stand still."

Crowley's breath whistled between his teeth. "Blood! Look! All over her hands—"

Doan knelt down beside Joan Greg. Her hands were spread out awkwardly beside her, as though she had tried to hold them away from herself even while she fell. There was blood smeared on her fingers and streaked gruesomely across both her soft palms. Doan poked at the knife she had dropped with the barrel of his revolver.

There was blood clotted on them, too. On the handle and on the broad blade. Doan raised his head.

"Brill!" he called sharply.

Bed springs creaked somewhere, and Brill's nervous voice said: "Eh? What? What?"

The springs creaked again protestingly. Brill, looking tall and lath-like in white pajamas, appeared in the open door of the bedroom next to Doan's. His slick hair was rumpled now, and he held one hand up to shield his eyes from the light.

"What? What is it?" His thin face began to lengthen, then, as though it had been drawn in some enormous vise. "Oh, my God," he said in a whisper.

He came forward with the stiff, jerky steps of a sleep-walker. "Did she commit suicide?"

"I'm afraid not," said Doan. "She's fainted. Which is Miss Alden's room?"

Brill stared at him in pure frozen horror. "You don't think she—" He made a strangled noise in his throat. He turned and ran down the hall, his white pajamas flapping grotesquely. "Miss Alden! Miss Alden!"

The door at the end of the hall was hers, and Brill pounded on the panels with both fists. "Miss Alden!" His voice was raw with panic now, and he tried the knob. The door opened immediately.

"Miss—Miss Alden," Brill said uncertainly.

"The light," said Doan, behind him.

Brill reached inside the door and snapped the switch. There was no sound for a long time, and then Brill moaned a little.

Doan said: "Come here, Crowley. I want you where I can watch you."

Crowley spoke in a jerky voice. "Well, Joan—I mean, Miss Greg. You can't leave her lying—"

"Come here."

Crowley edged inside Shiela Alden's bedroom and backed against the wall in response to a guiding flick of Doan's revolver barrel. Brill was standing in the center of the room with his hands up over his face.

"This will ruin me," he said in a sick mumble. "I was going to get a partnership in the firm. They gave me full responsibility for watching out for her. Account was worth tens of thousands a year. They'll hound me out of the state—can never practice again." His voice trailed off into indistinguishable syllables.

This bedroom was as stiflingly hot as Doan's had been. Shiela Alden had only a sheet over her. She was stiffly rigid on her back in the bed. Her throat had been cut from ear to ear, and the pillows under her head were soaked and sticky with blood. Her bony face looked pinched and small and empty, with her near-sighted eyes staring glassily up at the light.

Doan pointed the gun at Crowley. "You talk."

Crowley made an effort to get back his air of British light-heartedness. "But, old chap, you can't imagine I—"

"Yes, I can," said Doan.

Crowley's mouth opened and shut soundlessly.

"It comes a little clearer," said Doan. "You were so scared you got a little rattled for a moment. Just how well do you know Joan Greg?"

Crowley's smile was an agonized grimace. "Well, my dear chap, hardly at all. I just met the young lady today."

"We can't use that one." Doan said. "You know her very well.

That was what was the trouble with her. She was jealous. You've been living off her, haven't you?"

"That's not a nice thing to accuse a chap—"

"Murder's not nice, either. You've been living off Joan Greg. You haven't any more got a place on Flint Flat than I have. Have you?"

"Well . . ."

"No, you haven't. Joan Greg told you that she had gotten a job as secretary to Shiela Alden and was coming up here. You knew who Shiela Alden was, and you thought that was a swell chance for you to chisel in and charm the young lady with your entrancing personality.

"You must have let Joan Greg in on it—told her you'd make a killing and split with her probably. But when it came right down to seeing you make passes at Shiela Alden, Joan Greg couldn't take it."

"Fantastic," Crowley said in a stiff unnatural voice. "Utter—rot."

"You!" said Brill, and the blood made a thick red flush in his shallow cheeks. "You rat! I'll see you hung! I'll—I'll—Doan! Hold him until I get my gun!" He blundered wildly out of the room, and his feet made a wild pattering rush down the hall.

Crowley had recovered his poise now. His eyes were cold and alert and hard, watching Doan. Brill's bedroom door slammed, and then his voice shrilled out fiercely.

"Get up! Get up, damn you! I know you're faking! I saw your eyes open!"

There was a scuffling sound from the hall, and Joan Greg cried out breathelessly. Crowley moved against the wall.

"No," said Doan.

Confused footsteps came closer, and Brill pushed Joan Greg roughly into the bedroom.

"There!" Brill raged. "Look at her! Look at your handiwork, damn you, you shameless little tramp!"

Joan Greg gave a stifled cry of terror. She held her shaking, blood-smeared hands out in front of her helplessly, and then she turned and ran to Crowley and hid her face against his chest.

"There they are!" Brill shouted. He was holding a .45 Colt automatic in his hand and he waved it wildly in the air. "Look at them!

A fine pair of crooks and murderers! But they'll pay! You hear me, do you? You'll pay!"

Doan was looking at the radiator in the corner. He was frowning a little bit and whistling softly and soundlessly to himself.

"Why is it so hot?" he asked.

"Eh?" Brill said. "What?"

"Why is it so hot in the bedrooms?"

"The windows have storm shutters on them," Brill said impatiently. "They can't be opened in a wind like this."

"But why are the radiators so hot? The water in that one is boiling. You can hear it."

"What damned nonsense!" Brill yelled. "Are you going to stand there and ask silly questions about radiators when Shiela Alden has been murdered and these two stand here caught in the very act—"

"No," said Doan. "I'm going to find out about the matter of the temperature around here. You watch these two."

"Doan, you fool!" Brill shouted. "Come back here! You're in my employ and I demand—"

"Watch them," said Doan. "I'll be back in a minute or so."

CHAPTER VIII
HI, KOKOMO

HE WENT DOWN the hall, down the steep stairs, and across the living room. The log fireplace was dull, glowing red embers now. The wind had blown some of the smoke back down the chimney, and it made a thick murky blue haze. Doan went on across the room through the archway on the other side.

Ahead of him light showed dimly around the edge of the swinging door that led into the kitchen. The hinges squeaked as Doan pushed it back.

Kokomo was sitting in the corner beside the gleaming white and chromium of an electric range. He was still wearing his big apron, and the tall chef's hat was tilted down rakishly over his left eye. He had what looked like the same toothpick in one corner of his mouth, and it moved up and down jerkily as he said:

"What can I do for you, sonny?"

"Don't you ever go to bed at night?" Doan asked.

"Naw. I'm an owl."

"It's awfully hot upstairs," said Doan.

"Too bad."

"I notice you have a central hot water heating system here. What does the furnace burn—coal or oil?"

"Coal."

"Who takes care of it?"

"Me."

"Where is it?"

Kokomo jerked a thick thumb at a door in the back wall of the kitchen. "Down cellar."

"I think I'll take a look at it."

Kokomo took the toothpick out of his mouth and snapped it into the far corner of the room. "Run along and roll your hoop, sonny, before I lose my patience and lay you out like a rug. This here end of the premises is my bailiwick and I don't go for any mush-faced snoopers prowlin' around in it. I told the rest that. Now I'm tellin' it to you."

"On the other hand," said Doan cheerfully, "I think I'll have a look at the furnace."

Kokomo got up out of his chair. "Sonny, you're gettin' me irritated. Put that popgun away before I shove it down you throat."

Doan dropped the gun in his coat pocket, smiling. "Aw, you wouldn't do a mean thing like that, would you?"

Kokomo came for him with quick little shuffling steps, his head lowered and tucked between the hunched bulk of his thick shoulders.

Doan was still smiling. He made a fork out of the first two fingers of his left hand and poked them at Kokomo's eyes. Kokomo knew that trick and, instead of ducking, he merely tilted his head back and let Doan's stiffened fingers slide off his low forehead. But when he put his head back, he exposed his thickly muscular throat.

Doan hit him squarely on the adam's apple with a short right jab. It was a wickedly effective blow, and Kokomo made a queer strangling noise and grasped his throat with both hands, rolling his head back and forth in agony. His mouth was wide open, and his eyes bulged horribly.

Doan hit him again, a full roundhouse swing with all his compact weight behind it. His fist smacked on the hinge of Kokomo's jaw. Kokomo went back one step and then another, shaking his head helplessly, still trying to draw a breath.

"I should break my hands on you, cement-head," Doan said casually. He took the revolver out of his coat pocket and slammed Kokomo on the top of the head with the butt of it.

The blow smashed the tall chef's hat into a weirdly lopsided pancake. Kokomo dropped to his knees, sagging loosely. With cold-blooded efficiency Doan hit him again in the same place. Kokomo flopped forward on his face and lay there on the shiny linoleum without moving.

It had happened very fast, and Doan was standing there now, looking down at Kokomo, still smiling in his casually amused way. He wasn't even breathing hard.

"These tough guys," he said, shrugging.

He dropped the revolver in his coat pocket again and stepped over Kokomo. The cellar door was fastened with a patent bolt. Doan unlatched it and peered down a flight of steep wooden stairs that were lighted dimly from the kitchen behind him. He felt around the door and found a light switch and clicked it. Nothing happened. The light down in the cellar, if there was one, didn't work.

Doan went down the steps, feeling his way cautiously as he got beyond the path of the light from the kitchen door. The cellar was a warm, dark cavern thick with the smell of coal dust. Feeling overhead, Doan located the warmth of a fat asbestos-wrapped pipe and judged from the direction it ran that the furnace was over in the far corner.

He started that way, sliding his feet causiously along the cement floor. He was somewhere in the middle of it, out of reach of either wall, when something made a quick silent breath going past in front of his face.

He stopped with a jerk, reaching for his revolver. The thing that had gone past his face hit the wall behind him with a dull ominous thud and dropped to the floor. Doan stayed rigidly still, his revolver poised. He was afraid to move for fear of stumbling over something. He listened tensely, his head tilted.

A voice whispered out of the darkness ahead of him. "Don't—don't you dare come any closer. I've got a shovel here. I'll—hit you with it."

Doan was a hard man to surprise, but he was as startled now as he ever had been in his life. He stared in the direction of the voice, his mouth open.

The voice said shakily: "You get out."

"Whoa," Doan said. "Wait a minute. I'm not coming any closer. Just listen to me before you heave any more of that coal."

"Who—who are you?"

"Name's Doan."

"The detective! Oh!"

"That's what I say. And who're you?"

"Shiela Alden."

"Ah," said Doan blankly. He drew a deep breath. "Well, I know I'm not drunk, so this must be happening. If you're Shiela Alden down here in the cellar, who's the Shiela Alden up in the bedroom?"

"That's my secretary, Leila Adams. She's been impersonating me."

"Oh. Sort of a game, huh?"

"No!"

"Well, I was just asking. What's the matter with the light down here?"

"I screwed the bulb out of the socket."

"Well, where is it? I'll screw it back in again. I need some light on the subject."

"Oh, no! No! Don't!"

"Why not?"

"I—I haven't any clothes on."

"You haven't any clothes on," Doan repeated. He shook his head violently. "Maybe I'm a little sleepy or something. I don't seem to be getting this. Suppose you just start and tell me all about it."

"Well, Leila and I came up here alone. Kokomo had come ahead to open up the place. Kokomo and Leila are in this together. When we got here they held me up and locked me in the cellar—in the back room beyond this one. Leila told me she was going to pretend she was me."

"Is Brill crazy? Didn't he know Leila Adams wasn't you?"

"No. Mr. Dibben in the law firm always handled all my business. I don't know Mr. Brill. He's never seen me."

"Well, well," said Doan. "Then what?"

"They just locked me in that cellar room. There's one window, and they didn't want to put bars over it, so they took all my clothes away from me. They knew I wouldn't get out the window then. If I did I'd freeze.

"It's two miles to the station and I didn't know which way. And Kokomo said if I screamed he'd . . ." Her voice trailed off into a little gasping sob. "He told me what he'd do."

"Yeah," said Doan. "I can imagine."

"Where is he now?"

"Kokomo? He's slightly indisposed at the moment. Go on. Tell me the rest."

"I broke a little piece of metal off the window, and I picked the lock on the door and got out here. I know how the heating system works. The valves are down here. I turned off the ones that controlled the downstairs radiators and opened the ones that control the upstairs radiators wide.

"Then I kept putting coal in the furnace with the drafts wide open. I thought if I made it hot enough in the upstairs bedrooms someone besides Kokomo would come down and look."

"Sure," said Doan. "Smart stuff. If I'd had any brains I'd have been down here hours ago. You stay right here and I'll bring you something to wear. Don't be afraid any more."

"I haven't been afraid—not very much. Only—only of Kokomo coming down here and—"

"He won't be coming down. Stay right here. I'll be right back."

Doan ran back up the steps. All his cheerful casual air was gone now. His lips were thinned across his teeth, and he moved with a cat-like, lithe efficiency.

Kokomo was still lying flat on his face in the center of the kitchen floor. Doan, moving with the same quiet quickness, opened the cupboard door and located an aluminum kettle.

He filled it with water at the sink. Carrying it carefully, he walked

188

over to Kokomo and, using the toe of one shoe, expertly flipped the big man over on his back.

He dumped the kettle of water in Kokomo's blankly upturned face. For a second there was no reaction, then Kokomo's pulpy lips moved, and he sputtered wetly. His eyes opened and he saw Doan looking thoughtfully down at him.

"Hi, Kokomo," Doan said softly. "Hi, baby."

Kokomo made noises in his throat and heaved himself up on his elbows. Doan took one short step forward and kicked him under the jaw so hard that Kokomo's whole lolling body lifted clear of the floor and rolled half under the stove. He didn't move any more.

"I'll have another present for you later," Doan said.

CHAPTER IX
BLACK SNOW

H E   W E N T   I N through the living room to the front hall. He had opened the door of the closet and located his snow-damp topcoat when he heard a little shuffling noise at the top of the stairs. He turned around to look.

It was Brill. The light behind him made him look grotesquely thin, sagging in the middle like a broken pencil.

"Doan!" he gasped.

He got hold of the railing with both hands, and then he came down the stairs in a crazily shuffling dance, his skinny legs wavering and twisting weirdly. He tripped and fell headlong down the last ten steps before Doan could catch him.

The skin on his face was yellowish, the cheekbones bulging out in ugly lumps. Blood was streaked in a long smear across his forehead. Doan straightened him out on the steps.

"Doan!" he said desperately. "That damned scoundrel, Crowley. Tricked me. Hit me—hit me—chair." He heaved himself up on his elbows, eyes glaring. "Doan! I'll hold you responsible! Got away! Your fault!"

"They didn't hit *me* with a chair," Doan pointed out.

"You!" Brill gasped. "Leaving me with them. While you wander off . . . They'll get away! They'll get to the station! Jannen will help them! Flat-car there—go down the grade . . ."

"We'll telephone ahead and stop them."

Brill rolled his head back and forth helplessly. "No telephone. Tried it upstairs. Line cut. You've got to go after them! They've got only a few minutes start! You can catch them! That girl—she can't go fast."

Doan said: "You mean you want me to go out in that storm again?"

"Oh, damn you!" Brill swore. "Don't you understand that my whole career is at stake? I hired your agency, and you failed me! I'll have you black-listed. I'll sue!"

"All right, all right," Doan said. "I'll go bring them back. Take another coat and give it to the girl you find down cellar."

He went to the front door and opened it. The wind whooped in triumphantly, driving a fine mist of snow ahead of it.

"Light," said Brill weakly. "They've got an electric lantern. You can see—"

Doan slammed the door shut. The wind came whipping down out of the black mouth of the ravine with a fierce howling intensity. Doan was struggling to get into his topcoat, and the wind billowed the coat out like a clumsy sail and blew Doan with it down the steps and across the black, rock-strewn ground.

He stumbled into a drift waist-deep before he caught himself. He stood still for a moment, one arm crooked up to shield his eyes from the cutting whip of the snow. The wind blasted at him, and then he caught the flicker of a light on the path that led up out of the flat.

Doan began to run. He was half-blinded with the snow, and the wind pulled and tugged at him, pushed him in staggering crazy spurts. He stumbled and half-fell, and then the gravel on the steep path grated under his shoes.

The light was high above him, much closer now, and as he watched, it flicked over the edge of the ravine and disappeared.

Doan fumbled under his coat and found the revolver. He went up the path at a lurching run. His breath burned icily in his throat. The air was thin and fine, with no weight to it, and his heart began to drum in a sickening cadence.

He was breathing in sobbing gasps when he hit the top of the ravine, sweat crawling in cold rivulets under his clothes. He paused there swaying, looking for the light, and found it off to his left.

He turned and plowed stubbornly in that direction, and there was no path here, nothing but thick drifts of snow piled against stunted brush that tore at his clothes with myriad clutching fingers.

The light tossed up high ahead of him, very close now, and showed stunted trees lined up in a ghostly gallery, leaning forward in the push of the wind as they watched.

Doan tripped over a snow-hidden log and went down flat on his face in powdery whiteness. He heaved himself stubbornly up on hands and knees, dabbed at his smeared face with his coatsleeve— and he stayed that way, half kneeling, rigid, staring into savagely cruel greenish yellow eyes on a level with his own and not a yard away.

"Hah!" Doan said, grunting with the exhalation of his breath.

The eyes came for him with the sudden slashing gleam of teeth under them. Doan poked the revolver straight out and fired, wondering as he pulled the trigger whether his fall had packed snow in the barrel and whether the gun would blow back at him.

The shot made a bright orange flare, and the eyes were gone. A heavy body kicked and squirmed in the snow. Doan struggled up to his feet, and another dark low form slipped sideways in the whirling darkness, circling him.

Doan leveled the revolver and fired instantly. A shrill ki-yiing yip echoed the smash of the shot, and the second dark form went tumbling over and over in the snow, contorting itself into desperate struggling knots.

The third one came in a black streak out of the darkness, up out of the snow in a long lunge, straight at Doan's throat. He fired going over backward. The flat-nosed .38 hit the animal in the chest and turned it clear over in the air. It fell back rigid and still beside the first.

Doan struggled in the snow, heaving himself up, and then Jannen loomed above him, yelling something the wind garbled into an unintelligible, frenzied scream. He had an ax in his hand, and he swung it back up over his shoulder and down at Doan in a full sweep that made its head glitter in a bright, deadly line.

Doan whirled himself sideways, rolling.

"Jannen!" he yelled frantically. "Don't! Don't! I'll shoot—"

The ax-head hissed past is ear, and Jannen caught it on the up-swing and chopped back down again with it.

Doan couldn't dodge this time. He didn't try. He shot Jannen just above the grassy gleam of the buckle on the wide web belt around his coat.

Jannen made a queer, choked sound. The ax stopped in mid-air. Jannen took one step back and then another, trying to get the ax up over his shoulder again.

"Drop it," said Doan.

The ax was going up inch by desperate inch. Jannen's breath made a high whistling sound. He made a clumsy step forward.

"All right, baby," said Doan.

He pulled the trigger of the revolver again. There was a dull, small click—nothing else. Before Doan even had time to grasp what that meant, Jannen reeled queerly sideways and went down full length on his face, as rigid as a log.

"Good God," said Doan in a whisper.

He got up slowly. The thing had happened in split-seconds, and the echos of the gunfire were still rolling lustily ahead of the wind.

Doan stared at his gun. It was bright and deadly in his hand, with the snow moisture gleaming on its thick cylinder, and he remembered now that he hadn't reloaded it. He had fired once at the metal case and once in the snow-shed. There had been four cartridges left in the gun. He had used them all. If he had missed just one of those four shots . . .

The wind whistled shrilly through bare branches, chuckling in its high, cruel glee.

Doan stumbled forward, leaned down over Jannen. The man was dead, and the snow already was laying a white cold blanket thinly across his distorted face.

Doan plowed back through the drifts and brush, found the hard surface of the path. He felt weak and numb with cold that was more than cold. His legs were stiff, unwieldy sticks under him as he went back down the steep path, across the flat toward the warmly welcoming glow of the windows that watched for him through the whirl of snow.

CHAPTER X
TOO MANY GUNS

DOAN WENT BLUNDERING across the porch with his head down and ran into the front door. He found the knob, fumbled it with numb fingers, finally turned it. The wind swept the door out of his grasp, banged it back thunderously against the wall.

Doan stamped through into the soft luxurious warmth of the hall, fought the door shut again behind him. Sighing in relief, he wiped snow moisture off his face with the palm of his left hand.

"Drop your gun on the floor."

Doan jerked to attention. Brill was standing in the doorway of the living room. He was wearing a blue dressing gown now over his pajamas. He lounged there, quite at ease, with the big .45 automatic bulking huge and black in his right hand.

"Drop your gun on the floor," he repeated in the same confident, quiet voice.

He looked very theatrical, with the white blaze showing up in his smoothly brushed hair, with his eyes narrowed. He was smiling in a dramatically sinister way.

Doan loosened the stiff fingers of his right hand and the .38 thudded on the carpet.

"It wasn't loaded anyway," he observed.

"Come in here," said Brill.

He backed out of the door, and Doan followed him into the living room. Someone had thrown kindling on the fire, and red flames crackled greedily in it.

"You know Miss Alden, I think," Brill said.

She was sitting on the divan. She was wearing a man's overcoat so big that it almost wrapped around her twice. She had brown hair cut in a long bob, mussed a little now, and the fire found warm glints in it. Her brown eyes were wide and scared, and her soft lower lip trembled. There was a smear of coal dust on the end of her short straight nose.

"Hello, again," said Doan.

She didn't answer, and Brill said:

"You're becoming a nuisance, Doan. What happened to Jannen? I heard you shooting."

"I was just target practicing," Doan said, "but Jannen, that dope, stepped right in front of my gun just when I happened to be pulling the trigger. I expect he's sort of dead."

Kokomo came in from the kitchen. There was a lopsided swollen lump on one side of his jaw, and his eyes glittered malevolently at Doan.

"You tricky little devil! When I get my hands on you—"

"I can hardly wait," Doan told him.

"Later, Kokomo," Brill said. He was watching Doan with gravely speculative eyes. "I suppose you are beginning to understand this now, aren't you?"

"Oh, sure," said Doan. "I figured it out quite a while ago."

"Did you, now?" said Brill sarcastically.

Doan nodded. "Yes. You were next in line for the management of Shiela Alden's trust fund after this gent Dibben. You had all the time in the world to figure things out and get ready for this little play. You saw that an accident happened to Dibben at the right time. You knew Shiela Alden was coming up here—probably suggested the idea yourself—and you made all your arrangements beforehand.

"First you got Leila Adams, Shiela's secretary, to throw in with you by promising to split part of what you got from Shiela with her. Then you got Kokomo to do the muscle-work, promising him a split too. When you were prowling around up here beforehand you found out that Jannen was a crackpot with a grudge against the Aldens.

"Now, there was an ideal fall-guy for you all ready-made. Anything that happened you could always blame on him. But Jannen talks too much, and this poor guy, Boley, the regular station master, got suspicious of what you were cooking up with him, and either you or Kokomo or Jannen—or all three of you—got Boley drunk and probably doped him and left him out in the storm to freeze.

"Leila Adams wasn't going to impersonate Shiela Alden unless it was necessary on account of someone like me coming around. You definitely didn't want anyone around—not with the real Shiela Alden locked in the cellar.

"And so—" Doan paused, ran a hand over his cheek.

"Jannen knew a lot about explosives, and so you got him to fix

up that little cigar case present for me. You knew I was going to
be on the job because the trust company hired the agency, and
Toggery told you he was going to send me up. So you dressed up
in a fancy costume and laid for me with your cigar case bomb."

"How did you know I was the one who gave you that case?"

Doan grinned. "I couldn't miss. You spent so much time trying
to cover yourself up that you stuck out like a sore thumb. You
wanted to be sure that if anything went wrong no one could prove
that you had anything to do with the whole business.

"That was the reason for your little fairy tale about the janitor
and the cigar case and why you put on that elaborate, nervous and
worried act and why you wanted to make sure that I knew you'd
just been assigned to handle Shiela Alden's business. You wanted
me to think that you were a jittery sort of a dope who couldn't
possibly know the score. As a matter of fact, you *are* a dope."

Brill's lip lifted. "So? And I suppose you can tell me what
happened tonight, too?"

"Easy," Doan agreed. "When you found out you hadn't put me
away and that I was coming up here, you had to get a girl to act as
secretary to the phoney Shiela Alden because you knew I'd expect
to find a secretary.

"You hired the first girl you could find—Joan Greg. She wasn't
in on the impersonation business. She thought Leila Adams was
actually Shiela Alden—and, more important, so did her boy friend,
Crowley.

"Crowley just messed the whole works up for you. He started
impressing his personality on Leila Adams. He's a slick worker.
She fell for him. She was a scrawny, homely dame, and she'd never
had anybody like Crowley tell her how beautiful, breath-taking,
marvelous and generally all-around wonderful she was before.

"She liked it fine. She liked it so well she began to get out of
hand, and you knew that if Crowley worked much more of his sex
appeal, she'd spill something to him. You killed her.

"Joan Greg was crazy jealous of Crowley, and she gave you the
idea by trying it herself. You knew, then, that you could put Leila
Adams away and blame it on Joan Greg.

"You had a master key. You could get into her bedroom. You cut
Leila Adams' throat and then went in and planted the knife on

Joan Greg and bloodied up her hands. When she woke up she actually didn't know whether or not she had killed the phoney Shiela Alden. As soon as I left you alone with her and Crowley, you told them to beat it. You planned to lay all the blame on them, knowing they'd keep under cover.

"Jannen was prowling around the place, and you tipped him off and then sent me out, thinking Jannen and his damned wolves would take care of me. You tipped your hand twice then. First by that phoney entrance coming downstairs. Nobody who actually got banged with a chair ever acted so screwy as you did. And then you weren't even interested when I told you there was a girl down cellar. As an actor, you stink. What crackpot notion have you got up your sleeve now?"

Brill said smoothly: "I've had to alter my plans slightly, Doan, but I don't think it will really matter—certainly not to you. You see, at first all I wanted to do was to force Shiela to give me her power of attorney for a week or so after she got control of the trust fund. If I could have done that, as I planned, I would have made a fortune."

"Sure. By selling her a few million shares of phoney stock."

Brill looked contemptuous. "Nothing so crude. Merely by forcing the market up and down by alternately selling and buying the huge blocks of stock she owns in several corporations and being on the right side of the market myself each time.

"There would have been nothing criminal in that, and no way for her to prove afterward that she hadn't given the power of attorney voluntarily, because it would have been her word against myself, Kokomo and Leila Adams. But due to the way things have happened, I've been forced—not very reluctantly, I must admit—to ask Miss Alden to do me the honor of becoming my wife."

Shiela Alden spoke for the first time. "No," she said in a small, clear voice.

Brill paid no attention to her. "You see, Doan? Even if my original plan did go on the rocks, I can still pull things together. I'll have control over Miss Alden's money if she's my wife—you can be sure of that. And more important, she can't testify against me."

Shiela Alden said: "I am not going to marry you—now or any other time."

"I think you will," Brill said. "It's really quite essential. Kokomo, will you take Miss Alden into the other room and see if you can—ah—reason with her?"

CHAPTER XI
GOOD BYE NOW

S H I E L A   A L D E N   D R E W in her breath with a little gasp. Kokomo was grinning at her meaningly out of the side of his mouth that wasn't swollen. He came nearer the divan.

"It's warm in there," Brill said. "She won't need that coat."

Shiela Alden wrapped the coat tighter around her, clutching the lapels with fingers that were white with strain.

"No! You can't—"

"Brill," said Doan.

He hadn't made any noticeable move, but now he was holding a flat metal case on the palm of his right hand, looking down at it thoughtfully.

"That's mine!" Brill exclaimed.

"No," said Doan. "No, Brill. Not yours. It's the one you gave me."

Silence stretched over the room like a thin black veil, with the crackle of the flames in the hearth coming through it faint and distant.

"Foolish," Doan said, still staring at the case thoughtfully. "Foolish trying to alibi yourself by carrying one like it and pretending some mysterious Mr. Smith gave it to you and that the cigars in it subsequently blew the janitor to smithereens. There aren't any cigars—explosive or otherwise—in this case. It's packed with explosive."

"Brill said stiffly: "How—how—"

"You're a dope," Doan told him. "Don't you know that the bomb squad on any city police force has equipment—black light, X-ray, fluoroscope—so they can look into suspicious packages without opening them? I took this case down to a pal of mine on the Bay

City bomb squad. He squinted into it and told me it was a very neat little hand-grenade, so I kept it for a souvenir. Here. Catch it."

He tossed the case in a spinning, glittering arc. Brill yelled in a choked, horrified voice. He dropped the automatic and grabbed frantically with both hands at the case.

Doan dived for him in a lunging expert tackle. He smashed against Brill's pipe-stem legs. The case was knocked whirling up in the air, and Brill spun around and fell headlong. His head cracked sickeningly against the edge of the hearth, and he stiffened, his whole body quivering, and then was still.

Doan rolled over and sat up and looked down the thick black barrel of the automatic at Kokomo's scared, sagging face.

"Hi, Kokomo," Doan said softly.

Kokomo held both big hands in front of him, fingers spread wide, as though he were trying to push back the expected bullet.

"Don't," he whispered. "Don't shoot."

"Oh, I think I will," Doan said.

Kokomo believed him. He had already had a demonstration of what Doan could and would do. His thick lips opened and shut soundlessly, little sticky threads of saliva glinting at their corners.

Doan got up. "Turn around, Kokomo."

Kokomo turned slowly and stiffly, like a mechanical doll that had almost run down. Doan stepped close to him and slammed him on the head with the barrel of the automatic.

"I'll bet even your cement knob will ache tomorrow after that," Doan said amiably. He winked at Shiela Alden, who was staring with wide unbelieving brown eyes.

"Weren't scared, were you? They never had a chance. They're amateurs. I'm a professional. That case was really Brill's—not the one he gave me. I picked it out of his pocket last night. Wanted to look at it more closely."

She continued to stare.

He went over to the door into the hall and picked up the telephone. It was a French type handset with a long cord attached to it. Stringing out the cord behind him, Doan brought the phone back to the divan and sat down on it beside Shiela Alden. He held the receiver against his ear.

"The dopes," he said to Shiela. "They didn't even cut the line."

She turned her head stiffly, little by little, and looked from Brill to Kokomo. "Are they—are they—"

"Dead?" Doan finished. "Oh, no." He was still listening at the receiver, and now he said:

"Hello. Hello, operator? Get me the J. S. Toggery residence in Bay City. I don't know the number. I'll hold the line."

He waited, smiling at Shiela Alden in a speculative way. She had begun to breathe more evenly now, and there was a little color in her cheeks.

"But—but you did it so easily—so quickly. I mean, it all happened before I knew what—"

"The hand is quicker than the eye," said Doan. "At least mine was quicker than theirs."

"I—I've never met anyone like you before."

"There's only one of us," Doan said.

The receiver crackled against his ear, and then J. S. Toggery's voice said:

"What? What? Who's this?"

"Doan—the forgotten man. How are you, Mr. Toggery? How is Carstairs?"

"You! That damned ghoulish giraffe! He pulled all my wife's new drapes down! He broke a vase that cost me a hundred and fifty dollars! He crawled under the dinner table and then stood up and dumped the dinner on the floor! I've got him chained in the garage, and let me tell you, Doan, if he pulls just one more trick, I'll get an elephant gun and so help me I'll pulverize him! You hear me?"

"He's young and exuberant. He probably misses me. You'll have to excuse him. Goodbye now."

"Wait! Wait, you fool! Are you up at the Alden lodge where you're supposed to be? Is everything all right up there?"

"Oh, yes. Now it is. There was a kidnapping and a couple of murders and some attempted thefts and a few assaults with intent to kill and such, but I straightened it all out. Get off the line, Toggery. I've got to call the sheriff."

"Doan!" Toggery screamed. *"Doan!* What? What did you say? Murders—kidnapping. Doan! Is Miss Alden all right?"

Doan looked at her. "Yes," he said. "Yes, Toggery. Miss Alden is—quite all right."

He hung up the receiver on Toggery's violent voice and nodded at Shiela Alden.

"You know," he said, "you're so very nice that I think I could like you an awful lot even if you didn't have fifty million dollars."

Shiela Alden's soft lips made a round, pink O of surprise and then moved a little into a faint tremulous smile.

FREDRIC BROWN

Blue Murder

THE POLICE IN *pulp stories were generally depicted in one of two ways: as Neanderthal types, slow of wit and quick of fist and rubber-hose, sometimes honest and sometimes as crooked as a dog's leg; or as dedicated, plodding, scrupulously honorable minions of the law, more tenacious than bright. These stereotypes were widespread in crime fiction in the 1930s and 1940s, and continue in some aspects of it, annoyingly enough, to this day.*

The hero of "Blue Murder," Detective Sergeant Peter Craig, is of the dedicated, honest ilk; but although the stereotype is in force (no pun intended), there are shadings in Craig's character. And in the tale of the baffling homicide at the Crescent Paint Company and how Craig solves it, there is a generous helping of Fredric Brown's spirited good humor. One suspects his tongue was firmly planted in his cheek throughout the story's composition.

"Blue Murder" (a title that appeared on more than a few pulp stories, as well as half a dozen mystery novels) was the second and best of only two stories Brown sold to Babette Rosmond of Street & Smith Publications (of whom more later), and is virtually unknown even to the growing number of aficionados of Brown's work. It has not been reprinted since its initial appearance in The Shadow *in 1943; and because* The Shadow *is an extremely popular superhero among today's collectors, as evidenced by the number of Shadow paperback and hardcover reprints that have been published in recent years, copies of the pulp are rare and quite expensive. Readers and collectors of general mystery and detective fiction seldom find them available—an unfortunate fact, for a wealth of fine stories are contained*

in their pages. "Blue Murder" is just one of the many that deserve republication.

Fredric Brown (1906–1972) began writing for the pulps in 1938, while working as a newspaper proofreader in Milwaukee, and soon began selling regularly enough to devote his full time to the craft of fiction. From 1938 to 1953, he published more than 150 pulp stories, most of them mystery/detective, with two score or so in the fantasy and science fiction field. His first novel, The Fabulous Clipjoint, *was awarded the Mystery Writers of America Edgar Award as the Best First Novel of 1947; he followed it over the next seventeen years with twenty nine additional novels, including such standouts as* The Screaming Mimi *(1949),* Night of the Jabberwock *(1950),* The Wench is Dead *(1955), and* Knock Three-One-Two *(1959). He also published seven collections during his lifetime—two mystery/detective (*Mostly Murder, *1953;* The Shaggy Dog and Other Murders, *1963) and five science fiction and fantasy; most of the stories in these books first appeared in the pulps.*

Brown was a master of the mordant short-short (some forty-seven of which can be found in his 1961 mixed-bag collection, Nightmares and Geezenstacks). *He wrote humor, straight detective stories, psychological suspense, and wild fantasy with equal skill. And his fresh plot concepts and narrative techniques made him one of the most innovative storytellers of his generation.*

THE PHONE BOOTH was a tight fit, but Detective Sergeant Peter Craig got into it without a shoehorn. Barely. He edged in sidewise because the phone faced that way and he wouldn't have to turn around once he was inside.

Sweat ran down his forehead and he mopped it off before he dialed headquarters and asked for Captain Marlow. And by the time Marlow was on the wire the sweat was running down again and about ready to drip off his nose and chin.

He said, "Hi, Cap, this is Baby." He grinned, even though the booth wasn't wired for television and the grin went to waste. "Listen, Slave-driver, my train leaves in ten minutes; but I forgot to leave the address where my next check gets mailed. Jerry's Fishing Lodge, Box 7, North Wilding. And with a cool breeze blowing in across the water. I'll think of you, Cap, every time I hook a fish. Got that address?"

"No," said the voice on the other end of the wire. "But, Craig, thank God you called. You'll have to postpone it. We're in a jam and I need you."

"Huh? You're kidding me, Cap! Golly, you couldn't do anything like that to me. Hell, it's all arranged. I've bought my ticket, and—"

"And you can turn it back. Listen—the whole Homicide bureau except you and me is tied up on that Booker business and the one on the west side, and we just got a new case. Patrolman Brian just phoned it in. Blue murder. You got to meet me there."

Craig howled: "Cap, you *can't* be serious! Those muskies are biting *now* and, dammit, I've slaved for a whole year just to get this trip."

"Yeah, but if you want to keep on slaving when you get back you'll meet me at the Crescent Paint Co., 613 North Vine, in fifteen minutes. Sorry, Craig, but that's an order."

Craig sighed. "How long'll it take? And what you mean by blue murder?"

"It'll take until we crack the case, whether it's a day or a month. And a guy *named* Blue was murdered. Henry Blue. He owns the company."

"Hell," said Craig, "couldn't he have waited ten minutes longer? All right, I'll be there."

Mournfully, he sidled out of the telephone booth and waddled back to the baggage room to see that his suitcases were held for orders, instead of being put on the train. Then he took a taxi to the address Marlow had given.

There was a small crowd gathered in front of a ramshackle, four-story building, there in the heart of the warehouse district. The excitement seemed to focus on a door that shut off the areaway leading back between the Crescent company's building and the one next door. The door was closed. And locked.

Peter Craig pushed through the crowd and hammered on the door until it opened from the inside.

"Oh, it's you," said Patrolman Brian. "Captain Marlow just got here. It's blue murder, all right. Lookit!"

But even before Brian had spoken, Craig was staring at what lay back in the areaway. It was hard not to look, and he felt a bit like echoing the gasps that came from behind him, from the spectators who'd caught a glimpse through the momentarily open door.

It was "blue" murder, all right. Back near the rear end of the areaway lay the body of a man; unmistakably a body, although you could hardly see it for the blue. Bright blue splashed all over it and splattered on the walls on either side, and in a wide bright pool all about it.

"The hell!" said Craig, wondering if the heat was making him see things.

Brian grinned. "Nope, sarge, he isn't a blue blood. It's paint; some kind soul dropped a gallon can of it out a window, right on his head. Cap Marlow says for you to go in. Coroner's on his way here."

Craig nodded and again wiped the sweat off his forehead—or tried to, because his handkerchief was wetter than the area it failed to dry.

He walked back until he stood just outside the blue pool, and stopped there, looking down. He noticed the can itself now—a gallon can lying on its side a couple of feet from the corpse, and the lid lying nearby.

There were footprints in the paint beside the body; not clear ones, of course, because the viscous fluid had flowed back. And, studying the body more closely, Craig saw that it had apparently been shifted slightly from the position in which it had fallen; rolled halfway over from its face-down position—probably to allow whoever had made the footprints to feel over the heart for signs of life—and then had been allowed to roll back into approximately the original position.

From the pool of blue to the short flight of steps that led to the door of the building, were blue footprints; and outside the door stood a pair of forlorn, blue-smeared shoes. Whoever had worn them had gone back into the building in his socks, rather than track it full of paint.

"Hey," said Captain Marlow's voice from overhead. "Come on up."

Craig looked up and saw the captain's derbied head sticking out of a third-floor window. He said, "Yeah," and the head jerked back out of sight.

Craig kept on looking up while he was at it. There were four windows, one on each floor and in a vertical row, from which the paint can could have been dropped. All four windows were in the building that housed the paint company; the building on the other side of the areaway presented a blank, windowless wall. Four possible windows, or the roof.

Only the one on the second floor was closed; the other three were wide open. A few drops of paint had splashed as high as the top pane of the window on the first floor. And through the glass of the top pane he could see splattered drops on the lower pane, now raised up so that the lower pane was behind the upper.

That would indicate that the first-floor window had been closed when the paint can was dropped, and opened afterward. And that narrowed the problem a little.

He looked down again. There was barely room to get around the outside of the blue pool without walking through the fresh paint. The body—and the center of the jagged pool—lay much nearer the paint-company building than the one opposite.

If one walked carefully— Yes, he made it. The door was only a few steps back; but before he went in, Craig walked the rest of the way to the rear for a glance around. There was a loading platform for trucks there, but it was empty.

He went on up the five steps that led him into the side door of the building. The door led to a hallway, and to his right, off the hallway, was an open door that led to the room behind the first-floor window above the body. The room contained filing cabinets, a safe with the door ajar, and a long, high bookkeeper's desk.

Craig walked on in and looked around; everything seemed to be in order. He crossed to the window and lowered the pane, to check on those drops that proved it had been closed when the paint had spattered. They were there, all right; and he put the window back up the way he'd found it and went out into the hallway again.

A few steps ahead was the shaft of a service elevator. He pushed the button and waited. Here, inside the building, it was hotter than the hinges of hell. Craig wondered why anybody would work in such a building on such a day. Come to think of it, where *were* all the employees? Then he remembered it was Saturday afternoon.

His shirt was soaking wet with sweat, and moisture from his forehead was trickling down the bridge of his nose.

There wasn't any sound of an elevator starting, but down the shaft came the stentorian tones of Marlow's voice. "Hey, Craig, the elevator's busted. Walk up!"

"Huh?" said Craig incredulously. "*Walk* up? Me? Listen, can't they fix that elevator? It ain't human to—"

"Walk up, you big lummox. We're on the fourth floor now. Snap it!"

Craig groaned audibly and started up the stairs.

Three flights, and on a day like this, and he'd thought it work to climb the five steps that led from the areaway to the first floor. And, dammit, right now he should be on the train pulling out for a week's fishing. If only he hadn't phoned—

By the time he reached the second-floor landing he was puffing like a locomotive, and on the third-floor landing he had to stop to rest. The third-floor landing was wet—very wet. A bucket of dirty water had been spilled and still lay on its side, a mop beside it.

"Hey, Craig"—Marlow's voice again—"what's keeping you?"

"On the third-floor landing, Cap," Craig called. "Somebody kicked the bucket here."

There was a startled exclamation from above, and Captain Marlow came running down the steps two at a time. He stopped at the bottom—and his face went red as he saw the spilled scrub bucket. He said, "Damn you, Craig!"

Craig grinned at him. He said, "Listen, Cap, I'm not built for a mountaineer. I gotta rest before I go that last flight. Meanwhile, what gives? Who all was around when it happened?"

"Four of them," Marlow told him, "besides the murdered guy, Henry Blue. Yeah, it was murder, all right. I checked the possibility of a gallon of paint happening to get knocked accidentally off a window sill. It couldn't have—wouldn't have been on a window sill. It was dropped or thrown out of the third or fourth-floor window."

Craig leaned against the wall and closed his eyes. He looked asleep, but he asked, "How about the second floor, or the roof?"

"Nix on both. Second-floor window won't open. Frame's warped; I tried it. Anyway, nobody was working on the second floor. Roof's out, too."

"Why?"

"Only way's up a ladder arrangement to a trapdoor. Dust on the rungs—hasn't been used for a month. Somebody could, I suppose, have got on the roof from next door, or used the roof of the building across the way, although that's pretty unlikely. Especially as the paint came from here. It's their own brand. Cans of it on almost every floor. Cases of it!"

"But, Cap, if the crime was maybe planned out in advance, somebody coulda stashed a can ready on that roof. Of course, they'd have to have a pretty close idea when this guy Blue was leaving here. Could they have known that?"

Marlow shook his head. "That's out. Nobody even knew he was coming around today. He didn't show up at all until two o'clock, an hour ago. Unexpectedly. He stuck around half an hour talking to Weger, the foreman; and Horvath, the bookkeeper. And nobody left the building while he was here. So the roofs are out."

Craig nodded. "Swell. Then nobody'll have to—"

"But maybe," Marlow cut in, "just for routine, you better go next door on both sides and climb up to see what the view's like."

Craig paled at the very thought, then saw that Marlow was grinning at him and didn't mean it.

He said, "Whew! Don't scare me like that, Cap. I'd melt into a blue puddle, myself, before I got halfway through." Then he was climbing the last flight, after Marlow, and he stopped talking to save his breath for the climb. Waves of heat seemed to ooze up out of the very boards of the stairway.

There were four men waiting in a room on the fourth floor, the room whose window was directly over the body in the areaway. One was a tall, gangly man whose sallow complexion was given a greenish tinge by the green eye shade he wore. He had carpet slippers on his feet, and that ticketed him as the one who'd gone out into the paint of the areaway and had abandoned his shoes before returning. And if, as the eye shade made probable, he was the bookkeeper, he'd have probably been working on the first floor.

The man leaning against the wall in the far corner and chewing on a cud of tobacco the size of a hen's egg, was unmistakably a janitor. Of the other two—one a thin-faced, middle-aged man, and the other a younger but better-dressed chap—Craig couldn't guess which would turn out to be the foreman, Weger.

Marlow was saying, "I got here just before you did, Craig, and I've hardly questioned these gentlemen yet except to get their names. Well, we can get the spadework over right here. Horvath, you found the body. Suppose you tell us your story first."

The tall man in the eye shade gulped and his Adam's apple bobbed an inch toward his chin and back again. He said, "Well, Mr. Blue came here about around two o'clock. He came in that side door; the front door's bolted after twelve on Saturdays, and looked into my office and said 'hello,' and then went on up—"

There was a yell from outside, "Hey, Marlow!"

Craig, who was nearest to the window, looked out and said, "It's Doc Rogers. He don't look happy." Then he stepped back and let Marlow lean out the window.

"Listen," Craig heard Rogers' voice, "how can I examine this stiff without getting full of paint? I was off duty, and I got my best clothes on. Can't I have him taken—"

"No," yelled down Marlow. "You can get yourself full of paint and like it. I want a preliminary report right now."

"All right, dammit, but I'll put a new suit on my expense account. Anyway, how can I look for bruises and abrasions through a layer of paint? He's dead all right, though; I felt—"

"We'll send you down some turpentine," called Marlow. "I guess there'll be some around. Craig, will you find some and take it down to him?"

The man who looked like a janitor said, "I know where it is. I'll get some and take it to him," and slouched out of the room when Marlow nodded. Craig's eyes followed him gratefully. "Cap," he said, "there goes a gentleman under the denim. If he's guilty, I hope it's an unsolved case."

"Quit driveling," said Marlow. "Now, Horvath, you were saying—"

The bookkeeper shifted nervously from one foot to the other. "Mr. Blue went on upstairs, like I said. I don't know what he did up here; I wasn't above the first floor all afternoon—until now, that is. He came down a little later—"

"How much later?"

"Um-m-m, maybe five minutes, maybe fifteen; I don't know. I guess it was nearer fifteen. He came into my office—I mean, the accounting room. He borrowed a hundred dollars out of the petty cash, and—"

Craig whistled. "Petty? A hundred marbles doesn't sound so petty to me. How much do you carry?"

"We do quite a bit of cash business on small orders. We usually have several hundred, but there happened to be only a hundred and fifteen today. Then Mr. Blue stayed and talked a few minutes about fishing. That was what he got the money for; he'd just decided to go on a fishing trip. After muskies. He told me they're biting swell right now."

Craig groaned again. "The poor guy. Him and me both, and darned if I don't feel as blue as he looks. Only he don't know what he's missing, Cap, and *I* do!"

Marlow glared at him and said, "Shut up, you dope! Go on, Horvath!"

"He was in my office maybe ten minutes altogether; then he left, by way of the hall, and turned toward the outer door. Half a minute later I heard a thump and a thud that seemed to come from right outside the window, and I ran across and opened it. I gave a yell and ran out the door to see if he was dead or just knocked out, and—well, he was dead when I got there."

"Thanks, Horvath," said Marlow. "And when you came in you left your shoes outside?"

The bookkeeper nodded. "We'd freshly painted the floors last week, and I naturally kicked the shoes off rather than ruin the floors. I had carpet slippers that I kept here and wore sometimes. But before I got them I ran upstairs to where the others were, and Mr. Weger here was already phoning the police. I'd yelled up to him that Mr. Blue was dead as soon as I found out. Then I cleaned my hands with turps and—guess that's all till you got here."

He sat down, and Marlow turned to the thin-faced, middle-aged man. "Mr. Weger," he said, "will you start with what you were doing when Blue arrived, and go on from there?"

"I'm afraid I haven't much to tell, captain," Weger said hesitantly. "I was staying to finish an inventory—the whole staff had started it this morning and we were almost done. So I kept Raymond Blue here to help me—"

Craig's eyes went to the younger man, and he interrupted the foreman. "Blue? Any relation of the boss?"

"Yes," the well-dressed young chap answered for himself. "I'm his nephew."

"We'll come to that, Craig," Marlow cut in. "Go on, Weger."

"I figured the two of us could finish the inventory by midafternoon and we wouldn't have to keep anybody else overtime. Well, I didn't notice what time Mr. Blue—I mean Mr. Henry Blue—came in, but if Horvath says two o'clock, I guess that's about right. He said he'd just dropped in on his way out of town, and asked how the inventory was coming, and was surprised we were nearly through. He talked a few minutes, about fishing mostly, and then went down—"

"Did he mention that he came to get money?"

"I . . . I believe he did say something about being broke to explain why he dropped in. Said he was glad Horvath was still here because then he wouldn't have to burgle the safe. Of course, he was just kidding. He knew the combination himself."

"And then—"

"That's all, until a little later, about ten minutes, I guess, I heard Horvath yelling to look in the areaway, so I ran to the nearest window. Mr. Blue was lying there, and Horvath, about the time I got to the window, was running out the door and I saw him wade in through the paint and partly turn Mr. Blue over so he could feel for a heartbeat; and then he called up that Mr. Blue was dead and stepped back, and I went to the phone to call the police."

"Did you think it was murder, then?" Craig asked.

The foreman wetted his lips with his tongue. "I—well, yes, that was my first impression. There just didn't seem to be any way it could have happened accidentally. The way the stuff had splashed you could see it had been dropped on him from a height."

"You were on this floor, the fourth floor, when you heard the yell?" Marlow asked.

Weger nodded. "But not near this window. Raymond and I had been working near the front of the building, and I'd just sent him to the back room, behind this, to check up on some tempera colors we'd almost overlooked. So the window I looked out of was toward the front of the building."

Craig looked toward Horvath and the bookkeeper nodded confirmation. "Yes, I remember he looked out a front window. And Mr. Raymond Blue out of a back one."

Marlow cleared his throat. He asked, "Were relations between you and your employer—um—perfectly friendly?"

There was another "Hey!" in Dr. Rogers' voice from down in the areaway. Marlow went to the window and looked out, and Craig leaned against the window frame and managed to look over the captain's shoulder.

Rogers, smeared with paint from head to foot, and somehow reminiscent of a blue bantam rooster spoiling for a fight, had cleaned most of the paint off the head of Henry Blue. There was a heavy turpentine odor in the air, and a gallon jug, almost empty, stood on the cement.

"What's the report?" Marlow yelled.

Arms akimbo, Rogers glared up at him. "The guy's dead!" He wiped sweat off his forehead with a handkerchief and left a blue smudge.

"We guessed that, Doc," said Marlow. "What we want to know is, what killed him?"

"What d'ya think killed him—snake-bite? He was hit on the head by an object that might have been, and damn well was, a can of paint!"

Craig got his head a bit farther out past Marlow's shoulder and grinned. He called down, "Hey, Doc, what color paint?"

Rogers cursed fluently and at length, and Craig pulled his head back inside, chuckling. Marlow said, "Here come the stretcher boys, Doc. Take him away and give us a full report later. Better get that paint out of your goatee before somebody takes you for Landru."

Marlow turned back into the room and saw the janitor just coming in the door. "All right, Blecz," he said, "what's your version?"

"My what?"

Craig sighed and sat down on a packing case. He said, "The cap means, what happened and where were you when it did."

"Oh," said the janitor. "Well, I was scrubbing the second-floor landing when Mr. Blue came in. He says 'hello' when he goes by me, but don't stop. I finish up there and I'm working on the steps when he comes down. I go up on the third-floor landing when I hear Mr. Horvath yell something about the areaway. I run to a window, and—"

"That was when you kicked over the bucket?"

"Yeah. I got to the window quick and looked down and there was Mr. Blue like you saw him, and Mr. Horvath just pulling his head back in the downstairs window under me, and a couple seconds later he ran out the door."

"You looked out the hallway window—directly over the body?"

"Huh? The hallway window, yes, but the window directly over the body is in the next room off the hallway. Right over the window Mr. Horvath had looked out of. I didn't mean he was pulling his head back into the window *right* under me, because on the first floor that'd be the doorway."

"Nobody else was on the third floor, and you had access to the third-floor window out of which the paint could have been dropped?"

Blecz scratched his head. "Well, yeah. But I didn't go in there. All the time I was in the second or third-floor hallways or the steps between them."

"Hm-m-m," said Marlow. "Then you haven't any alibi, but you can certainly give one to Horvath, if he didn't pass you. The available window on the second floor is stuck; he couldn't have reached the third or fourth floors without your having seen him. Isn't that right?"

"Yeah," said Blecz. "I guess that's right."

Raymond Blue asked, "How does that alibi Mr. Horvath? Not that I'm suggesting it, but just to keep the record straight, that first-floor window is higher than a man's head walking through the areaway, isn't it? If the paint can were thrown, and not dropped—"

Marlow grunted. "Nope, Horvath's eliminated, Mr. Blue. We've got proof the first-floor window was closed when the paint was dropped. Splashes on the outside of both upper and lower panes."

Craig grunted. "Dammit, Cap, you worked fast before I got here. I thought I had that up my sleeve. Did you examine the window?"

Marlow shook his head. "Noticed it from the outside. We should check—"

"I did," said Craig. "I lowered the sash and put it back up. By the way, did anybody besides Horvath—any of you who were on the top floors—hear the noise of the fall?"

Blecz and Weger shook their heads. Raymond Blue said, "I'm not sure. I thought I heard something while I was in the back room, just before Horvath yelled. But I'm not positive now."

Marlow turned to Blue. "Then, as far as you know, Mr. Weger could have been in that room on the fourth floor—the one over where the body was—at the time of the murder. And as far as he knows, you could have been there. Neither of you have alibis. Right?"

Raymond Blue nodded slowly. The foreman frowned and said, "I guess that's right, but— Are you sure it *is* murder, captain? I'll admit I don't see any way it could have been accidental, but—"

"Maybe it was suicide," Craig drawled. He wiped his forehead again while the others stared at him, startled for a moment, until Craig went on: "Maybe he took the paint down with him and threw the can up in the air and stood under it when it came down. But it seems a silly thing to do. Damn this heat!"

Marlow glared at Craig. He said, "If you want to go fishing so bad, you don't mind whether you got a job to come back to, keep it up. Be helpful, you dim-witted hippopotamus. Wipe that paint off your forehead and start the wheels behind it going."

"Paint?" asked Craig curiously. He rubbed his forehead with a handkerchief and said, "I'll be darned," and then looked at each of his hands. There were faint traces of blue paint on the side of his index finger, on the right hand. "How'd that get there?" he asked.

Marlow snorted. "You touched the wall coming through the areaway, you dope! Now, Blecz, was there any animosity between you and Henry Blue?"

"Any what?"

Craig said, "He means, did you and Mr. Blue like each other, Blecz? But never mind answering." He didn't shudder under the impact of the glare Captain Marlow gave him because his eyes were closed and there was a beatific smile on his face. There was still blue paint, a tiny smudge, on his forehead behind the beaded sweat, but despite it he managed to look like an oversize cherub as he droned on:

"Sure, Cap. Blecz, here, and Blue liked each other. Maybe they were brothers under the paint. I'll bet a nickel 'blecz' means blue in Persian or Scandinavian or maybe Polish. And once in a blue moon they'd go hunting bluebirds through the blue grass. Listen, Cap, this case is solved and maybe I got time to catch the next train and get out of this sweltering city this afternoon, after all. What time is it? And lay off the janitor—even if he's wearing blue overalls."

Marlow was staring at Craig, but Craig didn't stare back; he still looked asleep. A drop of sweat ran off the tip of his nose and added wetness to a gathering spot on his necktie. Marlow said, "Damn you, Craig! If you're kidding, I'll—"

Craig said, "That paint on my finger, Cap. There's only one way I could have got it just there."

"Sure. You leaned against the wall when you walked around that puddle in the areaway."

Craig opened his eyes. "Go try it, Cap," he said. "Try leaning against a wall on the inside of one knuckle. If you can do it—then maybe Horvath didn't kill Henry Blue. But there's only one way I could have got paint on that knuckle in that position—and that's when I put up the window on the first-floor accounting room after I'd pulled it down to verify those blue spots on the outside of the pane. I hooked my index finger under the hook-shaped handle, the way anybody opens a window that's closed tight. And it proves that Horvath had paint on *his* hand when he opened that window and looked out and yelled."

Craig looked at the bookkeeper. "Isn't that right?"

Horvath gulped and his Adam's apple jumped to a new high. But he said, "That's silly. How'd I have paint on my hand then?"

"From splashing it on the outside of the window the first time you went out into the areaway. Then you came back in and opened it from the inside and yelled. After you yelled, you had witnesses to your running out and handling the body—although you already knew Blue was dead—in order to account for the paint being on your hands."

Marlow looked from Craig to Horvath and back again and said,

"Dammit, Craig, I don't get it! Maybe I'm dumb, but—"

"Sure, you are," said Craig firmly. "Listen, let's start back a ways. On his way out of the building, Blue goes in the office where Horvath is doctoring the books. He goes to the petty cash and all the money isn't there. Horvath hadn't expected him today and maybe got caught with his pants down. Maybe he's been gypping and covering up for a long time, and something happened to make Blue suspicious today when he went to the petty cash. Maybe—"

"Skip the maybes," Marlow snapped. "I'll concede the possibility of a motive. If it's there, an audit will show it. Go on from there."

Craig said, "So Blue goes to the phone to call 'copper,' let's say, and Horvath—scared and desperate—picks up a heavy object and beans him with it. Probably it was a can of paint, although it might not have been the same one. No reason, though, why it wasn't, except that the can didn't come open then. But Horvath maybe hits harder than he'd intended and finds he's killed Blue, and he thinks fast to fix it so he can't be thought guilty.

"The idea he got was simple, and wouldn't take more than three minutes to carry out. He lowers the body out the window into the private areaway—damn little chance of being seen—and maybe goes outside to put it in position if it doesn't fall right. Then, from inside the window, so he won't get his clothes splattered, he slams down the can of paint with the lid loosened so it lands alongside the body, and splashes paint all over like it had been dropped from high up.

"But none of it splashed as high as the window. He closed the window and went out. He dabbled one hand in the fresh paint—standing at the edge of the puddle—flicked paint at the closed windowpanes, both of them, to prove both halves of the windows were closed when the paint splashed, see? Then he comes back in—opens the window from the inside and leans out and yells. He's got some paint left on his hand or hands, but that'll be covered if he's the first one outside to examine the body."

"I'll be damned!" said Marlow. "If there really *is* blue paint on the inside handle of that window, then the—"

The tall bookkeeper's leap was so sudden that it caught Marlow unaware. A left jab struck his jaw. Not with any great force, but with enough push to send him off balance, reaching for the wall to keep from falling. And Horvath's right hand darted inside Marlow's coat and jerked the captain's service automatic out of its shoulder holster.

His knuckles were white on the handle as he swung it in a wavering quarter circle that covered all of them. His face was white, scared, and his voice unsteady with tension. He said, "I'll shoot the first one that—"

Craig stood up slowly, and he raised his hands slowly—as slowly as he'd made every move of the afternoon, up to now. Then, as the automatic swiveled to the far end of its arc, he leaped at the murderer with a speed almost unbelievable in a man of his bulk. A speed that the bookkeeper obviously hadn't believed possible, else he would have stepped back farther from the bulky sergeant.

Craig's grabbing hand missed the automatic, but the sheer momentum of his rush carried both Horvath and himself off their feet, and the floor shook with the crash of their landing. The gun skittered and Marlow got it.

Craig grunted and got up slowly. "He's out cold. Hope I didn't— Nope, he's all right; just knocked the wind and daylights out of him. What time is it, Cap? The train's at three fifty-five."

Marlow looked at his wrist watch. He said, "You got only eighteen minutes to make it; I don't think you can. You better wait for—"

But Craig was running—actually running—out the door and they heard his elephantine footsteps thundering down the stairs, two steps at a time.

Marlow said, "Hey—" and started after him, then went over and leaned out the window instead.

He said, "Hey—" again as Craig came in sight out the door, but Craig kept on running. He skirted part of the big blue puddle of paint and tried to jump across—

Then came disaster. His heel came down in thick blue paint and slipped, and his feet went out from under him. He sat down flat with a splash, in the thickest part of the blue pool of paint.

For the moment he was too angry to start swearing, too angry even to realize the extent of damage and disaster. And Captain Marlow, grinning down out of the window like a derbied gargoyle grimacing from a frieze, took full advantage of the silence.

"You awkward lummox," he said, "I was trying to tell you you'd get north *sooner* if you took the fast through express that leaves at seven thirty. Incidentally, pal, it's called the Blue Streak. And if you'll go home and put on a new blue suit, I'll take you to dinner before you leave. Over at the Bluebell Restaurant, they got swell blue points on the Blue Plate Special. And three guesses what kind of modern music the orchestra's famous for."

DANE GREGORY

Hear That Mournful Sound

THERE ARE A number of unsung pulpsters—writers of considerable talent who, because they never graduated to books or the slick-paper magazines, and therefore never developed a readership outside the pulps, have languished in undeserved obscurity. John Lawrence is one such unsung author; G. T. Fleming-Roberts is another. But the best of them all, at least in this writer's opinion, is Rob Robbins.

Robbins, who wrote primarily under the pseudonym of Dane Gregory, was a prolific contributor to the pulps in the thirties and early forties. He was equally adept at humor, light sex fiction, crime stories, Westerns, and shivery weird menace yarns. But his finest work was in the mystery field; the bulk of it was sold to Rogers Terrill at Popular Publications and published in Detective Tales.

Under Terrill's editorship, Detective Tales (1935–1952) was a cut above the average crime pulp. The conventional tough private eye, so prevalent in the pages of rival magazines, was conspicuously absent from DT during Terrill's tenure; instead, he gave his readers off-trail stories with emphasis on character and atmosphere as well as fast-paced action. Since quality stories of this type were not easy to come by, he was quick to encourage the talent of the man who signed himself Dane Gregory, often featuring Gregory stories on the covers and praising them in interior blurbs.

Curiously, Terrill was not enthusiastic about "Hear That Mournful

Sound" when it was submitted; he felt it was too subtle for the pulp audience. But it is a mark of his editorial acumen that he recognized its obvious merits, and bought and published it anyway. It appeared in the November 1942 issue of Detective Tales, *under the title "Lynchville Had a Barber." Despite Terrill's reservations, which perhaps unfairly underestimated his readership, it is Dane Gregory's most accomplished story ("The Mandarin's Thirty-Third Tooth" and "The Silver Bell of San Gee," two fine novelettes with Chinatown settings, rank as close seconds). A masterful blend of horror, atmosphere, and unusual characterization, it is reminiscent of Cornell Woolrich at his most spellbinding. Once read, neither it nor its final sentence can be easily forgotten.*

Rob Robbins made his first pulp sales in the mid-thirties, to Breezy Stories *and* Droll Stories—*work he refers to as "haymow literature, but so dewy-eyed in its approach to sex that today any Boy Scout could read the stories to his mother." Later, after working as an itinerant newsman on the Pacific Coast, he settled in San Francisco and began writing for the pulps full-time, publishing more than 100 stories under a variety of names. His pulp career ended in 1942 when he took an air traffic job with the Civil (later Federal) Aeronautics Administration in Alaska, where he remained until his retirement from the FAA in 1970. Since then, he has returned both to the Pacific Coast and to freelance writing, mostly of nonfiction. In the past decade he has contributed unusual feature material to publications in the US, Canada, and England; some of his articles on psi phenomena and historic murder cases have recently been collected by a British publisher. He now makes his home in Oregon.*

CHAPTER ONE
HELL'S ORCHARD

When she is murdered, let no one mourn.
This was destined when she was born:
But save your tears for the slayer who
Weeps on the very blade that slew.
————Red-inked entry in Claybaugh's
Giant Scrap Book——probably by
Claybaugh his own-self.

WELL, I DON'T know. They held the services the second day after all this took place up on the Hill; but while that's crowding things a little for these parts, I suppose it was thought best on account of the unseasonable weather. Anyhow, the news had traveled far enough so there was a very good attendance.

Miss Eubanks had been a pleasant woman, given to a few whims in her later years (as who is not? I always say) but highly thought of by all.

After the main service there was a long procession out to the cemetery and then a brief graveside service where they tell me the widowed Mrs. Crownover——she'd been Miss Eubanks' dearest friend——created a little excitement by offering to throw herself in the open vault.

I wasn't there for that part of it, however. It being a Saturday morning, I had to get back to the barber shop.

Most of the time the shop kept me pretty busy on a Saturday, and that had been especially true since Copeland Powers put away his apron to take a houseman's job over at the Club. Not that I minded, you understand. I've always been one to like lots of company and baseball talk around me; and anyhow, it was just as Tookie used to say.

That was the wife: her folks had named her Tucker after some relation on her mother's side, but everybody called her Tookie.

"Chigger," she used to tell me in her laughing way, "a chink in the till is worth two in the plaster."

But I don't know. It may have been the strange weather or it may have been that a big funeral procession always seems to drag the quiet of death through a town. Whatever it was, I never passed a longer, slower Saturday morning.

It was not seeing Charlie at the shine-chair that got to me the worst. I put a good stiff edge on the razors and then I moved the Lucky Tiger calendar over to the south wall, but it seemed like the rest of the time there was nothing to do with my hands. Under the circumstances, I guess it was only natural I should think quite a bit about Charlie.

Let's see, now, he'd been working for me every Saturday—oh, it must have been all of six years—till the day he got his big hands on that axe. Charlie always did like sharp things, but of course nobody thought much about it *then*. It was six years, all right, because it comes back to me now that it was that terrible hot summer right after Tookie went to Wichita, Kansas.

Well, I don't know. As I was going to say, this particular Saturday morning I felt about as sorry for him as I had when he first came bawling into town with the slats of his dad's whip across his forty-year-old shoulders.

It's not that I'm taking up for murder-most-foul, as Colonel Murfree likes to call it. Whether by Charlie or by Adam's off-ox, it's a crime against nature and I guess we all see eye-to-eye on that. But Charlie had been a great outdoor man, you know; and we don't have Court Week here until late September. It gave me a shut-in feeling myself to think of spending three months in jail.

I made up a little package out of some funnypaper books and then I put on my hat and coat and hung up the "Back Soon" sign. I went upstreet toward the county jail, which is four blocks south along Main in what some call the old pecan grove. That way the wind was in my face.

It seemed like the wind would never let up. Six days steady now it had been blowing in from the south; but not hard and not hurried and not even hot enough that a man could break out in a good clean sweat. It had the smell of dying flowers on it, and it was slow and smooth. You could open your hand against it and it would run like a woman's hand through your fingers; and in the night when it slipped along the eaves it was like a woman's voice.

Even the sheriff seemed to feel it a little, though Claybaugh is scarcely what anyone would call an edgy sort. He was working away at a crossword puzzle. His coat and vest and shirt were thrown across the back of his chair.

"Chigger," said Sheriff Claybaugh. "Eight-letter word beginning with H and ending with E and meaning 'capital offense.' Any ideas?"

I said no; then added: "I brought Charlie some funny books, Clay. *Animal Antics*—they're the only ones that don't make him cry."

"That's thoughtful. Strange about Charlie going berserk on us, ain't it? Everybody knew he was a little turned, but nobody thought he'd ever turn completely berserkwards."

"Claybaugh, that ain't funny!"

"I know it ain't, Chig." The sheriff turned his blue eyes up to me and they were soft. "I'm fond of Charlie my own-self, and I just can't hardly see him taking the wrong side of an axe to a gentle old soul like Miss Eubanks. Nope. I can't hardly see it happen."

"Well," I said, "he likes sharp things, Clay. No getting around it, Charlie always appreciated a good cutting piece. And there's weather."

Claybaugh huffed out his cheeks. "Tell a man there's weather. She's a sirocco for fair."

"Come twice?"

"You ought to do some word puzzles your own-self. Sirocco is what they call it in the tropical places when a wind blows in from the south this way. Makes people jumpy as cats, somehow, and now and then one of 'em goes on the hunt like Charlie. It's like the same chord of music played over and over till it runs through your bones like a scream."

"Say, don't it?"

Claybaugh said, "But it don't come often here. Last bad spell was six years ago. I remember the time because that was the year somebody boiled up crow meat and ate it to pay off a mid-term election bet. And that was the year—"

He unhooked the star from his uppers and began to pick away at a little spot of egg-yellow that had hardened into the groove.

"Well, I can talk about it now," I said. "That was the year Tookie packed up her duds and left me."

Claybaugh shook his head. "Pretty little thing. Cute as a cardinal with all that red hair—but, Chig, she'd been a flirting girl from the first." He put his key-ring on the desk. "Guess I can trust you with these, boy, but you watch Charlie real close."

"Tell a man I will."

Claybaugh came clear out of his chair and slapped the roll-top like someone killing bugs. "Homicide!" he yelled. *"Homicide!* Dam' it, Chigger, all this time it's been plain as the nose on your face!"

I edged away from him a little and ran one finger up to the nerve that sometimes draws at my lip. "Come twice?" I said.

Claybaugh dipped his pen in the bottle of red ink. He sat down and began to scratch letters across the word puzzle. "Begins with H and ends with E, don't it? You watch Charlie, boy—never can tell what may be in a man's mind."

I went in there to Charlie's cell and Charlie said through his balled hands, "I just couldn't seem to eat 'er, sheriff. You can warm 'er up for my supper, though, can't you?"

I said, "It's me."

He took his knuckles out of his eyes and they were tender. "I said all the time you might come and see me, Mr. Deems. I told the sheriff so."

"Well, and why not, Charlie? I brought you a slight something, too."

He brightened his eyes at the funnypaper books. "Cub bear ones?

"Miss Eubanks thought maybe I could learn to puzzle out the short words. She said so, Mr. Deems. But they wouldn't let me go to the service—oh, no, not *them!* Wasn't usual, the sheriff said."

"Charlie," I said, "it really ain't. Claybaugh tries to be fair."

"But I didn't chop her!" said Charlie. "Not one lick, I didn't. Mr. Deems. I need some new clothes awful bad, but you just couldn't have hired me to chop Miss Eubanks."

I sat down on the edge of Charlie's bunk and loosened my collar some so I could breathe better. "Seems like you were up there on the Hill, though," I said.

"On'y because Miss Eubanks likes flowers."

"Come twice?"

Charlie said, "She was gonna put in a big rock garden there, people talked. She was gonna stump out that old crabble orchard she taken over from the bank. So I says I'll go up there and offer to chop for Miss Eubanks. I figured she'd leave me chop, Mr. Deems, because everyone knows how handy I am with—"

His face bleached tow and I thought for a minute he was going to yell. "But not that way, Mr. Deems," he whispered.

"Maybe we better talk about the cub bear books."

"The wind was on the back of my neck," said Charlie. He was shaking a little and hunting a place for his hands. "It was like someone breathing on me, Mr. Deems, and it was dretful up there and I wanted to turn at the gate. But that was when I heard the scream. *Jim sang his'n purty!*' it screamed. *Jim sang his'n purty!*' "

"Come twice?"

He said it again.

"Charlie," I told him, "that's wild. Miss Eubank never owned a talking crow in her life."

"Wasn't no crow that screamed it, Mr. Deems. It was pore Miss Eubanks her own-self."

"Charlie," I said, "that story would be plain poison in court. Miss Eubanks had taught school all her life, and everyone knows she made a chore of her grammar."

He clenched his big face and went on talking. "I wanted to go the other way, but Miss Eubanks had been my dear friend. I run and I run towards the house, and direc'ly I got to the door it was bad, Mr. Deems. She set there with her head up against the door and I thought right away something might be out of whack because the axe was in her— The axe was in— The axe, Mr. Deems."

"Charlie."

"And I was crying a little, I guess, and I says, 'Miss Eubanks,' I says to her, 'how come anyone would want to chop *you?*' " Charlie put his mouth too close to my ear. "And then there was The Sign," he whispered.

"The Sign?" I asked.

"It was dretful," whispered Charlie. "Dead as she is, *up* jumps her arm like this, Mr. Deems; and she points Out There! She points Out There to that old crabble orchard—and then *down* goes her arm like this. It on'y made a soft little spank on the step, though."

It was the way he told it, somehow. I said, "Charlie!"

"And I took up the axe and I mogged for the trees, but the wind could mog faster than me. It was dretful when I got to the orchard. There was a shadow sixty-five miles long that run through the grass like a snake, but I could have stood that, maybe." He put his mouth to my ear again. "On'y thing I couldn't stand was The Women."

"Women?"

Charlie whispered, "It don't get in the books, I guess, but maybe the millionaires have got some *reason* for keeping it from us. When that south wind shook the leaves, I knew. It blew the moon all silver and green through the crabble trees; and the trees kep' saying at me, kep' saying: *'Oo-h-h, Charlie! Ah-h-h, Charlie! Tell the boys hello-o-o, Charlie, and don't do a thing I wouldn't do."*

He pecked at my knee with his forefinger then, but I don't suppose I jumped more than two or three feet at the outside. "You tell Colonel Murfree and maybe he'll put it in the *Democrat*," said Charlie. "Them crabble trees up on the Hill, Mr. Deems, they're dead women lifting their pore lean arms to fluff out their hair and try to look purty again."

"Charlie," I said, "not another word! A man can stand so much and no more."

"That's what I know," said Charlie. "I couldn't have gone on into them trees if I'd been bare-naked and Pop behind me with the gad. I yapped like a pup and I made for the road, and there I was swinging that dretful axe and running off at the head when the Allisons come uphill in their car." His mouth reached for his ear-lobes again. "How's Mrs. Allison today? Hate to think of her being down sick."

"Now, Charlie, you don't want to be a cry-baby all the time, do you? Look, Charlie," I told him, "you haven't even opened up your funnypaper book."

He unrolled the funnypaper books and out rolled that old Navy Colt of mine—the one I got from Copeland Powers when he bet on the wrong sheriff.

CHAPTER TWO
LYNCH TALK

CHARLIE COOLED OFF his fingers on the leg of his cords. His mouth opened wide then closed very slowly. He leaned close to me, whispered: "Gun?"

"Gun," I agreed.

"No," whispered Charlie.

I rattled the key-ring at him and said, "The Allison boys are taking their mother up north awhile—they think maybe she'll get over her breakdown sooner there. Well, Charlie, they've got a nice cool cyclone-cellar where you could hole up for weeks. Would be a nice cozy place."

He turned his face to the window and *whuffed* like a dog. "But maybe you'd get in bad with—"

"I'll have a yarn for Claybaugh—don't you fret about that. Charlie, maybe you're guilty as sin, but other-hand maybe you're not. One way or the other, I wouldn't keep a cannibal shoat cooped up in weather like this. Not when the south wind is blowing."

Charlie moved his feet. "The sheriff give me a big cavalry sword oncet."

It was muggy as a swamp in that little cell, and the nape of my neck began to draw at the hairline. "Damn it," I said, "you don't think I'm telling you to shoot *at* him, do you? All you've got to do is pour enough lead around the place to keep him interested in his word-puzzle. And then you mog, understand? Man comes in here offering you a chance and you stand around thinking up crazy things instead of mogging."

Charlie coaxed, "Don't lay 'er on my old sore back, Mr. Deems." He took the gun and he took the key-ring and he opened up the door and he went.

I lay down on the floor near the cub bear books and looked up at the long crack that ran across the ceiling. The funnybooks had the root-beerish smell of Bigler's Pharmacy.

I guess ordinarily the Colt would have made a terrific *boom,* but in all that soft heat the shots had a lazy, rolling sound like a cowbell heard at dusk. I lay where I was and listened to Claybaugh's chair lean hard against the wall and something heavy turn over once to scratch at the floor like a Badger. Then things were quiet.

Claybaugh came in sweating a little and dragging Charlie along by the scruff of his shirt. "Dam' it, Chigger," he scolded. "I told you to watch him. Remember I warned you."

Charlie had never been much to look at, of course, but he was worse than ever with his shirt front stained red clear down to the old trunk strap he used for a belt. I came up onto my hands and knees and shook my head a little to put things back where they belonged.

"I was watching him like a hawk," I said, "but even a hawk can't see backwards. And who'd ever have thought he knew the rabbit punch?"

Claybaugh threw Charlie onto the bunk and wiped off his fingers with the cub bear books. "You didn't even say you were toting a gun," he complained.

"Tell a man I was. Think I'd call on Charlie without side-arms of some kind?"

"Well," said Claybaugh, "all I wish is he hadn't made me do it. What'd the poor stiff want with a gun, anyhow? He threw every one of his shots straight at the floor."

Charlie's feet looked only a little bigger than gravestones with his toes turned up.

I shut my eyes and said, "Well, there'd have been a lot of loose talk if Charlie had broke out of jail. I hate having this happen, Clay, but I guess you handled 'er the only way you could."

"The only merciful way, after all," said Claybaugh. He blew his nose and heaved a great sigh. "Dam' it, though, I'm going to give Charlie particular hell when he comes out of this! That bottle of red ink I slapped him with went all over my word-puzzle, Chigger."

Well, I'll say this for the shots: they warmed up trade a little. People usually come to my shop for the fresh news, and it made things even better that I'd been right there in the thick of the fray when Charlie put on his jailbreak. By first-coke time that afternoon I had a better than fair crowd.

"Oh, Charlie's not really a bad sort," I told them. "Another sheriff might have played 'er different, but I'm kind of glad old

Claybaugh is the easy-going type. I wouldn't want anything to happen to Charlie. I'd hate to think of Charlie stopping a bullet from Clay's gun."

Cotton Maxey made the noise he makes with his lips. That's the blonde Maxey boy—the one that wears the green suit and the old Settler's Day button reading: *I Love My Wife, but Oh, You Kid.*

"Charlie can't help from liking sharp things," said Cotton Maxey. "They tell me his mother once jumped on his head because he forgot to dig up a fresh batch of eating-clay."

"Well," I said to the stuffed raccoon up on the setback, "you can't hardly blame her for that. I understand she'd been planning a big charity supper for the Maxey family."

There was a sort of embarrassed silence after I said it. Neither the 'coon nor anybody else wanted to break out a smile, because Cotton packs around a barlow knife only a little less wicked than the razor I was holding. He decided to let it ride. But the look he gave me wasn't friendly at all.

We were most of us somewhat on the peck, I guess. The southerly wind had blown in all day, shaking the dry catalpas along Main so that they danced like fingers on a piano. I'd closed up my shop tight against the sound; and as Les Turnidge came in, the air in that place was scarcely a day deader than Adam.

"She's thinning out on top, Les," I told him.

"I'm paying you to cut it, not wear it." He looked up at the 'coon in the setback as if he would like to shoot it again. "So Charlie goes faunching in there with a couple of big guns and Claybaugh slaps him with a book. Wears a gun his own-self, don't he?"

"Oh, it wasn't quite like that, Les. Anyhow, Claybaugh hates to shoot at people he knows."

I oiled up the clippers a little; they had a baby-chick sound that wore on my nerves. "It's not that I'm saying anything against Miss Eubanks," I said. "There wasn't a better woman or a finer teacher in the world. I'll leave that to Cotton Maxey, there—he must've got to know her pretty well those five or six years he spent in the Fourth B. She taught your little ones, most of you, and I guess she'd have taught mine if Tookie and I— Well, she was a fine woman."

"Set up with my wife once," said Les. His strawberry mark had a hot, chafed look under the clippers.

"Set up with everybody's wife. Fed hungry bellies and clothed naked Maxeys—whether they wanted to be or not. Asked nothing more of life than the right to raise a few little flowers. But like I say, she's gone now—couldn't even smell the beautiful floral offerings at her own service—while poor old Charlie sits up there healthy enough to tear the neck off a horse. And it's the living we've got to think of boys. Remember that."

Cotton Maxey bent over to stare at the sleepy June bug that had blown in from the street. There was a sound of breathing in the room, thick and slow like the wind. Crabby old G. D. Harvison Murrow balled his hand on Cotton's new issue of *Ginger Snaps* and peered at me out of eyes that were only a little more glassy than the stuffed raccoon's.

"*You'd* have to take up for Charlie! Sure—you hired him in the first place. Well, it ain't gonna do you a lick of good, Chigger! He'll get *his* next Court Week, the axe-murdering—"

"That so, G. D.?"

"Ain't it?"

I blew on the clippers. "Few months from now," I told them all, "we'll look out there and see old Charlie swinging downstreet with a grin on his face from here to the Hollow. Yes, and his big old cavalry sword clunking along at his side. Well, that's all right. Charlie ain't a bad man at heart, you know."

Les Turnidge's neck twitched under the lather. "How do you mean, Chigger?"

"Why, man alive," I said, "there ain't a single one of those big-upstate-millionaire-lawyers who won't be fighting for the chance to take Charlie's case! Just for the fame of it, I mean. And then what happens? With the exception of Cotton Maxey, there, every man-jack of you would have to tell the truth on the stand."

Cotton opened up his barlow knife and began to strop it softly on the sole of his shoe.

Les Turnidge said, "*What* truth? Or maybe we ain't got the right to know. We're only taxpayers! It's root-hog-or-die for the poor man, but some big-fat-upstate millionaire-lawyer— Ouch!"

"You leaned on the blade your own-self, Les. Why, Charlie's a little *different*, that's all, and you'd have to say so, wouldn't you? They'll send him away to a *place* for a while, and in three-four months—oh, maybe six—back comes Charlie to his grindstone and his tools. Well, hell, I like Charlie. I'd hate to think of him being cooped up for the rest of his days."

The June bug tottered over to the fallen *Ginger Snaps* and looked at a row of letters reading: *Babes in the Woodshed, by Dodo Dare.* Cotton's knife went *whickety-whack* on the quiet. G. D. Harvison Murrow bawled:

"Released as cured, you mean? You mean a bunch of big-fat-bloated-upstate millionaire-lawyers can come down here and—"

"It's how things are done, G. D. Right or wrong, it's legal, and we've got to stand by the law. I'll always say the crowd done the wrong thing in that beast-man case up north.

"What beast-man case?" said Les. "Ouch, damn it!"

"Criminy, don't jump around so! Well, some of the papers called it the Frenzied Frankenstein case. Seems this poor stiff had just been released from a *place*—been there three-four months. He thinks, *'Well. Nothing like having a license to kill, is there?'* So they were having a sort of Settler's Day like the one we have in October, and— Oh, I hate to talk about it."

The June bug had turned west and crawled along a crack in the floor. He was trying to find air, I guess. "Tell it!" screamed G. D. Harvison Murrow. "Tell it, Chigger!"

"Well, it was the little girl's death that got the town worked up so bad. The other eight people were all adults, and they should have had sense enough not to get in the way of a killer armed with a scythe. But the little yellow-haired girl— Anyhow, they called on Mr. Killer that night and they took him out of the jail. No fuss, no ceremony—they just took him right out and hung him higher than Haman's headache on the nearest tree."

Les said, "But how did they—"

"Oh, the jailhouse was a small one—not much bigger or stronger than ours, I guess. And then it seems the sheriff was an easy-going sort of man, too. You know the kind of man that wouldn't shoot an egg-sucking dog or a ditto Maxey."

Cotton tested the edge of the knife on a match he'd had clamped between his teeth. It still wasn't sharp enough to suit him, though. "You mean there was no trouble at all?" said G. D. Harvison Murrow.

"Well, I guess a couple of rich lawyers blew off a little, but the county officials winked at each other and let 'er ride. Some people

thought it would have been better if they'd handled it that way
when the gorilla-man drew his first blood—but like I was saying in
the first place, I don't hold with none of that. Men shouldn't take
the law in their own hands, not even when it's a matter of protect-
ing their homes and dear ones."

"I've got four little tykes of my own," yelled Lester Turnidge,
"and, Chigger, I'm just sort of curious to know why! Yes, and one
of 'em's a little yellow-haired girl, too! Little Sunshine, we call her,
and only the other day she was saying, 'Papa,' she was saying, 'don't
call me Little Sunshine any more because sometimes the sunshine—
sometimes the sunshine goes—' "

"Well, Les?"

" '—out,' " whispered Les. "Why, Chigger? Why? Why?"

"Just ain't right, that's all. Shows poor spirit. . . . There you are,
Les—clean as the rim of a bowl. Next pair of ears to be lowered!"

G. D. H. Murrow ground his footprints into one of those sporty-
looking women they have in the magazine. "Poor spirit, says Chigger! Poor spirit! But it's fine and dandy for a whole slough of big-
fat-bloated-plutocratic-multimillionaire-corporation-lawyers—yes,
and upstate ones on top of that!—to come down here and lay every
horror in the handbook on us! That's all right, now ain't it?"

"Easy does it, G. D. You don't want to go around talking like a
sorehead."

G. D. shook his two fists at the stuffed raccoon. "Just like Claybaugh, that's *his* trouble! Red-handed Frankensteen monster goes
screaming in there with a gun in each hand and that big old
cavalry sword in the other—and Claybaugh he's too timid to do
any more than spank him with a word-puzzle! Afraid to buck The
System! Well, he's a part of The System, that's why—and I ain't
voted for him any of these past sixteen years without wondering
when he'd show his hand!"

He got in the barber-chair panting a little. It was stuffy in there,
you know.

I said, "You hadn't ought to talk that way about Claybaugh, boys.
Clay's all right—it's just that he don't like to shoot at people he
knows. Why, if a crowd of you was to go up there tonight and say,
'Claybaugh, we can't sleep a wink till we've taken care of Charlie'—
well, like I say, what would happen? Why, Claybaugh he'd just only

shake his head sadly and tell you: 'Guess it's your right, boys, but I hate to think of what the millionaires will say.' She's thin on tap, G. D."

"Why wouldn't it be? I'm only a poor man, not one of these big-fat-baldheaded—"

"But of course," I said, "we don't live in that kind of town. And Claybaugh probably wouldn't be there, anyhow—he comes in at ten o'clock for his Sunday shave. Reminds me, I understand he may see Cotton Maxey's pa tomorrow and make him promise to use a lighter bullwhip when his crippled old mother drags the plow."

I picked up the straight-edge again. "And personally, boys," I told them all, "I'm glad to be living in the kind of town where a sheriff can safely leave his jail. I'm glad for Charlie's sake if nothing else—I wouldn't want anything to happen to poor old Charlie. . . . Something bothering you, Cotton?"

Cotton crouched low and put the point of his barlow knife slowly through the June bug's middle. Just in time, too—another second and the bug would have found that crack in the door.

CHAPTER THREE
"HERE COMES TOOKIE!"

WELL, I DON'T know. This is a kind of quiet little garden spot where nothing much ever happens after dark, though we do manage to scare up a bit of excitement at the fall street dances, and I guess there's little or no point in my keeping the shop open so late on a Saturday. The twilight was nice. At dusk the wind had turned off to a whisper.

Cotton Maxey came upstreet putting one yellow shoe ahead of the other with the particular care of a cat on a clothesline. He was wearing an old carnival streamer around his green hat,—*Out For a Good Time,* was what it said—and even with the wind going north I could smell the green choc smell that came south.

"Chigger," said Cotton. "Don't mean to tell me you're missing the party."

I didn't say aye-yes-or-damn.

"Chigger," said Cotton. "I figured of course you had your invite, him being a special friend. I even brought him a something my own-self."

It was a fudget I guess he'd picked up on the wheel o' fortune for not more than ten or twelve dollars—a little black ball-shaped tiepin with the numeral eight on it.

"Wouldn't want him to go tacky," said Cotton. "When a man wears a tie only once in his life, seems like he'd ought to wear something *on* it."

"Cotton," I told him, "I hope some day you'll drop around and open your barlow knife close enough to me so I can make twins of my favorite barroom poet. And bring your dog. If there's a flea-trap cur sick enough to like your smell, I'll provide a cur for each poet."

The light of his cigarette blew across his eyes and they were crazy. "Oh, will you?" said Cotton. "Oh, peachy!" He crooked his wrists like an edgy girl and went on up towards the grove.

That would have been about half after nine, I'd judge. Yes, I remember it well now—I looked at the clock when I went back inside.

It was quiet and stuffy for a while after that, and there was nothing much to keep me interested but the new supply catalogue.

It was 9:55, as I recall, when I heard the first of the sounds. *Smack!* it went—*smackety-smack!*—about like that. It probably would have sounded much louder up-wind, but coming all four blocks downtown it merely had a kind of soft, flat note.

That soon shaded off into nothing at all; and it must have been anyhow five minutes before I heard this heavier noise which was more like someone beating the top of a barrel.

A man yelled once above the noise, but the wind had cracked his words to pieces long before they reached the corner of Main and Seminole. Or maybe he didn't say anything in actual words; it sounded like G. D. Harvison Murrow uncorking a little rage. For the most part, however, there was only this *tunkety-tunk* effect and the various small sounds in the trees.

I sat where I was and didn't say aye-yes-or-hell; but of course it was something a man couldn't gloss over altogether. Even the 'coon in the setback appeared to be edgy. The jailhouse was bound to give in before long.

Take it all in all, I was pretty well pleased when Claybaugh came in for his shave. A man likes company around him at such times, you know. That was close on 10:10, I believe, though Claybaugh insisted the clock was four minutes slow by evening alamo time.

He hung up his coat and his vest and guns and he got in the chair. "Not too heavy on the hot towels, Chigger. Seems like it's hectic enough already with this bad harmattan going night and day."

"Come twice?"

"Tramontane, mistral, levanter or sirocco," said Claybaugh. "The wind that walks in the leaves, as the poet says."

I laid on the towels and boiled him only to a scolded baby blush. I took off the towels and said, "You slung the bolts and came up through the skylight, I gather. Well, personally, I think you done the right thing. No use a man's going the roundabout way for trouble."

We couldn't very well pretend to ignore it, you know: that would just have embarrassed the both of us. Somewhere the boys had scared up what sounded to me like a crowd-sized ridgepole; and on that sleepy breeze it made a firm, whanging noise only a little more noticeable than the late drought. *Dum-dum-dum*—like that.

"Guess you're right, Chigger," sighed Claybaugh. "Anyhow, Charlie'll soon be out of it all."

"That's how I look at it, too."

"And it seems to be a good orderly crowd," said the sheriff.

"Well," I told him, "I could see 'er coming this afternoon, Clay—there was some talk against Charlie right in here. But after all, what's a man to do?"

Claybaugh huffed out a scallop of lather. He drummed his fingers on the sides of the chair and said: "Not much of nothing, I guess. And how I look at it is this: if the jail can be torn down, county needs a new jail bad. Well, it'll be a whole lot easier to talk up a bond issue when Charlie's out of his misery at last and people start feeling low-down about the whole thing."

"That's a businesslike way to look at 'er, all right."

"Blade seems a little dull, Chigger," said Claybaugh. "I'd feel sort of easier in my mind if Charlie had done more damage with his shooting-piece today; but there's this much about it, Chig—a hang-rope jerks practic'ly any murder case out of the road. I don't know—even the courts usually assume that the dead man was guilty as charged. Well; that's human."

They were really drumming old Charlie out of there for fair. A broken window-pane tittered high on the gust; but the only windows in the jail were well above a tall man's reach. The thing that seemed to draw on your nerves was the steady beat of that big old ridge-pole fighting at the door.

It worked a little on Claybaugh, too, though Claybaugh has never been the edgy sort. He traded stares with the stuffed raccoon and began to drone through his nose while I whipped a little new into the razor. It was that tired old down-country *Johnny Allen* tune that goes in one ear and always has such a hard time finding its way out the other.

> *Johnny, oh, Johnny, oh, poor Johnny Allen—*
> *Why does he shudder and what does he fear?*
> *Only a voice calling over and over,*
> *Crying: Oh, Johnny, my bonny, my dear!*
> *Crying forever to poor Johnny Allen:*
> *Johnny, oh, bonny, oh, dear,*
> *My dear,*
> *My dear.*

"Clay," I told him, "that's plain morbid for a Saturday night."

"Don't blame you much," said Claybaugh. "Is kind of lonesome, ain't it? There was another song you hated bad, as I remember. That was the one Cotton Maxey used to coo on the various pool-hall programs: *'Looky, looky, looky! Here comes Tookie! See you later, boys.'* . . . . Wup! Nicked me a little."

"That's a bad mole, Clay. It ought to come off."

"Didn't it?" said Claybaugh. He twiddled his thumbs. "Well, Tookie was a pretty little thing, Chigger. Never forget how she used to dance her way downstreet with all that bright hair burning on her throat and just the right do on her mouth to make it look like fireweed honey tastes . . . *Oh*, she was pretty! But, Chig, there was more than once I wanted to reverse the order and spank her till she barked like a fox—and I guess maybe it was even worse for an edgy kind of man like you."

I tapped a spot of lotion onto Claybaugh's nick. "Tookie has her faults," I told him. "As who does not?—I always say."

"Still and all, Chigger, it couldn't've been a whole lot of fun for you when Tookie came sneakfooting in with choc on her breath and her nice rozberry lipstick worn down to the quick. I felt for you, Chigger—I really did."

I didn't say aye-yes-or-what of it. It was like that line in McGuffey's reader: The barber kept on shaving.

Claybaugh said: "Must've been particular hell, I should think, with the south wind singing that old, old song: *I Wonder Who's Kissing Her Now*. You remember it, don't you? Tookie used to whistle it sometimes when she played the piano . . . . And you remember the wind, don't you, Chigger?—that strange wind six summers ago—the slow dark wind that poured over the world like sorghum over a cake. . . . Oh, by the way, Chigger, where *is* Tookie?"

"Puff out your cheek a little, will you? There. Oh, she went to Wichita, Clay—thought you knew. Understand she's going with some big-millionaire-lawyer now.

CHAPTER FOUR
CRIMSON SPLOTCHES

THE CROWD UPSTREET seemed bigger and noisier now. While I wasn't there at the time, of course, I have an idea the boys at the Club had broken up their pan game in a great big hurry when the news scattered out on the wind.

Cope Powers has always been quite an organizer, you know— he's president of the Hustle Up dinner group here in town—and now you could hear somebody with Cope's voice yelling: "*Way-y* back, fellows! *Way-y* back!" Then it would be *whoom*—rest—*whoom*— over and over that way till it seemed like the slam of old Charlie's heart against his ribs.

"Can't be much longer now," I said.

Claybaugh pulled in a cheek muscle under the scrape of the blade. "And I'll never forget the night Tookie left you, Chigger. 'Claybaugh,' you told me, bawling like a kid, 'my Tookie's gone and done 'er at last.' Didn't surprise me a whole lot, of course."

"Wish you wouldn't talk so much when I'm trying to make you presentable for—for church. Sets me on edge a little."

"There was something kind of odd about the house, though," said Claybaugh. "Queer. I didn't even notice it at the time, Chig, but later on it came back to me and plagued me now and then for years. Sort of like an old word puzzle you've had to put away unworked. . . . *If Tookie was going to leave him,* I says, *why would she have bothered herself to drag that big hooked rug out from under the divan and move it clean over to yonder side the room?*"

I gave the straight-edge a lick and a promise. "Women are strange things, ain't they? Like Pa Deems used to say: Never marry a woman."

Claybaugh said: "A man's mind keeps on playing with problems even after something dark spills over his word puzzle. I think I solved that one tonight at half-past eight by evening alamo time."

"Did you, now, Claybaugh?"

"Yes. That was when I found myself all-a-sudden moving an old scatterrug over to hide that great big red-ink stain on my office floor. It looked so much like blood."

The wind ran in the brown catalpas and clashed them together like rattlebones ticking off the beat of a song. *Bonny, oh, dear, my dear.* I hate those old sad pieces. Give me something lively every time.

"Must have been a bad spot on your parlor floor," said Claybaugh. "*Oh-h,* it must have been bad—and especially so if lye and sandpaper and a porcupine brush wouldn't scour it out of your thoughts. . . . Where is she, Chigger? Where's Tookie cooling off her little heels, Chigger Deems?"

I said: "Wish you wouldn't talk about her like that. She knew how to laugh, Clay. She knew how to play the piano. I don't know— maybe she knew how to live."

"And it's too dam' bad she had to die in order to prove it. I guess you know you're under arrest, Chigger."

"And I guess you know you're under a razor," I said.

It went—*whoomety-whoom*—sort of like that. Practically any barber might have a bad accident with so much noise going on upstreet. And then, too, people around here know I'm the nervous type. Have been for years. As Colonel Murfree sometimes says, "He jests at scars who was never shaved by Chigger."

Claybaugh's hands lay big and flat and still on the arms of the chair. He turned his blue eyes up to mine and they were chiding. "Chig," said Claybaugh, "alongside you the meanest Maxey smells sweeter than baby's breath to me. You're a wicked little man, Chigger Deems."

"She's been quite a sirocco, Claybaugh."

"That's like a man blaming his weakness on the liquor he drinks to get weak on. I could excuse you Tookie, maybe—she was the kind of girl that whistles her way to a lonesome grave. But there's old Charlie, a man that thought more of you than of Bolivar Bear."

Whoom went the maul.

"And there was Miss Eubanks up on the Hill, a poor old thing trying to fill her life with jonquils because she had a set of teeth that once scared Harvison Murrow witless in a kissing game. Never got over it, either—listen to him howl!"

I opened a button on his shirt. "I tried to reason with her, Claybaugh."

"And I never saw a more convinced corpse."

"Wish you wouldn't talk like that, Clay. 'Miss Eubanks,' I says to her kindly, 'you don't want to stump out all those lovely crab-apple trees. Why, there's good rich shade there,' I says to her. 'Plant you some ginseng roots between the trees and you can make yourself a mint of money when the Chinese market opens up again."

"And then?" said Claybaugh.

"Oh, no, not Miss Eubanks! It was posies or nothing for her. 'Ginseng isn't pretty,' she kept insisting. *'Ginseng isn't pretty!'* she screamed and I guess she was still screaming it some even when I—"

"Take note you'd fetched up her axe from the chopping-block just in case. So Tookie's under the crab-trees, is she? Thought so."

"Won't have people digging there, Claybaugh."

His eyes were round and steady on mine. "Seems like you'd have done a little digging your own-self when you lost that piece of land to the bank."

"I'll tell you, Clay. I hate all this like billy hell, and maybe you'll think less unkindly of me if I—if I tell you the whole thing before I— It's Tookie's voice. It lives on and on in the crab-tree, Clay, and I know it's there because Charlie Weller heard it his own-self."

"The wind that walks in the leaves," said Claybaugh. "When a man's fear is too big for his brain, it always takes a voice outside him."

"It wasn't fear that sent me kiting home with my spade. *'Chigger,'* says Tookie. *'No! No!'* And, Claybaugh, I knew what she meant. There was something she didn't want to spoil for me, you see."

He was watching me dry off the blade; but his hands were quiet. I kept an eye on them, I'll tell a man I did. "That don't sound a whole lot like Tookie," said Claybaugh.

"Sometimes she's still in the house with me," I said. "And don't you go looking at me like I'm crazy! I know it ain't real. There's one part memory of how she was and five parts memory of how she should've been. But, Claybaugh, it was my own tears that finally washed the stain off the parlor floor. It's away to hell-and-gone better than nothing."

The shadow of my hand stopped like a spider on his face. "And that was what she didn't want to spoil for you, Chigger?"

"That was it. She was always so proud of how she looked, you know. She wouldn't want anyone—and me least of all—to see her with her long hair tangled in the— No one can dig around up on the Hill, Clay. Not while *I* live above ground."

His eyes were only a little softer than smoke. "Dam' it, Chigger, I'm almost sorry for you!" The ridgepole went *whoomety-whoomety-whoom.* He added, "Not quite, though."

"Think I wanted to turn old bear-loving Charlie into a million-aire-corporation-lawyer? There's a kind of a thing called fear, Clay, though you wouldn't know what it's like."

He watched the blade turn slow in the light. "You're the best little teacher in the world, Chigger Deems."

"I've got to do 'er," I said. "It ain't the way I'd have had it, Clay, but we quit being old acquaintances when you started working out the wrong kind of puzzles."

"Still don't think you can do 'er, boy. Not to me."

The jailhouse let go at last. You could hear the long, thin scream of the hinges tearing down-wind like a cross-cut tearing through a knot in a Judas tree. *Scre-e-e!*—sort of like that.

"Get the cowardly axe-killer—" yelled Cotton Maxey. And even above the *tunk* of the door, his voice had a bright wet edge like the thing that leaned on my knuckles.

"The years roll on," said Claybaugh. "Don't they, Chigger?"

It burned red and white and red on his neck, the ragged old scar he'd picked up from somebody's sunken drag-line long before the dark winds blew. That had been the afternoon he scraped me off the sticky bottom of the Bear, where I'd just settled down for the second time and had made up my mind to raise particular hell with a tradition.

"Won't do you a lick of good to talk," I told him. "She's got to be done."

I could sweat a little now, though the wind was still heavy with unshed heat. I swung the razor and put plenty of arm behind it. I threw the blade at the stuffed raccoon and put out one of its eyes. "Seems like a man as tight as you would get himself a safety-razor, anyhow," I said. "Guess there are things even a bad coward is worse afraid of than his fear, Claybaugh. Old Man Deems was quite a hellion his own-self, but I guess he never raised that sort of Cain."

Claybaugh huffed his way out of the chair and began to fiddle around with his shirt-buttons. "Hoped you'd put it like that," said Claybaugh. "Wanted to get the straight of things from your own lips, of course, but I think maybe that was the big reason why I came over for my regular close shave." He drew the back of his hand across his forehead and added: "Dam' it, though, Chigger, couldn't you have said it a little sooner?"

Up in the old pecan grove there was a kind of dull, dark *boom* and then we could hear a man's scream raise up and scatter out and die to nothing on the wind. While I wasn't there at the time, naturally, I sort of figured Les Turnidge had brought his new shotgun along.

"Sounds like we're a little too late to do anything for Charlie," I said.

Claybaugh said, "Sounds like Cotton Maxey to me, I hope. Though Copeland Powers would do 'most as well—I been dreading his talk on good fellowship at the club dinner Monday noon. I had a shotgun trap loaded with rock salt and mustard seed in Charlie's cell."

"Well," I said. "Well. But—"

"Oh, I let him out hours ago—soon after he shot three times right square at the floor and didn't even leave any bullet-holes in that. He's close by . . . Charlie!"

Charlie came in through the north door dragging that big old cavalry sword Claybaugh had given him; and it seems he'd been standing there all this time with his elbow cocked for the throw. He was always so handy with sharp things, too.

"I'd have hated to do 'er, Mr. Deems," he bawled, "but I'd have hated worse to see you do 'er to your own brother!"

"Well," I said. "Well."

I knew they were going to take me away; but I felt easier in my mind already, somehow. Maybe the south wind had turned off a little, or—well, it may have been such a relief to get the thing out of my veins at last. It had all been a terrible chore from the first. But I don't know, it seems like once a man gets started he just can't stop.

D. L.
CHAMPION

The Day Nobody Died

THE LOCKED-ROOM murder, that classic puzzle device of detective fiction, was not often used by pulp writers. Their heroes were generally much too busy chasing buxom blondes and dodging bullets to bother with such cerebral activities as piecing together puzzles. And the writers themselves were much too busy turning out reams of copy, in order to satisfy both their editors and their creditors, to bother with the construction of intricate plots, fair-play clues, and the other demanding trappings of the traditional detective story.

Cerebral sleuths were not entirely absent from the pulps, however; nor were ingenious plots that, occasionally, utilized the locked-room gambit. D. L. Champion's Inspector Allhoff is one such rare sleuth. And "The Day Nobody Died," in which Allhoff solves, among other mysterious happenings, the locked-room murder of a midget, is probably his greatest case.

The Inspector Allhoff stories, which ran more or less regularly in Dime Detective *from 1940 to 1946, are pulp pastiches of Rex Stout's famous Nero Wolfe (whether consciously or unconsciously on the part of the author is unknown). Allhoff, a former New York City Police Inspector, seldom leaves his apartment; his two assistants, Simmonds and Battersly, gather evidence and round up suspects for Allhoff, who then uses his superior intellect to get to the bottom of things. But series characters in the pulps had to be more unusual than that—and D. L. Champion was nothing if not an inventive writer. He took the Nero Wolfe formula and gave it a perverse twist: Allhoff has no legs, the result of a machine-gunning incident for which one of the aides, Battersly, was responsible; that is why he stays inside his apartment. Simmonds and Battersly are, quite literally, his legmen. Allhoff has also become somewhat unhinged by the loss of his lower extremities. He hates Battersly and torments him (and Simmonds, for other reasons) mercilessly; and he uses guile and some highly unorthodox methods to wrap up the loose ends in his baffling cases.*

In lesser hands than Champion's, the Allhoff stories might have been grim and unappetizing fare. As written, though, they are some of the cleverest pure (if rough-edged) detective stories to be found in the pulps. As is the case with the Nero Wolfe series, the characterization of and interplay among the three principals make them especially good and worth reprinting.

Born in Australia just after the turn of the century, and educated in New York City, D. L. Champion was a soldier with the British army during World War I, a seaman in the merchant marine, and a manuscript reader for a string of magazines before turning to story-writing in the early years of the Depression. During the next two decades he produced several million words of pulp fiction. In addition to Inspector Allhoff, he created two other memorable detective characters: Mariano Mercado, the detective partic-ular *of Mexico City who lives in mortal terror of germs and whose adventures also ran in* Dime Detective *in the early 1940s; and Rex Sackler, the "Parsimonious Prince of Penny-Pinchers," whose genuinely funny escapades graced the pages of* Black Mask *from 1940 to 1950. After the collapse of the pulps, Champion published one paperback novel,* Run the Wild River *(1952), and then went to Hollywood to work in films and television. No particulars on the subsequent years of his life, unfortunately, have surfaced to the time of this writing.*

CHAPTER ONE
ASPIRIN-PACKIN' MAMA

ALLHOFF HAD A cold.

It was utterly incredible to me that any germ, no matter how low its antecedents or moral standards, would voluntarily take up abode in Allhoff's snarling sinuses. Yet, apparently, several hundred thousand had.

His prominent corvine nose was the color of a lobster which has boiled for three hours. His lips were dry and cracked and his eyes were rheumy. Thus far I had had no external evidences of the condition of his temper. But I certainly knew the way to bet. Allhoff in the pink of condition was no beaming lover of mankind. With a running nose and a slight temperature he was going to be something more than a trial to Battersly and myself.

It was a little after nine o'clock in the morning. Allhoff was inhaling his fourth cup of coffee and cursing that it had no taste. From without, the cold gray light of a winter day oozed reluctantly through the grimy window pane.

Allhoff's tenement flat was in its customary chaotic disarray. The floor was unswept. The sink was piled with dishes. A platoon of cockroaches had established a beachhead upon the edge of the uncovered garbage can and reinforcements were arriving on the double.

A pile of dirty laundry wearily climbed the north wall and through the open door of the bedroom, the unmade bed could be seen, in all its flop-house glory.

Allhoff refilled his cup. He sneezed and expelled a thousand germs. He cursed and drained his cup with the delicate sound of a jeep passing through a swamp. Then Battersly came in.

He was tall and rather handsome in his patrolmen's uniform. He eyed Allhoff, with what I took for apprehension, as he passed on the way to his desk, took off his cap and sat down. Allhoff paid him no attention whatever. He alternated between slugs of coffee and sneezes. He cursed again and picked up a handkerchief. He buried his nose in it and the room was filled with the sound of a bomb exploding.

Battersly cleared his throat and said, deferentially: "You really ought to see a doctor, sir."

Allhoff swung his body around in his swivel chair and set his cup down with a bang. He said, "Doctors!" as if it were an obscene word. Then he drew a deep breath and let go.

"Out of every ten patients they get, five would recover anyway. Three are beyond help. The others may be remotely aided. But do they ever tell you that? Do they ever tell you they can't diagnose a case? The hell they do! I admit they can do surgery. They can set a broken leg and remove a perfectly good appendix without killing the patient. But they can't cure a cold. They don't even know its cause. But, by God, they prescribe for it. And they'll send you a bill. It's one racket where you get paid for your mistakes, too. If you're dead, they'll send your estate a bill. If you haven't an estate, they'll attach your tombstone. The bill and pill boys! By God, I'd sooner call in a Haitian voodoo man to burn a chicken wing in the full moon. His fee will be more reasonable and the result will be precisely the same. Doctors! God, they're worse than lawyers. And you know what I think of lawyers!"

I assured him hastily that we knew exactly what he thought of lawyers. He grunted furiously and turned again to his coffee cup. He thrust his nose in it and sucked in coffee.

Battersly blinked. From his expression I gathered that he had something to ask Allhoff and the query regarding the doctor had been intended as ingratiating.

Now Battersly stood up and approached Allhoff's desk with all the aplomb of a junior office boy about to put the question of a raise to the irascible senior partner.

"Inspector," he said nervously, "how would you like to handle a murder case Homicide knows nothing about? They don't even know the man is dead yet."

Allhoff put his cup down and looked up at Battersly, mixed emotions in his face. He disliked Homicide just a fraction of an inch less than he liked Battersly. He delighted in showing up the squad across the street. He delighted even more in crushing Battersly. He hesitated for a moment, then the copper in him came to the fore.

"Who's been killed?"

"I don't know, sir."

Allhoff lifted his eyebrows. "Well, where's the body?"

"Well—I don't exactly know that either, sir."

"Then," said Allhoff, "who's the killer?"

Battersly shuffled uneasily and hesitated.

"So you don't know that, either," roared Allhoff. "Then how the devil do you know anyone's been murdered?"

Battersly licked his dry lips. "Well, sir, it's like this. I met a girl last night in a bar. And she told me she knew that someone had been killed and that the police didn't know of it yet."

"And what did you do about it?"

"Why, nothing, sir."

Allhoff flung his arms to heaven as if asking the Deity to bear witness to Battersly's idiocy.

"My God," he said. "He's a copper and he meets a tramp in a barroom. She tells him she knows where a corpse is. So he buys her a drink and goes home. Are you so much in the habit of meeting dames who have corpses hidden somewhere?"

Battersly's face was red now. He cleared his throat nervously, and said: "If you'll let me explain, sir. . . ."

"*Let* you?" roared Allhoff. "I demand that you explain."

"This girl's name is Harriet Mansfield," said Battersly. "As I told you, I met her in a bar last night. She's good looking and tough. I guess her morals aren't all they should be and she's been in one or two jams with policemen. She doesn't like them."

"Neither do I," said Allhoff, superfluously.

"She's scared of coppers. And she doesn't trust them. But right now she's even more scared of this murderer."

"Damn it," yelled Allhoff, "what murderer?"

"I don't know exactly. She knows this murderer. She knows he's killed someone. Now she's afraid he'll kill her because she knows too much. She wants to tell about this killing to some policeman she can trust. Someone who'll investigate the killing, have the killer put away and protect her until he's in jail—protect her later from any pals of his."

"Did she know you were a copper?" asked Allhoff.

Battersly shook his head. "I was wearing civvies. But I told her I knew you. I told her to come up here this morning. I told her you'd keep her name entirely out of it, that you'd give her a fair break."

The idea of Allhoff giving anyone a fair break was something which caused my imagination to totter. Allhoff, however, beamed proudly as if he had never dreamed of doublecrossing anyone in all his career.

"When's she coming?" asked Allhoff. And the entrance of Harriet Mansfield answered the question for him.

She was a tall girl, and blond. She was under thirty, but a pair of dark circles beneath her blue eyes made her look older, and there was a shadow in their depths which indicated she knew more of life's seamy side than any woman should ever know. All in all, however, she was damned attractive.

She looked first at Battersly in his uniform. She said in a dull, expressionless tone: "So you were a copper, eh?" She turned to Allhoff. "And you're the Inspector. You don't look like no Galahad to me, but, hell, I just got to trust someone."

She sat down, sighed and opened a cavernous handbag. She withdrew a bottle of aspirin. She said to Battersly: "Son, get me a glass of water, will you?"

Battersly handed her a glass of water. She crammed half a dozen aspirin tablets in her mouth and washed them down. Allhoff emptied his coffee cup and regarded her oddly. It was obvious he disapproved of her, but if she was going to give him something which would enable him to sneer at Homicide, he was willing to listen.

She put the half-emptied glass on Allhoff's desk. In her monotonous voice, she mentioned a Greenwich Village address. She said: "Down there, in a studio on the third floor, you'll find a dead man. The studio is a big barn-like room with one window facing a blank wall. That window is locked on the inside. There's a wooden bar on the inside of the door. It's in place. It's all locked from the inside and the little guy is there with a bullet in his head."

Now, Allhoff was registering intense interest. For that matter, so was I.

"Do you know who killed him?" asked Allhoff.

Harriet Mansfield nodded. "I know who, how and why. That's what I'm here to tell you, but first I want to make a deal."

Allhoff nodded impatiently. "I understand. I'll guarantee that nothing happens to you. I'll keep you out of it altogether, if possible. Anyway, I'll see that this killer doesn't harm you. Is that enough?"

The girl nodded. "That's good enough for me. Now, this is what happened—"

She broke off for a moment and reached in her vast handbag again for the aspirin bottle. Quite obviously, she ate them. She was an aspirin addict. As she withdrew the bottle, she also took a small tin box from her purse.

"Oh, sonny," she said to Battersly, "here's that stuff I promised you. Try it. It works wonders."

Battersly stood up. His face was a fiery red. He moved toward the girl and took the tin box from her slim hand. Allhoff watched him with his shrewd little eyes.

"And what's that?" he asked.

"Nothing," said Battersly, hastily, "nothing at all."

"Oh, that," said Harriet Mansfield, dumping aspirins out into the palm of her hand. "It's corn cure. The kid was complaining to me that his corns kill him—drive him crazy with pain. Said he could hardly stand it. I got this stuff for him. It's wonderful."

Battersly sat down and closed his eyes. I drew a deep breath. Allhoff inhaled sharply. His eyes narrowed cruelly. He looked very much like a cat about to spring upon a particularly succulent mouse.

"So," he said, "his little corns hurt him? Now isn't that a damned shame? His tiny pink tootsies ache! Well, well."

Harriet Mansfield, the aspirins still in her hand stared at him in amazement. I said sharply: "Allhoff!"

He ignored me. He pushed his chair away from the desk, revealing a pair of leather stumps where his thighs should have been. His eyes, hot and frenzied, fixed themselves upon Battersly. He opened his mouth and his words filled the room like smoke from an exploding shell.

"You miserable rat! You whining, yellow dog! You dare complain about corns! What about me? Do I complain? You, who amputated my legs, have the cast-iron gall to squawk. Why, you—"

At this point Allhoff's vocabulary slid off into the sewer. He hurled slime and filth upon Battersly and all his ancestry back to

Adam. Harriet Mansfield blinked at him in amazement. She stood up and said: "Hey, lay off him. What's the idea of talking like that to—"

"Shut up, you tramp," roared Allhoff, and without any punctuation at all turned his attention back to Battersly.

Harriet Mansfield, apparently, had undergone many such rebuffs as this. She shrugged her stooped shoulders, sat down again and crammed the aspirin into her mouth. She emptied the water glass, crossed her legs, and sat silent.

Allhoff went on like a man who is never going to run out of breath. From long experience I knew he would continue until he was short of lung power. I turned my head away and closed my ears as best I could.

The reason for Allhoff's insane diatribe went back several years. In those days he was an up-and-coming police officer with two good legs and first-rate brain cells. Battersly was a raw recruit.

We were tipped off one day that a pair of murderers whom we had been seeking, were holed up in a West End Avenue rooming house. We had been tipped, further, that they were in possession of a tommy gun which commanded the front door from the inner stairway.

Battersly's assignment had been to effect a rear entrance and close with the machine-gun operator at precisely the same moment Allhoff burst through the front door at the head of the raiding squad.

Battersly got in the house, all right. Then he underwent a quite understandable case of buck fever. Instead of carrying out his task, he fled precipitately up the stairs to the roof. Allhoff came charging through the door at zero hour into a hail of machine-gun bullets.

A dozen of them lodged in his legs. Gangrene set in and after that, amputation was necessary to save his life.

Naturally, civil service rules did not permit an inspector of police minus his legs. But the commissioner, a stubborn man, was of no mind to lose his best man. By devious bookkeeping devices, he arranged it so that Allhoff was paid his old salary and continued to work under the department's sponsorship—unofficially, of course. Allhoff moved into this slum apartment across from headquarters.

He insisted that Battersly be assigned as his assistant. The commissioner, with a strong sense of poetic justice, had agreed. I had been sent along as an old hand who had come up with Allhoff, to pour oil upon the waters when they became too troubled.

I had no doubt that when Allhoff lost his legs he also lost something of his mind. He hated Battersly, unreasonably and relentlessly. He lost no opportunity to persecute the younger man.

Too often had I heard this same crazed diatribe which was pouring into my ears at this moment. Yet I had never become used to it. Were it not for a family and an impending pension I would have quit years ago.

At last Allhoff, out of breath, came to a stop. Breathing heavily, he turned to his coffee cup, filled it and lifted it to his lips.

I looked around again, glanced over at the girl to see how she had reacted to Allhoff's mania. I blinked, then looked at her more closely.

She sat slumped down in her chair. Her face seemed unnaturally bright and there was the tiniest speck of froth at the edge of her mouth. Her arms hung loosely down at the side of the chair and it seemed to me that her crossed, shapely legs were limp.

I sprang out of my chair and crossed the room. I found her pulse with my finger and there was no beat in it. I stepped back in utter amazement and said: "For God's sake, Allhoff!"

He put down his cup and said: "What's the matter?"

"She's dead."

CHAPTER TWO
MIDGET-MURDER

ALLHOFF'S BROW CLOUDED. He glared at me as if I, personally, had killed her.

"Dead?" he roared. "She can't be dead. Not here in my office. Besides, she was going to tell me about this murder."

His attitude was the epitome of all the arrogance in the world.

No one could die in *his* office. No one could die if they were about to tell him about a murder case.

"Have it your own way," I said ironically, "but if you're going to get any information from her you'll need a priest or a spiritualist. Or you might try cutting your own throat. Then you can join her in Heaven and get the whole story. After that, you can come back to earth and haunt the murderer. You—"

"Shut up!" yelled Allhoff. "Revive her."

"Are you crazy?" I shouted, losing my temper. "I tell you she's dead! She must have had a stroke or something."

Allhoff pushed his chair out and slid to the floor. He clumped over to the girl. He felt her pulse and listened to her heart. Across the room, Battersly toyed with the box of corn cure and watched interestedly.

Allhoff picked up the aspirin bottle from his desk and peered into it. He went back to the girl, put his face close to hers and sniffed.

"Stroke, hell," he said. "Cyanide."

"You mean among the aspirin tablets?"

Allhoff nodded. "That's right. Someone must have planted one poisoned tablet. It was just a question of time until she ate it. Of course, it had to happen here just when she was going to tell me about this killing!"

"Good old Allhoff," I murmured. "Sympathy drips from his heart like water from a spring. The fact that the girl is dead doesn't seem to bother you."

"Of course, it bothers me," he snapped. "I wanted to hear about this killing. It sounded fascinating, if it's true. Door barred, window locked and a corpse inside."

He clumped back to his chair and climbed into it. A thoughtful frown wrinkled his brow. He snatched up the aspirin bottle and put it in a desk drawer.

"Battersly," he said, "call the morgue. Have this body put on ice and tell them to keep it under cover for a couple of days. Don't let the newspaper stringers know anything about it."

"You can't do that," I began. "Maybe she's got relatives. Maybe—"

"Maybe," said Allhoff, "you're sucking around for a fine. Do as I say. Then you guys get down to that Greenwich Village address and see if there really is a little guy who's been murdered."

I shrugged my shoulders. Battersly called the morgue. As I saw it, Allhoff was merely trying to cover up the fact that the girl had been killed in his office. That, he knew, would be the cause of raucous laughter across the street at headquarters. Harriet Mansfield had come to him for protection because she didn't trust ordinary policemen and she had died in Allhoff's chair. Well, I had been in Allhoff's company long enough to have learned that minding one's own business was a most profitable pastime.

It was a little before noon when Battersly and I went down the rickety staircase, hailed a bus and journeyed uptown to Greenwich Village.

The address the girl had given us was that of a little crooked alley off MacDougal Street. The sidewalks were unswept and garbage cans lined the pavement. The street itself was cold and deserted.

We entered the building and climbed to the third floor. At the head of the stairway was a door. Battersly rapped on it hard with his knuckles. There was no answer. He tried the knob. It turned but the door did not open.

We exchanged a glance. Under the circumstances it was quite possible that a wooden bar *did* block the doorway. I nodded at Battersly. He moved a few feet away from the door and smashed into it with his shoulder. The door trembled but did not open.

"I think there *is* a bar there," said Battersly. "And I think it's a thick one. I nearly broke my shoulder."

"Wait here," I said. "There's a fire house down the block. I'll borrow an axe from them."

I went down to the fire house, returned a few minutes later with the axe. Battersly swung it against the door panels three times. The door broke down—it did not open.

The bar across its center was a solid two inches thick. We crawled under it into the room. My nostrils told me of the dead man's presence before my eyes. The stench of death permeated the studio. The room was stuffy and it seemed to me almost devoid of oxygen.

At one end a huge stone fireplace had been built into the wall. It was piled up with ashes attesting to the fact that a tremendous fire had been burning there some time ago.

Lying before the fireplace on a mangy scatter rug was the corpse.

"My God," said Battersly, "it's a kid. Who the hell would want to kill a kid?"

I moved closer and knelt at the side of the decomposing body. It wasn't a kid. It was a midget. He was, or had been, something well under four feet in height. He had been dead, I judged, for some time.

The method of murder would have been obvious to a ten-year-old. The midget had an ugly bullet hole in his head. Dried blood clung to the skin of his temple, stained the scatter rug and formed a winding streak upon the floor.

Battersly spoke from the window. "Say, sergeant, the window *is* locked. And the door certainly was barred. How do you figure it?"

I stood up. I examined the window. The catch was in place and beyond the pane, as Harriet Mansfield had said, there was a blank windowless wall. I shrugged my shoulders and looked around the room.

I found nothing much save candle grease. There was no electric light in the studio. There were, however, a hundred candles. Candle grease was everywhere. Smeared on the table and mantel-piece, all over the floor and spattered on the walls. Even the panels of the door were covered with it.

Battersly sat at a battered desk going through the papers in the drawers. "Find anything?" I asked.

"Routine stuff. It seems this dead guy's name is Robert Daintley. He's a partner in an antique shop on Greenwich Avenue. There's nothing beside that."

I sighed. I looked from the bar across the door to the locked window. "This," I announced, "is a beauty. We'll dump it in Allhoff's lap with pleasure. You wait here while I go out and call him for instructions."

I went down the stairs to the corner drugstore. From there I phoned Allhoff. I gave him what meager details we had picked up. Then, following his orders, I reported the murder to Homicide. After that, I went back to the studio.

"Homicide's coming down here," I said. "We'll send the beat copper up to stand by. In the meantime, Allhoff wants us to visit this antique shop, have a little chat with this Daintley's partner."

Battersly nodded. He did exactly what I had done a few minutes before. He looked from the bar across the doorway to the latch on the window.

"For Heaven's sake, sergeant, how in the name of—"

"Don't worry about it," I told him. "It's Allhoff's baby. For years I've been waiting to see him outwitted. I think this is it."

We pounded down the stairs over to Greenwich Avenue. Within ten minutes we entered a gloomy antique shop which bore the legend on its window: *Daintley and Grimes.*

The first thing I noticed was the portly special copper sitting in a chair which may or may have not been an antique. It certainly was old. He stood up as we came in, peered through the crepuscular light of the shop, and looked relieved when he saw the uniforms.

"Oh, Mr. Grimes," he called. "Someone here to see you."

Mr. Grimes emerged from the darkness at the rear of the shop. He reminded me very much of a mole. Weak blue eyes blinked from behind a pair of thick-lensed glasses. He was almost bald. His manner was fussy, his teeth obviously false. Mr. Grimes, I figured, was no man to stand up in the face of adversity. I found myself hoping he wouldn't be too upset about the death of his partner.

"Yes?" he said in a high pitched voice. "What can I do for you? I assure you we have no building violations here. We—"

"Where," I said, "is Mr. Daintley?"

Grimes blinked and looked rather like a helpless, fluttering hen.

"That's what I'd like to know," he said. "I haven't seen him for days. I simply can't understand it. I—"

"He's dead," I said, watching him closely for the effect of my words. "Murdered."

Grimes uttered a little cry and wrung his hands. "No," he said. "Why, I've been to his studio time and again knocking on the door, and receiving no answer."

"The reason was that he's dead," I told him. "Have you any idea who could have killed him?"

Grimes shook his head. "None at all. He had no enemies. God knows he had no money."

"What about this place?" I asked. "Does it yield a profit?"

Grimes shrugged. "We split perhaps eighty to a hundred dollars a week. You can check the books if you like. Certainly Daintley had no money. There's no sense in his murder."

We snooped around for a little while. The special copper buried his nose in the *Racing Form* while Grimes, apparently overcome by the news of Daintley's fate, sat down in a Windsor chair and mopped his brow with an effeminate lace handkerchief.

A few minutes later we took our leave and returned to Allhoff's office. He was blowing his nose furiously as we entered. He removed the handkerchief from his face and lifted his coffee cup.

"Well?" he demanded.

"Nothing," I said. "Everything the girl told us is true. The door was barred. The window was locked. There was absolutely no way for the killer to leave the room. Grimes, Daintley's partner, is a fussy old woman. I'm sure he knows nothing about it."

"I don't want your opinion," snapped Allhoff. "Give me the facts. Give me each detail your hazy brain can recall. Battersly, you listen and check him on it. Now, get going."

He picked up a pencil and held it poised above a pad as I began my recital. He made an occasional note as I unfolded my story. When I concluded, he grunted and refilled his cup.

Battersly got up from his desk and approached Allhoff with shining eyes. "Inspector," he said, "I have a theory."

Allhoff looked at him as if he'd announced he had leprosy.

"Look," said Battersly, "anything can happen in an antique shop. Suppose they got hold of something really valuable, worth a lot of dough? Suppose Grimes knocked his partner off so he'd own this thing all by himself?"

"This is positively brilliant," said Allhoff. "Army Intelligence needs men like you."

"Wait a minute," I said, "maybe it's more brilliant than you think. What about that special copper? Is it likely they'd employ a guy like that unless there was something valuable in the joint?"

"I was considering that," said Allhoff, "but from an entirely different angle. Did you notice which agency that cop was from?"

I nodded and mentioned the name of the agency.

"Call 'em. Find out how long he's been on the job. I'd guess it hasn't been more than a few days."

I checked that on the telephone and rather to my surprise discovered that Allhoff was right. The special copper had been on duty at the antique shop for precisely three days.

Allhoff nodded with such smug satisfaction when I told him this that I became nettled.

"So," I said, "I suppose you now know who killed the midget, why, and how the murder was committed."

He beamed at me. "You over-rate me," he said with false modesty. "I don't know who did it. I don't know the motive. All I know is how it was done."

I stared at him. "You mean you can explain that barred door, that locked window?"

"Sure," said Allhoff blandly, picking up his coffee cup. "That's easy."

I wracked my brains for a moment, then came up with the only answer I could get. "You mean the killer escaped through the chimney?"

Allhoff revealed his discolored teeth in an unpleasant grin.

"Simmonds," he said," aren't you thinking of Santa Calus?"

Battersly and I arrived together the following morning. We halted upon the threshold, stared transfixed at Allhoff. Here it was, nine by the clock. Certainly, he had not yet imbibed over a pint of coffee. Yet he was grinning.

Battersly and I looked at each other. We came warily into the office, each of us suspecting a trap. Allhoff said heartily: "Good morning."

"Do you feel well?" I asked solicitously. "Or has some dear friend just died?"

"Neither," said Allhoff equably. "I'm amused by the fact that Homicide is up to its neck in the midget murder. They've combined your theory with Battersly's."

"And come to what conclusion?"

"They figure, in line with your Santa Claus theory, that the guy went out through the chimney, and that it was Grimes who killed him to gain possession of some invaluable antique. They've got an expert casing the shop now to find the priceless article."

He went off into a paroxysm of laughter which was shattered abruptly by a sneeze.

Well, I *still* thought there was something to that theory, though I had no intention of saying so and ruining Allhoff's astounding merry mood.

"Have they found anything else?" I asked him.

"Yeah. The M.E. says the guy was dead about four days. And after combing the neighborhood they found a saloon where this Daintley and another guy had a drink on what appears to be the day of the murder."

"Do they know who the guy was?"

"Yes. The bartender knew him. Didn't know Daintley, though. But he remembers this other guy was in there with a midget. This guy's name is Strouse. He's on the way up here now."

Allhoff returned to the matter of brewing fresh coffee. I gave my attention to the onionskin reports which were sent over from headquarters each day, while Battersly sighed with pleasure and scanned the adventures of Dick Tracy, a vice I could never understand in a professional copper.

About eleven o'clock footsteps sounded on the creaking stairs outside. There was a rap at the door and two men entered.

CHAPTER THREE
WATCH-HUNT

THE FIRST WAS slim, clean-shaven, clad in a double-breasted suit. His eyes were dark, his face intelligent. He approached Allhoff's desk and said: "I'm Dan Strouse. You sent for me?"

Allhoff nodded and waved him to a chair. Strouse half turned and indicated his companion. "This is a friend of mine, Dr. Warburton."

Warburton bowed. He was portly, gray, and exuded success. I had heard of Warburton. He was an M.D. who had made a fortune in the past few years. Moreover, he was a famous collector of Washingtonia. His private museum was said to contain more relics of the Washington estate than any other collection. He owned more letters written by George and his half-brother, Lawrence, than once were believed extant.

He seated himself beside Strouse and looked at Allhoff. Allhoff sniffled with the sound of a weary vacuum cleaner.

"Ought to do something about that cold, Inspector," the doctor said.

Allhoff regarded him hostilely. "Why?"

"Might get worse. I'll examine you if you like."

Allhoff laughed unpleasantly. "What the devil do you know about colds?"

Warburton bristled. "Something more than a layman," he said coldly.

"I don't believe it," said Allhoff. "I will, however, concede you know more about corpses. I may have seen as many of them as you, but I never made any, save in the line of duty."

The doctor opened his mouth to reply. Strouse came pacifically into the breach.

"Now, then, Inspector," he said, "suppose you question me."

"I shall," said Allhoff. "Why did you bring him along?"

"Well," said Strouse, "at the moment the doctor and I are engaged in a business deal. Besides, he's my alibi, just in case you might accuse me in that midget matter."

"Your alibi?" said Allhoff. "What do you mean?"

"Last Tuesday I went to a barroom with Daintley. We sat around for about an hour. Daintley went away, leaving me there. The bartender, a friend of mine, gave me a lift to Doctor Warburton's. I remained at the doctor's house all night playing cards."

Allhoff nodded slowly. "So if Daintley was killed on Tuesday, you couldn't possibly have done it. Is that it?"

"That's it."

"You knew him well?"

"Fairly well."

"Any idea who killed him?"

Strouse shook his head. Allhoff took a long time to think it over. Then he jerked his head contemptuously in Warburton's direction.

"What's this business deal you're in? Is he trying to talk you out of a perfectly good appendix?"

Warburton flushed. "Damn it, sir," he said, "I decline to be insulted! I am about to buy from Mr. Strouse a most valuable document written by George Washington regarding the death of his half-brother, Lawrence, some six weeks after the latter died."

Unimpressed, Allhoff gulped more coffee. Warburton, carried away by his subject, went on.

"Yes," he said, "there are no other known letters written by Washington upon that subject. Lawrence died in the Barbados in 1752 where George—"

"He would have died sooner if he'd had a modern physician," snapped Allhoff. "All right, Strouse, that's all. Leave the sergeant there your address in case I want you."

Strouse gave me his address. A moment later he and the doctor walked to the door. As they gained the threshold, Allhoff said sharply: "Do either of you guys know a woman named Harriet Mansfield?"

I watched their faces carefully. They both registered a perfect blank.

"Never heard of her," said Warburton. "Who is she?"

Allhoff shrugged. "I don't know. She phoned me from New Jersey about an hour ago. Made a date with me for tomorrow morning. Said she knew something about Daintley."

Strouse shook his head. "I don't know anyone of that name," he said.

The door closed and our two visitors went down the creaking stairway. I looked over at Allhoff with interest.

"What's up your ragged sleeve?" I asked him. "What was the idea of that story about Mansfield?"

"You'll find out," said Allhoff, "tonight. Battersly, you go down to that antique shop at once. Chat with Grimes and that special copper. Let drop, casually, that same lie I just told about Harriet Mansfield. Do you think you can do that?"

"Yes, sir," said Battersly. "Of course, sir."

"Then get going," said Allhoff, "if it isn't too hard on your delicate little corns. If the pedal anguish isn't too much for you to—"

Battersly left the room like a gust of wind before Allhoff could get started. He put down his coffee cup and turned to me.

"You," he said, "are not going home tonight."

"Now, listen—" I began.

"You listen. They've got that Mansfield broad's address over at the morgue. Get it. She lived with another girl. When you leave here tonight, go up there. Introduce yourself and stay there."

"For how long?"

"All night."

"All night? Are you crazy? I'm a married man. What's my wife going to say if I stay at the apartment of some dame all night?"

Allhoff grinned oilily. "She'll probably praise you for your devotion to duty."

That was a beautiful thought, indeed.

"What am I supposed to do there?"

"Wait," said Allhoff.

"For what?"

"For whatever happens. I'm leaving the method of coping with things up to your own judgment."

"Why the devil can't Battersly do it? He's single."

"That's just why. He's a sucker for a girl. I want a man who'll stick to business. I figure you're too damned old to be concerned with sex."

That complimentary remark ended the conversation.

At six o'clock I called my wife and told a wild and blatant lie about some special duty to which the commissioner had assigned me. From her tone I judged I hadn't quite got away with it. I sighed, hung up, and took the subway to Broadway and 96th Street.

Betty Wasmuth was a suspicious brunette with a magnificent figure and skin as soft as her eyes were hard. She admitted me when I showed my badge and sat nervously on the edge of a sofa while I explained my mission.

Which wasn't easy since I hadn't the slightest idea what it was.

But the instant I mentioned Harriet Mansfield she was on me like a cat.

"Where is she?" she shrilled. "You lousy coppers got her? And for what? You ain't got no right—"

I decided that if she was scared she would be more inclined to have me hanging around.

"She's dead."

The shrew oozed out of her. Her face became deathly pale beneath her rouge. She sat down again and her hard eyes were suddenly softened with tears.

"Oh, my God, the poor kid. I knew she was scared of something. But I never thought—"

She was a pathetic figure in that moment. Clumsily, I leaned over and patted her shoulder. I uttered a half dozen idiotic consoling words and cursed Allhoff for putting me in this unreasonable position.

After a while she calmed down and went into the bedroom. She came out shortly before midnight and offered me a cup of coffee which I gratefully accepted. We chatted hesitantly. She wondered why I was here, why I was going to stay. I did not enlighten her, for the simple reason that I did not know myself.

About one o'clock the girl went to bed. I lolled on the living room sofa, smoking, killing time and wondering what the devil my vigil had to do with a midget who had been murdered down in Greenwich Village.

At three o'clock my eyes grew heavy. The room was filled with smoke and the neighborhood seemed as quiet as a sleeping child. I stretched out on the couch, put out the light and lay there in the dark resting my eyes.

Heaven only knows just when I dropped off to sleep. I came back to consciousness at the same moment the creaking of a floor board sounded in my ears. For a moment I lay absolutely still. I heard furtive, creeping footfalls in the dark. I heard the sound of tense, labored breathing.

I swung my feet down to the floor and sat up. My hand reached out for the chain on the floor lamp. I missed badly and the lamp went crashing to the floor. Something flashed in the darkness. The room was filled with the sound of a shot and a bullet whizzed past my ear.

I knelt down and reached for my Police Special. Footfalls raced toward me. A flashlight shone full in my face. I thought, for an instant, that this was my last moment on earth. I ducked my head down and charged into the flashlight.

How that second bullet missed me, I shall never know. I swung a wild fist into the darkness and it found its mark on a human jaw. The flashlight clattered to the floor. I clawed out at my adversary's right wrist, found it, and held on grimly in order to render his gun useless.

It suddenly became an out-and-out test of strength. Somehow I had hold of both his wrists—right and left. We grunted and strained against each other. Then suddenly he wrenched his right hand free. He brought the barrel of his gun down on my skull. I was aware of nothing except the abrupt buckling of my knees.

I regained consciousness to find Betty Wasmuth wiping blood from my brow with a wet towel. Her face was pale and there was terror in her eyes.

"I heard the brawl," she said, "but I was scared to come out of the bedroom. I remembered what happened to Harriet. Who was it? What did he want?"

Of that I had no idea. I got up, took my throbbing head to the bathroom, pulled myself together and left the house. I figured that what Allhoff had sent me up here to cope with had already happened. I took a cab downtown to his place.

Allhoff slept like a cat. He was awake before I had even turned the knob of his bedroom door. He pulled himself up in the bed, looked at the bump on my head, and said: "You fool. Did you let him get away?"

I sat down and unfolded my story. His little eyes grew hotter and hotter as I went on. When I had finished, he banged his fists on the muddy counterpane and cursed me bitterly.

"You idiot," he snarled. "You and Battersly have the intelligence of a pair of rather bright lice. You just let the killer get through your clumsy hands."

"What killer?"

"Daintley's killer. I planted the fact that the Mansfield girl was calling on me tomorrow to spill what she knew. No one knew she was dead. The murderer went uptown to kill her tonight. He figured that somehow his poisoned aspirin didn't work. He went to her flat to attend to it personally. I figured you'd bring him back with you."

"Well," I said defensively, "why the devil don't you tell me what's going on in your head when you send us out on an assignment like that? How the devil did I know what was going to happen?"

Allhoff shook his head. He clumped out of the bed into the other room, climbed into his desk chair and flicked on the switch beneath the coffee pot.

"All right," he said at last, "call Battersly. Get him here right away. Then I want you two guys to go out and pay early morning calls upon Strouse, Grimes and Warburton."

"For what?"

"Collect their wrist watches. Bring them back to me."

"Their *what?*"

"Watches. Their wrist watches."

We had no trouble with Grimes. He wrung his hands a little and fluttered around the shop. But he handed over his watch after we promised it would be returned to him in its original condition.

While we were still in the antique shop the phone jangled. It was Allhoff asking for me. His harsh voice drilled over the wire: "Simmonds, ask that Grimes if his partner drank much."

He clicked the receiver back on the hook without waiting for my answer. Dutifully, I put the question.

Grimes nodded his head dubiously. "Well," he said, weighing the question, "he wasn't a drunkard, if that's what you mean. But he did drink more than I thought was good for him. I told him often enough."

Taking Grimes' information and his wrist watch along with us, Battersly and I set out for Strouse's place. We got him out of bed and he raised hell. I argued with him for half an hour. Then by delicately pointing out that Allhoff was a bad man to have as an enemy, that refusal to let us borrow his watch might be construed as a tacit admission of guilt, we got it.

A taxi took us uptown to Doctor Warburton's. He was easier than I expected. I gathered that he regarded Alhoff as a somewhat amusing charlatan, which, incidentally, was just about Allhoff's opinion of him. He gave us his watch with a sort of amused tolerance.

Battersly and I returned to Allhoff's bearing the loot. Allhoff downed a cup of coffee, took the watches from us and made a telephone call. A moment later, a messenger came over from across the street and took the watches which Allhoff had carefully packed in an envelope. He handed the runner a second envelope in which he had enclosed a note.

For the next twenty minutes he drank coffee earnestly and noisily. Then he swung around in his chair and said: "Hey, I called that bar where Strouse and Daintley were on the day of the killing."

"So?" I said.

"So," said Allhoff, "he tells me that Daintley was drinking root beer and kept an unlighted cigarette in his mouth."

"Well, well," I said. "And did he tell you what kind of a hat Daintley was wearing?"

"Sure," said Allhoff, "a derby."

"And that, of course, clears up some important points about the killing," I said sarcastically.

"Of course," said Allhoff. "I'm surprised you noticed it, though."

Naturally, I had noticed nothing at all. I said so, but Allhoff had relapsed again to mysterious silence.

A little before noon, he looked up and said: "You fellows go down to Noonan's now and get your lunch. By the time you come back I'll have the principals in the case here and we can get to work."

"To work on what?"

"The murder solution, of course. Now get out and leave me alone."

CHAPTER FOUR

CHOOSE YOUR POISON

WHEN I FOLLOWED Battersly back from lunch, the guests had gathered. Doctor Warburton, pompous and obviously annoyed, had difficulty arranging his bulk comfortably on one of our narrow-bottomed chairs. He fidgeted and glared at Allhoff through his glasses.

Even so, however, he seemed more at home than Grimes. Grimes appeared as nervous as an aspen leaf with financial troubles. He perched on the edge of his chair like a bird. He never took his watery eyes off Allhoff.

Allhoff drank coffee, ignoring the company. On the far side of his desk, Strouse smoked a cigarette blandly. Of the three of them he was most at ease. Battersly was at his desk, regarding the entire

264

scene expectantly. He nodded to me as I came in and cast a significant glance across the room.

I followed his gaze and found that my own swivel chair was
occupied by Sergeant Sligo. That fact occasioned some surprise in
my breast. Sligo was a tough copper. He was built like a brick wall
and his hands were like a pair of red boxing gloves. His nose had
been broken in two places and there was a scar on his cheek from
a knife cut.

Sligo had broken a number of tough cases in this town—all by
the same method. With a baseball bat, a rubber hose and a sound-
proof room, Sligo was almost as effective as Allhoff himself. Sligo
was strictly strong-arm. There was a sadistic streak in him and he
would knock a citizen's teeth out with as little compunction as I
would step on one of the cockroaches beneath the Allhoff sink.

I got myself a chair from the bedroom and sat down, puzzled.
Allhoff decried the strong-arm boys. He invariably boasted that
his brain was more valuable than every rubber hose in any precinct
house basement. Why he had called Sligo in baffled me.

However, my being baffled by Allhoff no longer came under the
heading of spot news.

Allhoff set his cup down with a bang. There was a frown upon
his brow and a glare in his eyes. These, I well knew, were symp-
toms that he was angry. I watched him closely to see upon whom
his wrath would fall.

It fell on me.

He swung about in his swivel chair and glared at me. "I regret,"
he said, in tones which indicated that he regretted nothing at all,
"that I have been compelled to drag all of you down here to my
office. It is only because I am saddled with moronic assistants."

Everyone, including Battersly, looked at me. Allhoff took a deep
breath and called me a name that you shouldn't call your sergeant.

"Imbecile!" he roared. "I sent you uptown to catch the killer. I
knew he'd go to Harriet Mansfield's apartment after I planted the
fact that she was going to call on me the following day. But you go
to sleep! Moreover, you didn't even hold the killer's wrist steadily
when you fought with him."

That one dazed me. "I didn't what?"

"Hold his wrist steadily. You told me that at one period during the brawl you had hold of each of his wrists. If that were true. I figured there'd be a good chance of your fingerprints being on his wrist watch. That's why I collected them. There are prints there, but they're all too damned blurred to tell us anything."

"Oh," I said weakly.

"So," said Allhoff, "I had to figure out something else."

"You mean," I said incredulously, "that you now have the answer to the why's, how's, and who's of the murder?"

"I have the why's and the how's. I will have the who's before anyone leaves here today."

I glanced over at Sligo. "You mean you're resorting to Sligo's methods of detection?"

Warburton blew his nose into a silk handkerchief with a blast that sounded like Allhoff roaring at Battersly. He said: "I didn't come here to listen to you quarrel with a subordinate, Inspector. In fact, I don't know why I'm here at all. I don't—"

"Look," said Allhoff, "I'm very much afraid you'll thank me before this is all over. I was going to let you take your beating. However, my moronic subordinate has forced me to help you out."

"Help me out?" said Warburton. "Why—"

"Look," said Allhoff again, "this gadget you're buying. This letter from George Washington regarding the death of his half-brother— you say it was written some six weeks after Lawrence Washington died?"

"That's right."

"And Lawrence died on July 26th, 1752?"

"That, too, is correct."

"And what is the exact date on that letter?"

"September 8th, 1752. But what in the name of God all this has to do with—"

"Suppose," said Allhoff, "you shut up and let me do the talking. We are all gathered here to discuss the murder of Daintley. First, let me tell you how he was killed."

I screwed up my brow. To my certain knowledge, Allhoff had not left his apartment for weeks. If, while seated at his desk, he had figured out how the murderer had killed Daintley, barred a door and locked a window after the deed was done, I was prepared to admit that he was about fifty per cent as good as he actually believed he was.

He spilled coffee into his cup and drained it with the sound of a Saint Bernard lapping up a bowl of water.

"All right," he said, "this is what happened. Daintley knew his life was in danger. He knew from what direction, too. That is why Harriet Mansfield shilled him into opening the door."

"How can you know that?" I asked. "How can you know the Mansfield girl was even in that studio?"

"How the devil did she know a murder had been committed?" yelled Allhoff. "The killer was obviously no fool. Do you think he went around confiding to everyone that he'd killed a guy? It was impossible for the girl to have looked through the window and seen the corpse. There was nowhere to look from. Obviously, she was there."

He was still sore at me. He glared at me like a headlight. I decided to let him tell it in his own circuitous way.

"She got the door open," he went on. "Then the killer came in and blasted Daintley through the head. Simple, isn't it?"

Grimes wrung his hands and looked bewildered. "But anyone could have figured that out," he said. "The point is, how did the killer get away?"

"Through the door," said Allhoff, picking up the percolator.

Despite my resolve to keep my mouth shut, I came in again. "How?" I said. "Metempsychosis? Or did he float through the panels?"

Allhoff set the percolator down with a crash. "He went out on his feet," he roared. "He walked out—on two legs." He turned his head an inch and stared at Battersly.

This time I came in quick to cut him off. "But how?" I asked. "How could he bar the door after him?"

To my relief, Allhoff did not pursue the matter of people who walked out of rooms on their own two legs.

"The grease," he said. "The candle grease."

Warburton blew his nose again and blinked. "Candle grease?"

"Of course," said Allhoff. "He melted some candle grease. He smeared the entire length of the wooden bar with it. He stuck the bar to the door with the grease, held it there until the grease hardened."

I thought that over for a moment and felt like all the morons Allhoff had ever called me when Battersly, who was no Einstein, got it before me.

"Click," he said, "the fireplace."

"Right," said Allhoff. "Before he left the room he piled up the fireplace with kindling-wood and coal and lighted it. Then he closed the door and left. The fire lifted the temperature of the room high enough to soften the candle grease. The weight of the bar pulled it down and it dropped into its sockets."

Warburton nodded in Allhoff's direction with reluctant admiration. Allhoff sniffled, reached for a handkerchief and blew his nose. Warburton leaned forward professionally. But if he had been about to offer medical advice he thought better of it.

Allhoff replaced his handkerchief. He regarded Warburton maliciously. "God," he said, "I'd like to take you. It's a damned shame—" He broke off and shook his head sadly.

There was a long silence while he gulped more coffee. Strouse lit another cigarette. He said, politely: "You say you figured all this, Inspector? I thought you said you were about to obtain the information from Harriet Mansfield?"

"She's in the hospital," said Ahlhoff. "Nervous breakdown. The doctors say she's evidently scared to death of something. She's unable to talk. May remain in that condition for a couple of weeks."

I stared at him. Not because he had lied. But Allhoff was no character to pass up an opportunity for bluff. And if the killer was in the room, why hadn't Allhoff pretended that Mansfield *had* talked—that she had told him everything?

"Then," said Grimes, "you really don't know who killed my partner?"

"I have a damned good idea," said Allhoff. "However, I'm a soft-hearted fool. I like to be sure in capital cases. Sligo!"

Sligo pulled his vast girth out of my chair. He grinned happily. He pounded his huge right fist into the open palm of his huge hand.

"Are you ready?" asked Allhoff.

"All ready, Inspector."

"You understand thoroughly what you are to do?"

"Thoroughly."

Allhoff nodded. He jerked his thumb in Warburton's direction. "All right, doctor, you first. Go into the bedroom with the sergeant."

Warburton looked mildly astonished. "What for?"

Allhoff did not find it necessary to reply. He signaled Sligo with his eyes. Sligo laid his heavy hand upon the doctor's collar, dragged him to his feet. He pulled the vigorously protesting Warburton into the bedroom. The closing door shut off the doctor's enraged sputtering.

Battersly and I looked at each other. Was Allhoff directing Sligo to beat a confession out of Warburton? Grimes glanced around the room and wrung his hands again. He knew as little about what was going on as I, but he was a damned sight more worried. You didn't have to know Sligo's reputation to realize he was a bruiser. It was written all over his face.

Strouse sighed and lit another cigarette. Allhoff busied himself refilling the top of the percolator with fresh coffee.

In less than three minutes, Sligo and the doctor reappeared. The doctor wore an expression of utter amazement. Sligo seemed somewhat disappointed. I examined Warburton carefully. His face bore no mark. Apparently, Sligo had not hit him.

Allhoff caught Sligo's eye and the latter nodded. "O.K.," said Allhoff. "Grimes, you're next."

Grimes fluttered his eyes. "Inspector," he said, "I am an innocent man. Besides, I'm not quite sure that all this is legal. I—"

Sligo smiled without mirth. He put his fist under Grimes' nose and said: "Will you come quietly?"

Grimes swallowed something in his throat. He went quietly.

We sat around in complete silence, all save Allhoff utterly baffled. Then the sound of Sligo uttering a hearty curse emanated from the bedroom. A moment later he came out with Grimes behind him.

Again it occurred to me that Sligo wore that same expression of disappointment. Grimes, like Warburton, looked unharmed but a little stunned. He sat down again on the edge of the chair. I observed that Warburton was watching Allhoff much in the manner of a psychiatrist staring at a patient who may well become violent.

"All right," said Allhoff, after noting Sligo's nod. "You, Strouse."

Strouse shrugged his shoulders calmly, got out of the chair and followed Sligo into Allhoff's bedroom. The door slammed shut behind him.

A minute ticked by. Suddenly, we heard a thudding sound, followed by a louder thudding sound. A yell of pain burst through the panels of the door. A minute later, the door flew open and Strouse ran into the room.

One of his front teeth was missing. There was a darkening mouse beneath his right eye. Blood dripped from his split lip down on to his tie. Sligo strode along behind him, his little eyes glinting and an expression of vast satisfaction upon his face.

Strouse pointed his right index finger at Allhoff, his left at Sligo.

"This is illegal," he shouted. "It's third degree. Besides, it's insane. You've invaded the rights of a private citizen. I'll have you all broken. I'll have you—"

"Sit down," said Allhoff.

Strouse opened his mouth as if to toss around a few more threats. Sligo advanced happily upon him. Strouse shut up and sat down.

"Do I understand," asked Warburton of Allhoff, "that Mr. Strouse was given the same proposition in the bedroom as were Grimes and myself?"

"Exactly," said Allhoff. "But he refused to take one."

"Why?" said Warburton. "The entire procedure was ridiculous. Any man would prefer to take a harmless aspirin tablet than a beating."

"An aspirin tablet?" said Battersly and myself simultaneously.

"Of course," said Allhoff. "You wrecked my plan to have you take Strouse red-handed uptown. So I had to resort to chicanery."

"I'm listening," I said.

"Well," said Allhoff, "since he didn't know that Harriet Mansfield was dead, he figured the poisoned aspirin would still be in the bottle where he planted it. Sligo simply took each one of them into the bedroom. He offered them a choice of taking one aspirin tablet, which was taken from a bottle found in Harriet Mansfield's bag, or a beating. Naturally, Grimes and the doctor were outraged. But to any sane or innocent man, there is only one choice. They took the pill."

"But," I said, "Strouse didn't. He knew one of them meant sudden death. He'd rather take a beating than risk dropping dead."

"Too, too apparent," said Allhoff, affecting jaded boredom. "And equally apparent that Strouse murdered Daintley and Harriet Mansfield."

CHAPTER FIVE
NOT A LEG TO STAND ON

STROUSE STARED AT him. He patted his handkerchief to his bleeding mouth. He didn't get panicky. There was shrewd calculation in his eyes. He said: "You're as dumb as that palooka who slugged me, Allhoff. You're stuck with a few lovely textbook theories. You haven't got a thing on me that the D. A. would bother to keep in his files."

It seemed to me that this was true talk indeed. Allhoff's experiment with the aspirins and Sligo's heavy fist may have been conclusive as hell to us, but it wouldn't get into a court record even if Strouse had the dumbest lawyer in the country as his cousel. And that was a fact Allhoff must well know.

"You see," said Allhoff blandly, as if the case was tied up and in the bag, "Mansfield was probably Strouse's girl, or ex-girl. He prevailed on her to get Daintley to open his door. After that she got panicky. She knew Strouse was a tough, ruthless character. She knew her life wasn't safe as long as she knew what she knew. That's why she tried to get me to help her. But Strouse's lethal aspirin beat her to it."

"It all sounds wonderful," said Strouse, "but what are you going to do with it? You can't pin a murder on me with that aspirin gag. And I got an alibi for Daintley."

I recalled that Strouse had been in the saloon with the midget and was completely covered until after the killing. I nodded my head sagely.

"My God," said Allhoff, "do you think, Strouse, I haven't seen through that one?"

"I don't know what you're talking about," said Strouse. It was quite obvious he did.

"If I was right about the killer having to get the Mansfield girl to induce Daintley to open the studio door because he feared

Strouse, it was obvious the midget wouldn't casually visit saloons with Strouse. No, that, like the ingenious device of locking the studio door, was put in to make it harder."

"I don't see it," I said. "Daintley *was* in the saloon with Strouse, wasn't he?"

"No," said Allhoff. "The instant the bartender said Strouse was accompanied by a midget we leaped to the conclusion that it was Daintley. Midgets aren't too common. However, it wasn't a midget, at all. It was a child."

"A child?" I said.

"A child," said Allhoff firmly. "Probably hired from a theatrical agency, dressed in long pants and a derby hat. You will note the midget drank root beer, although Grimes stated his partner drank pretty heavily. You'll note also that he held an unlighted cigarette in his mouth. Cigar smokers do that often. Cigarette smokers don't. After baffling us with his locked room murder, Strouse figured on baffling us further with a perfect alibi."

Allhoff reached for the percolator. There was a long silence in the room. I turned everything he had said over in my brain. It sounded good. It sounded perfect. But it still didn't sound legal. Strouse's point was as well taken as Allhoff's. There was plenty of good theory and damned little good evidence.

Across the room Strouse smiled confidently and I knew thoughts similar to mine were passing through his head.

"Inspector," he said, "I don't think you can convict me of disorderly conduct. You can't lay conjecture before a jury, you know."

"And there's another thing," said Warburton. "I don't know much about law—"

"Or medicine," Allhoff interrupted blandly.

Warburton glared at him and went on: "I don't know much about law, but it seems to me the prosecution must establish a motive for a crime. You've completely overlooked that, Inspector."

I realized that I'd overlooked it myself. "That's right, Allhoff, you've given Strouse no motive for killing Daintley."

Allhoff banged the percolator down upon its electric base. "Idiots," he snarled. "The motive is so damned obvious, I didn't bother mentioning it. It's that damned letter. The George Washington letter."

"You mean the letter belonged to Daintley and Strouse killed him and stole it?"

"Obviously."

"My God, is the letter worth that much?"

"Ask Warburton what he intends to pay for it."

I looked inquiringly at the doctor.

"The price agreed upon," he said, "is one hundred and fifty thousand dollars."

Battersly whistled. I was impressed. Allhoff turned to the doctor.

"And despite the fact that I tell you murder was committed to gain possession of this letter, you'll still pay that price. You will, in short, finance Strouse's trial. You may well enable him to go free."

Warburton shrugged. "That's your business, Inspector, not mine. I want that letter. I'm willing to pay a good price for it. I don't care how Strouse got it. All I care about is its authenticity."

"And are you sure it's authentic?"

"Quite. Two experts have assured me so. One, a man who knows paper and ink—the other, a handwriting expert."

Allhoff inhaled deeply. "I wish I had a better case," he said slowly. "I just hate to do you a favor, doctor, but I guess my hand is forced."

He heaved a regretful sigh and turned to Grimes. "You," he said. "You knew your partner had this letter, didn't you?"

Grimes swallowed something in his throat and shook his head wildly.

"I had no idea," he said. "I knew nothing about it. I—"

"You're a liar," said Allhoff amiably. "But you wouldn't be a liar for nothing, would you?"

Grimes was bewildered. "I wouldn't be a liar for nothing?" he repeated dazedly.

"Look," said Allhoff, "you engaged a private copper as soon as you knew Daintley was killed. Why? There was nothing of any value in that store. At least, nothing any of Homicide's antiquarian experts could find. You hired that special to keep Strouse from killing you, too. He made a financial agreement with you to keep your mouth shut. You're getting a piece of Warburton's dough, aren't you?"

Grimes shook his head again. Not very convincingly, I thought.

"So that's what I mean," said Allhoff. "You wouldn't be a liar for nothing, would you? But you would be a liar for a slice of a hundred and fifty grand."

He looked over at Sligo, who returned his glance hopefully.

"I even believe you'd take a bad beating for that kind of dough. You're no hero, Grimes, but for a pile of money a man can steel himself to keep his mouth shut even under the pressure of Sligo's fists."

Allhoff leaned forward in his chair and fixed Grimes with a reptilian gaze.

"But would you do it for nothing?"

Grimes did not look happy. He bit his lip and wriggled in his chair. "I still don't understand what you mean, Inspector."

"I'll clear it up," said Allhoff. "I concede Sligo couldn't make you talk if you knew you'd make a fortune by suffering in silence. But would you still keep your mouth shut if you weren't getting a cent? Would you keep quiet merely out of your great love for Strouse here?"

Grimes patted a handkerchief against the cold sweat on his forehead.

"What I'm asking," continued Allhoff, "is what would you do if Warburton welshed on the deal—it he refused to buy the letter?"

Grimes didn't answer.

"I'll tell you," said Allhoff. "Without the incentive of money you'd talk like a back fence gossip the instant Sligo lifted his bullying hand. So, as you all see quite plainly now, in order to obtain a key witness, all I must do is prevent Doctor Warburton from buying that letter."

Warburton took a cigar from his vest pocket and lit it. He seemed to be enjoying himself immensely.

"Inspector," he said, "you appear to be as bad a detective as you claim I am a doctor. Your job has nothing to do with me. I am buying that letter. You do what you will."

Allhoff shook his head sadly. "This is like cutting off my right arm," he said. "I just hate to do you a favor, doc, but justice demands it."

Warburton exhaled smoke happily. He was putting one over on Allhoff. He was getting even for the insults he had suffered. Better than even, I decided. For if he bought that letter, Allhoff's case wasn't worth the paper the indictment was written on.

"Very well, doctor," said Allhoff. "Suppose I told you that letter was a fake?"

"A fake?"

"A forgery. A damned skillful forgery."

Warburton took the cigar from his mouth and laughed. "Rot. What about my experts? My parchment man? My handwriting expert?"

"Your parchment man is a fool. Your handwriting expert is an ignoramus. You, doctor, are a sucker."

"Very well," said Warburton calmly. "Since you possess so much knowledge of these matters, suppose you prove it's a forgery."

"All right," said Allhoff. "Now what is the date on that letter?"

"September 8th, 1752."

"That's what I thought," said Allhoff. "Now, do any of you bright boys know what happened on September 8th, 1752?"

"Sure," said Warburton. "George Washington wrote a letter to Governor Dinwiddie of Virginia, concerning the death of his half-brother, Lawrence."

"He did not!" yelled Allhoff.

"Well," I put in, "what did happen on September 8th, 1752?"

"Nothing," said Allhoff. "Nothing at all!"

"That's a rather ridiculous statement," said Strouse. "How could nothing happen on any date?"

"Nothing happened," said Allhoff, "because there wasn't any September 8th in 1752. There were not dates at all from September 3rd until September 14th."

We all looked at him as if his mind had gone. He grinned back at us, evilly and triumphantly.

"You fools!" he yelled. "You ignorant fools! On September 3rd, 1752 in all the British possessions, of which we were one at the time, the calendar was changed from the Julian of the Caesars to the Gregorian calendar of Pope Gregory. In order to make up for the lost days of the inaccurate Julian calendar, the dates September 3rd to the 14th were omitted. So, George Washington never dated a letter September 8th. There wasn't any! So nothing happened on that day. No one was born and no one died."

Warburton took the cigar from his mouth. His face was white as its ash. He said: "Is this true?"

"There's an encyclopedia in my bedroom," said Allhoff. "Look it up."

I went into the bedroom and did so. I brought the volume out to Warburton.

"Show it to Grimes," said Allhoff.

I showed it to Grimes. He read it blinking and trembling. Allhoff said: "O.K., Sligo. See if he'll lie for nothing."

Sligo took one step toward Grimes when he cracked.

"No," he yelled. "No, I'll talk. The Inspector is right—"

Strouse sprang our of his chair and headed with great speed toward the door. Sligo's speed was even greater. His hamlike fist hit Strouse on the side of the face. Strouse spun around like a top, then Sligo had him by the throat.

"Don't butcher him here," said Allhoff. "Take him across the street. Book him for murder. Take Grimes, too."

Sligo took the pair of them and dragged them out the door. Warburton stood up.

"I don't know what to say—" he began.

"That's fine," said Allhoff. "We won't have to listen. Boy, I sure would have enjoyed seeing you clipped for all that dough. You know what I think of doctors? They—"

Warburton got out at top speed to avoid hearing again what Allhoff thought of doctors. Deprived of that victim, Allhoff thought for a moment, then grinned. He opened his desk drawer and took out a small container.

"Oh, Battersly," he said, "I asked the morgue to send me over the contents of Harriet Mansfield's pocketbook. There was another tin of corn plasters in it. Doubtless, she intended it for you. Her dying wish, you might say. Here."

He held it out. His eyes met those of Battersly. Battersly averted his head.

"Don't want it, eh?" said Allhoff. "Well, I'll keep it myself. You never can tell. With wet weather coming, I might need it myself. Never know when my old corns are going to bother me. Never can tell when—"

"Allhoff," I said, "for God's sake, shut up. Lay off the kid for once. This constant harping is unjustified. It's—"

"Ah," said Allhoff, who always got the last word, "are you telling me I haven't got a leg to stand on?"

JOHN D. MacDONALD

Fatal Accident

THE VENERABLE CONCERN of Street & Smith, the leading purveyor of dime novels in the late 1800s and early 1900s, was one of the "big three" of pulp publishing (the other two being Popular Publications and Leo Margulies's Thrilling Group). They brought out a large number of mystery and detective titles during the heyday of the pulps, the most successful of which were Detective Story Magazine, Clues, Crime Busters (later Street & Smith's Mystery Magazine), and two hero pulps, Doc Savage and The Shadow.

The last two titles were under the editorship of Babette Rosmond, whose name was listed on the contents page as "B. Rosmond," presumably because it was felt that the predominately male readers of pulp crime and adventure fiction would be put off if they knew the red-blooded stories they were reading had been selected by a woman. Rosmond (herself an accomplished writer and the author of a very good novel with a pulp-publishing background, The Dewy, Dewy Eyes) was among the best of pulpdom's editors. She preferred unusual, nonformula stories to the standard pulp fare, as she stressed in her frequent market reports for such trade periodicals as Writer's Digest. And she strongly encouraged new and innovative writers, the most prominent of which was John D. MacDonald.

Rosmond purchased many of MacDonald's early pulp efforts written after his discharge from the army in 1946—some thirty-five stories all told. "Fatal Accident" (The Shadow Mystery Magazine, Fall 1948) is an example both of the type of stories Rosmond published and of the type MacDonald wrote: lean prose, excellent characterization, a tightly knit, *nonformula plot (and, as a bonus, a decidedly unstereotypical portrait of a working policeman). It is also distinguished as the first piece of fiction to use a form of a certain well-known (nowadays) piece of automotive equipment.*

John D. MacDonald *has been called* the consummate storyteller of our time. *He contributed more than 200 stories to the pulps in the late 1940s and early 1950s, before graduating to such slick magazines as* Cosmopolitan, Ladies Home Journal, Redbook, *and* The Saturday Evening Post, *and to the paperback original market that blossomed in the fifties, where he quickly established himself as a superior suspense novelist with such gems as* The Damned *(1952) and* Murder in the Wind *(1956). He created his most celebrated character, Travis McGee, in* The Deep Blue Good-By *(1963), and has brought him back for nineteen encores to date, including the recent bestsellers,* Freefall in Crimson *and* Cinnamon Skin. *Among his short story collections is* The Good Old Stuff *(1982), which contains some of his best work for the pulps and in the foreword to which he speaks warmly of his association with Babette Rosmond.*

BANNING KNEW HOW it was with me, knew I couldn't get the dead face of the Miller kid out of my mind. It was he who talked me into taking two weeks off in the spring.

I had taken my time packing; so, well after dark, I was roaring up Route 14 north out of Williamsport, my hands light and easy on the wheel of Banning's car. Mine was in the shop and he had insisted.

There was one of those Pennsylvania fogs. It was just heavy enough so that I didn't dare pass the car ahead of me, and was content to cruise along just far enough behind him so that his twin tail-lights made a red glow on the fog that tore by in shreds from the breeze of his fast travel.

It was hypnotic, driving behind the other car, and, as I drove, I thought back over the last ten years and wondered why I had become a cop. Lots of security, sure, but damn low pay. And you never manage to get tough enough to keep things from getting to you, from getting down through your thickened hide and stinging the few soft parts you had left.

I thought of the Miller kid and of the hammer murders in the shanty down by the river, and the gray, bloated look of the bodies that came out of the river. Violence. Diseases of the mind. Shifty eyes. A thousand lineups. You walk into small, dingy sitting rooms and you can smell the blood in the air and hear a woman moaning. It's a dirty business. Thankless.

The guy ahead of me had Pennsy plates. I was looking ahead to Jack Farner's lodge in the hills where I could sleep twenty hours a day and eat like a horse and come back to life.

A few miles north of Roaring Branch, Mr. Buick ahead of me slowed down and I dropped back, figuring he was about to turn. A light rain had started, cutting the fog, and his tail-lights were clearer. The road made a gradual bend to the right. He had dropped down to about forty. I held back, waiting for him to let me know what he was going to do.

He went part way around the turn, and the tires on the right side dropped off onto the wet shoulder. I braked, realizing that he'd have to slow down to get back onto the road. He didn't. He kept on going, right across the shoulder and the right front of the big car smashed into a mammoth tree with a noise like a million bricks falling into a greenhouse. The smash threw the big car onto its side and it slid forty feet in the mud, wheels turning in the air.

I jammed on my brakes and fought to get Banning's coupe out of a long skid. I pulled off onto the shoulder a hundred or so feet beyond the smashup and ran back through the rain, a flashlight in my hand.

The rain pattered on the black metal of the car. The front end was a complete mess. There was no sound. The door stuck. I managed to yank it open and pry it back. I climbed up and flashed the light down in there.

A man moaned. He was at the bottom of the heap. A bleeding woman was across him. The fresh blood matted her light hair. I bent down through the open door and felt for her wet arm. No pulse.

I flashed the light on her face. It was impossible to tell what she had looked like, but when I saw the depressed fracture of the frontal lobe, the pale, shell-like bones of the temple protruding through the skin, I knew there was no use in fooling with her. I pulled up hard on her arm, got her body up through the door, and put it on the grass.

The man's face was covered with blood. His mouth opened as I held the light on him and he moaned again. Ambulance business.

I crawled in with him, hearing the glass of the window on his side crack as I stepped on it. I checked him over to make certain he wasn't bleeding to death. No big holes in him that I could find.

Another car stopped. I climbed out, sent them down to the gas station to phone for an ambulance and the highway patrol. I handed the kid driving the car a buck and told him to bring back a couple of red flares.

He jumped the car away like a scared rabbit. I flashed my light back on the wreck. The guy was slowly climbing up out of the door I had propped open. I ran to him and steadied him as he climbed down.

His eyes were very wide and he was saying hoarsely, "Sleepy. Fell asleep."

I found a blanket in the back of his car and wrapped him in it and made him sit down, leaning against the bole of the tree he had hit. There was a big gouge in the bark and the white wood underneath was ragged and splintered.

Another car stopped and a man hollered out the window, "Trouble?"

"All under control, unless you're a doctor. Are you?"

"No."

He started to climb out. I said, "Run along, friend." He got back in, slammed the door and drove off.

The kid I had sent to the gas station came back and told me he had put the call through. He had a flashlight. He stared at the dead woman while I set the flares out on the shoulder.

When I got back to the man he said, "Janet! Where's Janet?"

He tried to get up. I put my hands on his shoulders and held him down. "Relax. She's hurt bad. A doctor'll be along in a minute."

Sirens growled in the distance, singing over the hills and around the curves. They bounced to a stop on the shoulder. Two of the

Pennsy state cops, young, blunt, and efficient. They gave the woman one look and turned to the man.

At their request he tugged his wallet out of his pocket and handed it to them. One flashed his light on the license and papers while I explained what I had seen and what I had done. The other looked the car over, got a camera and flash bulbs out of his car, and took pictures of the tracks in the mud, the scar on the tree, the overturned car.

The ambulance pulled over close to the tree, right through the shallow ditch beyond the shoulder.

The man was moaning again. They got a stretcher and made him stretch out on it. The intern went over him with quick, careful hands. More cars stopped. People got out, their eyes big with curiosity.

They carted the woman into the ambulance and one trooper told me to report to the barracks near Canton while they got a formal statement from me.

I sat in the small front room of the trooper station after the questions were finished. They had, of course, learned that I was one of the brotherhood, and, after a drink, they asked me to stay overnight; one of the troopers was on leave and I could use his bed. I was too tired to object.

In a short while the younger one of the two, named Sid Graydon, came back from the hospital in Canton. He tossed his hat on the hall table, came into the room, and sat down wearily.

The older one, Charlie Hopper, asked, "Get much, Sid?"

"Not a hell of a lot, Charlie. They gave him a drug to quiet him. He isn't hurt. Just shock and being shaken up. A fool nurse told him his wife is dead. He cried like a baby. Damn fool to drive while he was sleepy."

"Where's he from?"

"Philadelphia. Upper Darby to be exact. He and his wife were driving up to Elmira to visit her cousin there. His name is Walker Drock. He's a broker. Just another statistic to write up, Charlie. Nothing to pin on the guy. His wife's death is enough punishment for him."

Charlie sighed. "Probably both of them were asleep. According to the coroner, she didn't even get her hands up in front of her face. Just slammed her face right into the dashboard beside the glove compartment. Dented it right in. Funny about him slowing down. Usually they speed up when they fall asleep."

"Foot probably slid off the gas. By the way, Charlie, I've got to call Kell's garage in the morning and tell them not to touch the car. Drock was insistent about that. He told me that about four times."

"That's funny."

"No, these accident cases, they get an idea in their head and you can't get it out. He probably heard about some guy who had his car towed away by the police and then got a couple of hundred-dollar repair bill. I don't think anybody is going to do much repairing on that crate."

They gave me another drink and I sat with them and talked about the homicide cases in Philadelphia. I didn't tell them about the Miller kid. I won't be able to talk about that case for quite a while.

In the morning I drove on to Jack Farner's place, and spent two long weeks there. I put ten pounds back on and got a little tanned in the sun and cut Jack enough stove wood to last him for six months. The calluses on my palms felt good and the new strength in my shoulders felt even better.

I stopped off to see Charlie and Sid on the way back. Charlie told me that Drock had stayed in the hospital for two days and then had gone back to Philly with the body of his wife. The car had been counted out as a total loss, and sold for salvage value. The thing was open and shut. A simple, tragic accident.

And yet, somehow, it bothered me. Curiosity is an occupational disease with a cop, I suppose. I still couldn't figure out why Drock had slowed down before hitting the tree, why the jar of going off the pavement hadn't awakened him, why he was so insistent on the car not being touched.

Banning is the guy who taught me the cop business. Banning says to always assume the worst and work a case from that end. It was none of my business. And it was silly. If you want to kill your wife, and you drive your car head on into a tree, you'll probably end up knocking yourself off, too.

It bothered me and I know how I'm put together. I have to

283

follow every little thing up or I can't sleep nights. Maybe that's why I'm a cop.

I drove to Kell's garage. A guy climbed out from under a car and looked at the records and told me that the Drock car had been sold to an outfit named Higgins and Rigo.

Higgins was a puffy little man with watery eyes and a soiled shirt. He gave me the busy-man routine and I flashed the badge and watched him become very affable. He left me alone with a boy named Joe Baydle who had pulled the Drock car apart.

Joe acted very nervous until he found out that I wasn't interested in him. He leaned against the bench and said, "Anything funny about that Drock car? What do you mean?"

"I don't know what I mean. You've got to help me, Joe. I don't know what I'm looking for. They told me over at Kell's garage that Drock had got his stuff out of the car while it was there, and that he had brought a suitcase to carry off tools and things in."

"He must have had a hell of a lot of tools."

"How so?"

"The crate hasn't been sent to the bailer yet. It's still out in the back. Come along and I'll show you."

It was barely recognizable as the same car I had followed on that dark foggy night. It had been stripped.

Joe yanked the front door open on the driver's side and said, "Look here."

I bent over and looked where he pointed. The car was a four-door and a wide special compartment had been built under the front seat with a drop door that would open right under the driver's thighs.

I borrowed a flashlight and stretched out so I could look in there. It was empty. At first I thought there was no clue to what it had contained. Then I noticed a small fragment caught in a front corner. I pulled it out.

It looked to me like a piece of sponge. I showed it to Joe. He shrugged and I put it in my pocket.

The nurse at the hospital, a pretty little thing with a turned-up nose and wide, wise Irish eyes, said, "Yes, I took care of Mr. Drock. He was very upset about his wife."

"Did he make any phone calls?"

"Why, yes, he did. The morning after he came in here. He called the garage where his car had been towed and told them not to touch the car or anything in it until he had seen it. He called his wife's parents and her sister and her cousin in Elmira. He sent a few wires."

"Was he hurt badly?"

"No, he was very lucky. He didn't even get badly bruised. Just shock."

"How do you tell about shock?"

"The patient perspires a great deal, losing the body fluids from the pores. That fluid has to be replaced. Plasma."

"Did they use that on him?"

"No. Dr. Flanagan said that it wasn't a bad case of shock and just to keep him warm and give him a lot of fluids to drink."

"Thanks a lot, nurse. You've given me the information I want."

"You're quite welcome."

Banning drummed his fingers on the desk top. "It's wild geese you're after, Tom. I can give you one explanation. You say he's a broker. Well, for some reason he was carrying some negotiable securities and he had them hidden in that compartment."

"Ed, all I want is your permission to work on it for a couple of days."

"Go ahead, Tom. Go right ahead. Get the doubts out of your thick skull so you can come back to work. The couple of days, my boy, will be leave without pay."

"So be it."

The little green house in Upper Darby had a "For Sale" sign on it. Walker Drock had moved down to an inexpensive apartment hotel on Chestnut.

I picked him up the first night he left the office and followed him to his apartment hotel. I waited up the street and he came out in different clothes an hour later. He went to a cocktail bar on Woodland and fifteen minutes after he arrived, a good-looking blonde joined him.

They got pleasantly tight and then went up and took a room at a cheap hotel on Market near Thirty-eighth. He left her there at dawn and I let him go. She came out at quarter to eleven and walked two blocks toward town before she found a breakfast spot.

She sat at the counter and I went in and sat beside her, in spite of the empty stools on both sides of us. In the mirror I saw her give me a long, skeptical look while she ordered a big breakfast. She was the type who always have trouble with citizens trying to pick her up. A long lean girl with abundant curves in the right places, pale, go-to-hell eyes, and a wide, heavy mouth.

I didn't say a word until she had her coffee cup to her lips. Then I said, "Known Walker Drock long?"

She sputtered and the coffee ran down her chin and she sponged it off with a paper napkin.

"Who the hell are you?" she snapped.

"Just a cop, honey. A plain, dumb cop. Known Walker Drock long?"

"For a year. What's it to you?"

"Mrs. Drock didn't like Walker Drock knowing you, did she?"

"She didn't know—" She stopped suddenly. "What's this all about?"

"All about the sad and untimely death of Mrs. Drock. Very unfortunate, wasn't it? Or maybe fortunate. Depends on how you look at things."

"Mister, if you want to know anything, talk to my husband. His name happens to be Walker Drock."

"Sure and husband and wife sneak off to a cheap hotel. That sounds good."

"You think so? It happens that Walker has a certain position to maintain and it wouldn't look right if he married too soon after his wife's death. So we were married secretly in Maryland, and after a decent period we'll be married all over again."

I could tell she wasn't lying.

I said, "You'll have a great future, honey. You can wait for him to get tired of you and get chummy with some other gal. Then he'll kill you the same way he killed his first wife."

That was a shock to her. Her eyes widened and her hands shook. She glanced nervously at the counterman standing ten feet away. She said hoarsely, "You're mad! It was an accident. Walker was in it, too! He could have been killed."

"Could he? Suppose you ask Walker."

I turned away from the look in her eyes. I threw a dime on the counter for my coffee and walked out.

I used the badge on the resident manager of Drock's apartment hotel and got myself a room across the hall from his door. I propped the door open a crack so that I could watch his door.

I had nothing to go on. Just a hunch.

I didn't have a long wait. She probably met him for lunch. He came storming in at two o'clock. He looked down the hall behind him as he fumbled with the key. His face was white.

He went on in. I gave him three minutes. Then I took the passkey and let myself in. He was bending over the fireplace. I slammed the door behind me. As he spun around, his mouth open, I said, "Hot day for a fire, isn't it?"

You've got to give him credit for spunk. He rushed me. I rolled away from his punch, feeling the wind of it on my cheek. I dug a left hook deep into his gut and crossed a right to his face as he bent over.

He dropped on his back and was still. I dragged the smoldering, stinking mess out of the fireplace and stamped on it until it no longer smoked.

I sat on the other side of Banning's desk. He tapped his fingers on the edge of the desk and said softly, "I'll be damned!"

"Yeah, he got tied up with this Miss Eletha Forrest and his wife didn't like it a bit. She wouldn't give him a divorce. He planned it nicely. What he forgot to do was to get rid of the gimmick while he had a chance. But I suppose it wasn't too easy to get rid of, at that.

"He waited until another car was following him, and then he picked out a deserted locality. His wife had gone to sleep. That was essential. He had to slow down to about forty going off the road, and probably had it down to thirty-five when he hit the tree.

"He hadn't figured on it tipping over. That made it tougher for him, but he managed. I was the sucker witness—to tell people that he was in the car when it happened. He came out babbling about having fallen asleep, you remember.

"As soon as he had the general locality selected, he reached down and got the gimmick—the big thick sheet of sponge rubber out of the compartment—and kept it ready by his feet. He slowed down to forty, and as he headed for the tree he yanked it up between him and the steering wheel, leaning hard against it to kill the shock. The nurse said he didn't even get badly bruised.

"His wife was asleep. The smash into the tree threw her against the dashboard with killing force. The car turned over. He had a few minutes to wedge the sponge rubber matting back into the compartment under the seat. That's why he didn't want anybody poking around the car.

"He had read that people get killed when they hit unyielding surfaces. He made sure he had one with some give to it, and he probably realized that he had to force himself to relax against it. She had no protection at all."

I found the tall blonde signing her statement. She looked up and saw me, and her lip curled. "You fixed everybody good—real good," she said.

"I can't help that. Isn't it better to know?"

Her eyes were puffy and red. "I suppose so. I hate him, now. I hate him!"

"Come along and I'll buy you a drink."

She looked into my eyes and I saw that there was something about her that I hadn't seen. A sort of integrity. She said, "I hate him, but I'm married to him. I'll stick around and do what I can for him until the State of Pennsylvania electrocutes him. Maybe some day you can buy me that drink."

I walked out, remembering the look in her eyes, adding it to the looks in other eyes, the expressions on other faces.

A cop never grows a hide that's quite tough enough. You always end up hating yourself, too.

WILLIAM CAMPBELL GAULT

See No Evil

STORIES FEATURING ETHNIC characters were uncommon in the pulps; writers wouldn't write them because editors and publishers seldom bought them for fear of alienating their readership. Just as uncommon were corpseless character studies, because pulp readers demanded rapid-fire action and bodies galore.

Every now and then, however, a story would come along that, even though it broke one of the above taboos, was so good editors could not bring themselves to reject it. Dane Gregory's "Hear That Mournful Sound" is a case in point. But it was a rare day that saw the publication of a story that broke both of the above taboos—a story such as William Campbell Gault's "See No Evil."

First published in the September 1950 issue of New Detective, one of Popular Publications' string of detective pulps (and a magazine generally reserved for newcomers and non-series stories), "See No Evil" is a strong character study of two Mexican-American brothers trying to deal with hard times, racial prejudice, and hot-rod hoodlums in Southern California. Poignant and powerful, it proves that sensitivity and social relevance can indeed be found in those yellowing pulp pages.

William Campbell Gault is the author of any number of fine stories and novels, some of which deal with other ethnic characters and many of which combine the themes of crime and sport. A native of Milwaukee, he began his career in 1936 by selling short-shorts to the McClure Newspaper Syndicate and to such mild sex magazines as Paris Nights and Scarlet Adventuress; he went on to write sports fiction, and in 1939, sold his first criminous story to Ten Story Detective. *Gault's work appeared in all the leading mystery/detective, adventure, and sports pulps, a total of more than 300 sales. He also published three auto-racing stories (one with a racial prejudice theme) in* The Saturday Evening Post.

It was in the novel form, however, after the collapse of the pulps in the early fifties, that he gained his primary reputation. His first novel, Don't Cry for Me, *was awarded the Mystery Writers of America Edgar Award as the Best First Novel of 1952; and there followed such other high quality mysteries as* The Bloody Bokhara, The Canvas Coffin, The Convertible Hearse, *and* Day of the Ram *(the last two featuring his best-known series character, ex-football player turned private eye, Brock Callahan). Although he abandoned crime fiction in the 1960s, to concentrate on the more lucrative juvenile market (where he has published thirty three novels), Gault has happily returned to a life of fictional crime in recent years with such new Brock Callahan adventures as* The Bad Samaritan *(1982) and* The Cana Diversion *(1982). He lives in Santa Barbara, California.*

AT BREAKFAST, THERE was the story again, in the papers. I looked over at my brother, and saw his eyes on me. Big, brown eyes, Manuel's got, and a quick smile, and his brain is quick, too.

"Where were you last night, Manny?" I said.

"Out. Riding the heap around."

The heap is a '36 V8 with a cut-down solid top and two pots. With a Turbo head and Johannsen ignition. Too much car for any punk, but he'd built it. It had cost him many a skinned knuckle, and I couldn't say much about that.

"Around Pico, were you riding?" I asked him.

"Some. What's bothering you, Pete?"

"Kids bother me," I said. "Kids that got a grudge on the world. Kids that ride hot rods around, looking for trouble. In Pico, last night, seven of them beat up a guy; beat up one guy. They held his wife, while she watched. His sister had her baby with her and she ran away, but she fell in running away, and the baby's condition is critical. The man has a broken jaw and he lost three teeth and his back has been cut in seven places. It's all here in the paper, Manny."

"So? You don't have to read it, do you? You could read the sport page. Who's asking you to read it?"

"The kids were dark with brown eyes. Mexican kids, maybe."

"Maybe they're mad at the world, Pete. Maybe they figure they're not getting the break the *gringos* get."

"And that's the way to get a break, beating up strangers with tire irons?"

"I don't know, Pete. What's it to me?"

"I don't know. But this I know. If I thought you were one of them, I'd kill you where you sit."

"Would you? Who's mad now, Pete? What kind of talk is that?"

Mama had gone next door, to Sanchez's to borrow some eggs. Now she said, "That's what I'd like to know. What kind of talk is that, Peter Montello? Why don't you lay off Manuel? He's a good boy."

"He'd better stay a good boy," I said. "Where does he get his spending money?"

"There's ways of making a buck," Manny said. "I don't have to punch a time clock to make a buck."

"You had a black eye last week. Get that making a buck?"

"Maybe."

Mama said, "Peter it's time for work. Never mind about it, Peter."

"Who's the man around here?" I asked her. "Me or him?"

"What does it mater who's the man?" Mama answered. "I'm the boss. Here's your lunch, Peter."

I stood up and picked up my lunch. I looked at my brother. "You remember what I said."

"Which part?"

"And don't get flip." I got out before he gave me an answer to that.

Ah, he's all right. What kind of a break did he get, Papa dying when he was in seventh grade? High school, Manny had, but how could I send him farther, wrestling freight for Arnold's Cartage?

He's a bright kid, and should have gone to college.

But hot rods. Hot rod hoodlums now, running around like maniacs, insulting people, beating them. Wolf packs, some of the papers called them, and the sheriff was adding more deputies.

It was a hot, heavy day and I wore a pair of gloves to rags. Handling sole leather, and it cuts you all to hell.

Gina was sitting on her front porch when I went by on the way home, and I came up. She gave me a glass of lemonade.

"When we're married," she said, "I'll have a glass of it ready for you every night when you come home from work. I'll have a pitcher of it."

"When we're married—that's good," I said.

Her eyes are too soft for this world. She bruises too easy. "Why do you talk like that?" she asked me.

"When are we going to get married? What's wrong with a fact? What have you got against a fact?"

"What have you got against the world lately? Grouchy, grouchy, grouchy all the time. Tell me why should I love a grouch?"

"I don't know," I said. "I don't know."

"Oh, but I do, Peter," she said, and her soft hand stroked my cheek. "Oh, we won't fight. You've had a bad day."

"And Manny," I said.

"Now what?"

"These hoodlums, these hot rod hoodlums. Manny's got a hot rod."

"So?"

"And he had a black eye the other day."

She shook her head and looked at me with the soft eyes, like Manny's. "You're always hunting trouble, like those hoodlums. You don't know Manny's one, but you've got to think he is. Why do you always want to think bad?"

"I don't know. He's so—smart."

"You should be proud he is, not resentful. He's never given you any trouble."

Her brother Christy came up on the porch and poured himself a glass of lemonade. "Hi, Pete, how's the feet?"

Short and broad and perfect teeth. Was a fullback at Fullerton High, but no college made an offer.

I asked him, "Were you with Manny last night?"

"That's a good question," he said. "I forget. Ask Manny."

I reached over to grab him by the shirt, but Gina was quicker, and between us. "Peter, for heaven's sakes!" she said. "You're like a wild man."

Christy was looking at me, and his eyes were shiny and his mouth working. Both his fists were clenched.

I could have crushed him with one hand. I went past them and down the steps. I went home, and got in the shower Manny had put in the back yard.

Lots of things around here Manny had fixed up. He was handy with tools. And with tire irons?

Manuel. Manuel, my baby brother. When he was three, I was twelve, and watching him all the time, because I wanted to. Smart, always smart and quick and smiling.

About eight, Gina came over. She said, "You forgot your lunch bucket." She had it in her hand.

"I'm sorry, Gina," I said. "I feel better now."

"I thought you would. Let's go to the park. There's a concert tonight."

We sat on the grass, where it's free. Ortiz had a big voice, and you could sit in Palos Verdes and hear him. A poor man's singer, he must be; you can hear him in the cheap seats. What a voice, what a man.

I held Gina's hand and forgot about her brother. I almost forgot about Manny. Where had he been at suppertime?

Next morning, there were no new troubles in the paper. But the sheriff said there was a possibility the increase in housebreaking might be tied up with these hoodlum gangs. The city police were inclined to agree.

Manny was reading the sport page.

"Why weren't you here for supper?" I asked him.

"Wasn't hungry."

"Look at me when I talk to you."

He put the paper down.

"Did you call Ma that you wouldn't be here for supper?"

He nodded. "She knew about it."

She came from the kitchen with more pancakes. "Now what?"

293

"Nothing."

"Punching the clock, that's what's the matter with him," Manny said. "If you don't like it, why don't you quit, Pete?"

"And how would you two eat, then?"

"We'd find a way. We don't want to be a burden, Pete." He was grinning at me, that smart grin.

"Be quiet, both of you," Mama said. "I don't want another word out of you two this morning."

Another hot day. Loading refrigerators. The guys you get to work with these days, you might as well be alone. At noon, I sat near the north door, in the shade, with my lunch and the paper.

The voice was Shultz's. Big, round guy with a round head. Thinks he's the original Atlas.

"It's these damned Spanish-Americans, they like to be called. Most of these punks got Mex names, you notice? Manuel, or Leon, or—"

"Or Shultz," I called over.

"That's one of them," he told his buddies. "If I had my way—"

I was up and walking over there now. "What would you do, cabbage-head?" I asked him quietly.

"I'd shoot every one of those punks," he told me. "Beating up innocent people, scaring women into hysterics."

"You've got a big mouth, Shultz," I told him. "If you worked like you talked, we'd all be laid off."

He stood up, his face red. He rubbed his big hands on his cotton pants, looking me over. "Fight?" he said. "You want to fight, Mex?"

I nodded, and he came in.

He came in with a right hand I should have ducked, but didn't. It hit next to the ear and put me down. I saw his foot coming for my jaw as I scrambled on the concrete, and I twisted clear of it.

I was on my feet when he closed again. I put a fine left deep into his belly, and heard him grunt. His head crashed my mouth, and the blood spurted.

I caught him on the nose with a wild left, and he paused for maybe a second. My right caught his left eye.

He started one from the floor, and I beat him to it. It was a button shot, and I hit him twice more while he was falling.

His buddies were still sitting there. One of them said, "Don't get us wrong, Pete. We didn't ask him to sit with us. Sit down, Pete."

"It's cooler over here," I said.

It had been all right while it lasted, but it didn't do any good now. My hands trembled and I couldn't eat my lunch, and I was sick of myself. Hating wasn't any good; fighting wasn't any good. Why was I like this?

Gina was on the porch again. Mrs. Sanchez was there too, but not Christy.

Gina looked at my swollen lip, and her big eyes asked questions.

"Got caught by a packing case," I said. "Lucky it didn't tear my head off."

Mrs. Sanchez rocked in her rocker, saying nothing.

"Peter, poor Peter," Gina said.

"I'm all right," I said. "I'm no poorer than the rest in this block."

Mrs. Sanchez sighed, and said nothing.

"It must be hot in that warehouse," Gina said. "Should I make some lemonade?"

"Not today, not with this lip," I said. "I'll see you later."

"Tonight?"

"Sure. I suppose."

What was there in it? I could sit on her porch the rest of my life. Five years I'd been going with her and not a dime nearer to the priest. What was there in it? Pa hadn't left anything and Manny wasn't good for anything. I had Mama to take care of.

Manny was home for supper that evening. We didn't have any words for each other.

"Some home," Mama said. "Brothers not talking to each other."

Manny grinned. "He'll grow up some day, Ma. He was always the baby."

I looked at him and said nothing.

"Forget to duck?" he asked me.

Mama said, "It was a packing case. Peter is not street brawler, Manuel."

"Oh," Manny said, that smart way.

I asked him, "Don't you believe it?"

"Sure. If you say it. You wouldn't lie, Pete."

Red, things got, and I could feel his steady brown eyes on me. But I remembered Shultz, and how I'd felt after that.

"And if I did fight," I said, "I wouldn't use a tire iron. And I wouldn't need a gang."

Manny said quietly, "What the hell do I care what you'd do? You think you're some kind of an example?"

His eyes were burning; I'd never seen him this way before. He was breathing heavy; you could see his chest going in and out.

"Manuel—" Mama said warningly.

"Well, tell him to lay off of me, then! Picking, picking, picking all the time! I—" He got up and went out of the dining room.

The front door slammed.

Mama was shaking her head. "Peter, Peter, Peter—what is it? He's just a boy."

"He's old enough to work. I was working at his age."

She looked at the tablecloth. She was crying.

"Ma," I said, "I'm—oh, I don't know what I am. I'm sorry, Ma."

She nodded. "I know, I know—Peter, it's not good to hate. It's not good, being suspicious. Is it because of Gina? Because you've waited so long? You think I've been happy about that? Peter—"

"What's the good of talking?" I asked her. "It's a rat race, Ma." I got up, too, and went out.

It was cooler now. I could see Gina, in her kitchen, helping her mother with the dishes. I went over to Fourteenth Street, to Barney's.

I only had two bucks on me, but my credit was good. I drank a lot of whiskey, and it didn't do any good at all. I wasn't happy now, or mad—just sour, dead, empty.

The lights were out at Sanchez's. There was a light on in our house, though, and a prowl car in front. I hurried up the walk.

There was a cop there. Ma was sitting in the big chair, and crying. Manny was sitting on the davenport, looking mad.

The cop had a book in his hand, a bank book. He turned as I came in. He sniffed, and looked at me suspiciously.

"What's the matter?" I said. Sick, I was now, and mad.

"You the brother?"

"That's right. What's the matter?"

"Found this little book in a home that was robbed tonight. It's a bankbook showing a total deposit of eleven hundred dollars, made out to your brother."

"Eleven hundred dollars?" I stared at Manny. "You—"

"It's mine, but I lost it, Pete. I lost it over two weeks ago."

"Eleven hundred dollars," I said, and took a step his way.

"Peter—" Mama said. Her voice was deep and she glared at me. "This is the time, Peter. Now, I'll know if you're a brother."

Manuel, Manuel . . . I fought the whiskey and the hate in me. What a baby he'd been. What a smart, quick, smiling baby. I took a deep breath and faced away from him. I faced the cop.

"He says he lost it. Two weeks ago, he says."

"And reported the loss?"

"The very next day," Manny said. "You could check that at the bank. You want to see the new one they gave me?"

The cop shook his head. "You've got a '36 Ford, a convertible with a cut-down, solid top?"

"Every other rod in town's a '36 with solid top. That's the best model to cut down."

"Maybe. I think you ought to come down anyway. Just a few questions, you know, like where you were tonight."

Well, a test. I turned around and said, "I'll go along, Manny. Don't let him scare you."

"I'm not scared, I'm mad," Manny said. "I'm so mad I'm not scared to admit where I was tonight, though you won't like it, Pete. I was at Gilmore Stadium, driving the Art Willis Special. I won the feature in it. There must have been a couple thousand watching me."

"You, in a race car?" I said. "Manny, baby, you're just a—"

"Pete, I won. I win a lot of races. You should read the sports pages, Pete, not the front pages; you'd learn an awful lot."

Now I saw, and took a deep breath. "And the eleven hundred?"

"Was for you. A truck for you, I was saving for. So you could be in business for yourself, and wouldn't have to punch the clock. Ma knew I was driving, but we were scared to tell you, the way you've been."

"Sounds very fine," the cop said, "but I'm afraid it would sound better if the lieutenant heard it."

"Beat it," I said. "Go someplace and blow your whistle. You're not taking my brother anywhere."

"Peter—" Mama said.

The phone rang.

"That would be for me," the cop said, and went over to pick up the phone.

"Right," he said, and "Oh—I see. Admitted it? Let's see, that would be next door. Makes sense, all right. Sure, I'll run over and talk to his folks."

He hung up, and faced us. He didn't look comfortable. "A—a Christy Sanchez admitted finding that bankbook, and admitted being a member of the gang that robbed that house. Said he left it behind on purpose. Had some kind of grudge against your brother." He looked at me. "That would be you."

I didn't say anything.

He shook his head. "I don't know what's the matter with these kids."

"Christy hasn't a father," I said. "When you're ready to go down with the Sanchez's, I'd like to go along, officer."

"All right. I'll drop back." He went out.

"Manny," I said. "Oh, Manny, baby."

"It's all right, Pete," he said. "You work hard, and it's been rough. But for gosh sakes, don't—ah, Pete."

But I couldn't help it. I was crying. And Pete was crying and Ma too. It was wonderful.

JOHN D. MacDONALD

Crime of Omission

THIS SECOND SHORT piece by John D. MacDonald first appeared in Detective Tales *for August 1951, a year and a half before the demise of that fine magazine (and of all the other Popular Publications pulps). It is a simple story with a simple plot built on the classic theme of the eternal triangle; but in MacDonald's hands, with his impeccable characterization and his knack for creating suspense, it outclasses the vast majority of longer, more complex pulp fiction.*

"Crime of Omission" has not been published anywhere since its initial appearance, an oversight that is happily rectified here.

PAUL PRENTICE SAT on the camp porch at midnight, deep in the brooding knowledge that his world had faltered, stopped, surged in a new direction at three that afternoon, in the sunglare on snow. He had always been a quiet, amiable man and he could not accustom himself to the recurrent cycles of anger, hate, disgust.

His law partner, Jay Alber, widower of seven months, sat bundled in sweaters and jackets in a porch chair a few feet away. They both looked out at the hard grey sheen of the frozen lake, pallid in the moonlight. Inside the camp the fire roared in the chunk stove and the sides glowed dull red in the darkened room.

Anne was in there, warmly asleep by now, the blankets pulled over her head. From the four years of marriage he knew precisely how she would feel to his hands, the scent of her, the sleepy murmur of welcome.

He wondered how she could sleep with the sound of the frozen lake. The temperature was still dropping. The lake thundered, rattled, cracked with startlingly loud reports. It was a monster, stirring under the moonlight.

"How cold you think it is now, Paul?" Jay asked. His breath made a pale plume in the night.

"Thirty below at least," Paul said. His voice sounded old and rusty and tired.

That was the bad thing—that it was so dirty, and so sordid. The sort of trite and nasty situation relished by the authors of the cheaper love novels. Eternal-triangle stuff with all the fixings. The husband, getting a bit thick through the middle, a bit thin on top. The young partner, almost ridiculously good-looking. The young wife.

But Paul couldn't make his young wife fit the standard pattern. Not Anne. There had always seemed to be such a desperate honesty about her. And his abiding trust had been built on that honesty he saw and felt. And all that honesty, that level-eyed sincerity, had been false.

The lake made a low growl that ended in a crack like the sound of a rifle.

Paul thought back to the Thursday when they had planned this weekend. He remembered Anne taking his hand and saying, "Darling, let's ask Jay if he'd like to come. He's still pretty lonely, you know. He doesn't get out enough."

Incredible deceit! How long had she played him for a fool? He wondered if there had been . . . others. The very thought brought nausea.

Oh, the trip up had been very gay. All of them singing as Paul drove the car, the skis racked on top. Anne in the middle. Jay with his arm carelessly across the back of the seat. Had subtle signals been exchanged? Was there an unholy glee in their hearts at the wickedness of the situation?

"I guess every other camp is empty," Jay said. "What a weird night!"

"A very weird night, Jay," he said.

The strangest night of his life, when all values had to be re-assessed, re-weighed, sorted anew.

As a laywer, he thought, I should have carried professional skep-ticism over into the home. I should have known what people are. All people. Even Anne. Maybe if there had been children . . .

"Like a landscape on the moon, eh?" Jay said.

"I see what you mean." He remembered how he and Anne had joked about this good-looking partner, how Anne said that she would never trust a man who looked like that.

"You go for the old-shoe type?" he had asked.

"Hi, old shoe," she had said.

Good-bye to the laughing years. But what now? What was the next step? Face them with it? That seemed so feeble, so reasonable, so civilized. The anger that clotted in his throat frightened him with its virulence.

If there were only some possibility that he had misinterpreted what he had seen. The increasing cold had driven most of the skiers down to the hot buttered rum and mulled wine at the lodge. He and Anne and Jay had been on the far side of the intermediate slope, over near the dips and hollows of the open trails. The scene was driven hard and clear into his mind, as though etched there with acid.

He had missed them and he had come down in his usual conser-vative stem turns, the cold biting his lips, pinching his nostrils. He had made one turn so sharp that it had thrust him against an up-slope and he had lost momentum. He decided to go over nearer the fringe of woods to take the last part of the drop. He angled over and then saw them in a hollow beyond the crest, not fifty feet away. They stood motionless, gay figures against the snow. Jay's broad back was toward him, and he could tell by the head-tilt strain of her figure that their lips were together. Jay's gloved hand was at the nape of her neck.

It was a long, incredible, frozen fragment of time before he backed with exaggerated caution, crouched, turned his skis down the slope and went all the way down to the lodge in the most reckless schuss of his short skiing career, the wind freezing the unexpected tears on his cheeks, tears that seeped under the lower edge of the goggles.

They were not out alone long. They came into the bar not over ten minutes later, stamping their feet, slapping their arms, grinning at him with their bland conscienceless faces. He could not say anything then. He tried to drink too much. He ordered so many drinks that Anne began to watch him with an odd expression. But the drinks made no effect other than a numbness of his lips.

Later, as they went into the dining room Anne took his arm and whispered, "Are you all right, Paul?"

"I'm fine. Dandy."

"I thought you acted a little glum, darling."

Brandy after dinner and then the drive back here to the camp. It seemed quite a bad joke of the fates that this was the camp Anne had inherited, the camp where they had spent the long sweet days of honeymoon in an eternal August of the past.

They sat on the porch until Anne said, "I give up, gentlemen. To be vulgar, the lady is pooped. A nice day was had by all."

He noted that she patted Jay's shoulder before coming to him to kiss him good night. In spite of the cold on the porch her lips tasted lax and warm and sleepy.

And now she was asleep. Did she dream of Jay? Paul, with a hard feeling of shock, remembered the trip he would have to take the following week. He remembered Jay saying, "I'll hold down the fort." Three days. And three . . . nights.

Jay said softly, "Barb would have liked this. She liked crazy landscapes and strange places."

It was only lately that Jay seemed able to speak of his dead wife. Paul remembered how he had secretly rejoiced when first Jay had been able to speak of Barbara. He had been glad for Jay, glad that there were signs that Jay was coming out of it. Now he was sardonically amused. For Jay to speak of Barbara was a pleasant way to allay the suspicion of one Paul Prentice, husband.

"Can you walk on that stuff?" Jay asked.

"It's thick enough to drive on," Paul said absently.

Jay stood up, the earflaps of his ski cap pulled down, his mittened hands shoved into the slit pockets of his jacket so that his elbows were out-thrust.

"I'm going out and walk on that thundering stuff. Crazy idea, isn't it? Want to come along?"

"No, thanks. I'll stay here and watch you."

He heard Jay slip and grunt as he went down the snow covered steps. The wind of the previous morning had swept the ice clear of snow. Soon Jay appeared out from under the overhang of the porch, walking carefully out across the slippery surface.

Paul sat on the porch and looked at the dark figure in the moonlight. Hate was like one of those directional hands painted on a sign. A huge hand, suspended above the lake, the finger pointed at the dark figure walking slowly.

I'm supposed to think you're thinking of Barbara, Paul thought. You, my loyal partner, my friend.

And his mind swooped back to another day, a summer day. Rifle on the porch. Railing for a rest. Splashes around the dancing can. Then the direct hit, the can sinking out of sight. They had brought a rifle. Anne loved to shoot. Right now it was standing by the side door of the camp, under the edge of the porch roof for protection. He got it and sat down again in the chair.

Paul slid his chair into a better position. He took the glove off his right hand. The metal of the rifle seemed to radiate cold like that of imagined outer space. Softly he worked the bolt, slid it forward, locked it down. Ninety to a hundred yards. A simple shot with a target that size, with the moonlight aiding the sight pattern. The rifle had a peep sight. He breathed heavily and the metal turned frosty white as the moisture condensed on it. He laid his cheek against the metal, centered the little dot within the circle on the middle of Jay's back.

His finger was on the trigger. The lake made another series of loud reports. Like artillery fire at close hand.

Anne would not hear the shot. Off to the left was a dark place, an air hole now skimmed by new ice, thin enough to break easily.

He aimed carefully and exerted gentle pressure on the trigger. And then knew that he could not pull it all the way, could not fire, could not commit murder. He knew that even had he found them together committing the very act, he could not kill. And he despised himself for the softness that made this true.

And then Jay dropped from sight.

For one moment he thought he had fired. His mouth went dry as he thought he had fired. But there was no huddled spot of darkness on the ice. Instead a hole and a frightened cry, hoarse. A faint, echoing nightmare cry.

"Better!" a voice said in the back of his mind. "You fell asleep on the porch. He wandered out and stepped on the thin ice over an air hole. He'll die in minutes."

The metal of the rifle was stuck to the skin of his cheek. He was but faintly conscious of the sharp pain as he pulled it away. He fell on the steps, rolled out onto the ice, and scrambled to his feet. In one still part of his mind he sat up on the porch, waiting, listening for the cries to cease.

He ran recklessly, and too fast. When he neared the hole he thought for one moment he wouldn't stop, that he too, would plunge in. He lay on his belly and extended the rifle. Jay grasped it and Paul worked his way back. Jay came out over the edge of the firmer ice, his feet splashing madly at the black water which froze into a crackling, glistening sheath on his clothes.

He got Jay up onto wobbling feet. He supported him with an arm around him. The heavier man lurched against him with each step, shaking uncontrollably, unable to speak.

I cannot commit a murder of commission, or of omission, Paul thought hopelessly. I shall have to let him have her.

He got him through the door and over by the stove, as close as he dared put him. He shook Anne awake roughly. "Help me! Quick! Jay fell through a hole into the lake."

She came awake at once. Together they worked at the stubborn frozen clothes. Jay tried to grin at them, but his teeth chattered so badly that it was a grimace. His hands were so curled and helpless with the cold that he could not help them. Paul threw more wood on the stove, picking thin pieces that would give off the maximum of heat. They striped him and the strong body had a white, waxy look. Paul pulled a cot close to the stove, rubbed Jay with all his strength with a big towel. Anne uncorked a bottle, filled half a tumbler, supported Jay's head while he drank it. His teeth chattered on the rim of the glass. A few moments after the whiskey was down, the shudders quieted.

Paul helped him into two pairs of long woolen underwear from Jay's luggage, first heating them over the stove. They gave him two more drinks of whiskey, rolled him in warm blankets and watched over him.

"Thanks, fella," Jay said weakly just before he dropped into sleep.

"How close, and how horrible," Anne said.

"It was close," Paul said dully. She sat near the stove, warming her hands. The light picked out glints in her hair. Her face was that of a sleepy child.

"What on earth happened to your face, darling?"

He lifted his fingertips mechanically to his cheek. "This? Oh, I was fooling around with the rifle. The metal stuck to my skin."

"Let me get something for it. I think butter would help. It's sort of like a burn. You should have let Jay help you, darling."

"What do you mean?"

She turned in the kitchen doorway. He knew, looking at her, that the same weakness that kept him from killing Jay would keep him from hating her. He was forever trapped in his love for her.

"I forgot to tell you, darling. This afternoon like a clumsy fool I touched the metal tip of the ski pole to the corner of my mouth and it stuck there. Jay came up and diagnosed the trouble and breathed on the tip until he warmed it so that I could pull it free without taking half my mouth with it."

She came back with the butter, softened it by the fire, rubbed it gently on the torn place on his cheek.

"Now that's a strange expression!" she said, sitting back on her heels.

He smiled and fought back the sting in his eyes. "Love," he said.

JOHN
JAKES

The Girl in the
Golden Cage

BY 1953, ALL *the great mystery and detective pulps were extinct:* Black
Mask, Dime Detective, Dime Mystery, Detective Tales, Detective
Story, The Shadow, Doc Savage. *Only a handful of pulps remained,
and they, too, would soon become victims of television, and of the burgeon-
ing paperback book industry which offered the same kind of reading entertainment in smaller, handier packages and spiced with the kind of straight-
forward sexual content that had always been taboo in magazines.*

Two of the few remaining crime pulps were Thrilling Detective *and*
Popular Detective, *the patriarchs of the once flourishing Thrilling Group.
(Ned Pines, Thrilling's owner, could afford to keep magazines afloat longer
than most publishers; he and his editorial director, Leo Margulies, had
founded one of the major early paperback houses, Popular Library, in
1943.) Such stalwart pulpsters as Carroll John Daly and Norman Daniels
were still appearing in* Thrilling Detective *and* Popular Detective *in
1953, but these titles also featured stories by young writers, many of whom
later made names for themselves in books and/or in the digest-size crime
magazines. Writers such as Louis L'Amour, Jonathan Craig, Fletcher Flora,
Gil Brewer—and John Jakes.*

"The Girl in the Golden Cage" appeared in the Summer 1953 issue of
Thrilling Detective, *under Jakes's pseudonym of Alan Payne, and was
one of his few sales to the detective pulps. It is a private eye story in the*

hard-boiled pulp tradition, and yet it also reflects the changes that both the pulp formula and the private eye formula were undergoing in the early fifties. There is a flavoring of Mickey Spillane, whose Mike Hammer was at the peak of his popularity in 1953; and, more importantly, there is a strong emphasis on emotion and character, two elements which some contemporary detective writers have stressed to good benefit. For these reasons, "The Girl in the Golden Cage" makes a fitting final entry in this anthology.

John Jakes made his first professional sale (of a science fiction story) in 1950, at the age of eighteen, and was soon regularly contributing science fiction, Westerns, and an occasional crime story to the pulps and to the digests. His first novel, a Western juvenile, appeared in 1952; his first adult novel, also a Western, was published in 1956. Among his more than fifty additional novels are mysteries (the amusing Johnny Havoc private eye series), science fiction adventures, fantasies, sword-and-sorcery sagas, general historicals, and of course the bestselling American Bicentennial Series— The Bastard, The Rebels, The Titans, North and South—*that has made him one of today's most widely read authors.*

THAT SUNDAY STARTED gray and didn't change. The early winter clouds piled up over the skyscrapers and just before noon, a cold windy rain began slashing at the windows of my apartment. I stayed inside, eating toast and drinking big glasses of milk and going through a western novel. I felt good; safe and peaceful. Business was at a low point, which came as a relief after a couple of hectic months; I got a kick out of doing nothing. My apartment sealed itself off from the rain of the chill day. A gunman stalked through the pages of my book, hunting the marshall. And every time the heroine made an entrance I saw the face of the girl I'd slept with last Wednesday night. The face was a rich, warm image for such a Sunday. It made the apartment seem even more secure.

I looked at the clock when the phone rang. Twelve twenty-one. I picked it up and said hello and all of a sudden, the gunman and the marshall disappeared and I heard the rain on the windows, sharp as a rattle of bones. "Johnny," a voice said. I'd heard that voice often enough to know it. Lt. Hans Broekman. Homicide. I didn't say anything so he went on, "Johnny, did you know a girl named Lorraine Perau?"

Past tense. That jolted me right down to the bottom of my gut. "I knew her," I said, wondering how he'd made the connection. Then I remembered. I'd given her one of my cards the first time I met her, a month before. But nobody was supposed to know that I knew Lorraine Perau. She wanted it that way. You see, Lorraine owned the face that floated warm in the middle of this Sunday gloom. Lorraine owned the face that belonged to last Wednesday night, and other Wednesday nights stretching back over the month.

"You have any connection with her, Johnny?" Broekman asked.

"That depends."

Broekman signed. It was a habit; he tired easily. He had a wife who stayed up every night watching the late movies on TV, and besides that, he had insomnia. "A girl answering to the name of Lorraine Perau was found this morning in the Twelfth Street Freight Yards, inside a refrigerator car." He lowered his voice deliberately. "Somebody shot her to death."

The sickness hit me then, full and strong. In this business, you try to tell yourself that death is commonplace. But in the dark hours of the night you get to thinking. A human life ended. A miraculous machine broken. And when it's a girl you knew, a girl who came out of nowhere into a bar, who seemed afraid, yet who turned a handful of nights into something fine, the horror hits like a sledge.

"She had one of the agency cards in her pocketbook," Broekman said. "They didn't try to remove identification. You want to answer questions over the phone, or you want to come down?"

"I'll come down."

"We're still at the freight terminal. Twelfth Street." I stood staring at the dead phone. Finally I put it down and put on a tie. Black eyes watched me in the mirror. The gray hair said, Hood, you're thirty-one and you're a wreck. Lorraine Perau is dead and there won't be any more Wednesday nights. I wanted to call Romo Spain, but the big man, the brains of the agency was vacationing down in Miami Beach, wheeling his wheelchair along, cigarette holder sticking up jauntily from the corner of his blunt mouth as he eyed the girls switching their hips in the sun. Romo couldn't help me now. Someone had short-circuited the world, and it was turning cold and the life was seeping out of it and freezing me.

I practically ruined my coupe getting to the terminal. I knew all the homicide boys on the scene. Broekman stood under a tin-shaded light, a sloppy, sad-eyed man with a fleck of tobacco on his lower lip. He was questioning the switchman who'd found Lorraine. I stood in the doorway and lit a cigarette. The old switchman shuffled his feet and said that, Hell, he'd never have noticed if the refrigerator car door hadn't been open and there was this red high-heeled shoe sticking out.

Broekman said, "That's all for now." He turned around, knowing I was there. "Hello, Johnny. Fast trip." He didn't waste any time either. "What's your hook-up with the girl?"

I told him. How she walked into a bar and we talked. How we spent the night together, and several more nights after that, unknown even to Romo Spain. How she seemed afraid; how I never knew where she came from or where she went; how I somehow understood that if I tried to find out, I'd never see her again. How the only thing I did was look for her in the phone book and draw a blank.

"What was the name of that bar? The first one?"

"The St. James, on Dearborn."

He looked at me. A wind blew in from the freight yards, moving the tin-shaded bulb. Light-flecks showed in Broekman's weary blue eyes. "It's not a very pretty story, Johnny."

"For Christ's sake, Hans, who are you to pass on my morals? Who was she? Do you know?"

"Yes, I know. She wore a lot of makeup, thick pancake stuff. So I followed a hunch that she was in show business."

"Lots of women wear pancake makeup who aren't in show business."

"Lorraine Perau wasn't one of them." His eyes pinpointed, hard. "You're in cheap company, Johnny. She was a stripper at The Golden Cage."

His words cut me up inside. Sure, he was so tired he could hardly stand up, and the rain had soaked through his frayed suit coat, but he said the wrong thing and I slammed him on the point of the jaw and brought a thin line of blood glittering out of his mouth into the glaring light. One of the homicide cops said, "Hey, damn you!" and rabbit punched me so that I slammed against a crate and stood holding my head, watching the comets behind my eyes slowly trail away.

I looked up. I felt like a guilty little kid. "I'm sorry, Hans."

"It's okay, Johnny. People get mixed up with other people and sometimes you can't judge how they feel." He took a pad out of his pocket and wrote something down. "I haven't got anybody to tag with her killing, but there's no sense in my trying to tag you. I guess I'm all finished with you."

"I'm not finished." He turned back to me when I said it. "I want the guy who put the gun to her."

His eyes hardened to little chips of blue ice. "No dice, Johnny. You weren't hired by a client on this one. I wanted to know your connection, I found it. If I want you, I'll call you. Otherwise, steer clear. We'll handle it all right."

"Okay," I said. He stared at me levelly and his face didn't change. He knew me well enough to know I was lying. But he didn't say anything. "I'd like to see the body, if it's still around."

He hesitated, frowning. Then he jerked a finger for me to follow. We went out of the shed and down the platform through the rain. The refrigerator car, with two cops on guard, stood about a quarter of a mile away. We tramped across the tracks and the cops opened the door for us. The refrigeration was off but the air still had a flat, frozen smell. The pipes were thickly frosted.

The bulk under the sheet didn't seem real. I lifted one corner and saw her face and it was enough for me. I didn't want to remember her that way at all, lips whitened and drawn. I wanted to remember the Wednesdays, the taste of our steaks, the tang of late fall air in Lincoln Park, the warm room and the warmer arms. Just a couple of people who met as strangers in a bar and wound up having something pretty fine.

The Girl in the Golden Cage

I got out of there and drove slowly back to the apartment. The wipers ticked back and forth and I got to work, thinking. I had wondered about her, of course. Where she came from; what she did. But it had never been necessary to find out when she was alive. Now it was necessary because she lay in a refrigerator car with all the strange frightened life shot out of her. I found the Golden Cage in a phone book. The far north-west side. I drove out there. A big house, an old one, decorated with neon and a doorman. I knew that Broekman had been right. On the poster outside were the words, The Girl in the Golden Cage. Above the legend, Lorraine in a bra and g-string looked out at me.

Inside, I ordered a steak sandwich and a drink and motioned to the bartender. "Who owns the place?"

His mouth looked like a steel trap. "Steve Lannes," he grunted. That name I knew. I'd heard it in other bars, from men who get their cash outside the law. Steve Lannes had more than one club, plus a flock of rumors trailing after him. Steve Lannes had been mentioned once or twice in connection with call girls and making money from dirty literature which could sometimes pay off almost as well as a spot like the Golden Cage.

When the floorshow started, I saw what Lorraine had done here. A yellow-painted cage descended on a chain from the ceiling and a big-hipped girl did a strip in there, high up, where everybody could get a good look. That was Lorraine a few days ago. But somehow it didn't ruin the memory of her. I knew her in a different way. I listened to the small combo grind away, saw the flesh of the big-hipped girl in the cage sweating in the round yellow tunnels of the spotlights and it didn't make any difference. After the number was over, I left.

The rain was coming down harder than ever as I drove back toward the Loop. The wipers worked fast, and I made my mind keep up with them. I wanted Romo Spain, because he would have helped me. But I was on my own this trip. So I worked on it, sweated it out, and little by little, I got something.

Lorraine had been running, hiding when we were together; hiding from something on the outside. Now I figured a girl wouldn't hide from the fact that she took off her clothes for a living. To do that, she'd have to have to be pretty screwy, and Lorraine wasn't screwy. I reasoned that it had to be something bigger.

So what does a woman hide from? Sometimes from another man. That was the easiest answer. But it could have been anything. Maybe she'd poisoned her old maid aunt to get the family fortune. Romo would have looked over the possibilities and picked the right one, however obscure. Johnny Hood, the dumb leg man, took the obvious answer.

I locked the door of my apartment behind me. I turned on the light in the kitchen and got out two pints of liquor. I sat there, staring at the bleak unshaded window pane with its dapple of rain. Tears. Black tears from a cold night. I lit a cigarette and opened the first pint.

I poured it down steadily, one drink after another. I thought about her. I thought about her face and her mouth and her arms on those Wednesdays that were real and yet as unreal as the fall smoke of burning leaves hazing the park where we walked. The rain kept raining. I kept drinking. And I saw her face, right up to the moment when I fell off the chair and hit the floor.

Morning brought a clearing sky. I climbed out of the sack about nine, feeling that the worst of the shock was over. I fried some eggs, drank a quart of milk and took the coupe down into the Loop. I parked two blocks from city hall and hoofed it over. The air had a sharp, cool tang down there in the shadows between the buildings. The movements of people in the crowd seemed crisp; alive. A girl in a green woolen suit that fit tightly over her body clicked on by high spiked heels. I looked away fast. I thought of Lorraine when I saw her.

The clerk in the marriage license office was a gray-haired old bird with a lardy belly and rear end, the kind that grew heavy when the city hall crowd stayed in power too long. I knew him. I pulled two tens out of my wallet and laid them on the fresh white page where the couples signed their names.

"I want to go through the records, dad."

He blinked and shoved his specs up higher on his nose and shook his head, as if to say, I shouldn't do this. Then one veined and mottled hand slithered over the page and clamped around the bills. The hand disappeared in his pocket. "What was your name again?"

I showed him my license. "John Hood. The firm of Hood and Spain."

"Oh yes, oh yes." He nodded vigorously and put on one of the smiles reserved for times when it was necessary to smile. "You've been here before. Well, you know your way around. Help yourself." He even did me the favor of opening the wooden gate in the counter.

So I got to the records. I broke out a fresh pack of cigarettes. You see, I didn't know where I should start. I picked a year ago, arbitrarily, and started backwards from there, flipping pages, discarding the endless names that meant a lot when they were first put down there; names that meant loving and money and a house and kids but didn't mean a thing to me because I was looking for the name of a girl who was dead. When I finally found her signature, a week before Labor Day two and a half years back, I stared at it for a whole minute.

I had never seen her handwriting before. But there it was, small yet bold, as she had been. Lorraine Perau, twenty-four. I had her age, another unknown quantity. Slowly, I moved my eyes across the page to the spot where the man signed. Steven Aubrey Lannes, thirty-three.

I slammed the book shut and kicked the chair back and jammed my cigarette into my pocket. Now it fitted together a little bit. She not only worked there, she lived with the man who owned the place. Somehow, I couldn't imagine her loving him. If she had, she'd never have let it go beyond a casual drink in a bar. With me, I mean.

Just as I walked out into the hall, I saw the elevator door open and I recognized Ted Fishlin, one of Hans' boys. I stepped into an open doorway, my back to the hall, ducked my head and lit a cigarette. Fishlin's steps clacked by. I turned and watched him go into the marriage license office. I ran for the elevator.

The cage seemed to take a year getting down. I shouldered my way out to the street and a woman punched me angrily with her elbow as I went by. I kept going. Hans Broekman of Homicide was right up with me, playing the hunches. His leg man was only about ten minutes behind me. Fishlin would talk to the old man, find out I'd been there, and probably discover the book on the table where I'd left it. Fishlin would go through the book. Then we'd be neck and neck, heading for the wire where Steve Lannes was waiting.

I unlocked the glove compartment of the coupe, took off my

jacket and slipped on the .38 in the shoulder holster. The attendant gave me the eye as I drove out of the lot. I didn't pay any attention, swinging the car wildly into the line of cars. A gray sedan slammed on its brakes and somebody swore but I kept going.

I roared through the first traffic light a second after it changed from yellow to red. I pushed down the accelerator, weaving in and out of traffic. Once across the river, I turned left into a bad section. The little bar was open, the sidewalk in front littered with papers. But Index Harry sat at his table in the corner, a wine bottle before him and his eyes bleary. I waved to the bartender and jerked a chair around, straddling it. Index Harry put down his book and offered me a drink. I shook my head. He brushed an imaginary speck of dirt off his threadbare but clean gray suit and sniffed. I gave him a ten. "Who is it this time?" Index Harry said, pouring himself wine.

"Steve Lannes, owner of the Golden Cage." I leaned forward. The cops would use the phone. Lannes wouldn't be at the club this early, and Broekman, for all his professional experience, didn't have a goldmine of information like Index Harry. According to the legends, the blotch-faced old man across from me had been a college professor, Phi Beta Kappa and Ph.D. before he started drinking, God knows why. Now he had only a photographic memory and unknown sources of information to keep him in drinks. But he knew the address, private phone and whereabouts of every big shooter in the city, from the mayor to the leading hoods.

"Lannes is not in town," Harry said. He sniffed again and turned a page of his book.

"Is that all I get for ten bucks?"

He drew himself up haughtily. "My mind commands a high price, Johnny. A man who knows Milton and the other great thinkers of the world can't be bought cheaply."

"How much more does it take?"

"Twenty-five."

As soon as I paid him, his mouth flew open and the words rattled out. "Lannes went to his home on Coldwater Lake sometime Saturday night or early Sunday morning. So far as I know he's still there. That's all I have." He sloshed more wine into his glass. He reeked of it. One carefully trimmed fingernail pointed to his book. *"Paradise Lost.* Wonderful poetry here, Hood. You should read it some time. Satan's by far the best character. The righteous ones are weaklings and uninteresting. Which is frightfully close to the truth of life."

"Sure. Thanks." I walked away and left him as he got up, reeling a little, and started to recite poetry in a thick voice. The new sun hit me like a ball bat when I reached the street. The gears grated as I swung the coupe around the corner, heading north to the state line, and Coldwater Lake just beyond. I was ahead now. Ahead in the race with tired Hans Broekman; the race to reach the man who killed Lorraine and the Wednesdays.

I ate lunch on the road, crossed the state line at about two in the afternoon and hit the little town of Coldwater Lake about four. The blowsy woman who owned the combination gas station, diner and general store, gave me cold looks and the directions to Lannes' place out on the lake road. She also informed me that Lannes had roared through town at nine a.m. Sunday morning in his powder blue Cadillac and hadn't as yet left. "They been havin' a party out at that house ever since, believe you me."

Steve Lannes celebrating. What? Lorraine's death. I bought a hamburger and a shake from the woman and sat in my car until sunset, going through another whole pack of cigarettes. Then I started the coupe and went bumping along the dirt road that led around the lake. Night came down, cold and hinting of winter. The big expensive vacation houses bulked against the sky. All were dark except one, up ahead through the pines. Every light in that one was turned on. I swung off the road onto the shoulder, put out the parking lights and closed the door quietly. I moved through the trees, tight inside, my coat hanging open. In spite of the temperature the palms of my hands were sweating.

The pine needles crunched under my feet. There the pines stopped, opening a vista of blue-black sky dotted with stars. I stopped too.

The house was a modern ranch, with plenty of picture windows. The curtains were closed, but every window glowed. By now my eyes were accustomed to the dark.

I heard a dance record from the house. My breath made little vapor clouds in front of my face. The cold crept into my bones. I waited. For what, I wasn't sure. I suppose I realized that I had come all the way up here knowing that Steve Lannes had killed Lorraine, and now there was a party going on and I was all by myself; stuck. Romo would never have let himself get into a mess like this. He would have known what to do. But Romo was on vacation, and Romo had never known Lorraine.

Abruptly, the back door of the house opened. I ducked deeper into the pines. For a moment a woman stood outlined in a yellow oblong of light, cigarette in hand. Then she closed the door behind her and came down a couple of steps. She walked over to one of the two cars parked behind the house, a Cadillac. She opened the door of the Cadillac, perched herself on the edge of the seat and dragged on her cigarette. I didn't know who she was, but she was alone, so I circled the cars and came up beside her.

"Hello there," I said softly, trying to act like I might be one of the guests.

She swiveled around and I got a good look at her as she drew on the cigarette again. Blonde, but the bottled kind; heavily made up face; lips thick with paint, drawn in a precisely edged line. She had big breasts inside a dark, tight sweater and her stretched-out legs were long and heavy. She stank of booze. She was too drunk to be surprised to see me.

"Hello yourself." She swayed in the seat. "Do I know you?"

"I don't think so."

"My name's Gert Carter. Have you slept with me this weekend?"

"I'm afraid not."

She waved her cigarette in the house. "You been in there?"

"Not yet."

"My God, it's a madhouse." She leaned closer to me and I smelled heavy perfume mixed up with the booze odor. "C'mere, I'll tell you a secret. Steve and those two boys of his have put me through the wringer. I ache all over. My God, I couldn't stand any more. I lost count. They're really celebrating but I just couldn't take it. I had to get out for some air. I threw up twice tonight, it got me down so." She announced it matter of factly. "Am I talking too much?"

"I don't think so. I'm a friend of Steve's. Are you a friend of Steve's?"

She grimaced, and something bitter flicked in her eyes for a second. Then it vanished behind the bottled dullness. "Sure, I'm a good friend. A two hundred dollar a night friend. Could you afford me?"

I took hold of her shoulder. "Are you one of Lannes's call girls?"

She made a maudlin face. "Sad, ain't it? The primrose path. Well, it's money. Steve wanted a piece for the party and he picked me. I don't get any pay. That's the worst of it." She shuddered. "My God, he gives me the creeps. He's inhuman."

"Look," I said, still keeping my voice down. "Tell me something, will you?"

"Sure. You're a friend. All you want to do is talk."

"Why was Steve's wife afraid of him?"

She laughed, loudly. I stiffened, afraid someone would come out. But no one did. "Everybody knows that. You ought to know that, being a pal of Steve's. That dumb little twist thought all he did was run nightclubs. She was married to him for two years before she found out he handled girls. Then she found out about the pretty pictures and books he sells, and it—well, it turned her. The dumb twist. She stripped in his club because she was his wife, and he's a funny guy with funny ideas and he liked to watch her, but she couldn't stand the other stuff."

"Did she threaten to tell the cops?"

"Oh, no!" she said hoarsely. "Just told him she was leaving him. But it's the same thing. If she does go ahead and leave, she might talk about Steve's business. So I don't think she's going to be around much longer. You know how she is, don't you?"

"Sure, Gert," I said. "I know how she is."

Gert Carter didn't know Lorraine was dead. Gert Carter had been brought along for the celebration; the wake for Steve's dead and now unthreatening wife. My guess said maybe the two boys Gert had spoken of were the actual killers. But they didn't matter. Lannes mattered. He'd given the order. I patted Gert's hand.

"Wait right here for me, will you? I want to go see Steve."

She grinned drunkenly and ran her palm over my cheek. "Sure, I'll wait. You're nice. I might even find some more strength before the night's over. Hurry back."

I said I would. I turned my back and took out the .38. I walked up the steps and opened the door. The music hit me. The lights glared. Down the hall, somebody shouted. An empty liquor bottle lay on the carpet in front of me. The air curled with blue smoke.

I closed the door. One of the boys came out of the kitchen carrying a drink. I grabbed the drink and gave him the .38 barrel along the back of his thick neck. I caught him with my free arm and let him down gently. I started down the hall.

The second boy came out of a door on my left, his face warped into a scowl. "Hey, Louie, for the Christ's sake hurry up with—" His mouth flew open.

I grabbed his coat collar and pulled him forward and pistol-whipped him the same way. I let him bump as he went down, though. Good and loud. When I stepped around the door, Lannes was out of his chair. He got a look at my gun and sat down again, behind the desk, outlined against another picture window. This one didn't have the curtains closed, and it looked right out on Coldwater Lake.

The room was a den. On the desk was an ashtray, topped by two plaster figures. I looked at them for a second and caught my breath. I looked at the photographs and drawings on the walls. And when I looked at Steve Lannes again, the greasy-haired head bulking out of the rumpled white-on-white shirt, the bulb eyes and the liverish lower lip, he seemed old, and goatish in a dirty sad way.

"What the hell are you doing in here?"

I pointed at the ashtray. "Lorraine didn't like that kind of stuff, did she?"

"Who are you?" he shouted, jumping up.

"John Hood. I'm a detective. A private one. I'm looking for the guy who killed Lorraine Perau."

His eyes told me everything. In an instant. They said, Sure, Lorraine didn't like it and she threatened to get noisy about it so my boys bump her. They said, Sure, there's good money in stuff like that, and besides, I like that kind of art work myself. They said, You must be the guy Lorraine was running around with. I knew it was some guy. She wasn't the kind to go off by herself for very long. All he actually said was, "You're a pretty smart son of a bitch, aren't you?"

He tried to open his desk drawer. He got the Luger out and fumbled with it as if he didn't really know how to use it. I shot him. He fell over his chair and waved his arms and crashed through the big picture window and tumbled down a rip-rap slope into the lake. I walked over to the mess of broken glass and stared down. His head bobbed in the water like some kind of sputtering cork. I stood there while he drowned.

Then I went to his chair and sat down in it. I knew I was nothing but a dumb sap and Romo Spain would never have let me do a thing like this. Steve Lannes lay dead somewhere down in the lake. But it couldn't bring Lorraine back. It didn't erase the memory of her face, either. *As if it ever could, you goddamned fool. What were you thinking? What in Christ's name were you thinking?*

I shouted out loud. "I don't know. I don't know!"

Louie and the other boy got away. I heard their car start. I holstered my .38 and went back outside. I walked Gert Carter to the coupe. We drove back south toward the city. I stopped in a grocery and called Homicide long distance and told them what I knew. I hung up when they started asking too many questions.

Gert Carter talked on and on but I didn't hear. In Evanston I dropped her at an el station and made a promise to call her. Then I went to my apartment and got out two more pints. I didn't pass out this time. Broekman came through the door before that.

"Goddam you, Johnny. Goddam you for sticking your nose in." He glared down at me, looking tireder than ever. "This wasn't your business."

"I'm sorry," I said. "You want a drink?"

"No, I don't want a drink." He started pacing, letting out sighs and slapping his right fist into his left palm. He wheeled suddenly and stabbed a finger at me. "We got the guys who actually shot her. After you called, we staked out all the terminals. They tried to get a plane for Mexico City. A couple of dumb punks. They got scared and admitted the killing, but that doesn't make you any less guilty."

"No, it doesn't."

"I wish I could pin something on you. But if he's got a gun in his fist when we get him out of the lake, I don't know what I can do. I wish to God I could stick you, though. Wait till Spain hears about this. He'll burn your tail off. A dumb private cop trying to take over my job." He was jealous and sore, but he was right. I had gone over my head. And it wouldn't bring Lorraine back.

"What time is it?" I said.

"Dawn. Six-fifteen."

I had sat up all night. "I guess I better go to bed."

"I guess you better." He walked out and slammed the door hard behind him.

Romo got home a week and a half later. By then he knew it all; Broekman had written him a letter, airmail special delivery. Still, I had to go see Romo. I was scared, but I had to go. I rang his bell and waited. The voice roared, "Come in, Johnny."

He sat in his wheelchair, cigarette holder tipped up jauntily from the corner of his mouth. He had Broekman's letter on his lap. I could see the police department seal and the special delivery stamps. He wanted to let me know he knew the story, but otherwise he ignored the letter. I stood fiddling with my hat. "How was the vacation?"

"Exceptional. There's milk in the icebox. Pour yourself some."

I did. I fiddled with the glass instead of the hat. He stared at me. "Do you want a shopworn phrase?"

I nodded.

"Time," he said. "It will take time."

Silence hung between us for a long space. When he spoke again, his voice had softened. "You loved her, didn't you, Johnny." It wasn't a question. Something snapped inside of me, broke like a spring breaking.

"Yes," I said. "I loved her." I drank the glass of milk. I pulled up a chair. I sat down and told him how it was.